I0595953

PLAYING WITH FIRE

△

Book Three
THE POWER OF FOUR

PLAYING WITH FIRE

D.A. HENNEMAN

This book is a work of fiction. Names, characters, places, and incidents
are the product of the author's imagination or are used fictitiously.
Any resemblance to actual events, locals, or persons, living or dead,
is coincidental.

Copyright ©2018 by D.A. Henneman and Saray Books LLC.
All rights reserved, including the right to reproduce, distribute, or transmit
in any form or by any means. For information regarding subsidiary rights,
please contact the author at da@dahenneman.com.

ISBN-13: 9781735360232

Content Editor: Jennifer Meltzer
Book & Cover Design: Sumo Design
Cover photos © Getty Images

Manufactured in the United States of America
First Edition: May 2018
Second Edition: December 2020
Published by: Saray Books LLC

TO NETTIE

There are too many memories to count, and there will never be enough years for us to be friends. Thank you for the stomach cramping laughter, the bear hugs through the tears, and for sharing your fiery passion for life with me. Having friends like you is what magick is all about — love you to the moon and back.

1

The radio woke Sera Cardoso with a start. "Four alarm at 89A and East Cornville, all units respond. EMT in route." As she shook off the fog of sleep, Sera kissed her day off goodbye. She replied to the call on her handheld while she searched through the dirty laundry on the floor for something to wear.

"Cardoso responding, ETA five minutes." She pulled on a pair of gray sweatpants and a wrinkled white tee, trying to recall if it was once or twice that she had worn them. Wouldn't matter much since, once she donned her turnout gear, she would sweat like a cold beer on a hot day.

"All units, fire at 800 Wellness Center Drive. Station three on site, setting up command."

Sera swept up her ebony curls and secured them with one of the clips she kept in a basket on her dresser. She didn't need to look in the mirror to fix it; she had been wearing it in the same style since she was little. By the time she was done with the messy updo, she was in her living room. She scanned the floor for her shoes. Where the hell were they? She heard the radio crack with another message, this time from her chief.

"Station one waiting for responders, ETA ten minutes."

"Copy that, station one."

Damn. She should have spent the night at the station, even though she wasn't technically on the schedule. With one co-worker out on medical and the other on his honeymoon they were extremely short-staffed. Guess the gynecologist visit she had scheduled for later would have to wait another few weeks. Not that it would matter; it wasn't like she had been seeing any action lately anyway.

She found her shoes on the other side of the couch, where she had kicked them off the night before. Her back ached from the broken sleep she endured on the ancient piece of furniture, before she finally took herself to bed, just hours before. It was definitely bitching to her as she bent over to slip on her shoes.

"Crap," she muttered, "just what I need." She rubbed the knotted twinge in her lower back and grabbed her go-bag off the kitchen counter. She prayed it still had enough Motrin and snacks to get her through. She needed to grocery shop. That was yet another errand she wasn't going to get done on her non-existent day off.

Sera wasn't sure how much longer her body could take the abuse, she really needed to get that promotion. She hoped she would hear by the end of the week, and then her plan was to take a nice long vacation.

She raced out the door, slamming it behind her, and jogged to her truck. The engine hardly started before she screeched out of her assigned parking space and ripped onto the highway with her siren blaring and lights ablaze. She was halfway up the street before she realized she hadn't swished any mouthwash. She looked at the empty pack of Trident in her center console and shook her head with a laugh.

"Shit, well that figures."

She lived five miles from the station, which typically took less than ten minutes travel time when she didn't have her lights and siren on. It was always a battle getting through the tourist traffic in Sedona, especially on highway 89A, but there wasn't an easy way to get there.

Her radio cracked with updates from dispatch and her chief. "Station two on route to the Wellness Center. All units report."

"Station one responding. Cardoso, where the hell are you?"

"Cardoso ETA one minute."

"Dispatch, station one to scene in five."

At times she wished she lived closer, but purchasing a house wasn't something she was willing to do — at least not yet. Everything in her life hinged on getting the Arson Investigator position. It would determine if she grew roots in Arizona or moved on. She really wanted to grow roots; she was getting too old for the alternative.

Sera squealed into the staff parking, hopped out of her truck, and hustled through the door held open by one of her co-workers. They were already geared up and preparing the second engine. She stowed her bag in her locker and pulled on her gear as she received a brief update from her friend Nathan.

"Second station is almost there," he said abruptly. "We need to haul ass."

She grabbed her coat and helmet. "Ready. I can finish in the truck."

Sera and Nathan piled onto the engine and prepared for the ten mile ride. Lopez was already in the driver's seat and pulled out as soon as they gave him the thumbs up. The blare of the siren never ceased to make her heart race and her pulse flutter. It had affected her that way since riding with her father when she was a kid.

Station three had established the command center. They were one of the smallest stations, but were the closest to the scene. The man barking over the walkie sounded like her sparring partner Mark.

"Station one, we need you here yesterday. What is your ETA? Over."

"ETA four minutes. Over," Sera responded.

"That you, Cardoso?"

"Yes sir, it is."

"Good. I'll give Captain Williams a heads up. And Cardoso?"

"Yes sir."

"You need to be here in three."

The Wellness Center complex was on the outer edges of Sedona, surrounded by desert on all sides. Since it was so close to one of the area vortexes, its walking paths were open to the public and were often used for meditation. The complex acted as a buffer to the ancient burial grounds behind it and the staff members took great pride in maintaining its integrity and honoring the traditions of the tribes buried there. Sera had spent hours in the common room appreciating the artwork that had been donated by some of the most talented local artists in the area. It would be a shame if the fire destroyed the gallery, since many of the pieces on display were created by tribal elders who had passed on years before.

Luckily, traffic was light so they made excellent time. Sera and Nathan finished gearing up and checked their equipment as best they could in the speeding engine. As Lopez turned onto the access road, they saw the smoke pooling close to the building's roofline like mist on dry ice. A billowing column rose straight into the turquoise sky, which made Sera thankful for the windless day. It would make their jobs easier.

There were a number of ambulances waiting to receive patients. On her way to the command center, she noticed a few of the emergency techs working on people with minor injuries. She placed her hand over the tattoo on the upper part of her left breast and said a small prayer that there would be no fatalities. She had promised her abuela years ago that she would carry a thistle with her into every fire for protection. The tattoo she had near her heart had been the only way she could think of to honor that request. So far the symbol had done its job.

The Wellness Center offered on-site care for patients with addictions, psychological disorders and anxiety stemming from post traumatic stress disorder. Sera knew the building well. She volunteered on a regular basis in the counseling center and was extremely familiar with the layout. She knew they needed to contain the fire quickly so they didn't have to relocate the patients. Many of them were traumatized enough.

She spied Mark with the captain and reported in with the rest of her crew. When the captain was finished with the others, he turned to her and Mark made the introductions.

"Cardoso and Miller from Station one, sir. Cardoso was the one I was telling you about who volunteers here. She'll be the most familiar with the site."

He nodded abruptly and went right into giving orders. "We have word that there is one patient in wing two who has not reported in and we're unable to reach their location from the outside. We need you to get the vic out before the roof collapses."

"Got it," Sera responded.

"Your team is on search and rescue and if the building is compromised, you get the fuck out. Is that clear?"

"Crystal, sir."

Sera ran to catch up with Nathan who was already making his way to the main entrance. Even though there were no flames present, the space gave her a bad feeling. Something wasn't right. The pit of her stomach churned with a liquid heat, and her lungs seized, halting her breath. It wasn't heartburn; she hadn't eaten anything spicy. As a matter-of-fact she had only had a bottle of water and a granola bar on the way to the station. The tips of her fingers started to tingle as did the tattoo of the small purple flower that decorated her chest. That was the last sign she needed. Whatever force looked out for her was sending her a warning. She had learned the hard way to heed them.

"Nathan, hold up." She ran up to him and caught his arm, tugging back slightly. "There is a better way in that brings us closer to the wing. I think we should head around the south side of the building and go in through the entrance there."

"Okay, but this way seems clear."

"I know, but I am having one of my feelings. You know how I get."

He nodded. "Yup, I do. And I am also smart enough to know your feelings have saved our asses more than once." He waved his hand toward the edge of the building. "After you."

Sera sighed in relief. The warning feelings were becoming more and more frequent, and although she wasn't sure what triggered them, they did seem to be accurate. A few months back, after warning everyone out of a building that later exploded, the rest of the station started paying more attention to her intuition. She loved all the guys like brothers; it would kill her if anything happened to any of them.

"This access point looks clear," Nathan said, as he waved to a firefighter nearby. As the man came closer, Sera saw from his helmet that it was Summers. Lopez came up right behind him.

"What's going on?" Summers asked. "The captain sent us around to this side to help anyone who might be trying to get out from the windows."

"We are heading in, but using this access point," Sera explained. "Just want you to know where we are in case shit goes sideways."

"We've got your back," Summers replied. "Keep your comms on."

"Affirmative."

She and Nathan pulled down their face shields, checked the seals for leaks and made sure their Bluetooth comm system was working before entering the building. From her vantage point she couldn't see any flames, but Sera knew that could change in an instant. From the looks of the activity on the roof, they wouldn't have much time to check for survivors.

The smoke was thin, and she thought she heard coughing down the hallway toward the cafeteria. Nathan was already heading in that direction.

"There's a common area at the end of the hallway," Sera said through the comm-link. "We should start there."

Nathan nodded and took the lead, peeking into the rooms along the way to see if anyone was in them. Sera remembered that the end of the building they were in was primarily used for storage. It was highly unlikely they would find anyone, but it didn't hurt to check.

A voice cried out from the end of the hallway. "Is anyone there?"

Nathan looked back to her and gave a nod, signaling with his hand that he would move in first. She responded with a thumbs-up and a nod and followed closely behind as they made their way deeper into the building. It was definitely hotter in this part of the building, and Sera wondered how close they were to the outer edge of the fire.

The coughing stopped and Sera was unsure about the direction of the victim. Muffled through her helmet, she barely registered a popping sound and turned her head to see dust pouring from cracks in the ceiling.

"Nathan, watch out!"

Sera barely pushed him out of the way before the ceiling collapsed and separated them. She saw him through the flames. He had fallen with her shove but gave a thumbs up to let her know he was okay. He shook his head and touched the side of his helmet.

"Cardoso, report."

"We're okay, sir. Separated in the cafeteria by fiery debris. We'll need to come out separately. Looks like Miller has something wrong with his comm."

She heard another muffled cough. There was someone nearby.

"Get out of there now, both of you."

"On our way, sir. Think I found the vic."

"Secure the vic only if you can do it safely."

"Understood."

Nathan stood on the other side of the debris looking for a way across. From the height of the flames and the pile of rubble present it didn't look like he would be able to.

She yelled as loudly as she could in an effort to communicate over the roar of the fire, and used hand gestures to indicate he should head down the hall then exit left.

Nathan nodded as if he understood her, but stayed in place to wait until she secured the victim.

She looked to the wall of flames once more, trying to gauge how far the victim might be from her location. The flames weren't acting like any fire she had ever seen. They were staying in place like a wall. Why wasn't it spreading? Were the floors wet? She hadn't thought they made it this far with the hoses, but perhaps they did. She called out to the victim.

"Hello? Sedona Fire, is anyone in here?"

Sera felt the tattoo on her chest start to burn and her fingers tingle, something was wrong. She moved into the room toward the area where she heard the voice, pushing aside chairs and tables along the way to clear an exit path. On the wall to her right there was a hole encircled with flames that should have led to the room next to the cafeteria. But from her vantage point it looked as though it led nowhere. Why couldn't she see through to the other side?

The ring of fire swirled around the edges and crackled with a lightning-like energy. It started to spin, the outer edges spitting orange and red flames, while the center faded to black. The darkness lightened and she saw a shirtless man in the center staring at her from the other side. He wasn't in distress; he didn't call out to her, merely cocked his head in a dog-like fashion and stared her down with his golden eyes.

Her reflexes were dulled, as if she had worked a 48-hour shift with no sleep. The tattoo on her chest stung. Did she have a hole in her coat? She needed to get out of the building to check but wasn't leaving without the vic. She shuffled forward and her hand came up of its own accord. He was reaching for her too.

"I'm here to help you. Take my hand."

The man cocked his head again and then graced her with a dazzling smile. He sure wasn't acting like he needed saving. And was that a kilt he was wearing? Just as she reached the edge of the flaming hole, she heard a cough in the corner and glanced toward it. When she looked back, both the hole and the man in the kilt had disappeared.

She shook her head, not understanding what she had just seen and even more convinced there was something wrong with her gear. Perhaps her oxygen levels were off. It was either that or the sweat dripping into her eyes was making her see things.

"Over here," came the coughing voice and through the smoke she saw a shadow of movement. As she drew closer, she realized the man, fully clothed, was pinned under debris he was trying to move off his left leg.

"Command, I found the vic. Caught under debris. Getting him out now."

"Move it, Cardoso!" She couldn't help but roll her eyes. *No shit, Sherlock.*

She crouched closer to him to get a better visual. He looked to be in one piece, although his leg was bent at a weird angle. "Don't move, sir. I'll get you out."

"Beam's too heavy at this angle."

Was that a British accent she detected? It was hard to tell over the whooshing sound of the flames, but she could swear he sounded just like Benedict Cumberbatch. "I'll be right back."

Sera scanned the room, looking for something she could use as a lever. A leg from a broken table looked as though it would work. She pulled it from the pile and tucked it under the beam, yelling at the victim to pull himself out when she moved it. Sera pushed down on the table leg with everything she had, and the man pulled his injured leg out with a scream. He was pale and close to fainting. She would have to carry him out. The leg looked bad. She was surprised with all the smoke in the room, and the bone sticking out the way it was, that he was still conscious.

"Put your arm over my shoulders. We're going to head up the hallway." She honestly wasn't sure how long she had before he passed out. "Sir, I need you to stay awake as long as you can."

He nodded weakly, his eyes closed but his arm gripping securely around her shoulder. She could tell it took all of his strength to do as she requested. His limbs were starting to shake from the shock.

She hoisted him up as far as she could and took as much pressure off his leg as she was able. Once she got him in a semi-standing position, she leaned up under his stomach and pushed up until he was across her shoulders. As she straightened she pulled down on his uninjured leg and one of his arms. The man cried out in agony, then passed out. She was thankful they didn't have far to walk; he needed medical attention stat.

Sera trudged up the hallway, slowed by the load she carried. The sweat ran along her forehead and dripped into her eyes as she blinked to clear them. Nathan made his way around the building and was just coming in to help her when she got to the entrance. Summers and Lopez came up and took the victim from her shoulders, and Nathan led her away from the building.

Nathan grabbed her arm and lifted the shield on his helmet.

"You okay?" He lifted her shield and handed her a water bottle, which she drained in record time.

"Yeah. Just need to rest. Think there may have been something weird with my oxygen levels."

"What do you mean?"

Sera looked at the concern in Nathan's eyes and decided that whatever she saw in there, if it was anything at all, shouldn't be shared with him. He worried too much, and besides he was sweet on her.

"It's nothing, I'm just tired."

Nathan scanned her eyes for the truth and nodded. Apparently he believed her. "Okay, head over and get checked out. I'll check on the vic. Oh, and by the way, good call on the front entrance. It collapsed shortly after we entered. I had to go out through the back."

"Good to know I haven't lost my touch," she said with a smirk.

He gave her a soft smile that warmed his eyes and then ran toward the medic to check on the man she pulled from the building. Yup, definitely sweet on her. She needed to put a stop to that. He was the only one in the station that looked at her as a woman; to the rest of them she was just another guy. They all knew her rules. She didn't date anyone she worked with, but Nathan was new. He didn't know any better. Besides, he was ten years younger than her, and she wasn't sure she had the energy.

She wandered over to another emergency medical unit and sat down just as they finished a woman who had a shallow cut on her head. The injury wasn't bad, but there was a lot of blood. Sera was feeling better, and she realized as she sat calmly that her earlier feelings had all but disappeared. Her stomach was back to normal and her tattoo didn't burn. She looked down to the front of her coat, no hole. It was almost as though she had imagined the entire thing.

As the medic checked her oxygen levels and blood pressure, Sera found her mind returning to the image she saw in the fire and wondered what it symbolized for her. She never dismissed a dream, vision or hallucination. Her abuela taught her years ago that they all had meaning. She often said it was the mind's way of working out its destiny. She couldn't for the life of her imagine what a man in a kilt standing in a flaming ring of fire could mean, but she knew from experience that if she was open to the message the universe was sending her, it wouldn't be long before she found out.

2.

Logan Blackwood stood motionless, gazing into the campfire he built in the woods far from his homestead in Wisteria. The cycles of the moon pressed upon him as he weighed his options. With only two of them left to find her, and no word from the witch who promised she'd bring her, he suffered in edgy silence alone.

As he stood brooding and watching the flames, he wondered if the vision he saw earlier had been a trick of his mind. There was no explanation for it, and certainly not one for the feelings it awakened in him. While one could argue that he lived in a land full of magick, and that this would be something akin to witchery, he knew his fair share of sorcerers. None of them could build an elemental portal, not without an element of course. And there was no one who could have lit the fire inside him other than the one destined for him by Fate. That was the most confusing thing of all.

He poked the fire again, willing the flames to swirl and circle as before, but to no avail. The blackened void was gone and the strange yellow creature with it. Just over a moon ago, when the sorcerer Erebos pulled the bonnie lass Amie through Air's portal, Logan was close enough to see firsthand what it looked like. Since Amie was gifted the powers of air when she was brought through the portal, he assumed the same might be true for the one he saw in the flames. His gut told him what he had seen was similar to the elemental portal Erebeos conjured, the only difference this time was that it was surrounded by flames, not a cyclone.

After no luck at prompting the portal to rematerialize, he sat down on a nearby stump and opened his kit, pulling out an iron skillet and the scran Mila made for him. His mouth watered in anticipation of the meal, and while he waited for it to heat he consoled himself with a small piece of shortbread she put in his pack for dessert. Although she was human, Mila was like a mother to him, and she took amazing care of the homestead when he was away. The pack members and humans who called his village home adored Mila, and heaven help anyone who tried to harm a hair on her head. That was precisely why he was sitting in the woods alone re-heating three-day-old haggis.

He didn't dare make his change near the pack since his temper was volatile at best. He had one more night and then he could head back. It would be safer when the moon was in the center of its cycle. At least that was what he hoped.

What was it he had seen in the flames? Was it real, or was it his exhausted mind playing tricks on him? And why would hearing the yellow beast's voice cause his breath to catch? His reaction confused him, since the vision was nothing like he imagined his intended to look like. It hadn't even looked remotely human, or lycan for that matter, yet the feelings coursing through him couldn't be denied.

Could it be the beast was the key to finding his mate? Perhaps that was why its voice excited him. The more he thought about it, the more he convinced himself that it had to be so. If he had just taken its hand quicker and pulled it through the portal into his world, he would truly know.

He was irritated he hadn't pulled the creature through. If he didn't mate by the completion of the next two moon cycles, he would lose his ability to transform back to a man. And as full wolf, he would be unable to see to the safety of his village. There wasn't anyone fit or young enough to take over his duties as alpha and merging with another pack wasn't an option. Most of his village members couldn't shape-shift, and other alphas he knew weren't as open-minded or as accepting of humans as he was. He needed the image in the fire to help him find his mate. He was running out of time.

He decided he would only return home long enough to replenish his supplies, and then he would head right back to his campsite. If the yellow creature showed up, he would be ready, and then he would put himself in the best position to ask for help. He needed to come up with an alternate plan; he wasn't sure the witches would come through.

As if he had willed her to be present, the sorceress known as Zilla sauntered up and posed by the fire.

"How's it going, handsome? Did you miss me?"

She was just as stunning as ever, her jet-black hair loose to her hips and her emerald green eyes crackling in the light of the fire. The placement of her hands on her hips only managed to push her breasts up precariously to the top of her corset. While he wasn't one to ever look away from a beautiful woman, especially a half dressed one, he had already placed Zilla in the "okay to look but watch your fingers" category in his mind. As far as he was concerned, she had three things going against her: She was a powerful witch and no one in their right mind would mess with her; she wasn't a wolf, although some would argue that lycan blood was similar no matter the animal you connected to; and lastly, and most importantly, she wasn't his mate.

He groaned, which she must have heard, since she spoke again with an offended tone and a crinkle in her nose.

"If you are going to be like that, I certainly don't need to stay. I could find much better things to do with my time."

"Don't be like that, lassie. Have a seat."

"Don't mind if I do," Zilla said with a smile. She looked around the campsite full circle and held back her comments momentarily to examine her surroundings. Her voice was quiet and soft, as if the next comment was meant for her own ears. "Curious place for your campsite. Dead center in a clearing surrounded by a circle of trees."

"I suppose I would typically prefer more cover, but I like to see who's coming toward me. Fat lot of good it did me with you."

She laughed as she shot him a wide-mouthed look of shock. "Well!"

He shook his head and rose, indicating she should sit on the log near him. He had cut and moved several of them to use as seats around the fire. "I meant no offense. The past weeks have been drainin'." He sat back down after she perched on the log nearest the fire. As she reached her arms out to warm her hands, he noticed bruises dotting her fair skin. She pulled the sleeves of her shrug down over them after realizing where his eyes landed.

"I can certainly relate to that, as you well know. Sevilla only just managed to wake me from the sleep I was in."

"Ya fared well. I'm glad of it. Your injuries were severe and your sister was worried."

The smile on her face was faint, and her eyes shimmered with the beginning of tears. "Yes, I suppose she was. We've come a long way but have miles to go, not that you are interested in our relationship and its dysfunctions." She waved her hand as if swatting a fly; the uncomfortable topic was immediately dropped. "I would like to thank you for saving me, by the way. She told me it was you who carried me to her even though you were injured yourself."

"Aye. My injuries were but a scratch and I healed quickly. You would have done the same for a fellow lycan."

He looked into her face, her eyes downcast and a rosy tint highlighting her cheeks. Once again she changed the subject quickly. From what he knew about Zilla, it wasn't a surprise. She would be the last person he would expect to put her pretty little neck on the line…for anyone.

"I needed to talk to you, about our agreement."

"Aye."

She looked uncomfortable; he could tell he wasn't going to like what she had to say. *Shite.* He knew he shouldn't have trusted her. She was squirming, just like Annabelle did when he caught her taking extra treats before dinner. He could tell the conversation was headed in a direction he wasn't prepared for.

"I am just going to say it… I am unable to use my powers. I won't be able to help you find your mate."

His heart dropped into the pit of his stomach and he was unable to catch his breath. She had unmanned him with a single sentence. The truth of her words caused his throat to close and his voice to barely rise above a rasp. "I must find my mate. Ya know time is against me."

"I realize that, Logan, but there is something draining the magick of our land, and it has affected our powers. Sevilla and I need to see what we can do to rebalance it. In the meantime, you will need to do what you can on your own."

What the hell would he do now? His life and the lives of his pack depended on finding her. His mate. He took a deep breath, trying to tamp down the anger squeezing his chest. It was too close to the end of the most recent moon cycle, and he still felt the pull of his wolf. The tips of his fingers vibrated and he responded in a snappish growl.

"On me own? How the hell am I ta do that?"

"Logan, I am going to leave if you can't calm down."

"I am calm," he snapped.

"You could have fooled me! Tell that to your hairy knuckles and pointed ears."

He looked down at his hands; sure enough they had started to change. What was frightening was that he had hardly noticed. Closing his eyes and taking a deep breath, he centered himself with a picture in his mind. He imagined finding his mate, as impossible as that might be now, and what she might look like. In his mind she was wild and beautiful, and only had eyes for him. Imagining the love he would feel when gazing into her eyes, he managed to calm his beast and regain control.

"Much better, darling," Zilla twittered nervously.

He could tell she wasn't any happier telling him she couldn't help, than he was hearing it.

"Controlling your beast will be important moving forward."

"Aye. And it's getting harder by the day."

"I'm sorry, Logan. I realize this isn't the ideal situation, but it isn't as though you won't have help."

"I thought you said…"

"I did say I wouldn't be able to help. However, I didn't say I was going to completely bail on you."

"What do ya have in mind, witch?"

"That was rude."

"How is it rude? Ya are a witch." He closed his eyes and shook his head. He always felt as though she talked in circles and today was no different.

"I realize I am a witch, but you shouldn't call me one with that tone. You make it sound like it's a bad thing."

"Okay, lassie, I'll try to manage me tone." He was losing his patience; he needed to end their conversation. "Do ya have a point, or should I just go back to warming dinner?"

Zilla rolled her eyes; apparently, he was just as exasperating to her as she was to him. "The elements of Water and Air, Brooke and Amie, have been given the task to find the next two powers. According to what I have seen, and the few things my sister has told me, I believe one of those elements is your intended mate."

"Me mate is one of the two that are left? Fire or Earth?"

"Correct."

"And Brooke and Amie are looking for the next element?"

"Yes."

"I have less than two cycles of the moon left. What if they don't find her in time? Or they don't find my intended first?"

"This is our only option, Logan. I am truly sorry."

He looked into her eyes to gauge her sincerity and saw pity in their depths. He worried not only for his pack, but of the wee one that called him "papa"… his little Annabelle. He knew Zilla was fond of her as well.

"I shouldn't go back to the homestead. My powers are hard to control, but I need supplies."

"I am still able to work some simple magick. I should be able to find you a stone to wear to help you with your powers. In the meantime, I agree it will be safer for everyone if you stay here alone."

"Aye."

"Give me a list of things you need and I will get them from Mila. It will be nice to see her again, it's been some time." Zilla stood up, brushing the loose debris from the back of her skirt. "After I deliver your supplies to you, I will speak to Sevilla about how to get you updates from Brooke and Amie."

"And you'll continue to keep me plight from Mila?"

Zilla looked at him affronted. "Of course I will. Do you seriously think I want to have an alpha tear me in two?"

"I suppose not," he chuckled and shook his head. "You do realize the last time I saw Brooke she turned me to a chunk o' ice. Oh, and Amie's man bashed me face in. We don't exactly get along."

"Saying you and Aleck don't get along is like saying fairies aren't annoying. Simply not true. You will all just need to kiss and make up, darling," Zilla said with a shrug. "Just the same as I have. There are much more important things to worry about than who has a harder punch or a bigger haggis. Speaking of which, I will assume you will want more of that horrible smelling stuff."

"Aye. And I will need you take a message to my Annabelle. She needs to know not to come looking for me."

"It will be done," she replied with a nod. "Of that you can be certain."

Logan looked into her eyes and trusted she was telling the truth. Zilla would be sure to keep the members of his pack safe. He could rely on a fellow lycan, even if she was a cat. He wrote a list of supplies that he would need to get him through a longer period than he originally intended, along with a short note to Mila explaining that she needed to keep an extra eye on Annabelle. Confident he explained himself adequately, he gave the note to Zilla and she walked off in the direction of his village. He knew he wouldn't see Zilla until the morning, there would be no way Mila would let her return without cooking her a meal and insisting she rest. Besides, he had requested more shortbread, which would take Mila a little time to make.

It was best to limit his interaction with others while his mood was volatile. Time alone would allow him to concentrate on finding answers in the flames. He thought again about the strange yellow creature and the melodic voice that came to him muffled beneath a faceless mask.

I'm here to help you. Take my hand.

It gave him hope all wasn't lost. That there was still time to find his love and save his people. If it involved taking a yellow beast's hand and following it blindly through a flaming ring of fire, then he would do it. Who was he kidding? He was desperate enough to do anything at this point.

3

The cloaked figure made his way down the damp stone steps into a cavern designed to hold a great number of captives more powerful than he. The emptiness of the space echoed back to him with each step he took. The stones were slick with moss, and the smooth, damp walls curved downward, lowering him step by step to the levels far beneath the caves he now called home. The symbols etched into the walls were remnants of an ancient magic, unknown to him and telling of the beings that used the caves before his arrival. When he happened upon the space all those years ago it was long deserted.

He stepped off the final stair into the enormous hallway. Torches along the wall lit his path, as did the bright green glow from the substance he stole several months back. The mage he held captive had used the same material in his own dungeons, so the sorcerer knew their effects. Weakened and drained of his magic, he had once been held in a cell similar to the one he kept the mage in now. He hoped Ryker was awake; they had much to discuss.

The cell bars glowed bright, like the luminescent light of a thousand fireflies. The sorcerer felt the hum of magic under his skin and kept a few steps back from the bars to prevent it from draining his strength. There were chains of the lit substance crisscrossing Ryker's chest, and he knew from experience it would be some time before the effects on Ryker wore thin. Not that he planned on letting him leave, since he now realized the true source of Ryker's power. Wrapped in the magical chains, Ryker fed the sorcerer's abilities and allowed him to retain a firmer control of the body he now inhabited. In essence, Ryker served as magical fuel.

For what he had planned, tapping into the powers of a mage wasn't going to be enough to build up his stores of magick; he needed to drain the primal source. He learned from the carvings on the wall that the ancients used elemental magick for spells he had yet to conquer. He believed Ryker was the key to finding a way to harness that magick. He looked into the cell and noted that even though his guest could reach the nearby table, his meal was left untouched. Ryker was seated but slumped over, as if sleeping in his upright position. He knew better.

"Weeks have passed and still you sleep," the sorcerer said gruffly. He waited for a response. Nothing came. He decided on a different approach. "I only have need of answers. Once given, you will be free to go."

The man's head slowly lifted, his hollow eyes looked at the sorcerer with mistrust. "Why would I believe you, Erebos? As long as I have known you, you have never been a man of your word."

The comment took the sorcerer by surprise. He had known most of Erebos's thoughts, had inhabited his body for years, and had even done some of Erebos's dirty work. Ryker was someone Erebos had just started interacting with — wasn't he? It made the sorcerer wonder just how far back their true relationship went and, more importantly, why he couldn't remember it.

"It's Roy," the sorcerer corrected with a growl. "Erebos is no longer in charge of this body."

"Whatever you call yourself, the man is still the same," Ryker murmured. "Where is Erebos? He can't be far away."

The mage was too perceptive. The thought of it unnerved him. "His essence is nearby, that is all you need know."

Ryker nodded and sighed, apparently too tired to fight. "So what is it you want, Roy?"

"I need to know more about the witches, the ones that control the fates. Much like the rest of the past, Erebos's memories of them are fractured."

"They haven't been part of my life for decades. I have nothing to tell."

Roy shook his head; he didn't trust him. "See, that is where I think you're mistaken. I believe your connection to the past runs deep. You know more than you are letting on."

"Even if it did, it runs no deeper than the connection you have with the present. Where is Zilla, by the way? Has she found another life to destroy?"

"How do you know about…"

"Leopards don't change their spots, Erebos."

"She's a cat."

"I know precisely what Zilla is."

"And the name is Roy!"

The man had the audacity to chuckle before continuing. "Okay, Roy."

Roy fought his compulsion to open the cell and pound his captive to a bloody heap. Much as he would like to beat him black and blue, his powers would drain if he did. He didn't want to give Ryker the opportunity to escape. He was much too valuable.

Ryker closed his eyes and spoke quietly from a place in the past, almost as if he were picturing the memories in his mind. "Zilla was in love with Erebos long before you ever came to be, Roy. It's part of the reason we're all in this mess to begin with."

He felt his pulse quicken at the mention of his lover's name. It still angered him that she favored Erebos over him. Ryker's comment about a past he couldn't remember, either through his memory or Erebos's, intrigued him. "Tell me what you mean."

"I mean we've been here before, and Zilla's choices led to the destruction of the elements. Not to mention the death of my wife."

Roy was confused, this part of the past he did remember. "The elements weren't destroyed. You captured Air and had her in a cell just few down from mine. And Water has found its match as well. She was there the day your fortress was destroyed."

"I remember," Ryker responded with a sigh. "But they weren't the first to harness the elemental powers."

"Meaning?"

The pause before he spoke was almost indiscernible, yet enough for Roy to realize the mage was holding something back. "Meaning, everything is cyclical. All that once was shall be again."

"That sounds like the nonsense the witches spout," Ryker grumbled. He hated cryptic messages almost as much as riddles. He never understood why the Universe had to be so damn evasive.

"That's because one of them always said it. They also believe if we don't learn from our mistakes, we are doomed to repeat them."

Roy had firsthand knowledge of that; Erebos followed the same path and always expected different results. Zilla's involvement was the only reason he had been able to change his course thus far. The problem was Roy didn't know how much longer he could trust her. It had been some time since she visited his bed. It made him wonder just how well Ryker knew the sisters. He hoped he would fill in some of the holes in his memories.

"My understanding is Zilla's sister Sevilla is mentoring the elements as they come into power, and Water and Air are searching for the final two."

Ryker's face turned to ash and Roy realized he had shared knowledge of something that struck him at the core. Ryker's body crumpled upon itself and his shoulders drooped. His mistrust of Zilla and his reaction to Sevilla's name slid a piece of the puzzle firmly into place.

"Sevilla's your wife," Roy said knowingly. "The one you thought was dead all these years." He watched as Ryker's sobs shook his shoulders, fueling the labored intakes of his breath which echoed from his cell. Ryker's reaction surprised him.

"You didn't know she was alive?"

Ryker shook his head, and then responded in a pained voice. "No. I didn't. Last I knew she had been killed, and her sisters were the last to see her alive. I was told it was Zilla's fault." His voice was desperate as he met Roy's eyes from his cell. "Where is she now?"

Roy couldn't help the smile that split his face. He had finally found the key to unlock the secrets he needed to move forward. He sensed that Ryker would do anything to learn about Sevilla's whereabouts; he might do much more if Roy could promise a visit from her. It was time to negotiate.

"We will get to that. But, before we talk about her, let's talk a little more about the elements. Why would the sisters be so interested in them?"

4

Things finally calmed down at the station and Sera took advantage of it by scheduling some much needed time off. The Wellness Center fire had taken a toll on her, and she spent the following twenty-four hours in bed with the curtains drawn. It made her wonder if her father suffered the same aches and pains that found her in middle age. She shook off the fog of extended sleep while opening her room darkening shades and thought about the lifestyle she had chosen for herself.

She tried hard not to resent the fact that she had put her entire life on hold for her career, a career that spanned over twenty years and two failed relationships. But at age forty-five, and looking back on her life, she realized she might have overlooked opportunities that could have made all the difference. Perhaps she should have taken the lateral move to the station in San Diego when it was offered, or taken the extra classes that would have secured a Master's degree in fire science. There was a multitude of other "what ifs" that crowded her brain and made her question the life she found herself living.

She was single with no children and nothing to show for her ambition except a career that beat her body up on a regular basis. She wasn't getting any younger and her job affected her in ways she didn't want to think about. It stemmed far beyond the pain in her back. Although she was extremely fit and stronger than most men her age, her small 5'4" frame couldn't continue to take the abuse her position demanded of it. Maybe her dear, sweet abuela had been right. Sera should have been a school teacher. Of course, her grandmother also thought she should be a psychic, so there was that.

She had been around stations since she was old enough to walk and came from a long line of firefighters. If the promotion went through, she would be the first in her family to have Inspector status, which would have made her father really proud. It was at times like these she missed his sound advice and calming presence. He had been taken from her life much too soon. So had her mother.

Sera pulled some sweatpants and a wrinkled tee-shirt from a nearby pile on the floor and got dressed quickly. No time for a shower,; there were things to do. Her hair was generally so unruly she hardly wore it down, but today was a good hair day. She stood in the mirror deliberating between clip or no clip. When she wore it down it got a lot of attention. Her dark spirals fluffed out like a lion's mane, and often times she found herself on the receiving end of curious admirers. People couldn't help themselves she supposed, running their fingers through it. At times, she swore it almost reached out to people. She likened their attention to the same compulsion that drove strangers to touch a pregnant woman's belly, something which she herself was guilty of on more than one occasion. Decision made, she had no time for delays. Clip.

She loaded up the Keurig with her coffee choice and brushed her teeth in the kitchen sink as it brewed. After pouring the first cup into her thermos she popped in a different coffee cartridge and set it to brew. She liked concocting her own flavored coffees, especially since she could brew one cup at a time. This morning's choice was a blend of Dark Magic and Carmel Vanilla Cream, and her caffeine deprived body was screaming for it. She skipped applying the light makeup she typically wore; she'd be working out anyway. Half the time she skipped it entirely since it only managed to drip into her eyes when she responded to a call.

By the time she gathered her purse and keys, her coffee was done brewing and she was ready to go. Her plan was to get in a quick spar and shower at the gym before running the endless list of errands she had. She planned to check on the vic from the Wellness Center fire, James Fisher. He was still in the hospital, since the damage to his leg required a fair bit of surgery. She always felt personally responsible for the people she saved, and wanted to be sure he wasn't traumatized by what had happened. He'd be one of the first stops after her workout.

When she arrived at Frankie's Place, the warehouse smelled of musk and men. Sera found herself taking in a deep breath and letting it out with a sigh. Was it weird she loved that scent? She supposed it was, since most women would only smell stale body odor in a place like this. It was probably why she was the only woman who worked out there. Well, that and most women she knew didn't box. Especially at her age.

Her sparring partner Mark came sauntering up to the corner where she stowed her gym bag. She was already dressed for their workout, but still needed to wrap her hands.

"Here, let me help you with that."

"Thanks."

"No problem." He looked up briefly with a grin. "You ready to bring some heat into the ring?"

She had to laugh; he was such a pain in the ass. "Why, your girlfriend giving you trouble? Have some aggression to work out?"

"If only it were that simple," he chuckled. "Naw, just issues at work. Nothing that won't work itself out." He took one final tug on the bindings on her right hand before starting on the left.

"I know what you mean. I'm the same way. I tend to let shit go too."

"You hear anything on the promotion yet?"

"Not yet, and I'm beginning to get a bad feeling about it. It's taking the chief way too long to get back to me." Her slight intake of breath had him looking up. "Little too tight."

"Sorry." He loosened the straps, and then continued wrapping. "How's that?"

"Better, thanks."

"You know, part of the problem is you're way too qualified."

"I think part of the problem is that I don't have the right anatomy."

He rolled his eyes and shook his head with a smirk. "I think the reason you are way too qualified is because you are missing that particular part of the anatomy. You multi-task like a beast and are the most organized and driven person I know. Besides, you know Chief isn't like that."

"Yeah, I know, just easier to blame it on something like that. You know, instead of on the fact that I'm found lacking once more."

After finishing, Mark took both gloved hands in his, which caused her to look up into his confused eyes. "You are the last person on Earth I would call lacking, Sera." His sincere gaze brought a smile to her face.

"Thanks, Mark. But you're just saying that because I'm about to kick your ass."

His laugh was contagious. "Okay, spitfire. Let's find someone to tie my gloves and we'll just see about that."

"Oh, it's on!"

As he walked toward a few guys at a nearby ring, his muttered comment made her smile.

"I pity anyone who ever finds you lacking in any way."

Sera had a huge surge of energy during sparring and subsequently handed Mark his ass, as he stated with a grin after. He was always a good sport and never made her feel as though he was taking it easy on her. She would always ask for him to give it to her harder, and he would always huff back, "I'm givin' it all she's got, Captain." He got in a few good jabs with his jokes and references to Star Trek, but in the end she delivered some cracks that really set him back.

Early on, when they first started fighting, they danced around each other. Mark worried he would hurt her, only to find out quickly that she could hold her own. Now they boxed on an amateur level. They only fought when neither of them had to work the next day, since either one or both of them ended up with cuts, bruises or at the very least sore muscles that needed soaking.

She thought about the blows she gave him and worried the last one on the cheek might cause a black eye. He would be looking to get even next time, she thought with a grin. She would be ready.

Most of Frankie's early morning patrons had left to start their days, and Sera took advantage of the quiet locker room to get ready. Even though it would take the better part of the day to dry, she washed her hair using her favorite strawberry shampoo. Once out of the shower she tamed her curls with coconut-scented conditioner from the salon, which would reduce her frizz and make her tresses shine.

Her hair was one of those things she was proud of, but it was also simultaneously the bane of her existence. Once she had a man come up to her in a bar and put his face right into the back of her head. Her co-workers laughed as he pulled in a deep breath of her scent and sighed "delicious" in a velvet tone that only she could hear. There was no way she was giving up the wonderful way her hair felt after using the conditioner, so she got in the habit of keeping her hair clipped in the hopes of deterring stray noses. However, since today was her only day off, she decided it was going to be a hair down kind of day after all.

Before leaving the parking lot, she sat in her running pick-up and took a few minutes to check her phone for messages. She had appointments to reschedule, groceries to buy and a stop at the dealership for an oil change and tune-up. First on her list was checking up on the vic from the Wellness Center fire.

Sera loved volunteering at the Center; it fed her soul. She never had children, and aside from her abuela in Spain, had no family left. Her mother died shortly after giving birth to her, and her father passed in a fire two days before her thirtieth birthday. Even though his death had been fifteen years before, she still had a hole in her heart the size of the Grand Canyon. Not a day went by that she didn't miss her father. Helping the patients at the Wellness Center allowed her to process her grief. In many ways, they helped shed light on her own life and behavior.

She had kept tabs on the vic, James Fisher. The hospital let her know the surgery on his leg went well and he was able to receive visitors. He was lucky, for as bad as it looked it was actually a pretty easy break. When she pulled into the lot she spied a space right up front and pulled into it. Thanking the universe for the small favor, she locked her purse in her car and slid her identification into her pocket.

Sera introduced herself to the head nurse, and after explaining the story behind her visit, was told to wait while she checked with the patient. After a few minutes, the nurse escorted her to a private room up the hallway, not far from the visitor's center, and waved her in.

The man she came to see was seated in bed, propped up by the mattress and pillows behind him. The hospital gown, which would make anyone else look sickly or weak, only managed to make him look healthier and more robust. She wondered if perhaps they had given him the wrong size, since it was tight across his muscular chest. He gave her a dazzling smile, and waved his hand to a chair next to him.

"Please do have a seat. I'm happy you came," he said in a crisp British accent. "I want to thank you for what you did."

Sera took his hand in hers; he had a firm and steady grip. She didn't know what to say. The first meetings with a vic were awkward, especially when they were as nice looking as this one.

"You're welcome. I'm glad I was able to get there in time. My name is Sera, by the way, Sera Cardoso."

"Nice to meet you Sera, I'm James, James Fisher. My mates call me Jim."

"Ah, then Jim it is."

"Brilliant," he said with a grin. "So besides saving crazy ex-military blokes from burning buildings, what do you do for fun?"

"I can see we are going to have one of those friendships," Sera laughed. "We're going to get along just fine. Actually, I have a pretty solitary life, mostly fight fires, save handsome ex-military blokes from burning buildings and when feeling particularly frisky...I box."

"Impressive," he said with a toothy grin. "Well, we may have to wait a bit until I'm up to sparring, but would love a go with you."

She felt a slight blush. This man was very charming and definitely into her. She would need to proceed carefully for professionalism sake. Although, in her opinion, a little flirting never hurt anyone.

"Okay. You're on. But I don't want to have to deal with any lady friends coming after me when I kick your butt." His reaction made her pause. "What? Don't think I can?"

"The laugh wasn't for that. You carried an unconscious man out of a burning building, I'm pretty sure you can do anything you set your mind to. The laugh was more an expression of delight. You're a happy find, Sera Cardoso."

"Glad to hear it, and you, sir, are a delight as well. If you don't mind me asking, where are you from?"

"My accent is a dead giveaway then?"

"Pretty much," she nodded.

"I live in the west part of London, near Putney Bridge. I'm here on what I like to think of as a holiday, although my sister would call it therapy."

"I'm familiar with the Wellness Center, I volunteer there quite often. They have an amazing program."

His demeanor quickly faded. It seemed he wasn't quite comfortable with the topic yet. "So I've heard, especially for PTSD, which is what I'm there for. I had only been there a few days when the fire broke out."

"That makes sense actually, why you would have been a bit disjointed when the chaos started."

"Exactly so."

"You look surprised that I would get that."

"Not surprised as much as impressed. You are a very perceptive lady."

"Well-trained," she said with a shrug. "Although, I suppose some of it is perception at times. If there is anything I understand well, it is dealing with post-traumatic events."

"I suppose you do," he said quietly. "They will be releasing me in a few days. Will I see you at the Center?"

"My schedule is demanding, so it's hard to say."

"Oh."

"Now don't look so disappointed. I know you are there for at least 30 days. I'm sure we will run into each other."

"I'm counting on it," he said with a grin. He attempted to hide a yawn, and Sera took that as her cue to leave.

"I had better get going. I have a million things to get done today. It was really nice meeting you, Jim."

"It was lovely to meet you, Sera. I'm glad it was you who saved me."

She couldn't help the flutter in her pulse. The combination of his accent, blue eyes and dazzling smile was going to be dangerous moving forward. Her attraction was surprising since she didn't generally go for blondes. Her response warmed her face.

"Me too. I'll see you soon. Make sure you take good care of that leg… we have a sparring date to plan."

"You can count on it, lovey. I'm looking forward to it."

Sera gave him a final wave from the door, before heading down the hallway and out of the hospital. The flirty wink he gave her right before she left the doorway made her laugh and shake her head. He was going to be a handful; she could tell already. She was sure he wouldn't dish out anything she couldn't handle, but he was too young for her, and possibly even too flawed considering he was at the Wellness Center for help.

He was a charmer, she had to give him that, and their conversation kept her smiling throughout the day. A few hours into her errands, she started to question why she kept herself distanced from all possibilities. Perhaps hanging out with Jim wouldn't be so bad, especially considering he didn't even live in the U.S. A bit of fun without the ties could be exactly what the doctor ordered…for both of them.

5

Logan let out a sigh of relief; he was alone in the woods at long last. Zilla brought him enough supplies from Mila to last through the next moon cycle. For safety reasons, she didn't create a portal to his location from the pack's homestead. Instead she brought the supplies by wagon. He appreciated her foresight, as he would be able to keep most of his supplies up off the ground and away from woodland animals.

Zilla chatted incessantly while securing a leather strap with the stone she had promised around his neck. While he had not been sure that anything would help his edgy disposition, he had to admit that he felt the effects of the magical stone almost immediately. The white Halite crystal necklace was tighter than he cared for, but she wanted to be sure it stayed in place during and after his conversion. She mentioned that the stone helped to create inner balance and dissolve negative patterns such as anger. He hoped it worked; he didn't care for the feeling that he wasn't in control.

Before she left, Zilla let him know that she had spoken to his ward Annabelle directly, and that he needn't be concerned that the young one would try to find him. The dangers had been explained as much as they could be, without Zilla going into details that shouldn't concern her young mind. He was confident that he didn't need to worry about her, at least for now.

He thanked Zilla for her help and unharnessed his horse shortly after she left. Once the animal was free from the wagon, Logan sent him up the pathway with a gentle nudge and told him to go home to Annabelle. She would be sure to have an apple for him when he made it back.

As he unpacked and organized his supplies, he came upon a letter from Mila. She lovingly expressed her concerns for him and supported whatever decision he ultimately made. He hadn't shared all of the intimate details of the challenges he faced with her, but she knew enough to understand that the decisions he made would affect the entire pack. She wrote of the things she planned to do with Annabelle in an effort to keep her entertained in his absence. He hoped canning beets was going to be way more fun for his little girl than it sounded. There was nothing worse than an over-active child doing something dull. Describing Annabelle as over-active was putting it mildly; she was a force, and he hoped Mila and the beets survived her energy.

Mila's kind words warmed him; she had a positive effect on his life. She came and went at will, and some of her stays were longer than others. He didn't ask where she went, and she never offered an explanation, but he often wondered about the life she lived when she wasn't with the pack. Her stay had been several months this time, and in the past she would have been gone long before now. Logan hoped for the sake of the villagers he could find a way out of his current mess, especially if Mila was planning one of her trips. One of them really needed to be there and he was too edgy for it to be him. He folded the letter quietly and slid it into his satchel with the rest of his reading material. He would respond to it after he situated camp.

Among the supplies, Mila sent dried fruits and meats, several pounds of tubers and a healthy supply of ale. Logan would eat the more perishable items first, and because of his sweet tooth, the shortbread would be one of the first things to go. He propped the wagon level with a log and left the food items on it, taking off only what he needed for the night. He was in the process of shifting a few of the boxes around when the hair on the back of his neck started to creep. The spider-like tingling traveled down his neck and flared onto the tops of his shoulders. Someone was watching him.

Logan looked deep into the woods, his heightened sight competing with the shadows of dusk obscuring the thick tree line. He raised his head, sniffing the breeze in an attempt to pick up a scent. He continued to scan the area, side to side, even behind him, but nothing. The sensation was starting to fade, perhaps he was letting the solitude get to him. He needed to find his mate soon; he didn't care much for being alone. Unless Zilla was his only choice for company, then he preferred to be by himself. Cats weren't pack animals by nature, and she talked more than Annabelle did — if that were at all possible.

He pulled a few blankets and pillows from the wagon to place under the lean-to he created with the wagon. Mila had thought about his comfort, and he appreciated that. It was especially welcome after spending several nights sleeping on the hard ground with nary a blanket and his satchel to use as a pillow. During the last full moon, he felt the need to leave quickly, so hadn't had time to prepare properly. Knowing he would be staying for another few weeks, he took the time to build a proper shelter.

By the time he was done covering the supplies left in the wagon with canvas and building a fire, he had all but forgotten the eerie sensation of being watched, until he heard the soft snap of a tree branch.

"Who's out there? Show yerself," he snapped, as he bent to pull a blade from its sheath inside his boot. He sniffed the breeze, picking up a slight scent of musk and the faintest hint of garlic. But there was something beneath that as well. Not as much a smell, but a feeling.

Over the crackle and pop of the fire, the footsteps became more prominent. Logan could now tell which direction the stranger was coming from and prepared himself for a fight even though he had no idea what manner of creature approached. He slid behind the wagon, and called out again to the stranger.

"I'm armed, ya should know, and not expectin' company." Logan looked around the tree in the direction of the footsteps and saw a cloaked figure step into the dim light of the campfire. His hands were raised up near his head and all alarms that had been going off in Logan's mind ceased. The stranger seemed human.

The figure's response was calm and unconcerned. "I am unarmed, wolf. I am merely here to share your fire and hospitality on my way through."

"How can I trust you're tellin' the truth?"

The figure paused slightly then sat on one of the logs surrounding the fire. He slouched over, putting his elbows on his knees and responded with a laugh and a shake of his head.

"You can't."

"How did ya know I was lycan?"

"Didn't know for sure until now."

If nothing else, the man was honest. Logan couldn't help but smile. He stepped out into the light of the fire, warily looking at the figure across from him. Other than his face being covered by shadows and a hood, the man didn't seem threatening in any way. His body wasn't tense, and he didn't seem prepared for battle.

"I don't do well with strangers, so we best be introducing ourselves. Name is Logan."

"Kadar," the man replied as he pulled his hood down to reveal his face. Logan stepped closer, placing his knife in his left hand as he reached over to shake with his right. The man looked to be about the same physical age as Logan, although with a much slimmer and less muscular build. Logan had the impression that this man relied on his ability to quickly blend into the background and disappear. His otherwise nondescript features of dark brown eyes and dark shoulder-length hair were disrupted by a deep scar running vertically the length of his left cheek. It was recently obtained, as it was still puffy and red.

Logan nodded to the injury with his head, then bent to slide his knife back into his boot. "Looks like you got into some trouble. Lettin' you know, there'll be none of that here. So long as you don't start it."

Kadar shook his head and smiled with tired eyes that gave Logan the impression that they had seen too much. It made him wonder about his story. The man's voice was tired but firm. "I'm very capable of finishing it, but try never to start it."

"Aye. Know what you mean." Logan walked over to the wagon and pulled off a jug of ale. He showed it to Kadar as he walked back to the fire and located two mugs. "Ye mentioned hospitality?"

"I did. And I thank you," Kadar smiled. He took the mug offered to him and clinked it against Logan's before his first drink. "Cheers."

"Sláinte." Logan drained half of his glass before walking back to his makeshift kitchen near the fire. "Are ye hungry?"

Kadar nodded. "A meal would be most appreciated, thank you."

Logan started heating a frying pan with venison sausages as Kadar pulled his log closer to the fire. He handed his guest a large slice of Mila's homemade bread with honey, before slicing a piece for himself. "We'll have shortbread for dessert."

"This will be the best I've eaten in weeks."

"And why is that?" Logan was curious to know how his guest had come to find him in such a remote place. While he no longer felt threatened, Logan still didn't completely trust him. Trust took time and, in his mind, was always earned.

"I never stay in one place for long. I'm what you would call a lone wolf." Kadar shrugged his shoulders and took another swig of beer before continuing.

"Never understood that expression, wolves travel in packs."

Kadar laughed. "Guess you're right. Suppose we'll need to come up with a different expression."

"Aye. Lone cat, perhaps. Or bear."

"Just so," Kadar agreed.

"What brings ye through these parts?"

"Let's just say that I'm between employers at the moment."

"The last one give ya that nick?"

"In a round-about way I suppose," he said as he absently rubbed his cheek. He reached up and took the plate Logan handed him and nodded his thanks. "My former employer ended up in a situation that flattened his castle to the ground. I got the scratch making my way out of the rubble."

"Your former employer was Ryker?"

Kadar paused and tipped his head, his forehead creased in confusion. "You know him?"

"Aye. Worked for him meself," Logan admitted. "Not proud of it, but at the time I thought he would help me find something I've been looking for. Found out quickly he is only interested in helping himself and had to make new alliances."

"Ryker wasn't someone you could rely on, that is a fact. He may have been a different man before the death of his wife, but I only ever knew him after."

"Aye. The death of a mate would be the ultimate devastation in my mind. You knew her then?"

Kadar paused before he responded. "No," he said quietly. "I never even got a name, just knew her death was why he was after so much power. Almost like he could bring her back if he was able to gain enough of it."

"Too much power without the sense or compassion to wield it is never good for anyone involved."

Kadar raised his glass and nodded. "I'll drink to that." His mood seemed pensive, there was something troubling him. Logan knew better than most that lives had secrets and left the stranger with his.

Logan raised his glass in kind and took a drink. "I was in the same building with a friend of mine when it collapsed, barely made it out meself."

Kadar nodded in agreement. "I was in a corridor leading to the kitchenswhen the building started to collapse, but never knew what happened. I managed to get out through an access hall leading to the rear of the complex. Once I made it outside, I realized the devastation was all-encompassing. Did you happen to see anything?"

"I was in the courtyard when it happened. I witnessed a shadow come up from the depths of the dungeons and hover over Ryker's form. It was as if the shadow absorbed him, since the next thing I knew Ryker's body was gone. The shadow started glowin', like the great star on a cloudless night. It kept increasing in size until it took up the courtyard and released me from the spell I was under. Next thing I knew my friend was leading me down a hallway with the building crumbling around us. Thankfully, we were both lycans, so we managed to escape by changin' to our animal forms. We were able to squeeze through smaller spaces."

"Handy skill indeed," Kadar agreed. "So where is your friend?"

"Thankfully, she is back with her family," Logan muttered. "She can be a bit of a trial."

Kadar laughed and poured another round for them both. "I believe most women can at one time or another. Seems like fate has brought us together for a common cause that has yet to be determined, Logan."

"Aye. I would agree with that statement, I am never one to turn my head against a message from the fates. We will see where this friendship goes, Kadar..."

"Last name's Nagi."

Logan gave a quick nod. "Blackwood. Name's Logan Blackwood."

Kadar raised his mug toward Logan, who raised his in response. "Here's to friendships and new alliances."

"Sláinte."

Kadar nodded and clinked his mug with Logan's. "Fe Sahetek."

Logan must have looked confused; he had never heard that term before. It prompted a smile from his new friend.

"Means good luck in my language," Kadar said.

Logan gave Kadar's glass another clink. "Aye, I'll drink to that. I can use all the luck I can get."

After the final glass of ale, and one last check around the perimeter, Logan and Kadar both fell asleep quickly. Logan wasn't sure what woke him, but when he glanced over to Kadar he noticed he wasn't moving. He heard snoring from across the fire; it seemed his guest was still asleep.

Logan got up and put another couple of logs on the fading fire, stoking it to raise the flames. The night was cool and he welcomed the fire's warmth. He sat back down, pulled his bedding closer and laid his head on his pillow, watching the flames twirl and dance in the center of the pit.

Flames had calmed him since he was a young pup, and tonight was no exception. The fire was particularly soothing this evening, although he would have to admit that it might have more to do with the amount of ale he and Kadar knocked back. He watched the orange, yellow and greenish-blue flames wave and weave, reaching up toward the night skies like a woman reaching for her lover. Logan stared into the flames, his vision blurring slightly and his soul calmed by the colors. His eyes quickly came to focus when he realized there was something present in the flames. He sat up slowly, fearful that he would frighten whatever was in the fire. As he gazed into the flames the image became clearer, and as it came into focus, he realized it was the same yellow creature he had seen before.

The image reached for him, and once again he heard a female voice muffled beneath a faceless mask. "I'm here to help you. I'm going to get you out of here, just take my hand."

Logan shook his head and whispered. "Nae. I'll be stayin' here." He sat up slowly and placed his arms behind him and leaned back on them. She wasn't a threat. "You're a strange looking creature."

"Strange looking? Well that's rude!" The creature laughed as she pulled the covering from her face. Logan realized now that it was a hat of some sort, since the hair she had kept underneath came billowing out upon its release. Waves and waves of curly dark hair were shaken out and fluffed with her fingers. He didn't know what to say; all he could do was stare. His mind kept chanting that she was the one he had been waiting for. And if she wasn't, his mind would have a hard time settling for anyone else. She was the most enchanting woman he had ever seen.

The woman took a step closer and he could see her coffee colored eyes. He loved the auburn tones in her dark hair and noticed they were wider and more prominent than what you would see naturally. It was almost as though she had taken a paint brush and streaked them on. As he looked into her eyes, his heart recognized her importance. His sudden intake of breath made her demeanor change quickly, and her smile turned predatory and wild. It was clear she intended to toy with him, and he sensed that with her he'd be playing with fire.

Without losing eye contact, she moved her hands to the top of her coat and undid the latches. With a quick pull of the zipper and a shrug of her shoulders, the coat was off in record time and dropped to the ground. She pulled on some straps that went over her shoulders, and the pants that were attached slid down next. Her voice came out husky, as if it were made of the smoke from the fire.

"You still think I'm strange looking?"

Logan couldn't respond; he only shake his head and looked at the sculpted goddess standing before him. She was magnificent. He glanced over to Kadar's sleeping form only long enough to make sure he was still asleep, since she was scantily clothed, leaving nothing to the imagination. There was no way he would allow any man to share his dream. He wasn't sure what she had on, but it barely covered what it needed to and was tight-fitting to her form. He was licking his lips when her voice blanketed him once more.

"You like what you see, big boy?"

Thankfully he found his voice, although his first few words came out in a croak. "Aye lass… Aye lassie, I do."

"I take it you want to see more?" She moved a step closer and was at the very edge of the fire.

"I cannae think of anything I want more."

Her eyebrow raised and she responded with a laugh. "I'll just bet, my hungry Lobo. Tell you what, you show me yours and I'll show you mine."

He slid closer to flame and reached his hand forward for her, his cock so hard it pained him to move. She was definitely his mate; there was no denying the pull. He wished he knew what to do to bring her through the flame. There was a force in place preventing him from touching her.

"Well?" She questioned, as she looked directly at the bulge tenting the piece of fabric in his lap. He had all but forgotten about the kilt he laid over himself in the night. She was bold, and he was ever so glad he slept in the nude. He slipped the tartan down inch by inch, watching her face for signs of approval. Her chest heaved with shallow breaths as the fabric revealed the thin trail of hair that led to his treasure. It was her turn to lick her lips, and he imagined how they would feel wrapped around his…

"Mother Goddess!" she exclaimed, staring at his uncovered form. Her wide eyes stared directly at his penis, which stood proud and ready for action. Her smile was brighter than a hundred fires. Aye, she was the one for him!

He couldn't help the teasing tone in his voice as he rose to his knees and placed his hands on his hips. There was no hiding anything he had to offer, the kilt was pooled near his knees. He pulled his shoulders back and puffed out his chest. She was going to see everything the gods gifted him with.

"We had an accord, did we not?"

"An accord?"

"Aye lassie, an agreement," he grinned. "You show me yours, if I show you mine."

Her laugh was loud and deep, vibrating deep through his soul and shaking his patience. Logan wanted her now, he didn't want to wait. He held out his hand and waved back at himself. "Give me your hand, lassie, and I'll show you what I've got firsthand."

"That wasn't the agreement, sir. I hardly know you. But considering this is some sort of dream and an agreement has been made, I suppose I need to follow through."

Logan couldn't hold back the groan as she turned her back to him and unceremoniously removed the small black top from her breasts. She dropped it to the ground and glanced back at him over her shoulder, laughing as he grabbed onto his throbbing cock and squeezed. He hadn't gone off too soon since he was young; he wasn't about to start now. It was evident she liked games, and he was ready to play.

"Turn around, lassie, and let me see ya."

"In a moment, big boy," she said with a laugh as she peeled down the tight black fabric covering her ass and kicked it aside. With her back to him, he had a glorious view of her backside, and his hand immediately started to move rhythmically. The golden globes of her buttocks were more beautiful than any full moon he had seen in his lifetime, and he soon lost control between what he was seeing and what he imagined doing to her. She was slowly turning, her hands crossed over her chest to cover her breasts. His hand pumped and growls came deep from his throat. She was almost completely facing him now, but his eyes were locked on her face as she watched him pleasure himself with a soft smile. Her tongue swiped slowly between her lips and Logan gasped, his heart pounding as he threw back his head and howled at the night. His endless orgasm shook him to his core, breath rasping as he descended from the high. He hardly registered the voice that spoke to him as he came to. When the man's voice repeated itself, it snapped Logan back to reality and his eyes cleared.

"If you needed some time alone, I could have taken a walk."

Logan looked into the fire and on either side of it, but the woman was gone. His guest was across the fire staring straight at him. Logan was pretty sure the howling woke him up. Feeling the heat rise to his face, Logan stood quickly, wrapping his kilt around his hips and heading toward the tree line. He was not in the mood, and he had never done anything like that in his life. Doing it was bad enough, having it witnessed was horrifying. He decided to pretend it never happened; that would be the best way to proceed.

"I need a bath," he spit out gruffly.

"I'll bet," Kadar laughed, and then rolled and put his back to the fire.

Logan heard chuckles until he made it halfway up the path, at which point the chuckles became full-bellied laughter. As embarrassed as he was, he laughed as well, since the situation he was in was completely ridiculous. Yet for some strange reason, his soul felt lighter than it had in years. He knew was going to find her; it was just a matter of time.

6

Sera woke with a start, the covers kicked to the floor and her hair in a poufy, knotted mess. She must have fallen asleep while watching television again and wondered if she would ever finish the first season of Outlander. Considering her latest fascination with the show, it wasn't surprising she dreamed of him again, the man with the tummy-tingling accent and scotch whiskey eyes. She was really starting to have a thing for men in kilts, which was strange considering she had never given them a thought before.

She still tingled from the way he made her feel in her dream; how he warmed her blood and made her heart race. He brought out the naughty in her through bantering and flirting, although she supposed it could have also been the drinks she had after dinner. Had she seriously done a striptease for him? That was the first time that had ever happened. She must have been out of it, since every stitch of clothing she had on the night prior was dropped to the floor near her bed. She really needed to cut back on the scotch.

Sera padded naked to the kitchen to start the coffee maker, recalling some of the details from her dream. Closing her eyes as the coffee percolated, she sorted through the vivid images in her mind.

Her Scottish dream-hunk had been sitting at the time, with a blanket covering him from the waist down and nothing on above it. There was a thick leather strap circling the upper part of his well-formed bicep, and his chest was lightly dusted with jet black hair. Her dream-self thought he must work out, since his abs looked like he had spent the last several years doing sit-ups.

Although he was the size of a weight-lifter, he didn't look the part since he had facial scruff and shoulder length black hair. He definitely didn't manscape, and she wasn't sure she would want him to—since feral looked amazing on him. She supposed it was why the nickname "Lobo" came to her mind in the dream. He looked wild and untamed, just like a wolf, and she remembered the strongest desire to move her hands over his impressive chest and follow the line down to the massive bulge he flaunted.

She asked him to come with her and he responded with a laugh, calling her a strange looking creature. Even though she called him rude, she wasn't offended in the slightest. She was used to being razzed at work and could dish it out as much as she could take it.

His accent was Scottish, she knew for sure now, since he had sounded a lot like Gerard Butler. She wondered why he was calling her a creature, but then realized she was wearing turnout gear. She supposed it could look creature-like to someone not familiar with it. Dreams were strange that way, always messing with interpretations. The latest vision was so similar to the one she had at the Wellness Center fire, she wondered if they had some significance or connection. She would need to talk to her abuela soon; she was excellent at interpreting visions and dreams. And these dreams, or visions, were occurring too often to ignore.

She recalled the feeling discomfort; her gear made her hot and sweaty in the dream. When the tattoo on her chest started to sting, she thought back to the day of the fire. Just as before, there wasn't a hole in her jacket, and it was as if the stinging was a sign. But what was it telling her?

The shield on her helmet had fogged, and the only fire that had been present was the small one he sat near. Their banter made her brave and she had removed her helmet and shook out her hair. That was when it had really gotten hot. The intake of his breath caused her to look directly into the man's eyes, where she saw tiny flecks gold within their depths. They had been locked on her, absorbing every detail of her face. She had to be at least fifteen years older than him, but his heated gaze made the years melt away. Sera had never been admired like that in her life; it was as if his very existence depended on his ability to touch her. She relished the feeling, and she promised herself that from now on nothing less would do. If she were ever to get involved with another man, he was going to worship her. At the very least, he would have to look like the man she stripped for in her dreams; muscular, wild with a huge, throbbing…

Her eyes snapped open as the Keurig finished her coffee. Her reaction was ridiculous. She was panting and her breasts were heavy and on high alert. Not to mention she was boiling up. Had her furnace kicked on? Could she be having a hot flash? She pulled her hair up off her neck to try to get some relief. The glowing numbers on the thermostat reflected 68° but she sure didn't believe it, she was sweating like she did in her turn-out gear. She padded back and forth trying to create enough of a breeze to cool herself. Perhaps she was running a fever? Honestly, who was she kidding? She was probably just horny. She had been fine until she started thinking about the Scottish hunk. If she had gotten this hot in her sleep, it was no wonder she had torn off all her clothes.

Walking to the fridge, she opened the top door of the freezer and stuck her head inside, welcoming the frigid air that dropped down and cooled the front of her body. She was starting to feel better and gain some control of her senses, the hot flash seemed to be dissipating. Lord, help her if that was what it was; she was too young for those to start—wasn't she?

Sera rummaged around for a tray of ice cubes and pulled them from the shelf. There was no way she was drinking her coffee hot now. Finding some creamer in the back of her fridge, she quickly put her coffee on ice and took a few large swigs before heading into the shower. With the naughty way her mind had been acting, it would serve her right to subject herself to an icy spray.

Sera made the water as cold as she could handle, and the icy jets felt marvelous on her heated skin. She closed her eyes against the sprays and waited a few seconds for the water to make its way through the mass of hair to cool her scalp. It felt amazing; she didn't feel a chill at all, which was strange considering she had hardly turned the hot water on. After washing her hair, she tucked her head under the spray once again to rinse. Just as she got the last of the suds out of her hair, she realized she could no longer feel the water hitting her skin. It was as if the water stopped entirely, although she knew that wasn't right since she could still hear it spraying from the shower head.

Sera cracked open her eyes and could hardly see through the steam that surrounded her. She reached blindly for the knobs to turn the hot water down. Had she turned it on accidently? Extending her arms in front of her, she twisted the hot water off entirely and waited for the freezing jolt. It never came.

She watched in amazement as the cold water came out of the shower head, hit her skin, and steam rose up in its place. There was something wrong; she was no longer getting wet. The sprays came out as water, but immediately turned to steam anyplace they hit her. She had never seen anything like it in all her years as a firefighter and calmed herself with the thought that there must be a rational explanation. Water turned to steam over 212°, there was no way her body temp was over that. Was there? Logical explanation or no, she was unwilling to investigate the causes until she had some clothes on. She was starting to feel vulnerable and shaky.

Turning the water off completely, Sera got out of the tub and reached for a towel. She shook it out and realized immediately she wouldn't need it. Somehow, some way, her hair and body were both completely dry. Impossible. Her body being instantly dry was one thing, but her hair? It never took less than two hours to air dry, it was much too thick.

The steam in the room dissipated, and there were no signs of a hot shower on the mirror above the sink. If it weren't for the scent of strawberry shampoo on her hair, she might have imagined the entire thing. She was no longer feeling warm, like she did in the kitchen, but decided to take her temperature anyway. Maybe she was coming down with something and it was causing hallucinations. The digital display showed 101°, which surprised her; she didn't feel feverish. She decided with the mild temperature, and the way her mind was working, she had better call in sick and stay in bed. Obviously she needed a better night's sleep and to get whatever this was out of her system before it got any worse.

△

The hospital was quiet and James was bored. Thankfully, a breathless voice interrupted his third attempt at reading an article on fly fishing. He really needed to have someone bring him something else to read.

"Mr. Fisher, you have a visitor."

He looked up with a grin; it was Rebecca. She was by far the nicest looking nurse on the floor, and one of the most attentive to his needs. He wondered how attentive she would be if he took her to dinner after he was discharged. Perhaps if his plans to pursue Sera didn't work out, he would see.

"Thank you, love."

She dropped her eyes and flushed prettily as she backed out of the doorway to let his sister enter. Brooke rolled her eyes as she walked toward the bed, shaking her head with a grin. She nodded toward the empty doorway and leaned down to give him a kiss before addressing him with a sly smile.

"What was that all about?"

He couldn't help but laugh. "What was what all about?"

"Oh please, James, I could hardly walk through the pheromones filling this room. You have another staff member completely smitten with you."

"All part of my sinister plot to rule the world!"

"Well it seems that so far you will just be ruling the female nursing staff at Verde Valley Medical Clinic."

"I don't know, I was visited earlier by an Andrew who might be willing to give it a go as well."

Her shocked laugh made him smile, he loved hearing her laugh. "You are the absolute worst, James."

"Been saying that for years, love."

She pulled the nearby chair closer to his beside and sat. It seemed to him that she was planning on staying a while. He was fine with that since he didn't relish reading his only magazine yet again. He looked up into his sister's face and then followed her gaze to her hands twisting and squirming in her lap.

"What's on your mind, sweetest?"

Brooke looked up and gave him a soft smile, looking so much like the mother they had both lost so long ago. Their mother had long blond hair as well, although hers hadn't included the greenish blue streaks Brooke's did.

"You have always had that way about you. I could never hide anything from you when I was younger."

"You're easy to read. Always wondered if perhaps that was why you moved to the United States."

"So I could hide things from you?"

"So it would be easier," he laughed.

She nodded with a quiet smile. He had a feeling he had touched on something that would come out over time. After their parents died, he hadn't been there for her like he should have been. He knew that now.

There was so much he missed in his sister's life, and he hoped his plans would give them the time they needed to heal the past.

Brooke took a deep breath and shared her thoughts. "There is something I need to tell you, and I need you to keep an open mind."

"Is this about your fiancé? Do I have to give him what for?"

The smile was back. He was glad since the melancholy look broke his heart. "No, this isn't about Will, he and I are fine. He says hello, by the way, he wasn't able to come. He had a board meeting he couldn't miss after his last show of the week."

"Understandable. He has a lot going on between his magic shows and running his family firm." Brooke wiggled in her seat. She didn't look like she was excited to share whatever was on her mind. He got a sinking feeling and said a small prayer that it wasn't what he thought it was.

"Remember the dreams I had when I was younger?"

Shit. "Brooke, you aren't going to tell me…"

"They were real."

He closed his eyes and took a deep breath. Christ, he knew he should have been there for her. He really thought she had put this all behind her. He should have never let her move.

"James, I need you to believe me. So much has happened, and it is simply impossible for me to keep this from you any longer."

"Brooke, you remember what the therapist said…"

"Trust me, I remember," she snapped. "But the therapist had no idea that what I was going through was real. No one did."

"You had been through so much at the time. You had just lost Mum and Dad. It was natural that you would imagine replacements for them."

"I didn't imagine it, and I need to show you something."

She raised her hand and pointed to the glass of water sitting on his food tray. As she waved her finger, he heard a crackling sound and looked to the glass, which frosted before his eyes. He looked back to Brooke's face with surprise.

"Brilliant! You learned one of Will's magic tricks."

Disappointment scrunched her face and laced her voice. "It's magic, but not the kind you are thinking. It's not an illusion. It's real. Real magick."

"Right."

"James, it truly is." She pointed her finger at the nearby water pitcher, the contents of which also froze, then blew into her hands and held them clasped over his tray. A chunk of ice the size of a baseball fell from her open hands, and he tried to figure out how the trick worked. He looked up when she called his name and disappeared before his eyes. He looked around the room, questioning his own sanity, when she reappeared on the opposite side of his bed.

"How did you…"

"I am able to manipulate the element of water. I can travel in mist form and re-animate at will. I've also been practicing controlling the weather, although I'm not super great at it in this dimension."

"This dimension?"

"Yes. The place I dreamed of all those years was real, so were the people. Will and I traveled there through an elemental portal and have been unraveling our purpose ever since. Aleck has been there as well, James. His girlfriend Amie is the element of Air."

"Do you realize how mental this all sounds? For god's sake, Brooke, they will commit you alongside me if anyone overhears this rot. Difference is I get out in thirty days. You, they will keep indefinitely."

"What else can I do to prove it to you?"

"Short of making it snow in Sedona, I'm not sure."

"I would but it would take me days to recoup."

"Right."

He couldn't believe she was laughing. Didn't she realize how serious this was? It was as if she had never gone to therapy, and now she was pulling others into her delusion. Did his friend Aleck really believe this rubbish?

"James, I realize how it sounds, and I will take you there to see for yourself as soon as I can. I needed you to know just in case something happens. Things are starting to get a bit crazy and I'm not sure how safe you are here. Amie and I are looking for someone who can help, and from the clues that we have been given, we believe that person is somewhere in this area."

He picked up his glass to take a drink, realizing too late the liquid was entirely solid.

"Let me take care of that," Brooke said softly as she took the cup from his hands and blew into it. "Here you are."

James hesitated, shook his head and then drank the contents in two swallows. He desperately wished it was two fingers of scotch. It was the worst time for him to give up drinking.

Brooke gathered her purse from the chair and leaned in to kiss his cheek. "I'll give you some time for this to sink in. I'm sure once it does you'll have questions for all of us. I'll bring Aleck and Amie with me next time."

All he could do was nod his head as Brooke blew him a kiss from the doorway. When he saw the heart-shaped ice chunk on his tray, he shook his head in amazement. There was no way he could explain any of it logically; it had to be a trick. He hoped his friend Aleck would be able to make some sense of the situation, although he didn't hold out much hope. Not only was he worried that thirty days in therapy wouldn't be enough for him now, but also that the other people in his life might be joining him. If they were all buying into Brooke's dream world, every single one of them was in trouble.

7

Sera stood in her second bedroom, surrounded by her workout equipment and taking her frustrations out on the speed bag on the wall. Mark hadn't been available for a sparring session at Frankie's, which was probably best since she felt like punching something until her hands bled. She might have really hurt him after the beating he took from her just a few days ago.

The speed bag rocked and vibrated with each punch she threw. It flew back at her just as fast as the disillusionment did after the phone call she took earlier. The chief hadn't talked long and she didn't make the conversation comfortable.

After she heard that she hadn't gotten the promotion, every word he said was muffled by the disappointment that clouded her mind. After sixty seconds of awkward silence, the chief told her to take a few days off to process. She knew it was only because he didn't want to deal with her temper, especially since her snappish comments would be directed at him for the next few weeks. He didn't like it when people were upset with him, especially her, so taking a few days off was probably best for them both.

"How… the… fuck…" Her anger came out in breathless pants between punches. "…did… that… dipshit… Holden… take… it… from… me!"

Her punches, each more powerful than the last, landed in the identical spot on the bag.

"He…must… have… blown… the… chief!" The last punch was thrown with emphasis, and while she knew it wasn't true, it made her feel better to say it out loud. On top of being heterosexual, everyone knew the chief loved his wife; hell, even Sera loved her!

When she cooled off she would have to have drinks with Martha and vent; she was an extremely good listener. Maybe she would have some insight as to why the chief made the decision he did, at least from a female's point of view. Sera thought that might be helpful; if nothing else, she could drink through her anger, maybe even have some hot sex with a random stranger to cool her down. Hell, maybe not random, maybe someone she knew. She wondered if James would be available for a night out soon; he seemed interested. If not, there was always Nathan. Much as she hadn't wanted to go there originally, the rules for her changed moving forward. Now that she wasn't being promoted, all bets were off for future sexual activity. And there was no shortage of men in her life who would agree to help her out.

She felt reverberations in the floor as the bag pulled and tugged at its mounting. She would have to look into reinforcing the bar; it looked as though some of the drywall was starting to crack. She decided to give the speed bag a rest, and moved over to the heavy bag, giving it a few round-house kicks before settling in for more punches.

"Holden has only been with the department for two years. How the hell did he pull it off?" Sarah muttered as she readied herself. She took a deep cleansing breath, filling her body with oxygen, then started in with her punches. With each left and right hook she felt her anger rise. The workout wasn't relieving the pressure like it usually did. If anything, it was making it worse. Sweat poured from her body, and she wondered what she set the thermostat at. She had forgotten to check it again after what happened in the kitchen. She ignored the heat and kept punching; she was at the tail end of her work out anyway.

Bemoaning her loss of the fire inspector position and picking up the speed on her punches, she frantically tried to work out her frustration but to no avail. The heat was getting to her and playing tricks on her eyes. Was that smoke? As she punched, the pull and tug on her muscles felt too good to stop, but she knew she needed to. Sera was worked up. She felt stinging bile rising up in her throat. Her anger was palpable, and now she was seeing visions of flames covering the bag. Was she dehydrated? It couldn't be real; it had to be hallucination, just like the voice she heard over the crackle of the flames.

"Thig rium mo ghaol."

She shook her head, confused by the language but recognizing the voice just as if it were her own. His voice was already part of her psyche and the effects on her body both confused and frightened her. He was a shadow in the flames, the man from her visions, and she fought for her sanity with every punch to the bag.

"You aren't real," she said as the sweat stung her eyes. "You need to leave me alone."

"I cannae do that anymore than I can stop breathing," he said with a chuckle. "Don't make me wait too long, lassie."

She didn't need to open her eyes to know he was gone, and with him the flames. She felt it in her soul. As hot and bothered as he made her, he also provided a strange comfort that put her racing mind at ease. It made her wonder if she would ever be able to find anyone that made her feel that way in real life. Someone who made her feel connected to something greater than herself each time she was near him.

As her punches landed during her cool down, small white puffs billowed from the area she contacted. The thought crossed her mind that she may have created a small tear in the bag when the wrappings on her hand slipped from her palms and dropped to the floor. She stopped the punches and looked down, before flipping her hands palm side up and opening her fingers.

What she saw there confused her at first, and she ran her right finger through the soot on her left palm. Both palms were black, as were the ends of the wrappings that had fluttered to her feet. It was almost as if the heat in her closed hand was hot enough to burn the cotton strips and cause them to fall off, which she knew couldn't be the case. She was hot, but her hands weren't on fire; they weren't even red. Those flames she punched through hadn't been real.

There was something strange going on with her body and it wasn't anything any of her EMT friends could help her with. What was happening was otherworldly; she knew that since her abuela had taught her to recognize those signs. Sera knew sometimes smaller messages were hints to something larger and she didn't want to miss anything. Her occupation was too dangerous to take any chances. While there were any number of psychics in Sedona that could give her some guidance, her abuela seemed to be better at really getting to the center of a problem. Besides, she was long overdue in seeing her.

Sera called her abuela, but she didn't answer her phone. With the days off she had been granted, and taking a few more off for good measure, Sera decided a visit was in order. Her abuela wasn't getting any younger and a phone call wouldn't be enough. She needed to see her face to face. Something wasn't right. And it would be nice to be home for the upcoming holidays. Being single, she had always taken the holiday shifts, but not this time.

Sera stripped out of her workout clothes, looking over her shoulder to ensure that the gorgeous vision wasn't still there enjoying a peep. She wouldn't put it past him after the way he looked at her during her dream striptease. Wondering what he said to her, she wrote down what she had heard phonically on her way into the shower. Perhaps her abuela would know what it meant; she was pretty familiar with Gaelic even though it wasn't her first language. She used it all the time with her spellworks.

Her body was starting to cool from her workout and the sweat chilled her. She couldn't help but wonder if she would have a repeat of the crazy shower she had the other day, but decided to risk it. She smelled horrible, and she wanted to get cleaned up just in case she could find a flight to Spain after dinner. That would give her time to pack and get a hold of her grandmother before boarding. The more she thought about the trip, the more she knew it was the right thing to do. Her grandmother was a wise woman; she would know what was happening. At least that was what Sera hoped.

The shower cooperated, and she spent some extra time shaving and soaking in the hot sprays. It felt good on her aching muscles. After she towel dried her hair, she threw on a clean tee-shirt and shorts and separated the piles of laundry in her room between clean and dirty. There was really no avoiding it any longer; she needed to wash her clothes. She picked through the clothing and pulled out the items she knew she would need to take and loaded them in her stackable. The second load would have to wait, perhaps even until after her trip depending on when she was able to secure a flight.

With the laundry going and her bags down and ready to pack, she got on her laptop and checked out the flight schedule. There were limited flights, but because she was traveling alone she didn't feel like she would have a problem securing one. While it would cost her way more than she would have paid had she done a little pre-planning, she had plenty of money in the bank. What the hell else did she ever spend it on? Costly or no, this trip was definitely the right thing for her to do. She was tired of putting her life on hold for the "what ifs."

Sera lucked out on the flight; there was space on one leaving first thing the next day. It would mean 16 hours traveling time with two layovers, but since she still wasn't able to reach her grandmother by phone, she went ahead and booked it. Even though her grandmother was known to wander off from time to time, she was good about calling back.

Sera was getting worried, and she was glad she had taken the two-week vacation she had coming to her. The thought that she might need to stay longer to help the elderly woman made Sera anxious, and she prepared for a longer stay just in case. She spent the next few hours tidying her apartment, taking the perishable food items out to the dumpster, and paying her upcoming bills. By the time she finished packing and putting away her laundry, it was well past midnight. But, she felt better knowing she had things handled and could fully concentrate on enjoying time with her abuela. While she tried to remain positive and not imagine the worst, her sleep was fitful.

Δ

The next day, exhausted and sore, Sera swallowed three Motrin dry. She rubbed frankincense on her temples and the back of her neck while arranging for a rental car upon arrival at San Sebastián Airport. Since the small town of Zugarramurdi, where her abuela lived, was further inland, it would take Sera over an hour of driving and crossing through a portion of France to get there. She knew the first thing her grandmother would do would be to feed her a home cooked meal and then send her straight to bed. She couldn't wait; she loved to get spoiled and it had been much too long since she had visited. No matter how exhausted she was, her abuela would never forgive her for staying overnight in a hotel before traveling to her house.

The drive was lovely and passed through a small portion of France that jutted south into the top part of Spain. Zugarramurdi was located in the Province of Navarre, and was a small town with no more than 300 residents. It was best known for its history of the persecution of witches during the Inquisition, and stories of the 53 people found guilty of witchcraft during that time were shared daily at the Museo de las Brujas where Sera's grandmother worked. She walked visitors through the exhibits, describing the atrocities that took place at a time when fear of the unknown caused people to do horrific things.

The Cuevas de Zugarramurdi were nearby caves where celebrations of the summer and winter solstices still took place. Sera remembered attending with her grandmother years ago, and looking back, she realized that had her grandmother been alive at the time of the Inquisition she would have surely suffered at the hands of the senseless. Her grandmother's healing spells were harmless but would have easily been misunderstood in 1610. She supposed she herself could have been found guilty of practicing witchcraft, since many of the holistic remedies her grandmother swore by were now part of Sera's lifestyle. Because of her migraines, she was never without a bottle of Frankincense. She also regularly burnt white sage to remove negativity in her life, and the thought occurred to her that maybe it was time to do it again. She was sure her abeula would hook her up with some fresh herbs from her garden.

Sera pulled into the dirt drive that lead to her abuela's cottage and was surprised when she didn't see her out in the driveway to greet her. Her grandmother could generally hear people coming up the path; her windows were always open and sounds carried. Sera opened the trunk to retrieve her luggage and glanced into the yard over the trunk. Had she gotten rid of her chickens? They usually were out to greet her as well. She slammed the trunk, but still no Abuela, only whispers of the wind and sporadic chirping of the crickets could be heard. She left her luggage in the drive and went up the steps. Something was off.

The door was locked, so she searched for a key underneath the blue ceramic pot on the porch where her grandmother kept it. The plant in the pot had long since died, and Sera's worry started to burn a hole in her stomach. The key was where her abeula always kept it, and she hurriedly jammed it in the lock and swung open the door.

"Abuela, it's me," she called out. "Are you here?"

The house was orderly, but smelled musty and abandoned. No one had been home in a while. Was it possible that she was staying somewhere else? Her grandmother had never been gone for the length of time it would have taken for the house to be so stale. Sera searched the house, the small bedrooms upstairs, to the cellar below, calling all the while but there was no sign of her grandmother. She tried to recall their last phone conversation; had she mentioned a festival or some activity at the museum that caused her to stay with a friend in town?

Following that theory, Sera went to the shed to look for her grandmother's car and felt her heart stop. The car was parked where it always was with a thin layer of dust covering it. Even the bicycle she sometimes took instead was present, leaning against the wall and covered with shiny webs. If her abuela had gone off to do spellworks, or was preparing for an event, she would have used one of them to get to town. Sera tamped down her feeling that something was wrong. Perhaps her grandmother had been picked up by a co-worker at the museum? She had been doing that more often now that her eyes weren't what they used to be.

As Sera jogged back to the house she called out, but there was no response. She tried to recall some of the names of her grandmother's co-workers, and wondered if she had their phone numbers in her phone. She didn't think so, but checked through her contacts anyway. She had her abuela's work number, and even though it was late and the museum was closed, she called just in case someone was working late. As the phone rang, she searched her grandmother's drawers for a phone book, for something that might provide a clue to who she might be staying with. She came up empty.

She checked the cupboards quickly, noticing they were all extremely bare. Where had all of her grandmother's food gone? She was never without several jars of canned tomatoes and homemade pickles. When she opened the refrigerator, the light didn't come on and after a quick glance in the freezer she realized it was not only empty, but unplugged as well. Did her grandmother go on a trip?

Taking the stairs two at a time, Sera ran up the stairs to the bedroom and searched the closet shelves where her grandmother kept her luggage. Both bags were missing, and a wave of relief washed over her. So perhaps just a trip, albeit a long one. Why the hell hadn't she gotten her a cell phone last Christmas? She checked the drawers; it was obvious that clothing had been taken out, as there were only a few items left behind. She checked the medicine cabinet in the bathroom, which was completely empty, and noticed the only drug that had been left behind was a small bottle of Tums. She shook four into her hands and popped them into her mouth, chewing them into a stale paste on her way back down the stairs.

It was pretty evident her grandmother had gone somewhere, and from the amount of dust, it had been quite some time. It didn't make sense since Sera had just spoken to her a few weeks ago. Sera wondered if she would have gone through all the trouble to find homes for her chickens, or if they just found somewhere else to go. Perhaps while Sera was on her way to Spain, her abuela decided to surprise her in Sedona? Wouldn't she have mentioned the trip on the phone? The clues she was gathering didn't point to that. Just to be sure, after calling and checking the nearest hospitals, she contacted all airlines with flights out of San Sebastian. She wanted to be sure to check any flights within the last few weeks that her grandmother may have traveled on. The staff wasn't very helpful, due to privacy laws, but let Sera know that once they checked her credentials they would get back to her with any information they could via email.

Much as she hated to admit it, there was nothing more she could do immediately to find her grandmother. Her brain was shutting down from exhaustion and she needed sleep. It made her feel slightly better that her abuela had apparently gone on a trip, and she hoped after the museum opened, she would find that she was staying with one of her co-workers. Her gut told her she was okay, as strange as it was; her tattoo would have given her some kind of sign if she wasn't.

Sera went out to the drive to gather her luggage and took the bags up the stairs to the spare bedroom where she typically stayed. It still held memories from her childhood, framed articles from her achievements, and her most cherished possession, a photo of her parents when her mother was pregnant with her.

She picked up the framed picture, smiling softly as she traced her fingers lovingly along the glass. Her father had been so proud, his hand laying protectively over her mother's belly. Sera's mother beamed with her pregnancy and love was written plainly on her face as she rested her head on his shoulder and smiled into the camera. Sera had her mother's hair, dark, curly and untamed; however, her eyes were definitely her father's deep brown. She would have much rather had her mother's eye color, it was uniquely beautiful. They were a light golden brown, like the caramel her grandmother made, and in a trick of light in this particular photo, they glowed with a golden radiance. Sera had met a lot of people, but never saw eyes quite like her mother's. Her abuela always said her mother's love for her could be seen in her eyes, and it made Sera a bit sad that she had gotten her hair instead.

After changing for bed, she slid between the clean sheets for some much needed rest. She was going to need it since the first thing on her list in the morning was going to be to track down her grandmother. Goddess help her since her grandmother could pretty much be anywhere.

8

*Z*illa limped up the walk leading to her sister Sevilla's cottage, wondering how she was going to hide her latest round of injuries. She decided there was no use trying; Erebos was entirely gone and his darker half Roy was bound to get worse as time went on. The visits with him would need to be limited in the future. As his power grew, so did his impatience and Zilla was on the receiving end of it. Even with her lycan abilities, her injuries took days to heal.

She needed her sister's help to figure out what came next. It would be a minor miracle if they all came through this without killing one another. They were being forced to face the secrets of the past. Zilla was no saint; she was the first to admit it, but their other sister Fate sure had made a real mess of things.

Sevilla's humble stone cottage stood as it had for well over 200 years, surrounded by the plants and flowers she used to create her potions. Zilla had never taken to gardening the way Sevilla had, so for years she had her sister make her medicines or infuse her stones for her. Zilla was glad they were back on speaking terms, since for the last few decades her own potions hardly came out right and her stones were never fully charged. Zilla really should have paid more attention during lessons when they were younger but always had more fun turning into a kitten and chasing the field mice.

With a couple of quick knocks, she let herself in the front door and made her way to the nearest chair at the dining table. She walked from the pond and her leg was aching. Zilla didn't dare create a portal any closer to Sevilla's homestead. Her sister liked her privacy and Zilla respected that. Besides, they agreed that any magick they still had access to should be reserved for emergencies.

Sevilla was at the sink rinsing root vegetables from the garden; it looked as though Zilla would be staying for dinner. The smile on Sevilla's face quickly changed to worry as she turned to greet her sister.

"What happened to you?" The concern in her voice was clear. She put the vegetables down and wiped her hands on her apron as she came around the table.

"I'm fine, Villy, just a scratch," Zilla said with a wave of her hand and a laugh.

Her sister pulled Zilla's thick black hair off the side of her neck and her eyes widened. Zilla knew what Sevilla was seeing by the intake of breath. The last time Zilla looked the bruising had turned a mottled yellow and covered the right side of her neck to the top of her shoulder. There were also fingertip sized bruises running along her collarbone on both sides that she saw in the mirror while getting ready for her visit. She hoped her hair would cover the worst of it, but it seemed she had been wrong.

"Zilla, this isn't a scratch and you know it. You haven't been this bruised since the day Logan brought you here - unconscious."

"That bruising was so much worse, lovey. A building collapsed on us and we had to dig our way out."

"That is my point exactly," Sevilla countered. "I'm assuming this is Roy's work since Erebos was never this rough with you. You have dark circles under your eyes as well. Are you getting any sleep?"

Zilla nodded. Her sister knew the situation. She knew because they all had a hand in creating the mess they were in.

"You're right, Erebos would never hurt me. He would get irritated with me but never raised a hand. Until recently, I thought Roy wouldn't either. And no, not really sleeping lately, too much on my mind I suppose."

Sevilla ran her hand along Zilla's upper back, causing her to wince. Her skin was tender, and it was obvious Zilla had more bruising than she realized. She had thought about wearing something that covered her arms, but the corset style top was the only thing she could wear comfortably. Now she knew why.

Her sister sighed deeply. Zilla could hear vast disappointment in the sound. It made her wonder if Sevilla still blamed her for the choices Zilla had made all those years ago. They hadn't spoken of that day since it happened, but Zilla knew they would need to open that wound once more and air it out for good. She wasn't sure she or Sevilla were ready for that, and wished their sister Fate was present to take her part in the blame.

They might be triplets, but they were as different from each other as the seasons were from the earth. They all had their own way of handling bad situations and this, by far, was the worst they had ever faced. She blamed Fate the most for the place they had come to; after all, she was the one who could see into the future.

Sevilla bustled to the sink, gathering ingredients along the way. "I can make something for that, but you will have to stay the night. It takes some time to brew and once you drink it you will need to lie down. Perhaps you should hold some lavender compresses on the worst of the bruising while the potion simmers. You were limping as well. Is your leg injured?"

"You had your back turned to me, how did you…never mind." Zilla laughed and shook her head. She should know better than to try to hide anything from Sevilla. Like with all things in the past, if it happened, she was in tune with it.

"It isn't as mystical as you think, Zilla. I saw you in the mirror over my sink when you came in." Sevilla smirked over her shoulder. "A compress should probably be held on that gash first since that will be slower to heal."

As usual, Sevilla saw way more than could ever be reflected in a mirror. They each developed different gifts over time. Even though Zilla was the only one of the sisters who had shape-shifting capabilities, she had always been envious of Sevilla's skill with perception and insight. It was as if she could see right through to the truth no matter how well hidden it was.

Zilla shrugged. "You don't need to worry about it, Villy. You know as a lycan I'll heal quickly."

"Of course I know that," Sevilla scolded, as she handed her a cool scented compress. "But there's no sense in being in pain while you do it, now is there?"

"True." Zilla shrugged and pulled up her skirt. The compress was soothing against the cut she received during Roy's last fit. If she had been dressed at the time, chances are she would have only been bruised there as well. His temper was worse than Erebos' ever was, and without her powers, she was defenseless against him.

She already decided to stay with Sevilla, it wasn't like she had any-where to go and she needed to take a break from seeing Roy. Originally she hoped he would give her some clue as to Erebos' whereabouts, but he was only interested in sex…rough sex. While she didn't generally mind it a little spicy, the last few times he had been straight-up abusive. She realized now that he knew what she was after, and there was no way he was going to tell her anything.

"I planned on staying with you for a few days anyway, if that's alright with you," Zilla said. "I think we need to connect with Brooke and Amie and see if they have made any progress finding the next element. We need all the help we can get, and the only way the lycans will assist us is by keeping our promise to Logan and finding his mate."

"How did he take the news?"

"What? That we have no magick available to us and he's on his own?" Zilla shrugged and waved her hands in the air. "As well as can be expected, I suppose, considering we basically left him to find his mate within the next two moons, with no magical assistance whatsoever."

Sevilla filled a kettle with water from the small pump near her sink, and snipped selected herbs that were drying on a line above her head. She also added in a few pinches from some glass bottles she had in a nearby cupboard.

"Well, I wouldn't say no magical assistance," Sevilla countered. "Brooke and Amie are actively looking with the clues they were given by Fate and the drawings that have shown up in the Elemental Journal. They've managed to narrow it down to an area near the place Brooke's brother is staying. She and Amie felt a pull, so that was where they de-cided to start."

Zilla was relieved that the drain on the magick didn't seem to be af-fecting the two ladies chosen to embody the elements of Water and Air. Ever since the day at Ryker's when she and Logan had barely escaped with their lives, the powers she and Sevilla tapped into naturally had all but disappeared. It was as if the well of their magick had completely run dry. Thankfully, Sevilla was well trained in the old ways and made great use of the tools provided by nature. She still had a few things she could do, albeit the list was getting shorter as time went on.

"I told him they were looking, but I don't hold much hope they will find the next element in time for him. Even if they do, who is to say it will be his mate?"

"True," Sevilla replied. "I suppose all we can do is trust the universe."

"Oh, I trust the universe. It's all the other people in my life I am having a hard time with. Present company excluded of course."

Sevilla raised an eyebrow and smiled. "Of course."

Zilla decided to change the subject. There was no way they were getting into the topic of trust right now.

"So do you know when they are coming next?

"I believe they will be arriving tomorrow."

"How is Amie, by the way," Zilla asked. She was curious about the woman she had befriended months before. Their friendship dissolving still brought pain to her heart. She missed talking to her.

"Still angry with you, but she's coming around," Sevilla responded quietly. "At least that was what the crystal showed."

Amie, the element of Air, felt the sting of Zilla's lies. However, Zilla had only been following instructions at the time, and once she realized Amie was destined to be with Aleck, she stopped trying to keep them apart. Perhaps if she had been able to look into a crystal as well as Sevilla, she would have realized sooner that she had gotten Fate's message wrong. Or perhaps her love for Erebos clouded her judgment. Either way, Amie was still pissed and avoided speaking to Zilla at all costs.

"I always envied your work with the old tools. I never could get my crystal to show me nearly as much as yours shows you," Zilla said.

"That is because it requires a great deal of patience, of which you have none."

"Rude much?" Zilla's tinkling laugh filled the kitchen. She had really missed the bantering, especially since she and Amie weren't speaking. "The past is your thing and there is patience in retrospect. The present really has no time for that kind of thing."

"Which is precisely why you get into the trouble you do," Sevilla answered.

"Well there you go, sounding like Mother."

Sevilla smiled. "Well, I take that as a compliment."

"It was meant as one, Villy," Zilla said solemnly. "You would have made an amazing mother you know. So glad you had Brooke to fill that void."

"Me too," she said softly. Zilla watched as her sister lifted the kettle out of the sink and walked to the fireplace to set it. Even though they were identical in features, Sevilla had a fluid grace Zilla never felt she achieved. It was one of the things she admired most about her sister. While Zilla always stirred the pot, Sevilla was there to calm the waters.

"While we wait for this to boil, we should get out some of the tools you are better with and see if we can find some answers."

Zilla nodded in agreement. "Tarot and pendulum still work for me. Remind me what you asked Fate when she gave you the riddle."

"I asked if you and Ryker were still alive, which she confirmed with a nod. I also said that I would need help rebalancing the magick and needed to find you, which is when she gave me the riddle."

"Which was?"

Sevilla closed her eyes and took a deep breath, calmly reaching into the recesses of her memory. Her voice was soothing as it came to Zilla's ears, and she herself closed her eyes as well to receive its message.

"Always dark and on the run, without the sun there would be none."

The answer came to Zilla immediately, causing her to open her eyes. "Could that be a shadow?"

Sevilla nodded. "That is what I thought, and knowing your name meant Shadow didn't help, since you were the one I was looking for. So there was only one other entity I could think of."

"She must mean Roy, but he wouldn't willingly help us rebalance the magick."

"I think the key word in that statement is willingly."

Zilla felt her stomach knot. Erebos, and his darker half Roy, had been through enough. And while it was true Roy was a pain in the ass, he was still the other half of the man she loved. She didn't like where this conversation was heading.

"Villy, I am not going to help hurt poor Erebos. Don't you think we've done enough? His mind hasn't been the same since we split it."

"You think I don't remember?" Sevilla snapped back. "And frankly, my mind hasn't been the same either since my sisters killed my husband."

"Ryker isn't..."

"I know Ryker isn't dead, Zilla. But I haven't known that over the last several decades thanks to you both. I had just started coming to terms with his death and had even learned to live without him. I have a whole other set of issues to deal with now that I moved on."

Zilla teared up. This was exactly the conversation she had been trying to avoid. "I'm so sorry, Villy, I really had no idea. Fate is going to have a lot to answer for. In the meantime, I want to avoid hurting anyone else."

"Calm down," Sevilla said as she waved her hands in front of her. "The path I've chosen is not your doing and my journey is my own. I'm not upset with you anymore and no one is going to ask you to hurt anybody. But, I do think we need to find a way to make Roy think it is in his best interest to allow us access to magick. That way we can all work together to find a way to heal Erebos, merge his two halves and hopefully re-balance the elements."

Zilla took a deep breath. What Sevilla described was what she and Erebos had been trying to do during the time she and her sisters weren't speaking. The problem was Roy had become too strong and decided he liked being in charge of Erebos' body. While she used to see more of Erebos, now she was only ever seeing Roy. It had gotten out of hand, and she hoped the man she loved was still out there and could be merged with his other half. She hated to think of the alternative, especially since Roy was so power hungry. If he gained what he was after, they would all have a lot more to worry about.

"Sorry, Villy, I didn't mean to get so upset. I'm just at a loss as to what to do. It used to be that I was able to manipulate the outcome, and make Erebos and Roy both think that I was helping them gain the elemental powers. But something happened when Amie came through."

"What do you mean? What happened?"

"It seemed that when she got here Roy was able to fully take over Erebos' body. Since then he has been learning spells at a heightened pace. It's almost as though he has found a way to tap into another source of magick, something ancient. Perhaps he is absorbing powers from those around him?"

"If he has found a way to feed from other magical beings, it could explain why we aren't able to use our powers. What he is tapping into and how he is doing it is something we need to sort out. It is possible Roy is holding both Ryker and Erebos hostage and we need to find a way to stop him before he destroys everything that holds us all in balance. If we can't get control of him here, his next move might be to travel into other dimensions."

"I fear he may have already found a way to unbalance nature where Brooke and Amie are from. The weather there has been abnormally volatile."

"The girls mentioned an increase in storms," Sevilla agreed. "I can only imagine the chaos he would cause if he becomes stronger. Remember what happened all those years ago? We can't let that happen again, too many lives were lost. We need to find a way to stop him, and we need to hurry and find the other two elements. They will only be able to fight the powers in their dimension if all four of them are united."

Sevilla moved over to sit beside her and pressed a handkerchief into Zilla's hand. Zilla's shoulders bounced slightly as the tears dropped onto the small piece of embroidered linen their mother made. Zilla lovingly traced the stems of lavender that were sewn on the corners, and marveled that Sevilla had kept them in such pristine condition for so many years. Her sister truly did embody the past.

"I haven't seen Erebos in weeks and I'm afraid for him, Villy. It's all our fault he is this way, that he has lived his life with a piece of his soul missing."

"We will fix it, Zilla. We'll find a way."

"Well now, we really don't have a choice, do we."

Sevilla looked across the table into the fire and slowly shook her head. "No, we really don't."

The longing on Sevilla's face almost broke Zilla's heart, and she knew she needed to apologize for the part she played.

"I'm sorry Fate lied about Ryker's death all those years, Villy. I really had no idea."

"I know," Sevilla said softly, "In her way, Fate told me." Her body tensed, as though she wasn't ready to talk about the past even though it obviously weighed heavily on her mind.

"I loved him too you know, he was my brother-in-law," Zilla added.

Sevilla's smile was wistful. "Yes, I know." She cupped Zilla's pained face, and wiped a falling tear with her thumb. "First we will find Fate, then we'll find both Ryker and Erebos and fix this. I promise."

Sevilla stood up and walked to the hearth, gathering her basket of magical tools. Once placed in the center of the table, she poured two glasses of wine in the adjoining room and made her way back to the kitchen. Before sitting across from her, she handed one of the wine glasses to Zilla. She pulled out her tarot deck, and lit her sage from a nearby candle. It seemed that Sevilla was back to business.

"Now, what question should we ask the cards first?"

9

era slept soundly, comforted by the faded scent of lavender in her abuela's sheets. Although the dust on the furniture and the cobwebs in the corners were a sign the house had been abandoned some time ago, Sera still picked up whiffs of sage and lemon balm as she prepared for her shower.

A quick search through her luggage for her salon products confirmed that, in her haste to pack, she had left them at home. Her hair would be a riotous mess without them. After a peek in the shower to see what was available, she went downstairs to the kitchen. Looking in the cupboards put her mind at ease. During her brief inspection upon arrival, she had missed the unopened coconut oil in the back of the cupboard near the stove. Sera could use anything for shampoo, but she needed something with a high oil content to tame her curls.

After taking the oil down from the cupboard, she couldn't help but notice the dark symbols in a circular pattern on the inside of the door. They looked hand drawn, but not with anything like a marker since the color wasn't consistent. It was then that she caught the faded scent of burnt wood. Sera ran her hand across the symbols and they were slightly grooved, as she half expected, since they looked as though someone had taken a pyrography pen to draw them. The detail on the symbols was striking, and she was amazed her grandmother could create such artistic flourishes with such a rudimentary tool.

They were sigils; swirled symbols drawn with intent. Similar to what she would see on rune stones, each one had a different meaning. Sera had seen them enough over the years to recognize them. Her grandmother had her own unique style of drawing, and used them often for protection and healing. However, these were different. She ran her fingertips over the grooved drawings and contemplated what they could mean. They certainly weren't for protection, since other than the coconut oil, the cupboard was completely bare. Perhaps her abuela had stored something of importance stored here?

As she rubbed her hand over the sigils in a circular pattern, she started to feel the familiar tingle on her chest. Her tattoo prickled her skin, and while it wasn't painful, Sera took note as it was her habit now to do. She pulled her phone from her back pocket and took a picture of the inside of the cupboard door. Perhaps it would be a clue that would help her find her grandmother.

Sera closed the cupboard door and jogged up the stairs. She needed to hustle if she was going to have time to talk to anyone her grandmother worked with. She had slept longer than she intended. Hopefully, someone at the museum could help her decipher the meaning of the photo and set her on the right track.

While she was used to her abuela's independence and unconventional way of thinking, she was worried that something otherworldly was happening, especially since strange things had been happening in her own life. She couldn't help but tie the two things together in her mind.

After a hot shower, she ran the oil through her hair and combed through the curls with her fingers. Since her temperature generally ran warmer, she dressed in jean capris and a black tank top, finishing off her simple look with her favorite moonstone necklace. She checked her watch and noted there were still a few hours before the museum closed. The jet lag had given her a later start than she hoped for. With a quick brush of mascara and lip gloss, she laced up her hiking boots and packed up her purse.

Sera only took the necessities, identification, lip-gloss and her money clip. The chief's wife had always commented on how tiny Sera's purse was, once calling it a wallet on a string. Compared to the suitcase Martha carried, Sera supposed she was right.

She pulled a sheer gray blouse from her suitcase, then stacked her luggage on the antique table in the corner. Her plan was to unpack when she returned to the farmhouse. She locked up and slid the key she had taken from the front porch into her purse. Perhaps she would go to the hardware store and make a copy, just in case her grandmother had arranged for someone to check on her house. She didn't think that was the case, but having an extra copy wouldn't hurt.

Right before she loaded herself in her rental car, she slid the blouse on over her tank top. She was glad she thought to grab it since she knew the Cuevas de Zugarramurdi tended to be damp and the temperature was around the low-seventies. There was a small river running through the cave that kept humidity in the air. Even though it was weeks from the winter solstice celebration, the interior caves would be cool, especially after the sun went down. Sera's plan was to check the museum first, and then to check the caves. Hopefully her grandmother was at one or the other place, or someone would know where she was. If not, Sera would have to resort to getting the authorities involved, something her abuela wouldn't necessarily be comfortable with. She liked her privacy.

The ride to the museum was scenic but quick, with the only stop before town at an intersection blocked by a herd of sheep. An elderly farmer picked up a small lamb struggling to keep up with the rest of the herd. Sera watched him place the lamb across his shoulders and shuffle to the side of the road. His quick nod as he rubbed the animal's tiny head pulled a wave and smile from her. She wondered if he was the same farmer who had been sweet on her abuela last autumn, and if so, if he had ever made a move. Her heart warmed at the possibility.

Sera pulled her car over to the side and got out as he walked toward the back of her rental. After introducing herself in Spanish, the farmer smiled and was quick to give his name. While he hadn't seen her abuela in some time, he was very familiar with who she was. Sera was right, he was the same farmer her grandmother had mentioned. Apparently she cooked for him, since he spent three full minutes raving about her paella.

She had no idea how old her grandmother was; it wasn't something that was spoken of. However, if Sera did the math, there was a high possibility that her grandmother was in her late seventies. Sera hoped the same genetics ran through her veins, since her grandmother didn't look, or act, a day over fifty. On her last visit to the States, she had been mistaken for Sera's mother on more than one occasion. After promising Sebastián she would pass along greetings to her grandmother and giving the lamb a scratch behind the ears, Sera got back in her car and made her way into town.

The drive to the museum didn't take long. After she parked the car, Sera made her way into the building and stopped at the counter to speak to the staff. Even though she had often spoken to her on the phone, she hadn't been to her grandmother's in years. Sera only knew the people she worked with by name from the stories her abuela told. A quick glance to the woman's nametag showed the name Maria, which wasn't helpful. Practically everyone in the town was named that. Besides, the woman looked nervous, as if this was one of her first days at work. Sera requested information about her grandmother in fluent Spanish, and the employee said she would get someone who had worked for the museum longer. Edgy Maria, as she thought of her now, went into a door behind the counter and returned with an elderly woman who had a kind face. Sera noted her name was also Maria, which didn't surprise her.

"You must be Sera," the woman said softly. "Your abuela spoke so fondly of you."

"Thank you. I am so glad you know her. Does she happen to be here?"

A look of confusion shadowed the woman's face as she shook her head. "She hasn't worked here in over a year. Surely she told you she retired?"

Sera felt a wave of guilt as she tried to remember the last several conversations they had. Had she been so caught up in the promotion and bullshit going on at work that she hadn't listened to her abuela?

"No, she hadn't mentioned it," Sera muttered. A swear word slipped out under her breath, but it didn't go without notice.

Kind Maria was starting to look worried. "Is there anything wrong? Has something happened?"

She tried in vain to recall the phone calls. Had she monopolized them? With all the stress and pressure she had been going through, she wouldn't doubt it.

Sera shrugged her shoulders. "I'm really not sure. It looks as though my grandmother hasn't been home in months." Edgy Maria's interest in the conversation grew noticeably.

"I do know she still works at the caves, and they have been busy planning the winter solstice celebration," Kind Maria explained. "It's possible she stayed in a room at the nearby inn. They often give her a place to stay so she doesn't need to ride her bicycle back and forth."

Sera smiled; perhaps it was a simple as that. "She never was one to drive, was she?"

Kind Maria shook her head with a smirk. "Trust me, you don't want her driving. Let's just say everyone is safer if she is on a bike."

"I believe that," Sera laughed. "Oh, before I go, would you mind taking a look at this picture? I found it inside one of my abuela's cupboards. I thought maybe it was some kind of protection sigil."

Kind Maria took a look at the photo displayed on Sera's smartphone, with Edgy Maria looking over her shoulder. It was Edgy Maria who responded first.

"Doesn't look as though it's for protection entirely, since there are a number of symbols represented around the circle."

"Yes, you're right," Kind Maria agreed. "It is almost as though it is a number of words."

"Like a sentence?" Sera questioned.

"Exactly so," Kind Maria nodded. "Or a message."

"Is there anyone you know that could decipher something like this?"

"I would be happy to give it a shot," Edgy Maria said eagerly. "I love doing research on this kind of stuff." She pulled a handbag from beneath the counter and pulled out a phone. "Shoot me a copy of that picture and I can text you with any updates."

Sera punched in the numbers she was given and forwarded the picture as a first text. They each set up contact information in their phones, and Edgy Maria promised to get back with Sera quickly before she excused herself into the back office. Sera slid her phone back into her purse and jotted her number down on the back of one of the museum's business cards.

"I appreciate your help, Maria. Here's my number if you happen to see her."

The elderly woman took the slip of paper with a nod. "Of course I will call you if I do. The staff at the caves will have already gone home, but I'm sure you are familiar with the way in. Take my flashlight, just in case you decide to stay after sunset."

"Thank you so much," Sera said.

Maria placed her hands on either of Sera's shoulders, then on the top of her head and Sera prepared for her blessing. It seemed this woman had a lot in common with her grandmother.

"May the Goddess keep you safe within her sight. May the God protect you and bring things right." She dropped her hands and Sera opened her eyes.

"So mote it be," Sera whispered and gave the woman a small smile. She knew the phrase meant "so may it be," and while Sera didn't necessarily practice all of her grandmother's ways, she did recognize and honor them. Pagans said the phrase, just as a Christian would use the word amen. As far as she was concerned, she would take all the help she could get.

It didn't take her long to travel to the caves; she could have walked from the museum but felt the pinch of time. The caves weren't far from the parking area, and the platform-like stairs that led down to their mouth took her into another world step by step. She had always loved this space, and had fond memories of it as far back as she could remember. Her abuela had come to the caves long before she worked as a tour guide, and Sera would spend the better part of her summers helping her with her rituals. As she stepped down and entered the cave, she closed her eyes and pulled in a deep breath. The scent of a thousand fires and the magick of hundreds of years warmed her soul like a campfire at midnight. While she might not practice the craft, she truly appreciated the effects.

She had yet to see anyone, but did not call out in such a sacred place. Her abuela taught her years ago the caves were a place of worship, just like the grandest church, and as such they were to be honored with reverence. She walked through the aisles, her footsteps echoing back to her from the hollows of the cavernous space. The caves showed signs of people preparing for the festival, as the lights had been left on to light her path. Sera thought perhaps they had gone home for dinner and would be returning later to finish their work.

Some of the smaller crevices were dark, and she checked them quickly with the flashlight Maria had given her. Most of the more remote areas were being used for storage, in anticipation of the hundreds of people that would be present during the solstice ritual. One cave was filled entirely with wood logs for the fire that would burn in the largest of the caves. As she turned the corner, she saw that several logs had already been placed in the central area.

As she stepped closer to the unlit pyre, her eyes were drawn to the walls behind it. There were etchings on the rock, and on closer inspection Sera realized that these circular patterns were the same as she had seen at her abuela's house. Had she drawn the same symbols on the cave walls as well? They gave Sera the impression of a doorway, and she ran her hand over the symbols on the closest circle. They were grooved but extremely smooth. This wasn't her abuela's handiwork, of that Sera was sure; these symbols had been carved long ago. But why didn't she remember them from her childhood?

She stepped back and looked at the circles; there were a total of three, with the one in the center being the largest. The pattern was created with the same symbols as she had seen in her abuela's kitchen, with the center circle a little more ornate. She walked to it for a closer inspection. All the circles were enormous, spanning from ground level to well over her head, and the symbols seemed to be consistent between them all. As Sera ran her hand over the design on the largest circle, she realized the difference was that the pattern was edged on both sides with triangles. What she found odd was that the triangles, no matter where they were placed on the circle, were drawn pointing up. She looked up; first inclination was that the triangles represented arrows, but she didn't see anything out of the ordinary.

The carvings were tied to her abuela. As much as she knew in her mind she should continue looking for her, she was compelled to keep rubbing her hands over the symbols. She was mesmerized by the pattern and ran her hands lovingly over them, mimicking the triangle pattern repeated throughout.

She was so wrapped up in peace of the moment that she barely felt the tingle of her tattoo. When she heard the whoosh behind her, she turned just in time to see the pyre burst into flames. Sera looked side to side; there was no one present in the space, and she was confused as to how the fire could have started. She barely had time to register that there was no heat coming from the flames when she was grabbed from behind by a set of muscular arms and dragged backwards. How had anyone gotten between her and the cave wall?

"Thig rium mo ghaol."

Sera looked down at the arms gripping her and started to panic. Strangely they looked familiar. It couldn't possibly be the man from her dreams. They were just dreams right? She tried to turn her head, but it was locked tight against a rock-like chest. The only thing she could see was the leather strap he wore on his bicep.

"Are you kidding me right now? Let me go!"

She felt the vibration of his laughter on her back. It seemed the Scottish hunk from her dreams was as real as the cave she was standing in.

"I cannae do that, lassie. You need to come with me. The moon waits for no one."

"What is that you keep saying and what the hell are you talking about?" Sera kept trying to wiggle loose, but his grip was tight.

"What? Thig rium mo ghaol? It's an endearment."

"You don't even know me! Are you crazy?"

"Aye. Crazy 'bout you, my love."

Holy shit, he was dragging her backwards! How far did he expect to get before his ass ran into the wall of the cave? She tried to pry open his grip, but his arms were like small tree trunks. There was no way she would be able to overpower him without the use of her arms. Remembering her dreams, and the way he had made her feel, she wondered if in all honesty she really needed to try. Strangely she didn't feel threatened, his grip was firm but gentle and his tone was flavored with a smile. Sera was irritated more than anything else.

She turned her head, trying to see into his face, the closest she came was an intimate look at his thick neck. He smelled really good, and she had to catch herself from closing her eyes and getting lost in the scent. She noticed a black leather strap with a caged white stone hanging around his neck and she wondered what power he was hoping to gain from it. Curious about this man or not, she didn't like being forced to do anything. She much preferred to be asked - nicely.

"Listen here, shortbread, you need to let me go. I have no intention of going anywhere with you."

She felt his nose in the back of her head. She felt the intake of his breath that let her know that he was taking a deep pull of the fruity scent she had going on from her shower. With each sniff he took her another step backward.

"I love shortbread, but not as much as yer intoxicating scent. I could die a happy man right now."

"Let go of me and I can make it happen."

He let out a raucous laugh, one that sent lightning to her core and brought her nipples to attention. What the hell was wrong with her? She was literally being dragged away and she couldn't help reacting to him like a dog in heat!

"Nae, love, I'll not be letting you go now. Or ever. You are definitely the woman for me. The fates have been kind."

She felt him pull her back yet another step and realized they were no longer standing on a stone floor. The texture was different, and she looked down to a dirt patch sprinkled with small sticks and stones. When she looked up, they were in a large circular clearing surrounded by trees and grass. It smelled mossy and fresh here, and she wondered how he had been able to transport her to the forest surrounding the cave without her knowing it. She looked up and side to side as her captor dragged her further backwards, and that was when she saw it. A perfect circle cut out over a campfire that they had just stepped back from. It looked like a round doorway that led into the cave she just left.

The giant fire back in the cave was reducing in size and by the time it was out completely, the circle had closed in on itself. The cave scene disappeared, the doorway closed. In its place was a small bonfire in the center of a camp similar to the one she saw in her dreams.

The arms that pulled her back loosened. Sera took advantage of the moment and spun around in the man's arms and brought her fisted hands into a fighting position. She almost lost her nerve when she saw his incredibly handsome face smiling down on her with tenderness, and she breathed in his comforting scents of sage and musk. For a complete stranger and someone she had conjured up in her dreams, he sure had an effect on her. She was definitely attracted to him, and somewhat curious to know what the hell he was talking about. Nevertheless, she wasn't one to be manhandled by anyone, so she did what any girl in her position would. She pulled back her fist and let it fly toward his handsome face with a growl.

10

James was seated and waiting for his sister Brooke just outside the rear door of the Wellness Center. He told her to meet him behind the complex, which was where he had been spending most of his time since his release from the hospital. He gazed at the terrain laced with walking trails that led to the back of the property and enjoyed the soft touch of the breeze on his cheek.

James found great comfort outdoors, as it helped him escape the sounds and smells of the reconstruction taking place inside. Being around all that activity made his pulse race, and while it seemed like a ridiculous reaction, he finally understood why. His therapy sessions dragged out memories he had never been willing to face before, and the cracks from the hammer were transformed into artillery in his mind. It made him wonder if he would ever be able to hear everyday sounds in their proper form again. Or even without flinching for that matter.

Alcohol helped him in the past, but he had been sober since the incident in London that almost took his life. It wasn't easy, and he still had minor tremors from cutting it off too quickly. But he made a promise to Brooke and he intended to keep it. She was all the family he had left.

He quietly contemplated the red rock in the distance bursting from the ground in layered plateaus. It was mid-afternoon and the sun's rays hit the formations differently than earlier in the day. The moving shadows changed the look and feel of the formations; even the colors seemed more vibrant. It amazed him that layers of rock that had stood for thousands of years could be ever changing like the ocean his sister loved so much.

Even though it was desolate in areas, in many ways Sedona was one of the most beautiful and peaceful places he had ever been. It had a welcoming feel about it, as if no one judged you and your past didn't matter. The community was flamboyant, artistic and insightful, and slowly wove its calming presence in and out of his soul until it took root. For the first time in years he felt he might have a chance at peace.

He shifted in his seat. His leg was stiff, although his fused tibia was healing nicely. He had been fortunate that the break hadn't necessitated a cast and was only wrapped loosely in surgical dressings. Things were hard enough without having to deal with weeks of navigating showers around a leg covered in plaster.

While he wanted to avoid complications with the ladies at the center, it had been several days since he had seen the bewitching firefighter who rescued him. He was getting antsy and wasn't sure he could continue to wait. Especially since sex was the only other thing he could use to control his anxiety now that drinking was completely off limits. He considered who might be the most receptive and discreet of all the ladies he had met so far. He couldn't help himself; it had been much too long and he was craving a woman's touch. He needed the sense of normalcy and escape that only an enthusiastic toss in the sheets could provide.

In an attempt to change the direction of his thoughts, he shook his head and took a deep breath—time to focus on something else. His upcoming visit came to mind, which he was looking forward to. He hadn't seen Brooke since the hospital. He hadn't seen much of anyone really. The common area had been terribly damaged so the residents tended to keep more to themselves, staying in their rooms and reading instead of watching television or playing cards. It would be nice to finally have something to do.

Brooke was bringing Aleck, and he was bringing his new girlfriend Amie. She had come with Aleck to the hospital in London, after the gunshot incident that put James in ICU, but they hadn't met properly. By the time he was released, she had flown back to the States. In the weeks leading up to his stay at the Wellness Center, he spent a lot of time with Aleck talking about the past and making plans for his future. James had never seen Aleck so happy and he was looking forward to getting to know Amie better. In a lot of ways, his friend's happiness gave James the courage to finally face his demons. He hoped that one day he would be as fortunate and find someone who made him a better version of himself. He was tired of the old one.

"Everything okay out here, Mr. Fisher?"

The unexpected voice made him flinch. He must have been lost in thought; he hadn't even heard her steps on the pathway.

"Right as rain, Stephanie," James responded with a grin. The pretty blonde flushed at his comment and moved his crutches closer to his reach.

"Your sister just called to say they were running late. They had a run in with a neighbor cat."

James laughed. "Yes, well, I am sure Max had something to do with that."

"Max?"

"My dog," James answered. "He's an Irish Wolfhound and a bit of a handful."

"I suppose he is," she grinned. James imagined what she was thinking—like dog, like owner. "Well I will be sure to come out and say hi to him later. Enjoy your visit with your sister, Mr. Fisher."

"Please call me Jim, love."

He really liked the way her cheeks turned red at the smallest of intimacies.

"Okay. Jim."

She reached the doorway and he gave her a toothy grin when she turned to look at him. Yes, he had been watching her ass as she walked away, and he wasn't shy about it. Her glowing smile at his wink proved that she wasn't shy about it either. Perhaps after his visit with Brooke he would see if Stephanie might be willing to go off somewhere for a chat. He definitely needed some action; he was a walking, talking, divining rod.

In another attempt to calm his libido before he traumatized his sister, he took in a deep breath and practiced some of the meditation exercises he had learned earlier. "Breathe in the good, push out the bad."

With his eyes closed, he visualized a bright light slowly weaving its magic in and out of his essence and pulling the lost pieces of his soul back to him. Some of the concepts the counselors used were a bit out there, but he was desperate enough to give it a go. He mentioned there were some pieces of his soul he wasn't sure he'd want back, but the counselors assured him that they would work on those things together. He didn't need to keep the painful memories, but he needed to air them out and then decide what to do with them. They told him he would be in complete control of what he kept in his life moving forward. He liked that thought.

James had a few more moments to himself before the rumbling bark of his dog brought a smile to his face. He no sooner opened his eyes before Max came bounding up and caused his friend Aleck to yell out from a distance.

"Max, no."

Max sat down in front of James with a whimper and set his eyes on his master. James smiled at his furry friend, and explained the situation to him, since it was the first time Max had seen him since the fire.

"You need to be gentle, boy. My leg is healing and can't be bumped." James motioned for Max to sit on the side opposite his injury. "You can come on this side, Max."

Max wagged his tail and shifted closer, sniffing the dressings and giving one last whimper before placing his massive head in his owner's lap. James rubbed the wiry fur at the top of his head and gave a quick nod to his visitors as they walked up to the bench where he was sitting. Brooke leaned over and kissed his cheek, clearing way for Aleck, who shook his hand and then reached his hand behind him to bring a woman to stand beside him.

"I brought you some more clothes," Brooke said. "I left them with someone at the front desk. I think she said her name was Stephanie."

"Brilliant," James answered with a wag of his eyebrows. "I'll be sure to get those from her later."

"I'll bet," Brooke snorted with a shake of her head.

"Glad to see you are feeling better," Aleck said with a laugh.

"The scenery in Sedona is very inspiring," James bantered back. "Speaking of which, who is this lovely creature you have with you, mate?"

"You can turn down the charm, Jim, this one is mine," Aleck said as he pulled her into his side with a laugh. "I would like you to officially meet Amie."

Aleck's smile lit up his face. It was clear that he was extremely happy and James could see why. While James wasn't one for redheads, Amie was absolutely stunning. He was having a hard time wrapping his head around the fact that she was a pilot, since she could have just as easily been a model. She was tall and slim with classic bone structure that would make a marble statue of Aphrodite envious. James realized now why his friend had been so obsessed with seeing her again after the mishap with his phone during their last visit in London. He would have snatched her up too.

"It's very nice to meet you finally," Amie said with a smile. "Although between your sister and Aleck I feel as if I know you already."

"Hopefully they only shared the good bits," James said with a grin.

"Of course," Amie agreed, blushing prettily. A quick glance at Aleck's raised eyebrow had James immediately reining in the charm. While he looked at it as harmless flirting, it wasn't worth losing a friend over. Aleck was serious about this one.

"Oh, don't let him fluster you Amie," Brooke admonished. She sat next to James on the bench and motioned to the crutches next to him. "You good enough with those for the walk?"

James nodded. "Pretty sure I'll be fine with these. There are some benches once we get back there that I can rest on while we chat."

"Brilliant," Brooke said as she stood. "I'd like to go somewhere a little more private to chat about the topic I brought up in the hospital."

He looked up at Aleck to check for a smirk, at the small chance that they were having a go at him, but he looked serious. A quick glance over to Amie showed him she was buying into it as well.

"The topic of magic?" James couldn't help but keep the disbelief from his voice.

"That's right," Brooke agreed. "Max, move back boy, we need to get your daddy onto his crutches."

Max stood and rounded the rear of the bench, coming up on the opposite side of the group. James stood up with Brooke's help, and Aleck handed him the crutches.

"This whole situation is a right pain in the arse," Jim exclaimed.

"Quit being a baby," Brooke teased. "It could have been way worse considering the circumstances."

"Yes, but that doesn't mean I have to enjoy being treated like an invalid."

"I'm sure you wouldn't mind if Stephanie was helping you out," Aleck joked, receiving an elbow in the side from Amie.

James couldn't help but laugh. "True, mate. She is a wonderful caregiver."

"I'll just bet," Brooke said with a roll of her eyes. "Well, there will be no care giving in the sense you mean tonight. We have things to sort through. Let's go, Romeo."

Brooke walked alongside James as he hobbled the path leading further back on the property. Max ran ahead, happy to stretch his legs but stopping and looking back every few minutes to ensure everyone was still in sight. Aleck and Amie were hand in hand on the other side of James, passing nervous glances between themselves. For such a frivolous topic, it seemed his visitors were being pretty serious. Max reached the clearing in the center of a small rock formation that created an outside room which provided a certain amount of privacy. James had been back there before; it was where they had their group counseling sessions, especially now that the common room had been damaged in the fire. He was starting to get a little nervous about their upcoming chat; they all seemed so solemn. He decided, like paratrooping, it was best to jump in feet first.

"So Amie, you're new to this group. What do you think about this magick rubbish?"

Amie quickly glanced over to Brooke before answering. "Well, if I am being completely honest, I would have to say that sometimes it is a little hard to believe."

Aleck nodded in agreement. "That's putting it mildly."

"You don't believe it's real?"

"I didn't say that. I just agree with Amie that sometimes it is hard to wrap your head around."

James thought for a moment before making his next statement. "I'm assuming you've seen what Brooke can do."

"I have," Aleck responded. "And what Amie can do as well."

James looked over to Amie, who gave him a small smile. She was unassuming in her peasant skirt and flowing top. He glanced back up to Aleck before completing his walk to the benches. He had known Aleck long enough to know he wasn't pulling one over on him.

"I know you are having a hard time with this, James, which is why I brought Amie and Aleck with me. We've been gifted with these powers and, while we are still figuring out why we have them, we are learning to embrace them."

"Right then, show me what you've got," James said as convincingly as he could muster.

Amie gave Brooke a side glance, and moved closer to her after Brooke's quick nod. They must have anticipated his disbelief and had something arranged ahead of time. Aleck sat down next to him and answered the question wrinkling his brow with a laugh.

"Jim, you might as well buy into the whole idea, it isn't going away."

"You do realize how mental this all sounds?" James shook his head in disbelief.

"Of course I do." Aleck agreed. "But I also believe what I see, and I have seen some shit that would make you question your own sanity."

"Fair enough," James said. "So why are you sitting here? Aren't you going to show me what you can do as well?"

Aleck laughed, pointing at the women. "I can't do shit. The powers are all them. Although I suppose the magick not affecting me might be something. Will got some powers when he went through the portal, but I think he started out with some to begin with."

"Portal?" James had just about heard enough, and he was supposed to be the nutty one!

"Brooke and Amie can show you. It's how they access the other land we travel to."

"Right." Perhaps Max was the only sane one.

He looked back at the women, curious as to what they had planned. Brooke and Amie stood in the clearing facing each other with their eyes closed in concentration. Their hands were raised with palms flattened, but they didn't touch as they stood about six feet apart. At first James thought they were in a trance, and looked to Aleck for his reaction. His friend just shook his head toward the girls and whispered, "Keep watching."

James looked back and that was when he saw it. The sparkling glow coming from the palms of their hands and ballooning out from the center as it merged. The colors were distinct, turquoise-green from Brooke, and lavender-blue from Amie. The blended glow swirled and created a round field that completely covered the girls and then moved slowly toward the place where he and Aleck were seated.

"What the hell is that?" James said.

"Air Conditioning," Aleck said softly. "They learned if they combined their powers of water and air they could cool things down."

The rounded glow passed over them and extended behind to the edge of the seating area. Aleck was right; it had to be at least twenty degrees cooler in their bubble. The hair on his arms stood on end.

He looked through the bluish-green glow to the other side of the force field, and saw Max take off like a shot toward a shadow. Had he seen a cat? Was that a person?

"Max!"

"I'll get him," Aleck said, as he rose from the bench and jogged through the glow.

Out of the corner of his eye, James saw more movement. There were a number of figures standing to the side of the clearing, with more and more appearing by the second. He couldn't tell what they were from this distance, and the force field was causing his vision to blur, but they seemed to be human. He had no idea that some of the residents were out for a walk. Guess they would be getting an eyeful!

"Amie, watch out!" Aleck yelled out as he ran into something and then was pushed back.

Max's growl was vicious, he was attacking something or someone, and James grabbed his crutches and pulled himself to his feet. The women stopped their light show and looked visibly winded. They both turned their backs to James and put their arms out in front of them to prepare for a fight as they looked from side to side to determine what was happening. It was then that James registered exactly what he was seeing.

Rows of skeletons, some bare bones, some with shreds of the clothing they had been buried in, moved toward them. He saw more clawing their way out of the earth, sending the red dirt of the desert into the sky in puffs. Max bit at a few that strayed off to attack him, and from what James could tell, he was holding his own. Aleck fought his way through the corner of the mob, trying to reach Amie.

"Amie, see if you can push a gust," Brooke yelled, and then turned her head to bark directions at James. "You stay put. We'll take care of this."

"Since when are you in charge?"

Brooke rolled her eyes and turned to shoot a stream of energy from her palms toward the closest enemies. "Since I tapped into these powers!"

James heard a crumble behind him and turned in time to see a corpse rising from a hole in the red sand. He supposed now he had proof that the Wellness Center was indeed surrounding by old burial grounds. The mummified body wormed its way out and its progress was slow. He leaned on his good leg and backhanded his crutch at the creature as hard as he could. The skull went skittering across the patio stones, and the body collapsed in a heap.

"Remove the heads! Aleck, remove the heads," James yelled, and tossed Aleck one of his crutches. "Here, use this."

Aleck caught the crutch, and immediately swung it toward three skeletons nearing Amie. All three heads were knocked off in unison, and he took a step forward to swing at the next batch. James hopped up toward Brooke to help her, although she seemed to be holding them off on her own. The watery blasts from her hands froze the skeletons and prevented them from movement, but there were just too many. The light from her hands started to dim, and he remembered what she said in the hospital about using her energy in this dimension and it wearing her out.

"Brooke, there are too many. They just keep coming," Amie screamed. She unleashed a jolt from her fingertips that sent several skeletons shattering against a nearby boulder.

Aleck decapitated several more to give the women some space. "You need to get us out of here, ladies," he said with authority.

"On it," Amie answered.

"You're too tired to do it yourself. I'll help," Brooke said.

James wacked another skeleton sneaking up from behind. "Whatever you are going to do, you'd better hurry."

The women held hands, and with their free hands pointed the nearest area clear of enemies. Within seconds there was a hole surrounded by the same colored energy he had witnessed earlier. Within the blue-green border laced with lavender there was a wooded area. It looked precisely like someone had photo-shopped a picture centered within a picture. James wasn't sure what it was, but he knew immediately what the women intended.

"Hurry! Get in!" Brooke yelled at James, while Amie simultaneously called for Aleck.

"You've got to be kidding..."

"Get your ass moving, Jim, there's no time!"

Aleck took his friend's arm and pulled it tight over his broad shoulders. Aleck was taller than James and the height difference made it so Aleck was pulling him along.

"Max, come!" James belted out as he was being dragged into the hole. He could only tell the dog had heard him by his responding bark. The women beckoned to Max as well, and soon James felt Max's presence beside him. Aleck stepped through the doorway and James immediately knew he was in a different place. It was less stifling and not nearly as dry as the desert.

Aleck turned them around, to make sure the women made it through the portal, and James watched as the ladies ran through from the scene with the red sand and stones into the lush wooded area where they all stood.

Brooke and Amie turned together and clapped their hands, at which point the hole decreased in size and disappeared. Brooke bent at the waist, hands on her knees and her head lowered in an attempt to catch her breath. Amie came immediately to Aleck's side, and James pulled himself off of his shoulder so he could give Aleck and Amie a moment alone. Besides, he needed to check on his sister.

Max sidled up to him, allowing James to place a hand on his back for stability as they worked their way over to Brooke. Although she was clearly exhausted, James could hear the faintest hint of a smile in her tone.

"So, you believe me now?"

11

Logan pulled the woman from his visions through the portal and could hardly restrain his excitement. Finally, he would get the answers he searched for! He had hope for his future for the first time in several moons. He grabbed the feisty handful by the wrists before her punch landed on his foolishly grinning face.

"Hey now, lassie, there'll be none of that with us."

"Let me go you meathead!" The woman started to raise her knee, and Logan quickly circled his arms around her, wedging her tight across his chest. He didn't know what was worse, getting kicked in the man nuggets or having her wiggling against them.

"Ya need to calm your wee self. I'm not going to hurt ya." He had never seen any woman so irritated. If she was his mate why wasn't she falling into his arms? Wouldn't she feel the same pull he did?

"Well you could have fooled me," she spat into his chest. Her voice was muffled, but the tone came across loud and clear. She was certainly miffed.

"You need to calm…Gods, woman!" The stomp she gave him on the top of his foot gave him a start. Thankfully he had his boots on, otherwise her quick boot heel could have really done some damage. He pulled her tighter to his body; it was all he could think to do to stop her from moving.

"Let me go," she grunted. Her warm breath tickled his chest and, even though it was driving him mad, he was ever so glad he hadn't had time to button his shirt completely.

"You really need to stop wiggling, my love." While he had never forced himself on any woman, he couldn't help but be turned on by holding her so close. She had to be his intended, she smelled like heaven. If she didn't stop moving she would find out just how hot she made him. His attraction to her rattled his thoughts.

"I won't stop until you let me…" She stopped wiggling and stood rigid in his arms. Her sharp intake of breath let him know it was too late. She felt his reaction to her through the layers of clothing that separated them. Waves of guilt blanketed him. Gods, he felt like an animal. This was not how he envisioned meeting his mate. He had hoped she would come to him willingly, like she did in the visions. He loosened his grip slightly and felt the breath on his chest once more.

"I tried to warn ya," Logan said keeping his tone as soothing as he could while he struggled to control his thoughts. It would be some time before he would be able to share how he felt about her; he realized that now. She wouldn't understand the pull his species had when they joined with their lifemate. Much as he hated the thought, he needed to be patient.

"Are we going to stand like this all day, or are you going to let me go at some point." She was starting to tense up again. Gods she was prickly, just like the symbol he wore on his back. He absolutely loved it!

"I'll let ya go, but you need to promise not to run. Wisteria can be a dangerous place if you're not familiar with it." His grip loosened a bit more; he was calm and more in control of his libido.

"So where exactly is Wisteria? How close are we to Spain?"

Logan sized her up. Her tiny frame was rigid and her eyes, which were by far her most beautiful feature, snapped at him in anger. He was surprised to see her forehead crinkled in a frown. How could it be possible that he felt the pull when she did not? There were going to be some sleepless nights unless they came to an accord. More than likely, there would be some sleepless nights either way. She was the most beautiful creature he had ever seen.

She broke eye contact and lowered her head, once again face to his chest. He had to clear the passion from his throat before answering her question.

"All I know is that I pulled you through the window that opened above my fire," he said patiently. He needed to calm her down, she looked angry enough to come out of her skin.

"Window?"

"Aye, a portal."

"Portal?"

"Aye. The magick of it is out of my expertise, but I've seen them before."

"Magic," she said unbelievingly. He had heard that tone before. Typically when Mila knew he was full of shite. Actually, he heard it when any woman sensed he was full of shite.

"Aye. Earth magick." He was able to loosen his grip more and pull his chest away from hers. Perhaps she was intrigued by the conversation, since she felt more relaxed in his arms. Although there was still an underlying sense of irritation, he could no longer smell her fear.

"Okay, say I buy into the whole magick argument. What the hell would possess you to do that?"

"What, pull you through?"

"Yes."

"My reasons are complicated, my love," he responded gently. "Just know that it would be impossible for me, in any world, to hurt you in any way."

She paused, took a cleansing breath and loosened in his arms. It seemed she finally believed he was a man of his word. He felt her shift and reluctantly he took his nose from the top of her head. A tilt of her head was all it took for their eyes to meet once again. For as irritated and hot-tempered as she was, he was happy to see humor in their depths.

"So, Mr. Complicated, since it seems I am stuck here for the time being, what do I call you?"

"Logan, from the clan Blackwood."

"Of course," she laughed. "And tell me, Mr. Blackwood, is this another dream or am I really stuck here with you?"

Logan winced inwardly; the word stuck wasn't one that sat well with him. Was that how she truly felt? Couldn't she feel the bond between them? It made him wonder if he was mistaken—perhaps she wasn't the one. Perhaps she was merely a puzzle piece that put him on the path to his destiny. He hoped that wasn't the case. He didn't have a lot of time to waste. Besides, he was extremely attracted to her and couldn't imagine feeling like he did for any other woman. His emotions were raw when she was near him.

She huffed impatiently; she was still waiting for his answer. "Well?"

He looked into her eyes, and still saw hope in their depths. She was the key, she had to be.

"Nae, lassie, not a dream. And aye, you're stuck here with me."

△

Sera almost felt bad for him. He was acting hurt that she didn't want to be held prisoner by him. Not that she would have minded being held against her will in a dream state, but he said this was real, or as real as she could wrap her head around at the moment.

He made it hard for her to concentrate. His gaze was so intense and being wrapped in his arms depleted her will to move. He made her feel as if nothing on Earth could harm her, although one could argue that he might. And as crazy as it was, whatever it was he bathed in was driving her insane. If she didn't step back from him soon, she wouldn't put it past herself to start rubbing up against him. Best she could do was put as much snark into her tone as possible and get him to relax his grip more.

"So… Mr. Complicated."

"Logan," he said softly.

"Okay…Logan," she repeated. His eyes crinkled in the corners when she said his name. If he wasn't a complete stranger, it would have been endearing.

"And your name, lassie?"

She paused – as if giving him her name would give him a power over her she wasn't prepared to investigate. The thought left her mind as quickly as it popped in. Honestly, what did she have to lose? It might make him lower his guard which would give her a better chance to escape.

"Sera. It's short for Seraphina."

"Sera," he repeated in a soft lilt with an underlying tone that she couldn't place her finger on. It was a cross between a moan and a growl. She was a complete sucker for a man with an accent. Now she would have to avoid all future conversations where he addressed her by name. Her original train of thought was spot on. He was definitely going to have power over her and she wasn't prepared to investigate it.

"The name suits you," he said with a grin. "And your surname?" She could listen to his accent all day long. It was doing funny things to her tummy.

"Cardoso."

He pulled back and tilted his head. He looked like a dog listening to a whistle. He was clearly reacting to her name. It made her wonder how he would possibly recognize it since he was obviously Scottish. His hands fell from her arms and he took a step back. She noticed the thin leather strap around his neck and wondered once again about the properties of the white stone dangling from the small silver cage. Her grandmother taught her that certain stones provided certain attributes, and she was curious what he felt he needed balance in.

He closed his eyes and took a deep breath, pinching the top of his nose between his eyes. At the shake of his head and his deep chuckle, her curiosity got the better of her.

"What is it?" she said as she took a step toward him.

He took another step back and put his hands up in surrender. His laughter was making her mad. "I recognize the name is all," he said with a grin.

"What the hell is that supposed to mean?" She took another step forward to his step back. His laughter was full-bellied now, and she was irritated that she was the butt of some inside joke.

"I dinnae mean anything by it, love," he said as he gestured in a calming motion. "But some things are making more sense to me."

"Well, that makes one of us," Sera snapped in response. "None of this makes any sense to me. I am completely in the dark here and it's pissing me off."

"Aye, I can see that," Logan said. "If ya can calm yourself, I can take ya somewhere to get some answers. Later."

"What makes you think I am going to go anywhere with you?"

He placed his hands on his hips and puffed his chest, giving her a condescending look that made her blood boil.

"Well now, lassie, do ya really have a choice?"

"There's always a choice."

"Suppose that's so," he said with a grin. "Do ya even know where ya are?"

"Of course, I..." Sera looked around her, and he watched her face fall as the realization came to her. "Well maybe not, but I'll find my way around without you."

Logan chuckled softly and shook his head. He admired her spunk. "Good luck with that, lassie. I'll be over here when you come to your senses."

His playful grin and pompous stance infuriated her. She turned her back to him with a stomp and walked toward the treeline beyond the fire pit.

She'd show him just how capable she was.

At the edge of the woods, she glanced from side to side. The trees were never ending, and she could hardly hear the steps she took as she inched her way in. They were muffled by the moss that carpeted the forest floor and she knew instinctually she was far from the caves. The silence surrounding her was eerie, broken only by the sound of her breath and a patterned thunk resonating from Logan's campsite.

Her steps paused as her tattoo started to tingle. Perhaps wandering off wasn't a good idea. Her stomach started to growl and she slowed her pace. She looked back to the fire behind her where Logan was busy chopping wood. He didn't look up from his task, looked like he hardly was giving her leaving a thought. She looked back into the woods and made her decision. As much as it pained her, staying with him was the better decision. For now.

A few hours later, Sera was at the edge of Logan's camp, parked under a tree and sulking. She would call it formulating a plan, but if she was being honest with herself it was definitely more like pouting. While she knew she didn't really have a choice in her current situation, she didn't like the fact that Logan took great pleasure in being so smug about it. Well maybe not smug—perhaps cocky would be a better description.

After mentioning she needed to find a private place to commune with nature, he shrugged his shoulders and pointed her toward the nearest clump of bushes. He continued shaving thin slices of wood from the block he held in his hands and acted as though her leaving wasn't a thought in his mind. While she thought long and hard about running off earlier, she had no idea where she would go. She really needed to be better prepared when she did finally leave. Besides, she had to pee and was hungry. Whatever he had cooking smelled pretty good.

When she went around the backside of the bushes, was happy to see a small makeshift seat with a hole and even happier to see toilet paper hanging from a branch nearby. After doing her business, she sat with her back to an oak tree and had been there ever since. There was no way she would survive out there without him. She had rescued way too many people out in the middle of the wilderness who had been much more prepared to be on their own than she was. Besides, he offered to take her to speak to someone who knew more about what was going on. If he was true to his word, and took her somewhere with more people, she would have a much better chance at escape. So, she would wait.

She spent her time observing him quietly. Shortly after their conversation, he went about his business and acted as if she wasn't there. She could tell a lot about a person through their mannerisms, and she had come to know Logan wouldn't hurt her. In fact, she realized, he was much more than he seemed.

There was a wagon at the edge of the woods where he kept his supplies, and for the first hour after her arrival he tinkered with one of the wheels. It looked as though it wasn't moving freely. After wedging a log under the wagon to raise the corner, he removed the wheel and sat near the fire while examining every inch of it. At one point he took a knife to the center and whittled away at some of the wood, cursing when his hand slipped and he cut his thumb. The injured digit went right into his mouth without hesitation or glance her way. He was very much used to being alone. If she had done something like that, the first thing she would have done was to look around for witnesses to her stupidity.

Once Logan finished with the wheel, he went back to the wagon and checked every part of the axle. He was meticulous with his attention to detail; there wasn't a spot on his project left untouched. The calluses she felt through her sheer blouse now made complete sense to her; he was a man used to working with his hands. He also gave her the impression that he was extremely capable.

The style of the cart didn't surprise her, nor did the fact that it had wooden wheels, since she had seen enough of those at her abuela's throughout the years. But she was surprised Logan had a cart but didn't seem to own a horse. It made her wonder just how long he had been here in the woods alone and if he always camped. It also made her wonder if he had an actual home.

She watched as he finished his project, spinning the wheel and watching for sticking points. Satisfied that the repair was complete, he cleaned up his area. He took great care of the things that belonged to him. Each tool was wiped and carefully placed in its proper place within his leather bag. Once he stashed his tools, he pulled the log from below the wagon and set it aside.

He removed his shirt and pulled an ax from a nearby stump. He made quick work of chopping the wood he used to prop the wagon into smaller logs for the fire. She thought she saw something on the back of his shoulder, but she couldn't be sure due to the distance. More than likely it was dirt from cutting wood earlier. He finished chopping and placed more logs on the fire, never once making eye contact with her.

Thankfully, he pulled his shirt back on after wiping himself with a small cloth. There was no way on earth she would want him to catch her staring. He was the most chiseled man she had ever laid eyes on, and as large as he was, he moved with an unbelievable silence. It was hard to keep her eyes off of him. Even though he hadn't given her the time of day for the better part of the afternoon, she realized later that he was observant and had paid more attention to her than she had given him credit for.

The sun started to set, and while he had a nice fire going, she had been too stubborn to make her way over to it. She rubbed her arms through her sheer blouse and minutes later he laid a plaid piece of wool across her lap and brought one side up over her shoulder. Without saying a word, he turned and went back to the fire, picking up the small piece of wood he had been whittling. The whole interaction took less than a few seconds, but spoke volumes of his awareness. She realized he must have patience too, since he paid such attention to detail on the tiny pieces he was working on.

Her ass was numb, so she got up to stretch her legs. She pulled the plaid over her shoulders and held it over her body like a blanket. It smelled of musk and man and it didn't take her long to realize she was snuggling in one of his kilts. She decided she didn't mind, the scent actually calmed her. It reminded her of the firehouse.

As she walked by, he didn't look up, but she noticed his whittling came to a halt. She walked within the treeline of the camp and he resumed his work, obviously satisfied she wasn't going to take off. The campsite was strange and she realized, now that she was up and moving, that the trees grew in a circular pattern. The clearing was a perfect circle and Logan's fire was in the dead center of it. She wondered why that was; why Logan wouldn't want more cover if he was camping alone. How he would protect himself in the case of an animal attack? She wondered about the possibility of bears.

She ran her hands along the bark of the trees as she walked by them, feeling their texture and letting her mind wander. It was odd, wasn't it? Wouldn't somewhere more secluded be a wiser place to set camp? And what caused the trees to grow the way they did? She looked over the clearing for stumps or debris, something to indicate that the trees had been cut that way, but it was perfectly flat. She looked up; the trees reached high into the sky, their canopies spreading wide as if they had been there for a hundred years. It was the most unnatural, natural feature she had ever seen in her life.

It was then that she saw it, actually to be completely accurate she felt it first. The symbol carved into the tree where she sat all afternoon. She hadn't noticed before, since when she stood it was below eye level, and when she sat her head was covering it. It struck her as though she had seen something similar before and ran her fingers in the grooves as she considered where that might have been. It came to her in a flash, the symbol was something like she had seen in the cave and it made her wonder if there were more.

Curious about the symbols and acting as if she were going for another walk, she went to the next tree. Sure enough, there was a different symbol carved in the tree, and as she walked around the perimeter, she saw that each one of them had similar carvings.

"I don't know what they mean, only that they protect what's in them."

"Jesus! You scared the shit out of me!" Sera shrieked. "How the hell did you get behind me so quickly?"

Logan shrugged and gave her a lop-sided grin. "You were preoccupied. And you were mumbling."

Sera harrumphed. "Well, next time walk a little louder."

"Aye, lassie," he laughed. "I'll be sure to make lots of noise, so as not to startle ya, or any of the other beasties that may be lurking about."

Sera rolled her eyes, he could be so irritating. "Did you do these?"

"Nae. They were here long before I was. Long before most anyone I know. You recognize these?"

"I saw something like it in the cave that you dragged me from. Also in my abuela's house."

"Abuela?"

"My grandmother," Sera explained. "I was looking for her when you grabbed me."

"And these symbols were there?"

Sera nodded. "Yes. There were three circles of them carved into the cave wall. The center one had triangles around it on both sides. I think that was the one that we traveled through. Wait a minute!"

She walked over to the tree she had sat beneath and opened her purse, her phone was still in there and holding half a charge. She opened the photo she had taken of the cupboard door and showed it to him. He flinched, like he had never seen a phone before, then looked at the image she zoomed in on.

"Yer a sorceress then?"

Sera was confused, then followed his line of sight. "You mean my phone?"

"The image is like that of a crystal, is it not?"

"No. Just my phone," Sera repeated. "Nothing magical about it, just good old-fashioned technology."

Logan's eyebrows furrowed; he was clearly confused.

"Don't worry about the phone, just look at the image. See this one here? It is the same as the one on the tree here." Sera pointed to the tree then walked to the next tree in line. "I wonder if they are in the same order?"

Logan walked with her from tree to tree, verifying the symbol pattern matched what she had on her phone. "What do you think it means?"

"I don't know," he answered. "But I know someone who might."

12

James was disoriented and confused. Somehow their group had been transported from the desert to a lush green forest. Thankfully, none of the fighting skeletons from the Wellness Center property followed them through. Brooke started barking instructions before James had a chance to gather his bearings. It definitely showed a new side to his baby sister, who spent her young life crippled by anxiety and as quiet as a whisper.

He supposed finding out the therapists were mistaken and that all of her make-believe friends were actually real was the turning point for her. He was still having a hard time wrapping his head around it. While he was happy for her, he worried about his own sanity. Everything that happened so far made him feel very much like Alice when she went through the looking glass.

"Max, you need to help James, boy."

Max woofed in response and followed the direction of Brooke's finger to James' side. Max was just the right height for James to use his head as support.

"Suppose you will have to do until I can find a cane," James joked as he gave the dog's ears a scratch. Max barked sharply, then ran off into the tree line.

"Well, so much for that," James laughed. "As soon as he sees a squirrel I'll be toast."

"I'll find him," Aleck offered. He jogged in the direction Max bolted, calling his name in a hushed tone.

Brooke addressed Amie as she tucked herself under James' side. He leaned some of his weight on her by putting his arm across the top of her shoulders and relieving the pressure on his leg. "We need to get to

Sevilla's and we can't risk a portal. I have no idea what those things were and if they can get through."

"Agreed," Amie said with a nod. "They were definitely real, not an illusion like we came across in Fate's domain."

"I was thinking the same thing," Brooke agreed. "I don't think they were moving on their own. And they had been there a while. There was no smell of rot."

"You're right now that I think of it," Amie said. "And it was definitely like that day at Ryker's when Aleck was fighting the armor. I think there was someone, or something controlling the skeletons. Like puppets."

"Sorry, ladies, I'm completely lost. Having a hard time jumping full on into your fantasy. What the devil are you talking about? And who is Sevilla?"

Brooke helped James over to a stump. He was glad to get off of his feet; his leg was starting to ache.

"When Amie and Aleck came through the Elemental portal for Air the first time Amie was captured. She was taken to a fortress and we went there to save her. Sevilla and her sister Zilla helped us. Long story short, a wizard named Ryker brought armor to life with magick and used them to attack us."

Oh, he was well and good into the looking glass. He figured he might as well go all in at this point. "Right then. So what happened?"

"I turned into a turbine engine force and knocked Ryker out by pulling the oxygen away from him," Amie answered. "It winded him."

"And then I punched him in the face while he was distracted," Aleck said as he walked into the clearing from the tree line. He finished walking to Amie's side and slid his hand right into hers like a gun sliding into its holster.

"You always did have a hard punch," James quipped. "You get to add him to your one-punch list?"

"Naw," Aleck shook his head. "I don't think he was someone that was used to getting physical, so I don't really count it. He came off as someone used to having others do his dirty work," Aleck muttered.

"We are not going into that right now," Amie laughed.

"Yes, we don't have time for a Logan discussion," Brooke agreed.

Before James could ask what they all meant, Max came up behind Aleck with a massive stick in his mouth and sat down thumping his large tail against the ground.

"What you have there, boy?" James waved the dog over. For such a large dog, Max moved carefully to his side. He kept the stick away from his master's legs by turning his head to the side.

"Yeah, it took me a few to realize he was on a mission not just horsing around," Aleck said. "He was definitely looking for something specific. I tried it out. I think it will work pretty good."

James took the long, straight branch from Max's mouth and examined it. It looked like a small tree that had been cracked off at the roots. At the top there was a "y" shape made with two branches that were also broken off. The notch would work perfectly under his arm.

"I broke off some of the length on the branches," Aleck explained. "Max did really good finding something just the right shape. He really is an amazing dog."

James looked into Max's eyes, seeing more than loyalty in their depths. There was a wisdom there that couldn't be denied, and it made James wonder if there was more to him than met the eye. "Thank you, Max," he said with a smile. "This is brilliant."

Max responded with a bark and another thump of his tail.

"We really should get going," Brooke said nervously. "We've already lingered too long."

"Woof," Max barked as James stood. The dog stood and took a few steps back. He watched his master carefully, as if to see if the gift he had given him would be useful. When James put his arm over the notch and took a few practice steps, Max wiggled his entire body like an excited puppy. He barked again and ran toward the treeline.

"Looks like Max agrees," James said with a grin. "Lead the way, ladies."

Max took the lead, with the ladies walking side by side behind him and James and Aleck bringing up the rear. James was glad for the chance to catch up with his old friend without being overheard by Brooke and Amie. There were just some conversations they didn't need to be part of.

James was curious about the earlier conversation that was dropped open ended. He brought it up in a quiet voice, although the ladies were so busy chatting it up, he didn't think they would even pay attention to what he and Aleck spoke about.

"Who is this Logan you mentioned earlier? Ex-boyfriend of Amie's?"

"No." Aleck took in a deep breath and let it out before proceeding. "He lives here in Wisteria. He was there the day we came through the portal and Amie was taken."

"Was he the one that took her?" James asked.

"Not sure," Aleck answered. "I only know he told me to forget about Amie, and then knocked me out cold. When I came to, they were all gone. Amie included."

"Ah," James said with a smirk. "So he added you to his one-punch list."

"I think everyone is on that jerk's one-punch list," Aleck griped. "The man is a mountain. Not to mention he's a werewolf, so he's got this…"

"Hold on, mate," James interrupted. "A werewolf?"

"Yes."

"Are you mental?"

Aleck shook his head and laughed. "Don't I wish? No, I'm telling you, dude, there is shit in this place that will make your head spin. Logan spoke to me in wolf form and literally cracked into a man before my eyes."

"Which is when he decked you?"

"Pretty much," Aleck groused. "I got one in later, but it barely left a scratch. It was like hitting a brick wall. My fist hurt for a week after."

"Shit." James thought about it for moment. "So is he a liability or an asset?"

"Supposedly an asset," Aleck said with a roll of his eyes. "If you ask me he is just an ass."

"That is evident, my friend," James said with a laugh. "So where are we heading? Max seems to know where he is going."

"He's been there before," Aleck explained. "We are going to Sevilla's house. We use it to re-group since she has some pretty strong magical barriers protecting it. I think it is why the girls don't zap into the yard even though they could. They've mentioned something about the doorways being accessible to other beings if they were to do that."

"That could be bad, especially if what attacked us in Sedona came through. What the hell were those by the way? Have you seen them before?"

"Only in my nightmares," Aleck answered. "Whatever they were, I think the girls were right, they seemed to be following instructions—like our men did in the military."

"I thought that too. They were coming at us in waves and from all sides. Their attack was strategic. Did you see a leader?"

"I was too worried about getting to Amie. I think Max took off after someone set back from the action. He wasn't able to get to him before we opened the portal and called him through."

"Is this something that we need to share with the girls? Do you think this Sevilla can help?"

"I think for now we will take it all in and keep our mouths shut. I'm not sure we can trust Sevilla, or her sister for that matter. There is something going on with them I can't put my finger on. Besides, I would rather formulate a plan with all the data. Most of the time in this place the information takes a while to come to light."

"Ah, just like the good old days, right mate?" James laughed at Aleck's expression.

"What happened to the two of us retiring?" Aleck questioned.

"Well, you're the one that fell in love with a woman who can turn into a tornado," James laughed. "I was happily minding my own business back in London before you dragged me into this situation."

"Bullshit," Aleck laughed. "The military had you by the balls – you were losing yourself. The idiot that shot you actually did you a favor."

James laughed aloud at the comment. Leave it to his friend to hold up the blatant truth like a mirror. "I suppose he did, mate."

James knew that he and Aleck were both ready to put the life of espionage and bullshit behind them, but he wasn't sure that was going to be possible now. It seemed to him that he and Aleck had landed in the middle of a situation very similar to those they had dealt with in the past. Bottom line was every mission they were involved in had to do with a fight for power. He had the sinking feeling this wouldn't be any different. Except that the enemies wielded magical weapons and had the ability to raise corpses from the grave. There was that.

James looked up at the two beautiful women walking ahead of them and could only hope that the power contained in their willowy frames was enough to fight the battle ahead. He knew it was coming; the tightening in the pit of his stomach had never let him down before. It was the same feeling he had gotten at the point of no return in each and every mission he was assigned to. The only way out of this now would be to move forward - and he and Aleck were both acutely aware of it.

"I won't be much help in battle," James said softly. "We are going to need to find some weapons."

Aleck nodded. "Not sure they will help here, but I think they will make us feel better. I'll see what I can find. In the meantime, promise me you will take in everything that is said, and pay special attention to tone and body language. We will compare and deconstruct later when we have a chance."

"Beware of who you trust," James began and waited for Aleck's response. And just like every conversation that had begun that way between the two of them before, Aleck didn't miss a beat.

"Lucifer was once an angel. You watch my six, I'll watch yours."

"Wouldn't have it any other way my brother," James responded.

Aleck smiled and slapped him on the back before running up to Amie and taking hold of her hand. Brooke slowed up to walk beside James, leaving the couple alone for a moment.

"We're almost there," Brooke mentioned. "How's the leg?"

"A bit sore," James answered honestly. "I think when we get where we are going I should put it up and ice it."

"Well I can certainly help with that," she joked.

He laughed aloud. "I'll bet you can." They both paused, each in their own thoughts, before he asked his next question. "So who is this woman we are going to see? Sevilla is it?"

"Yes," Brooke nodded. "She was who I used to see after Mum and Dad passed. She helped me through quite a bit."

"You never talked about her," he said.

"Nobody believed me," she answered with a shrug. Her voice was small. "I decided early on it was easier to pretend I wasn't having the visions. Less therapy that way."

The weight of her words were heavy in his heart. In many ways he wished he could take the years back. He looked over at the beautiful and well-adjusted woman she had become, and decided perhaps they would have never made it to this moment if he had. He was glad that destiny had finally put them on the same track. He would be never doubt her again.

"Did she help you back then with the magic stuff?"

"Oh no," Brooke said. "I had no idea about any of this until Will and I came through the portal off the coast in Maui. After we got here, I realized the type of magick she practices was present all along. She just never shared it."

"What type of magic is that? Are you talking witchcraft?"

"Not in the way you are thinking," Brooke said. "It's more like what I understand some of the pagan practices to be. You know, honoring the old gods and goddesses. Connecting to the Earth and her seasons."

"Like Wicca?"

"Precisely. You're familiar with it?"

"Absolutely," he said with a grin. "I dated a girl once that practiced Wicca. I used to love it when the time came around for the full moons."

"Oh my lord, James," Brooke laughed. "Well there will be none of that here so you can get that straight out of your head! Although, honestly with Zilla, we never really know."

"Zilla?"

"Sevilla's sister. She comes across as being a little more on the wild side."

"Sounds like someone I might like to get to know."

"We tend to steer clear of her. She and Amie were close until Amie found out she was lying to her. I think she lies to her sister as well. I don't trust her."

"Good to know. All kidding aside, I rarely trust anyone."

"I know what you mean," Brooke said with a sad smile.

James heard Max's barks and looked up to see a quaint stone cottage centering a lush green clearing. It was obvious from the way Max was prancing about that they had made it to Sevilla's. He looked over to Brooke who was beaming like she had just won the lottery.

"Isn't it wonderful," she gushed. "I'm so happy to share this with you, James. You have no idea just how long I have wanted this to happen." Tears formed in her eyes, and he couldn't help but feel guilty that he hadn't been there for her when they were younger.

"I'm so sorry I didn't believe you all those years, lovey. But, I'm glad to be here for you now."

While James meant every word he said, he couldn't help but worry that they had all gone mad. He knew he and Aleck suffered from post-traumatic symptoms, and with the death of their parents, there was a good chance Brooke did as well. It made him wonder if group hallucinations were a thing. Perhaps Max was the only sane one in the bunch — a shame really, considering he was a dog. Sharing him with Aleck was good for both of them.

Brooke helped James through the gateway behind the others and walked up the stone pathway that led to the front door. A beautiful woman creaked open the oak paneled door and met them on the stoop, giving Brooke a long hug before greeting the others. She gave Max a hug as well, then handed him a nice sized bone that would keep him busy for the rest of the day. He scampered around the corner of the cottage, looking for a soft place to rest as he chewed on it.

She straightened and turned to look at James questioningly. Her clear emerald eyes were luminous, and her raven hair fell in soft waves to her waist. She was absolutely stunning, and nowhere close to the maternal caregiver he pictured in his mind when Brooke described her during her early therapy sessions. She couldn't be a day more than forty.

"You must be James," she said to him as she pulled him in for a hug. "It is so nice to meet you finally." She stood back and a line creased her brow. As quick as he noticed the question on her face, it was gone and replaced with a warm and welcoming smile. "I'm Sevilla, welcome to my home. Please come in and get off that leg. Brooke can make some ice for it while I brew some tea."

"Thank you," James said as Sevilla ushered him through the door and sat him at a large wooden table centered in a rustic kitchen complete with a working fireplace.

Amie ran up the stairs to the right; James presumed they led to a second floor with bedrooms. She seemed to be in a hurry.

Aleck looked slightly confused, then apologetic. "I'll just check on her. Amie and I will be right back," he explained, before following up the stairs behind her.

James hoped the stairway wasn't as narrow as it looked, he would have a hard time getting up there if he needed to.

Sevilla's curious gaze followed the couple up the stairs and offered a slight shake of her head. She took a deep breath before addressing her remaining company. "I sense something happened. You want to tell me what brought you here today?"

James pointed to Brooke as he shook his head. "I think she needs to be the one to explain, since I am not entirely sure this isn't a dream."

"We get that a lot here, darling," he heard a sultry voice say from the room behind the fireplace. After looking at the woman entering the kitchen from the archway, he had to look back to see if Sevilla was indeed still standing by the kitchen sink. "You aren't seeing double, handsome," the woman said with a grin.

"James, this is my sister Zilla," Sevilla said with exasperation. "She loves to make an entrance."

"Just be glad I have all my clothes on this time, since I was enjoying a lovely nap by the fire."

James was still trying to sort her comment out in his mind as she sashayed further into the kitchen and into the light. The two women were more than sisters, they were definitely twins. Even though at first glance they looked identical, in the better light he was able to see subtle differences in the way they stood and the moves they made. Sevilla seemed to be more delicate, where Zilla was edgy. Zilla's eyes were green like her sister's, but had more of a hazel effect in them. Sevilla wore a loose peasant style skirt and top, while Zilla had on a corset style top and tight fitting jeans. There was also an energy surrounding Sevilla's sister that he couldn't quite put his finger on. Where one was mysterious and calming, the other was blatant and energetic. If he had to guess, it just meant that Zilla was a bundle of trouble. In the past, he gravitated to women like her in the bars; they were always amazing in the sack and never asked for a commitment.

He attempted to stand for introductions, but Brooke came behind him and pressed down on his shoulder.

"Stay put, James. You've been on your leg too long."

"I can come to you, darling," Zilla said with a toothy smile. She leaned over slowly, giving him a long look at her ample cleavage, before giving him a chaste kiss on his cheek. He was positive he would find red lipstick there later.

"It's so very nice to meet you."

"James," he supplied. "Brooke's older brother. It's lovely to meet you."

"What brings you all here? Did you have any luck finding what you were looking for?" Zilla looked directly at Brooke when she asked the question, and Sevilla turned, clearly interested in her response.

"I think we should wait until Amie and Aleck join us. So much has happened and I want to be sure I don't forget anything."

"Of course, Brooke," Sevilla said. "Why don't you run up and get your journal. I will make us all something to eat."

"And I'll keep James company while you are gone," Zilla offered.

"Great," Brooke said as she rolled her eyes. It seemed that they were all used to Zilla's antics.

James was amused by the whole scene. While there was no denying Zilla was a beautiful woman, she was most certainly not his type. She tried too hard to convince others that she was more than she seemed. It made her come off as being conniving. Most definitely something he didn't have time for in his life. Aleck was right. They would need to keep an eye on her. There was something a little off.

"Brooke, about that ice," he called out before she took the stairs.

"Oh, of course, my apologies," she said shaking her head. She cupped her hands in front of her mouth and blew, forming a large piece of ice in her palms. "This should work for now."

She wrapped it in one of the napkins from the table and handed him the cold compress. "I'll be right back."

"Take your time," Zilla said with a grin. She pulled the seat out next to him and perched herself on the seat. James could tell from the way Brooke was holding her shoulders that she was irritated. Sevilla was over at the sink shaking her head. It gave James the distinct impression that they were in for a long night.

13

Between the clouds and the lush canopy of leaves, the half moon was hardly visible. Logan and Sera were still in the woods at his campsite, even after he said he might know someone who could help with the symbols. Sera knew it was late, but it still irritated her that Logan refused to take her to any semblance of civilization until the morning. She realized she was being unreasonable; no sane person would traipse around the woods in the darkness. But she couldn't help it, she was impatient by nature.

After their examination of the symbols, Sera sat down closer to the fire and waited while Logan finished cooking their meal. She offered to help, but he refused. It looked like he had a routine, so she didn't take it personally. It was probably better for him that she stayed out of the way.

The aromas from the pots on the fire smelled heavenly and her stomach rumbled. Sera was just getting ready to ask one more time if she could help with anything when Logan announced dinner was ready. She stood up from the stump she had been sitting on, and before she could take a step toward him, he rushed to her and swung her roughly behind his back. She attempted to pull her arm from his grip and had just started to argue when she heard a branch snap.

"Stay behind me," Logan whispered fiercely.

She snapped her mouth shut, understanding that in this strange place she had no idea what to expect. Sera snuggled up to Logan's back and looked behind her to the darkness in the trees. It made her wonder if he had ever had any trouble with bears.

A man's voice called out from the trees Logan faced. He sounded friendly. "Hello, Logan. Was hoping your offer still stood for some hospitality?"

"Aye." Logan responded cautiously. He reached behind and grabbed Sera's hand, pulling her to his side before letting go and placing his arm across her shoulders. The move was territorial, his grip tense. Before she had a chance to move from his embrace or say anything, the man came into the clearing. His pace slowed; obviously surprised to see her there. He raised his hands in surrender, clearly apologizing for intruding.

"Sorry, Logan, I had no idea you had company. I can go…"

"Nae. Don't be a fool. We've got plenty." The words coming out of Logan's mouth sounded amiable, but the grip he had on the top of her shoulder told her otherwise. Was this man friend or foe?

"Thank you," the man said as he came closer to where they stood. He stopped in front of Sera and dropped the hood of his cloak, revealing a beautifully masculine face with chocolate brown eyes. His shoulder length brown hair was clean but tussled, and he had a puckered scar running the length of his cheek. The scar only made him more intriguing to Sera.

She shifted on her feet to prepare to shake the man's hand and thought she heard a quiet rumble. The man's raised eyebrow and side glance at Logan confirmed what she heard. Logan had indeed made a sound, and she was pretty sure it wasn't his stomach. It looked like his friend was going to ignore it. He put his hand out and Sera took it in hers.

"It is a pleasure to meet you, my dear. My name is Kadar."

"It's very nice to meet you Kadar," Sera responded with a smile. "I'm Sera."

Kadar raised her hand to his lips with a smirk. He had hardly put his lips to her hand when Logan grabbed it from Kadar's grasp and pulled Sera toward the fire. He put her on the seat he had been sitting on himself earlier and sat on the stump directly to her left. The last stump was a few feet to Logan's left. He was effectively sitting between her and their guest.

Mouth agape, she shot Logan a sideways look as he waited for Kadar to settle on his stump. Before she was able to question why he was being such a jerk, Logan got up and loaded the plates. She decided to let his rude behavior go without comment since she was hungry and didn't want to take a chance that he wouldn't feed her.

"Thank you. This smells wonderful," Sera said, as she took the plate and fork he handed her. The tingle she felt as his hand brushed hers was hard to ignore.

"I'll get the bread," Logan said with a warm smile. He took a plate over to Kadar, before dishing some up for himself and leaving it on the stump.

"Do ya fancy some ale?" Logan called from the back of the wagon. He laughed and shook his head when both Sera and Kadar answered yes. He walked back to the fire with the handles of three mugs in one hand, and a loaf of bread in the other.

"Here, let me help you with that," Sera said, as she put her plate on her seat and took two of the mugs out of his hand. She walked over to Kadar and held one out to him, curious as to why he didn't take it right away. He was looking at something behind her, and his line of sight didn't change, even when he took the mug from her hands and drank from it. She wondered what held Kadar's attention and turned where she stood, locking eyes with Logan, who looked as if he was ready to burst from his skin.

She walked slowly toward him, never once dropping her gaze. Her tone was unbelieving. He was being an ass. "What is wrong with you? Are you okay?" When he didn't respond right away, she shrugged her shoulders and crossed back to her seat. "Whatever."

"I'll be fine," Logan answered grumpily. "Just stay put."

"So sorry," Sera snapped back sarcastically. She lifted her plate from her seat and plunked down on top of the cushioned stump. "I was just trying to help."

"I dinnae need your help, lassie."

She felt the heat rise in her face, and her fingers started to tingle. He was really pissing her off. "Well, next time you do, I'm sure not going to give it to you. You lug-headed, ungrateful…"

"The stew is amazing," Kadar said with a grin. "And the ale is refreshing. You should try it, Sera."

Sera stopped mid-sentence and looked over at Kadar who was leaning forward to speak to her from around a seated Logan. He was smiling from ear to ear. It looked as though he was taking great pleasure in egging his host on. Sera shook her head and laughed at Kadar's attempt to lighten the mood. He reminded her of her sparring partner, Mark, who always cooled her temper by diverting attention away from the issue.

She shot Kadar a conspiring wink, which only managed to make Logan's frown more prominent. What the hell had gotten into him all of a sudden? Were the two of them friends or not? Maybe Kadar was right; maybe she should just enjoy the ale. Perhaps she should get Logan to drink more of it as well; it might loosen the bug up his ass.

She took a few swigs from her mug before quietly diving into her stew.

Kadar was right, it was amazing.

"Did ya want some bread, lassie," Logan said softly. She looked at him, noting the sheepish look on his face and his hunched shoulders. Whatever was going on with him was confusing. It was like he was fine one minute and grumpy the next.

She decided to cut him some slack; he seemed embarrassed by his own behavior. Besides, she needed to be nice to him until she could figure out what the hell was going on.

"Thank you, Logan," she said softly. She took the bread from his hand, and looked back down to her plate. She decided looking at Kadar was something she needed to avoid. For whatever reason, it upset Logan, and she needed to stay out of the middle of it. They all ate in silence and drank until their mugs were empty. It wasn't until the second round of ale that the tension of the conversation was lifted.

△

Logan took the dishes Sera handed him one by one and scraped the few remaining spoonfuls of stew into the fire. He would rinse them in the morning; there was no way he would leave her here alone. Kadar had gone off to the river, and while Logan was desperate for a bath, he would wait until morning on that as well.

Kadar infuriated him; he had been smirking at him off and on all night. It made Logan wonder just how much he had seen that night Sera danced for him in the fire. He thought at the time that it was a dream, but now that he had passed through the image and pulled her into his reality, it seemed more likely that it had been real. The way Kadar looked at Sera made Logan think that perhaps he had seen just as much of her bare skin as he had. That thought made his hackles rise.

It wasn't as if he didn't trust Kadar — but, he didn't trust Kadar. Actually, there weren't too many men he did trust. And Sera was much too valuable to him to take a chance on leaving her alone with a relative stranger. Besides, Kadar mentioned working for Ryker, and as far as Logan knew, he could still be under his employ. It seemed strange that Logan had been at the same camp for a week with nary a soul to talk to, and now the same man visited him twice in a span of a few days. He also found it odd that Kadar started showing up around the same time Logan saw visions of Sera. Aye, he was right not to trust him, something didn't smell right; he just quite couldn't put his finger on it.

He tried not to react when Kadar took Sera's hand before dinner, but he couldn't help himself. Logan's growl had risen from the pit of his soul and came out of his throat before he could squelch it. He knew his behavior was irritating Sera, but his compulsion to protect her was all-consuming.

"…for the night."

Shite. He had been so caught up in his thoughts; he completely missed what Sera had said.

"Sorry, lassie. I dinnae hear what you said."

She gave him a soft smile, and even though he knew it was caused by the ale affecting her tiny frame, he pretended otherwise. He wanted it to be that she was warming to his attentions, but he knew better. Another step brought him close enough to see the tiny lines that creased the corners of her eyes. Logan took a deep breath and fought the urge to run his fingers along their path. He wanted to know what caused them, wanted to be part of the laughter and the tears that now reflected on her beautiful face.

"I just said I was going to wrap it up for the night. I wasn't sure where you wanted me to sleep."

"As close to me as possible," Logan responded automatically. He nearly cringed after he said it, especially after the intake of her breath and widening of her eyes.

"You make me nervous," Sera said quietly.

Earlier, he had spent the entire afternoon as far away from her as he could handle in order to give her time to adjust to him. He kept his hands busy, since his impulse was to run them through her hair and bury his face deep into her curls. He avoided thinking about her by fixing the wheel on the wagon and whittling three new animals for Annabelle's collection. None of these things helped, especially after he saw her walking around with his colors draped over her shoulders. The sight of her wrapped in his kilt confirmed what his heart already knew – she was meant to be his. The pull of his wolf merely confirmed it.

He glanced at her and continued scraping the dishes. He couldn't think of a way to respond to her comment without making her angry or more nervous. The things he wanted to say would probably send her into the dark woods screaming.

Sera's whispered voice took away his opportunity to say something soothing. "Are you okay with Kadar being here? Are we safe?"

Logan nodded. "Aye, lassie, you are most safe. I'll see that no harm comes to ya."

The irritation swept across her face and shot from her eyes. He almost didn't need to use his sense of smell to pick up on her emotions, since her face was so expressive. He wondered if she knew that about herself, how her face moved and changed like flames in a fire.

"That is not what I asked you, Logan, I asked if we were safe. I don't need a man to keep watch over me. Trust me I can hold my own."

He could watch the display on her face all day and never grow tired of it, especially when she laughed. The fine creases near her eyes deepened in humor, and the tinkling sound of her joy soothed him like nothing else could. She wasn't laughing now, though. She looked as though she was ready to rip his eyes out.

"Calm your wee self…"

"Do you have any idea how condescending and arrogant you sound when you say stuff like that?" She crossed over to one of the logs by the fire and sat in a huff.

"I dinnae mean anything by it," Logan said sincerely. "But ya are wee, there's no denyin' it."

Sera shot him a sidelong glance and rolled her eyes. Her laughter caused him to close his eyes and breathe in the soothing effects.

"Okay, you have me there. I am petite. But I can lift double my weight when I have to and can punch a full-grown man black and blue."

Logan sat on the log next to her and faced her, leaning his elbows on his knees and giving her his full attention. He wondered if she realized how incredible she looked in the light of the fire. Maybe one day he would tell her.

"Logan. All I am saying is that I am very used to working as a team and I would expect the same from you. I need to know you have my back, but if the shit comes down you need to know that I have yours as well."

"You've decided to trust me then," he said with a grin. His heart swelled in his chest at the thought.

She snorted softly and smiled. "It seems to be in my best interest to do so. You haven't given me much of a choice."

"Aye, I haven't," Logan inwardly grimaced. "To answer your earlier question, I do believe that we are safe, but I suggest we take precautions. I don't know Kadar well, and I would feel better if you stayed close to me."

Sera shot him a look, her eyebrow rising to the occasion. "And?"

"Not just to protect you, but for my protection as well."

She smiled; it seemed that he had won that battle. "What is your suggestion for the sleeping arrangements? And don't get any funny ideas about what will be going on. I can't be held responsible for what happens in my dreams."

Logan's pulse quickened and he smiled at the thought. She was right; there would be none of that tonight, especially not in front of an audience.

"Nae, my love, I'll be keepin' me hands to myself."

"Considering what happened before in our dream, I'm not sure that is a relief," Sera muttered under her breath.

He chuckled. Her head snapped quickly and she shot him a look, clearly surprised that he had heard her whispered comment. He decided to let it go; they had a lifetime to nurture that part of their relationship. For now, he needed to learn more about the fiercely independent creature he was bound to. He looked forward to peeling back the layers of her personality and getting to know every last one of them.

"You can sleep near me. I have plenty of room on my blankets. I can give you a few to wrap up in so there is a barrier between us if that comforts you."

"That sounds good. I'll be sleeping in my clothes anyway." Sera stifled a yawn behind her hands and looked at him with hooded eyes. She looked exhausted; it had been a long day.

Logan stood up and put his hand out to help her rise. Sera shook her head and smiled, placing her hand in his and allowing him to pull her from the stump. Their hands stayed joined as he walked her over to the pile of blankets he had spread out earlier in the day. Sera removed her shoes and chose to spread out on the spot nearest the fire. Logan was happy with the choice since he could hear noises in the woods behind him and would be able to see intruders from the front. He would be better able to protect her with his heightened senses. Not that he would tell Sera that.

He placed a few more logs on the fire and was just making his way back to the blankets where Sera laid when Kadar came out of the woods from the direction of the river. Kadar glanced across the fire and saw Sera stretched out on the blankets behind Logan. He shot a raised eyebrow Logan's way. Nods of understanding were exchanged between the men, and Kadar quickly rolled out his bedding and settled down for the night. By the time Logan made one last circle around the campsite and returned to Sera, she was on her side facing the fire, fast asleep.

Logan intended to take her home and leave her there with Mila and Annabelle where she would be safe. With the next full moon only weeks away, he was limited on time, but he didn't want to rush it. He wanted to be sure that Sera came into his life, and to his bed, freely and without reservations. It would take some time to woo her, and his plan to start tonight was somewhat dampened by the arrival of his new friend, Kadar.

He changed quickly into his pants, which were much less comfortable than his kilt, but more of a barrier against his wayward thoughts. Logan lay happily behind Sera, placing a rolled blanket between them and sidling up as close as he could without touching her. He took one last look across the fire at Kadar, whose covered form wasn't moving. Logan had earned Sera's trust, so he would stay up as long as he could to keep watch. He lowered his head close to the back of hers and took a deep breath. Her scent was a soothing balm to his nerves and he followed through with his compulsion to push his face into her locks, while keeping the rest of his body in check. Her hair felt like silk on his cheek, and as much as he had wanted to remain conscious and keep vigil, he wasn't able to. His beloved had finally come to him, and it would earn him the best sleep he had had in months.

△

Sera was startled awake, drenched with sweat, and pinned under an arm the size of a small tree. Logan was full-body spooning her, and as much as she regretted leaving the safety of his arms, she really needed to get away from him. His body was like a radiator, and between him, the wool blankets he had covered her in, and her hot flash, she was seconds from stripping down naked. She gently pulled his arm from around her waist and dropped it behind her before pulling the layers of blankets back and allowing the cool night to soothe her heated skin. The tattoo over her left breast was the only place she didn't find immediate relief, it stung like a mother.

A woman's voice called to her softly, and she realized that it had been that, not the heat, that had awoken her the first time. She looked across the fire and saw a tiny figure silhouetted in the treeline. She was about to wake Logan when the familiar voice spoke to her once more.

"Nieta precioso. Come to me."

"Abuela? Is that you?" Recognizing the voice, Sera got up and walked toward the fire to get a better look.

"It's me, my darling. I've come to take you home."

Sera was close enough to see the outline of her shape, and a few shadowed images. Her tattoo was on fire, and the tips of her fingers were sparking. It certainly looked like her grandmother, but something was off.

"What are you doing here?"

"That's it," the figure responded. "Just a few more steps this way."

Sera stopped, just as the figure hissed and she heard Logan's voice close behind her.

"Sera, no," he yelled, grabbing her hand and pulling her back behind him. She had left him sleeping, how the hell did he sneak up on her so fast?

"Logan, what are you doing? That's my abuela!"

"Nae, my love, it's not. You need to trust me."

Sera twisted her wrist from Logan's grip and took a step to the side so she could see around his immense frame. He was right, the figure wasn't her grandmother; she wasn't even sure it was human. It could have fooled her in every way in the light of day, but by night the eyes glowed blue and her grandmother's eyes were brown.

The figure shifted, growing taller in the fires glow and increasing in size by half. When it addressed her again, it was with a man's voice.

"Lycans are not to be trusted. You should come with me to find the answers you seek."

Logan once again took her hand and pulled her behind his shirtless back. He addressed the figure, but none too kindly.

"Erebos. The last time I saw ya, you were chained in Ryker's dungeon."

"The name is Roy," the man snapped back in anger. "And no man can contain me, not Ryker. Not even Erebos."

"What do you want?" Logan's grip firmed around her hand and settled her. If the being that called himself Roy wanted to take her, Logan wouldn't make it easy on him. As much as she believed in fighting her own fights, it was a strange comfort to realize he was willing to take a punch for her. Or whatever this guy would throw at him.

"You know what I want, lycan. Bring her to me and there will be no bloodshed."

"There'll be no bloodshed anyway, ya have no power here." Logan shifted on his feet and loosened his grip, letting go of her hand in the process. He bent at the knees and his hands fisted open and closed at his side. The muscles of his back were tense, bulging beneath the surface of his skin and creating the illusion of movement. She heard the cracking of twigs and realized the sound had come from Logan even though he hadn't taken a step.

"You can't keep her here forever. And you can't be in two places at once. I'll be waiting, lycan."

The figure disappeared in an instant, one moment there, the next gone. Logan stood facing the treeline, still tense and watchful, as if the man would return and make good on his threat. She touched his shoulder and felt him jump from the zap of electricity that sparked when her fingers touched his skin. When she pulled her fingers up she noticed a marking, the one she had noticed earlier from a distance. She could get a much better look at in now, and what she saw made her pause and drop the bottom from her stomach. She didn't believe in coincidence, but this had destiny written all over it. Before she had a chance to put her thoughts in order, Logan addressed her.

"We cannae stay here, lassie. I need to take ya home."

"You're taking me back to Spain?"

"Nae. I'll be taking ya to my village."

"Well, I guess that's something," Sera snarked. She was still nervous about the image he was marked with. True to her nature, she dealt with her nerves with sass and avoidance.

"Logan, you need to tell me what is going on. Who was that guy? And why would he be after me?" She moved around his side to face him, but he twisted in place leaving his back facing her.

"Logan, look at me." She moved again, and he twisted again. Why wouldn't he face her? "What the fuck is wrong with you?"

"I need a moment, lassie."

"What the hell is that supposed to mean? Some guy with glowing blue eyes, dressed as my grandmother comes here to abduct me and all you can say is 'you need a moment'? Are you serious right now?"

Sera heard the cracking twig sound again; it seemed to be coming from in front of Logan. She called out into the treeline. "Kadar, is that you?"

Logan's back widened with his breath and he let it out slowly, as if he was trying to find patience in the act. There was no response from the treeline; perhaps she was hearing things. Kadar must have left in the night; she saw no signs of him near the fire.

Sera took a step around Logan's side, and this time he didn't move but stood with his fisted hands on his hips and his chest puffed out. She was surprised to see him in pants, and wondered when he found the time to change. It must have been after she had fallen asleep. She was sure it had been for her benefit, since they looked way more constricting than a kilt would be.

Her eyes skimmed up his abs to his chest and she wondered how she hadn't noticed how hairy he was. He had been shirtless when he chopped wood; but she had been observing him from a distance. Maybe she had been too far away for it to register. Not that she minded since he was a beautiful specimen either way.

His head was tipped back, which made it impossible to make eye contact. Why was he avoiding her? The man was infuriating.

"Logan, look at me." Sera placed her hands on his chest in an effort to get his attention. His hands came up and covered hers, his fingers scooped beneath hers as he pulled their joined hands close to his chest. He slid her palm over to cover his heart, which felt as though it was going to burst from his chest. She pulled her other hand from his grip, reached up to his neck and pressed lightly. His pulse fluttered wildly. He pulled her hand down from his throat to the center of his chest once again and, taking a deep breath, looked down into her eyes at last.

She gasped. Logan's eyes were just like the man in the treeline, except instead of glowing blue, they were sparkling gold. They were mesmerizing, like a shiny kaleidoscope, swirling around his highly dilated pupils. More shocking than that were the long fang-like teeth poking from between his lips. It was almost as though his teeth were too large for his mouth.

"What are you?" Sera whispered, attempting to pull her hands from his grip and take a step back. He held her hands in place, and she left them there for his sake. He looked pained.

"A man," Logan answered quietly. "But also something more."

"The man called you a lycan," Sera said softly. "Did he mean like a..."

"Werewolf. Aye, that was what he meant."

Sera looked away from his eyes and down to where their hands were clasped. Strangely, there was less hair there now. She was curious as to where it had gone. When she looked back into his eyes, the glow was gone but the sadness remained. The fangs retracted, and his jaw looked more squared. He was looking more like the Logan she had first met in her visions. She felt it in her bones; no matter the genetics, he was a good and decent man. And he was lonely.

"When you get angry…"

"I start to change, although up until a few moons ago I could control it. Now it happens more often, and when I least expect it. Seems to be worse when there's a threat."

"That actually explains quite a bit," Sera laughed nervously. "When that man came here it caused you to start changing?"

"Aye."

"And at dinner with Kadar?"

"It was close, but I managed meself."

"I see." Sera pulled her hands from his grip and took a step back. She wasn't sure how she felt about being alone with him, even though her gut told her he wouldn't hurt her. The new information crowded her already overwhelmed brain. She needed answers, and she wasn't sure they should necessarily come from him.

"What now?"

"I need to get you to safety, but first I need to check on my village. The Shadowman threatened you both."

"Shadowman? I thought he said his name was Roy?"

"Aye, he did. But I have known him by other names as well. They are all one in the same."

"And what did he want with me?"

"I'm not sure, lassie, but we'll find out. I know just the person to ask."

14

Sera watched Logan as he hastily packed a small sack from his supplies on the wagon. Since they were already half-dressed, it didn't take long for them to get ready. Sera only had her purse with her, which she gathered from the place they slept. She looked across the fire, curious about Kadar's absence. Perhaps he and Logan had words after she went to sleep. The way Logan had been acting at dinner, she wouldn't put it past him.

She glanced up as he approached and drank in the amazing lines of his physique. Sera had come to realize that the chest hair she saw earlier was the direct result of Logan's change, since there was more of his skin showing now. Her vision traveled down his chest and followed the neat trail that tucked into the waistband of his pants. It was only when she looked up and made eye contact with him that he started to move again and released his breath. He had the audacity to slide on his shirt with a chuckle.

Sera rolled her eyes, slightly embarrassed that he caught her gawking, but there was no woman with eyes in her head that would blame her! The man didn't have an ounce of fat on him and was built like a tank. She glanced over after he finished putting his shirt on, which was almost as dangerous as staring at his bare chest. The soft linen stretched against his wide shoulders, and she wondered not only how he managed to wear something so tight without ripping it, but also who had made it for him. The shirt definitely looked handmade.

She needed something to do. "Do you want me to snuff the fire while you put on your boots? I'd be happy to, I'm ready to go."

For a fleeting moment, he looked as though he was going to tell her he didn't need her help, but then responded with a nod.

"Aye, lassie, that would be helpful. There's a pile o' sand on the other side of the pit, and the shovel is in the back of the wagon."

Sera smiled, he was learning. "I see it," she replied. By the time she was done putting sand on the embers and replacing the shovel, Logan was ready to go.

They entered the woods at the same point they had seen the Shadowman. Sera hoped that didn't increase their chances of running into him again. Looking over at the large bat Logan carried, Sera realized he must be thinking the same thing. The bat didn't look like it would be effective in a baseball game, but it sure looked like it could do some serious damage to someone's skull. Sera was happy to see that it looked relatively clean and that the only markings on it were designs that had been etched into the handle.

She wasn't sure how she felt about Logan's volatile behavior and the fact that at any moment he could change into a hairy snarling beast. But she couldn't help her curiosity either. For the most part Logan seemed receptive to her line of questioning, but didn't make eye contact with her. His eyes were busy scanning either side of the path they were on.

"Is it true that all werewolves are compelled to change on a full moon?"

"Not so much a compulsion as a desire. There's nothing better than connecting to your animal when the moon is round and the air is crisp. Except perhaps..." He stopped abruptly and looked into her upturned face. Was he turning red?

"Except...," she prompted with a grin. He was definitely turning red. She knew where his original train of thought was heading and she wasn't letting him off so easy.

"Well except for the times when...what I mean ta say is while having..."

"Sex," Sera provided with a smile. Where was the man that was all steam and innuendo? He was sure being shy all of a sudden, not that she minded since it was nice that they were taking things slower than they did in her dreams.

"Aye, sex," he answered and promptly cleared his throat. "The act can have some healing qualities."

"Healing qualities?"

"Aye, clears the head and provides focus."

"I guess I see your point," Sera chuckled. Time to get the conversation back on track. "So what about the silver bullet thing?"

"Silver bullet?"

"Yeah," she said. "Legends say that you can kill a werewolf by shooting him with a silver bullet."

Logan thought about it for moment before responding. "I suppose it depends on where you shoot him. Most of the lycans I know die of old age."

"No guns here?"

"Nae, lassie, no guns. There are things way more powerful than guns here, so no sense in havin' them."

"Like what?"

"Like the Shadowman. He's a powerful sorcerer who wields magick like a weapon."

"Why didn't he use magick last night? It was the circle wasn't it?"

"Aye, tis what I believe. Although I wasn't entirely sure of it until he left without attacking."

"And now that we aren't protected?"

Logan stopped walking and turned her to face him. She could feel the warmth from his palms through her sheer top. For an instant he looked down to her chest, which Sera didn't mind since she had done the same to him. However, the curious look on his face made her glance to where he was staring. The top of her thistle tattoo peeked over the top edge of her tank. It made her wonder if he too was making a connection.

He cleared his throat, and when she looked up he was smirking and responding to her question.

"What do ya mean we aren't protected? I thought ya had my back, wee one, and when the shite comes down, as you say, I'll have yours."

Sera laughed and shook her head; so he had been listening. "You're right, Logan, I do have your back. Just wait until you see my ninja moves!"

Logan grinned and started walking once again. "Not sure what a ninja is, but there's no denyin' I'll fancy your moves when I see them."

Sera was amazed that they walked for hours and saw nothing but trees, moss and rotting logs. Logan picked a small clearing with a large fallen tree to take a break. He shared dried sausages, fruits and the last of the bread from dinner the night before. The leather canteen they passed back and forth was filled with clear crisp water. With all of the hiking and fresh air, it was probably the best meal Sera had eaten in a long time. At least that was how she felt at that moment.

"Thank you for this, Logan," Sera said sincerely. "I was starting to get hungry."

"Aye, I could hear that," he said with a wink.

"I can't help it, my stomach has a mind of its own," she laughed. "Was it really that loud?"

"Nae, I just pick up on sounds a bit better than most."

"Handy skill, I'm impressed," she smirked. "So what other skills do lycans have?"

"Depends on the lycan," he answered with a shrug. "I suppose the ability to heal is common between species."

"That's interesting," Sera said honestly. "So cuts and bruises take less time to fade?"

"Aye," Logan nodded. "And broken bones mend in days." He cleaned up the rest of their snack and rose to his feet. Sera took it as her cue to get moving and allowed him to help her to rise. She continued the conversation as they walked.

"That is amazing. So have you had anything major happen to you?"

"Aye, there was the time about 50 years ago when I fell off a cliff and broke my…"

"Whoa…wait a minute! 50 years? How old are you? You can't be a day over 30."

"You would be accurate in lycan years, which are half as much as human. I'm almost 60."

"And here I thought I was too old for you," Sera joked.

"Nae, lassie, ya aren't."

Logan's tone and the harnessed passion that laced those four little words made Sera's heart stop. In another world he would be way too young for her in her mind, but in this world, a world where magick was available and freely given, perhaps they were perfect for one another.

Sera found her mind returning to the image she now saw every time she closed her eyes. There it was again, a smile touched with a playful dimple and golden eyes as warm as a summer's day. While their introduction had been less than stellar, he had been nothing but accommodating and gentlemanly. There was an undercurrent of attraction she felt in her dreams, and she knew they were mutually feeling the sexual tension. If she had been back home and met him in a bar, she would have had no hesitation taking him home and riding him like a pony. Especially after receiving the news she wasn't promoted.

This situation honestly wasn't any different, and she decided she wanted to learn more about the man who was now fifteen years her senior. She looked at his beautiful face again, jealous of the unlined skin around his eyes, and considered what it would have been like to have a different life at half her age.

"You're quiet, wee one. Have ya run out of questions so quickly?" Logan's tone was probing; he must have sensed something was wrong. He was right, and it irked her that a complete stranger could pick up on her emotions in such a short time. Obviously she needed to talk incessantly; he paid way too much attention to her facial expressions when she was quiet.

"Sorry, my mind was wandering," Sera said with a smile. "So how much longer until we get there?"

"A few minutes actually. It's just through this last cluster of trees."

"I'm not sure how you can tell we're close at all, considering these trees look the same as the trees we have walked through the entire day."

Logan laughed and Sera's heart paused in her chest. The sound erupted from his chest like thunder and humor lit his face like the sun. It was one of the most enchanting things she had ever witnessed in her life.

"I dinnae pay attention to how the trees look, but how they smell."

Sera frowned as she contemplated the comment. "So how do these trees smell differently from the thousands of other trees in the forest?"

"Well… ya see I… there is a way of marking…"

"Ooooohhhh!" Sera exclaimed with a blush. "Say no more, really. I totally get it," she said with a laugh.

"Not just that," Logan chuckled. "It is more about how each of the areas has its own distinct scent. One area may smell more musty and damp, where another area may have the sun's rays breaking through the trees and smell crisp."

"You can smell humidity?"

"Aye, among other things."

"What other things?"

"Fear, for instance, or happiness."

"I see," Sera said softly. "It seems you have the ability to zero in on someone's emotions without them even being aware of it. Seems as though it gives you a bit of an edge, Logan Blackwood."

Logan looked at her, his eyes squinting as if he was calculating just how to respond to her comment. Honesty won out over self-preservation. "Aye, it does, lassie, but I only use it to enhance my relationships, never to control them."

"Good to know," Sera said with a faint smile. She could sense Logan wanted to say more, but for whatever reason he decided to remain silent. Perhaps it had to do with the fact that they had just walked into his village.

The path they had been on the better part of the day led into a clearing that had small wooden houses on both sides. Some were made of logs, others were made of wooden planks, and while the colors varied, Sera assumed it only had to do with the age of the wood. There were a few stray chickens in the street, but most of them seemed to be contained in the fences surrounding the front yards. The grass near the houses seemed to be kept at the appropriate height by the goats that wandered in and out of the open gates. Sera doubted there would be a need for lawnmowers, even if they had them.

There were pens dotted between and behind the cottages that housed pigs, and Sera spied at least two cows from her vantage point. It looked as though most of the remaining space was absorbed by well-tended gardens. As first impressions went, the village was humble and well-maintained.

A squeal and a yell came from one of the first houses they came upon. The little girl couldn't be more than ten and ran toward Logan with her arms open wide.

"Papa, Papa!"

Papa? Sera looked between the two as Logan lifted the young girl into his arms and she covered his face with kisses. Papa? A smile lit up his face, just as it had when he laughed with her in the forest. He was right; she could almost smell his happiness.

"Annabelle," Logan admonished. "What on earth have you been into? You smell like a..."

Sera couldn't help but chuckle, it was obvious from the brown stains on her clothing and the distinctive odor wafting from her, just where she had been.

"I was in the pig-pen, Papa. I was feeding them like Nana asked, but the big one with the black spot came from behind and made me trip."

While they looked nothing alike, they did seem to share the same golden colored eyes. The girl's gaze locked onto Sera, and her head tilted before looking up into Logan's face.

She pointed her little finger at Sera. "Who's that?" she asked abruptly.

"Annabelle, manners," Logan said firmly as he set her on the ground in front of him.

"Sorry," she said with a sigh. The young girl turned to face Sera, straightened her shoulders and quietly waited for her introduction.

"Annabelle, I would like you to meet my dear friend Sera. Sera, this is my ward Annabelle."

Logan's tone during his introduction made Sera flush. She would need to investigate the "dear friend" title with him later. Sera took Annabelle's small hand into hers and was surprised when the girl pulled herself forward and hugged her around the waist. Her arms naturally came around her; Sera couldn't help but give the girl a gentle squeeze. She definitely smelled like a pig pen, but Sera didn't mind in the slightest. It was nice to be hugged.

"It's wonderful to meet you, Annabelle."

The young girl pulled herself out of their embrace and gave her a broad smile. "It's really nice to meet you too. You're really pretty."

"Well, thank you," Sera laughed.

"Isn't she, Papa?"

Sera looked at Logan, who gave her a quick wink before answering Annabelle's question. "Yes, sweetling, Sera is very pretty." His eyes softened and his next comment covered her like silk. "Beautiful in fact."

Annabelle yanked on Logan's hand, effectively breaking the eye contact that Sera and he had been sharing. Sera was glad for the disruption, she was starting to feel her temperature rise and wasn't sure it was appropriate. He had called Annabelle his ward, but she was calling him Papa. Was there a mother in the picture? And if so, why the hell had he been flirting with her?

"Are you staying home now?"

"Nae, my love, we're just here for a few days."

"All right," Annabelle said with a pout. "Well I suppose that will have to do. A short visit is better than no visit at all. That's what Nana says."

Logan reached into his pocket and held out some tiny wooden

figurines. "It should help to know I'm always thinking of ya. Would a few animals for your collection help ease the pain?"

"Yes, Papa! Thank you!" Annabelle snatched the figurines from his hand and held them up one by one to examine them. "I don't have any like these," she said with a grin. "I'm going to go show Nana and match them to her book!"

Annabelle ran off with the figures clutched in her hands, and turned and waved from the doorway of the second house on the right. "It was nice to meet you, Sera!"

Sera waved back. "It was nice to meet you too!"

She watched as Annabelle entered the house, and then turned to Logan, who was watching her warily. A slight raise of her eyebrow was the only prompt he needed.

"I suppose you'll be wantin' an explanation."

"Aye, laddie," she said with a smirk. "That I will."

Logan laughed and shook his head. "Well, before I do, I think there is someone you should meet."

"Okay," Sera said with a grin. "But don't think you're getting off that easy. I'll be wanting answers later."

"I know ya will, lassie, and you'll get them. Come this way."

Without hesitation he took her hand, and without pause she left it in his. Strangely, after all the things that hadn't felt right in her lifetime, this simple gesture did. She tried not to read too much into it, especially considering that he was practically dragging her to the doorway of the house Annabelle entered. He seemed anxious for her to meet whoever was in there.

The home was built with logs and had a covered porch that extended into the yard enough to have two rocking chairs on it. Wild roses crept along the sides of the entry, and climbed up to the roofline; their sweet fragrance reached her even at the distance they stood. There were window boxes on the side of the house near the garden, where the yard received the most sun. Sera didn't see any color in them, but could detect the strong scent of rosemary and mint. She assumed the boxes contained herbs for cooking.

Logan closed the gate behind them to keep the chickens contained, and pulled Sera up the path to the front door. He gave two quick knocks and shouted out just before lifting the latch. The mechanics creaked like the hinges in an old farmhouse.

"Mila, I'm back."

"Mila?" Sera repeated.

"Aye," he replied abruptly, as he pushed open the door and pulled Sera inside.

"That's my abuela's…"

The petite woman at the sink wiped her hands on her cotton apron as she turned to greet her guests. Her smile turned to confusion as she looked back and forth between Sera and Logan.

"Sera?"

"Abuela!" Sera pulled her hand from Logan's grasp and raced into her grandmother's open arms. "What on earth are you doing here?" Her grandmother held her tight, murmuring questions in a combination of Spanish and something else. Was it Scottish?

"I was so worried about you. When I didn't see you at the farm I feared the worst."

"You went to the farm?"

"Yes, it looked abandoned. I went looking for you at the caves, which is how I ended up here."

"I don't understand," Mila said. "How long have you been here? Logan, how do you know my granddaughter?"

A quick glance to her grandmother showed a look of confusion. Sera was sure it was the same look she had as she addressed Logan as well.

"Is this the part where you start explaining?"

"Aye, lassie," Logan shrugged sheepishly. "Now's the best time to start. Although I am sure Mila will have some things to add."

Sera looked at her grandmother's beaming face and realized he was right; she did have some puzzle pieces to provide. She wasn't sure she was ready for the enlightening and allowed her grandmother to usher her to a seat near the dining room table.

"I think you're going to need a drink for this," Mila said with a wink.

"I have the feeling that I will need more than one," Sera said.

"That makes two of us," Logan mumbled.

Sera watched as her grandmother opened and closed cupboards, pulling down glasses and a bottle of wine, before slicing up cheese and sausage and placing it on the table. She was at home here, this was definitely her house. It was apparent when Annabelle entered the room from a side room, and took instructions from her abuela in Spanish, that it was her house as well. Sera wondered how long they had all known one another. Annabelle nodded her head and quietly settled near the fire with a large hardcover book. If Sera wasn't mistaken, it was the Encyclopedia of Nature her abuela read to her when she was Annabelle's age.

"You have something stronger than wine?" Sera asked. "I think I'm going to need it."

"I believe I have scotch," Mila answered.

"Perfect! Make it a double!"

15

Sera helped her grandmother clear the dishes from dinner, while Logan took Annabelle outside for a walk. After Logan filled her grandmother in on a few details of how they met, it was clear during the meal that the conversation they needed to have shouldn't be shared in front of young ears, or male ones for that matter. Now that Logan and Annabelle were out of the house and otherwise occupied, her grandmother was much more open to a deeper conversation.

"So how long have you known Logan?" Sera asked. She was curious about the dual life her grandmother had led.

"For as long as I've known you," she answered cryptically. "I used to live in Wisteria as a child, although I didn't come to know Logan until much later."

"Wait a minute. You lived here? I thought you were from Spain?"

"I am, or was. It was where I built my life with your abuelo and raised your mother. She was so young when she met your father, but they were very much in love, so I gave them my blessing when they moved to the US. They wanted us to go with them, but my home at the time was in Zugarramurdi. After your grandfather died, there was no sense in moving, your mother had passed by then. Your father agreed to send you to me in the summers and during holidays, which helped him manage while you weren't in school."

"I enjoyed that time so much it continued after school." Sera smiled fondly at the memory. "I still love visiting you at the farm."

"I love having you, Nieta," Mila answered. "But the years stretch, and the visits haven't been as frequent. So, I started building a life here again. It is where I find purpose. Mi destino."

"And your connection to Logan?" Sera asked as they moved with their drink glasses to the cushioned seats that circled the fireplace. Sera recognized the chairs from the farmhouse. Now that she thought about it they had been missing from the living room.

"I knew his grandmother. We were friends when we were pups, but Logan doesn't know. He was born long after I left here. By the time I came back, Logan was already the alpha. You know, his father and your father were friends as well, although I haven't seen his parents in years. He tells me they live on the other side of Wisteria. Once Logan became the alpha, his parents basically retired."

"Pups? So are you…was Dad…"

"Lycan? Yes," Mila said with a smile. "I'm assuming you've come to know about Logan's heritage, he isn't much on pretenses."

"Yes. And I've learned that about him," Sera nodded. "He and I spoke a little on the way here. I'm still trying to make sense of it all. It's crazy not only that werewolves are real, but that he is one. It is also strange that I never knew about you and Dad."

"My capabilities are as dormant as they can be. And your father, well, he hid his. He wanted to raise you as a human. It was especially important to him after your mother passed."

Sera thought back to how young and virile her father always seemed to her. Now she supposed it made sense. She wondered if his heightened senses made it easier to fight fires. It tore her apart all over again, since if it hadn't been for the fire he would have had an entire lifetime with her. Hell, he probably would have outlived her.

"So that means that I'm…"

"Yes," her abuela nodded with a smile. "Although your powers seem to be dormant like mine." Sera thought her lycan heritage could explain some of the strange things that had been happening to her. It made her wonder what it meant for her moving forward.

"If you were raised here, was Mom a werewolf too?"

"She was dormant as well, but met your father during her trials. My family requires that all members return home for their sixteenth birthday and stay for entire moon cycle. It allows the pack to determine if there are lycan abilities, or if the child is human. In the pack I was born to, humans aren't allowed to stay, it weakens the bloodline."

"That's a bit harsh," Sera blurted out.

Her grandmother nodded in agreement. "Honestly, there have been more humans than wolves in the last two hundred years. I'm not sure why they even bother. Anyway, your mother showed no signs of conversion so I was free to take her home. By then, your parents had met and fallen deeply in love, and your father wouldn't let her leave without him. So he abandoned his pack and moved to Spain with us. It caused quite a stir at the time. He was from a very prominent pack."

"But I was born in the United States."

Her grandmother nodded. "Yes, you were, they moved there just before she became pregnant with you. He wanted to give her the best life possible. I think in a way he was looking for a fresh start."

Sera had a newfound respect for her father. Turning his back on his family for the love of his life spoke volumes of the passion he must have felt for her mother. "So did Grandpa know about you guys?"

"Grandpa Delgado? My husband? Heavens no!" Mila laughed. "I had been shunned from the pack and had to find my way as a human. That was all he ever knew me as. My mother was heart-broken when I didn't convert and took me to a witch to ensure I would have a safe place to live. The portal she created took me to Spain. I was fascinated with the witch's ability and Zugarramurdi embraces the craft, so I stayed and learned everything I could about spells, healing and Earth magick."

Sera nodded. "This is a lot to take in," she whispered.

"I know, Nieta. Just know that every choice that was ever made for you or your mother, was made out of love. We only ever wanted to give you the best life had to offer."

"I get it," Sera said quietly. "But it seems to me that the choices that could have been, were never mine to make. I wasn't brought here when I was sixteen to see this side of my heritage."

"Your father didn't want you to know. He wanted to keep you safe and he didn't agree with the politics of the pack at the time."

"And you never thought to tell me after all these years?"

"I only did what I thought was best," her grandmother sighed. "I wanted to honor your father's wishes and to do what I felt your mother would want as well. Please don't be upset."

"Well, I am upset," Sera snapped. "I'm upset that I spent the last forty-five years of my life living a life that has turned out to be empty and unfulfilling. Living a life that I made choices for, from a handful of options, instead of knowing all I had to work with."

"I had no idea you felt that way…"

"It doesn't matter, your lycan family sounds like they suck anyway."

"Sera Marie Cardoso!"

"Well they do," Sera said with a huff. She got up from the chair and paced in front of the fire. Her grandmother watched her quietly, and when Sera looked over she had a puzzled look on her face.

"Why are you looking at me like that?" Her grandmother's expression was making her more irritated as the seconds ticked by.

"Sera, is there something you want to tell me?"

"Like what," Sera growled and pulled at her shirt to billow it from her body. She was starting to sweat; she needed to get away from the fire.

"Well, how you got here in the first place. And exactly how you and Logan met?"

"It is roasting in here, Abuela. I think I should go…"

"Sera, Papa picked you some flowers," Annabelle said excitedly as she entered the house. She clutched a small handful of wildflowers, trimmed with fragrant herbs from the window box. "And I helped him."

Sera accepted the bouquet and leaned forward to give Annabelle a kiss. She didn't dare hug her, her tank was soaked through and stuck to her like a second skin.

"Adding rosemary was the perfect touch. That is my absolute favorite, thank you, sweetie."

"Annabelle, let's take them over to the sink and I'll help you arrange them in a glass," Mila said. "We should get them in water right away."

"Okay, Nana,"

Mila and Annabelle walked to the sink and trimmed and arranged the bouquet. Logan walked straight to Sera and cupped her face with his hands. He tipped it up, forcing her to make eye contact with him.

"Tell me what's wrong," he said firmly.

"It's nothing," Sera snapped.

Logan took the cool wet rag Mila offered him and patted it on Sera's forehead, and then on the back of her neck. She was starting to feel better with his ministrations.

"Is that better, my love?" He questioned softly.

Sera gave him a small smile and nodded. "Yes, much better. Thank you. And stop calling me my lo…"

"Look Sera!" Annabelle said excitedly. "We put a little of everything in here and even tied some ribbon here to match."

She gave Annabelle a hug; she was starting to feel more herself. "I love it."

"You can take it with you when you go back to Papa's house," Annabelle suggested. "Nana said it might be best if I stay here, so you can sleep in my bed there."

Logan looked into her eyes once more, then glanced up and nodded over her shoulder. Her eyes followed the direction he was looking in, her abuela looked worried. Sera decided it might be best to call it a night, and she was overwhelmed with the amount of information she had learned about her life in such a short time. It was probably best if she separated herself from her abuela, she wasn't sure she could take much more. Logan's gaze was on her again, she was positive all he could see was her exhaustion and fine lines, but who was she to say. He gave her arms a gentle squeeze before taking the vase from Annabelle and giving Mila a peck on the cheek.

"We'll see you in the morning," Logan offered. "It's been a long day for her."

"I'm sure it has," her grandmother agreed quietly. She gave Sera a soft smile and nodded her head slowly. Her grandmother was looking at her strangely, there was something on her mind, but Sera was too tired to deal with it.

Logan hugged Annabelle and kissed her on the top of the head. "Thank you for fixing these, my sweet."

"You're welcome, Papa," Annabelle said with a grin. "That was really fun, maybe tomorrow we can hunt for mushrooms with Sera."

"We'll see, lassie," he soothed softly, taming down her waves with his hands. "Guid nicht."

"Good night, Papa."

Sera walked to her grandmother and gave her a brief hug before turning to Annabelle and giving her the same. Logan took Sera's arm, and she allowed him to usher her out the door into the cool night air. As the hot flash dissipated, so did her edginess. She instantly felt better.

As happy as she was to finally know what happened to her grandmother, she needed a break from the roller coaster of emotions she had been on since her arrival in the village. She knew she would be more at ease spending the night at Logan's, even though he was ultimately a stranger to her. It helped that her grandmother trusted him, since it reinforced Sera's initial impressions of him.

Watching him interact with Annabelle during dinner also provided insight into his character. It was obvious that his daughter adored him, and he in turn was a caring and generous father. His banter with her grandmother was comfortable and loving, and it made Sera misty for what could have been. Logan was witness to her melancholy moment, and subtly reached under the table to clasp her hand and gave it a gentle squeeze. It instantly made her feel better, and they both ate one-handed for the remainder of the meal.

The relaxed interaction with him during their meal, and her grandmother's apparent love for him, made the decision to stay at his house an easy one.

16

Logan took Sera to a small log cabin further up the road from Mila's. It was small, similar in size to a large shed or garage, and like her grandmother's house looked well-maintained. There were window boxes beneath the glass paned windows, but instead of herbs, it looked as though Logan was growing tomatoes. Her grandmother and Annabelle must have been watering them while he was gone.

The walk wasn't long enough for the silence to be uncomfortable. Logan helped her up a shallow step onto a patio of sorts, built with slats of wood similar to a pallet. There was a small wooden bench to the right of the doorway, where Logan sat to loosen his bootstraps. Sera realized he was removing his boots before he went inside, so she sat beside him and removed hers as well. When they were done, he lined both sets of shoes along side of one another, tucked neatly beneath the bench where they had sat. He gave her a wink and a shy smile and reached for the door.

Similar to Mila's house, the door handle was a latch, but the door did have a bolt, which Logan swung over once they were inside. The curtains were drawn and it was dark, so Logan lit a nearby oil lamp to provide some immediate light. Her eyes were already adjusting to the dusk.

"I'll start a fire," he said as he stepped to the stone fireplace that centered the room. "It gets cold here at night."

The fireplace looked as though the opening went straight through to the room on the other side. That made sense to her since the fire would be able to heat the entire house that way.

"Can I do anything to help?"

"Nae, lassie. Just make yourself comfortable. It won't take me long to get this going."

Sera nodded and sat in one of the wooden rocking chairs near the fireplace. It was beautifully crafted, and one of the most comfortable chairs she had ever sat in.

"Is this oak?" Sera asked.

"Aye," Logan glanced up to her and smiled. The wood is from a tree that fell in a storm some years ago. I made the chairs when Annabelle was a wee lass. The rocking calmed her after her mother died."

"They are just beautiful, Logan. You do amazing things with wood. I assume those carvings on that shelf are yours as well."

"Aye."

"You have a great talent for whittling."

Logan puffed with pride before continuing with the fire. Sera finished her thought. "And I am truly sorry for your loss."

There was a slight pause before Logan spoke. "Tis Annabelle's loss, not mine," Logan said a-matter-of-factly. "I made a promise to my Beta that I would care for her when her mother passed."

"I'm confused. Annabelle isn't yours?"

Logan put one more log on the growing flames and sat in the rocking chair across from Sera.

"She's mine in every sense of the word but one."

"I see," Sera answered quietly.

They both rocked for a few minutes, the rhythmic sound soothed her jangled nerves from the conversation she had had with her abuela. Did she really want to get to know this man? Was it a good idea? Her grandmother knowing him definitely took the edge off, although Sera had already decided on her own that he was a decent and humble man. Her mind was a tangled nest of information, which Sera tried in vain to sort. She was on overload and needed to unwind.

"You have anything to drink?" Sera questioned softly. Happily, Logan got up and walked to a small standing cupboard. When he pulled out a bottle with a stopper and two glasses, she realized it was a liquor cabinet.

"I always have scotch," he said. "Two fingers?"

"Yes," she laughed. "Although I think I'll get a bit more than I'm used to with your hands."

He chuckled and handed her the drink before lighting a few more lamps and sitting back down. The warm fluid tingled in her mouth, and she swished it around as inconspicuously as possible. She supposed the alcohol would be similar to using mouthwash. What she wouldn't do for a toothbrush.

She looked around the room and made more assumptions about Logan's life by looking at the items he had in his home. A coat of arms was centered above his fireplace, presumably representing the Blackwood clan. There was a kilt draped over it in the same color and pattern as the one he had placed over her shoulders at his campsite. In her mind, both things held a high place of honor for him, as did the collected items decorating the mantle. If Sera had to guess, they were items found in the woods on the walks he took with Annabelle. The rocks, pinecones and small animal nests were all things that would delight a child.

The kitchen area was immediately to the right when entering the front door and was no more than a counter with a sink. A small wooden table with two chairs was lined up snug under the window and looked as though it could be increased in size by pulling up the flaps on either side. Logan had placed the glass jar with the flowers he had picked in the center. He must have done that before building the fire.

"I forgot to thank you for my flowers," Sera said with a smile.

"Your smile is thanks enough, my lo…lassie."

Sera smiled into her drink and looked up into his questioning eyes. He was extremely attentive and observant, had been adjusting how he communicated with her since the time they met. He was a quick learner, but he was still trying to figure her out - she could tell. Sera was more than happy to leave it that way, a little mystery never hurt any man.

There was a large room behind the fireplace which Sera assumed was Logan's bedroom. She could see the corner of a bed with more plaid and a number of pillows. Considering they had slept on the forest floor the night before, she was looking forward to sleeping in an actual bed. There was a small room to the left of the main area where they sat, and the glimpses of pink fabric and basket full of wooden toys, gave Sera the distinct impression that it was Annabelle's room.

"So are ya still wantin' an explanation? Or have ya decided you have it all sorted?"

Sera looked into Logan's face and saw humor, but in the depths of his eyes she saw something else she couldn't quite put her finger on.

"An explanation would be great," Sera said. "This Beta was what, your second in command?"

Logan cleared his throat before responding. "Aye."

"And where is he now?"

Logan's expression was heart-wrenching and Sera found herself leaning toward him. "He died shortly after his wife. He took her death especially hard. It is sometimes the way of our species who lose a mate."

"Even when there is a child to take care of?"

"Aye, lassie. Even when there is a child. In that case, 'tis the job of an alpha to fill in for his pack members."

Sera leaned back and started to rock, allowing the motion to ease the pain in her heart. She was overwhelmed with sorrow, but at the same time filled with pride. The man that sat across from her was probably the most loyal and honorable man she had ever met.

"That is very admirable of you, Logan," Sera said softly. "Annabelle seems to care for you very much, which speaks highly of the life you have given her."

"Thank ye, Sera," Logan said softly. They rocked a few more minutes, before Logan's rich baritone broke the silence. "Ya want to talk about what happened back there?"

"It was nothing," Sera said evasively. "Why?"

"Doubt that," Logan said shaking his head. "The tension was thick. Oh, and you were smoking."

"Smoking?"

"Aye. There was smoke rising from your curls like mist on a pond at sunrise."

"You actually make that sound like a good thing," Sera laughed with a blush. He could have told her she stank like one of the pigs in Nana's pen in his accent, and she would be fanning herself like Scarlett O'Hara. "I suppose I was a bit over-heated."

"My love, the wet rag I used to cool ya was dry in seconds." Logan's searching gaze met hers. His eyebrow rose as if challenging her to call him on his use of the phrase, "my love." She decided to let it go. Like him, the phrase was starting to grow on her.

She shrugged her shoulders and conceded. "Okay, there have been some odd things happening lately. It started with my tattoo tingling every time something bad was going to happen, and it kicked up into high gear when I started seeing you in my dreams."

"The tattoo there?" Logan pointed to her left breast. The top of her thistle was showing again over the edge of her tank top. "Does it tingle now.?"

"No. But it did when we saw the Shadowman dressed as my grandmother in the woods."

"A protection spell," Logan nodded.

"That's right. My grandmother wanted me to carry a thistle at all times, and the only way I could do that was to have a tattoo of one put on." Sera pulled her top down a bit to show Logan more of the design. Logan stared at the design and put his hand to his face and scraped his whiskers. It almost looked as though he was hiding a smile.

"Is something funny?" Sera said, as she pulled up the edge of her top and sat back in her rocker.

"Nae, my sweet. I just find destiny to be amazing at times."

"Meaning?"

Logan looked leaned forward, placing his elbows on his knees and looking directly into her eyes. He took a deep breath and answered softly. "Meaning, we were meant to meet, you and me."

Sera stopped rocking and leaned forward in like fashion. She knew there was truth in Logan's statement, just as there were stars in the sky. They were both marked with the same symbol; there was no denying the coincidence. The light from the fire sparkled in his golden eyes, and if she wasn't mistaken he was holding his breath. She looked down and noticed that he had an amazing view of her cleavage as she hung forward. The look on his face made her willing to show him more.

"You like what you see, my hungry Lobo?" Sera whispered to him softly. The Spanish nickname "wolf" had much more meaning now than it did when she called him that in her vision.

"Aye," Logan answered with a grin. "Show me yours and I'll show you mine."

She laughed aloud; he really did have an amazing memory. Perhaps he was right, maybe they had been meant to meet. Why else would they have shared those visions? There was definitely something going on that was greater than her and she needed to find out what it all meant. It made her wonder if it meant a second chance at happiness. If so, she'd be a fool not to take it.

Sera sighed and looked into Logan's beautiful face, he was so young and she wondered what he could possibly see in someone her age. Of course, she supposed since he was a werewolf, technically he was the older one. Maybe in some strange way, this was meant to be. She was tired of allowing opportunities to pass her by, and for life to make the decisions for her. There was no doubt there was a mutual attraction, and there was absolutely no doubt that her body screamed for release. One last look into his open and willing face was all it took.

She rose slowly and walked slowly around the backside of his rocking chair, pausing in the doorway that led to his bedroom. His eyes followed her every step of the way, and the warmth of his gaze stirred the fires of her soul. She decided she was tired of putting her life on hold, and undid the button and zipper on her pants.

Turning her back to him, Sera shimmied out of her jeans, leaving only the small piece of black lace that formed her thong. She looked over her shoulder at Logan, who stared at her unblinking. He hardly took a breath. His rapt attention made her feel like the most beautiful creature on earth, and only reinforced her decision. Sera crossed her arms and took hold of her tank top from the bottom edge, sweeping it and her bra clean off as she walked into his room. Logan was up behind her before the fabric hit the floor.

"You are a wee temptress," he whispered in her ear. "Your magick weaves around me and holds me prisoner."

His body was spooned up behind hers, she could feel his passion. "You don't seem to mind," Sera said with a sigh.

"I've waited so long for this. For you." he said as he lifted up her locks and licked the back of her neck to the lobe of her ear. His other hand circled possessively around her waist and slid below her thong.

"No more waiting," Sera whispered. Her breath caught as his hand dipped lower, and she spun in his arms to slow the pace. She wouldn't last long if his fingers made it to their destination.

Her hands cupped his face, his whiskers felt soft to her touch. She pulled his head lower, and shrieked in surprise when he lifted her off her feet and pulled her legs around to straddle his waist.

"That's better," Logan grinned.

"Much better." Sera wrapped one hand around his shoulders and the other she wove into the hair at the back of his head. She gave a slight tug on his thick hair, moving his head forward and gave him a full kiss on the lips. He opened to her, claiming her tongue with his and battling for dominance. He walked forward to wedge her against the wall, which allowed her to move her hips more freely. His gruff voice paused her grinding.

"I need ya to be sure, lassie."

"I need you out of those pants, Logan," Sera answered, kissing him again and laughing as he turned toward the bed and tossed her on it.

Sera didn't think she had ever seen a man take his pants off so fast. If she wasn't so horny, she would have made him put them back on and strip for her properly. That would definitely be happening later.

He slid off her thong and added it to the pile of clothes on the floor. When he looked back to her sprawled on the bed, his face reflected every happiness she had searched for her entire life. She lifted her arms and he slid into them naturally, his cock resting against the vee of her legs and throbbing warm against her core. His arms were on either side of her head holding his weight, and he kissed the tip of her nose before repeating his earlier comment.

"I need ya to be sure."

"I'm sure, Logan," Sera said with a smile. "We're both consenting adults, aren't we?"

"Aye," he said. "But, if I continue, I need you to know you'll be mine."

"I'm totally cool with monogamous…"

"Forever."

Sera laughed then stopped when she realized Logan was completely serious. "So your kind isn't able to have sex just because? I thought you… I mean, you mentioned you had…"

"Aye, we can have sex, lassie. But with you it'll be different." She raised her chin to give him access as he leaned forward to nibble her neck. His weight felt so good to her, like an impenetrable wall that kept out reality.

"How so?" Sera could hardly concentrate on what he was saying; his tongue was trailing to her breasts and giving each one of them his loving attention. He was breathing deeply, and whatever worries Sera had about scent were gone. He was sniffing her like a candle and loving every minute.

"Because you're my mate. My intended," he said softly as he tipped up his head to look into her eyes. "And once you find your mate, you are connected for life."

"And that means?"

"It means, once we have sex, we'll be wed."

"Wed? As in married?"

"Aye."

Sera closed her eyes; she should have known he was too good to be true. He was completely delusional. "You're nuts, Logan. Do you have any idea how crazy that sounds? How could you possibly know…"

Logan pulled his warmth from her and sat on the edge of the bed, showing her his back. "I have a tattoo as well," he said softly.

Sera sat up as Logan took her hand and placed it over the upper part of his back. "I've seen it," she said with a whisper, tracing the image with the pad of her finger.

The thistle tattoo was the same shape and color as hers, only slightly larger to fill the space of his shoulder. As she stared at the image, she felt the truth of his words burning on her chest. She plopped back down on the bed and put her arm over her eyes. It seemed that destiny wasn't through with her.

"I'll understand if you want to stop," Logan said with a pained voice. "I can stay at Mila's…"

"Don't be ridiculous, Logan," Sera said. "If anyone is going to Mila's it's me." Sera growled, beyond frustrated. There was no way she would be getting any sleep now; she was entirely too worked up.

She felt his fingertips warm on her skin, traveling along her left side. He was barely brushing her, but she felt the electricity from his touch running up and down her side, from her hip to the tip of her breast and back. His caress was soothing and hypnotic, and she dropped her arm back over her head so she was able to watch him.

Logan slid up higher on the bed so he could reach the entire side of her body from head to foot. Her assumption was right, his other hand was holding his cock, but his face showed no signs of impatience or urgency. He seemed content to touch her, nothing more. That wasn't going to be enough for her, she could tell already.

"I think that I need some time for all of this to sink in, Logan."

"I know."

"You have me at a disadvantage."

He looked curious, but at the same time delighted. She could tell by the added pressure to the movement of his fingers, he knew exactly what she meant. "How so, my love?" His coy behavior was endearing. He was going to be a handful.

"Well, when you touch me like that," Sera covered his hand with hers and stayed it, "it makes me want to do all sorts of things with you that we have now determined are off-limits."

"Aye," Logan grinned, as he moved his hand once more along her skin. "Although making love doesn't always include intercourse."

Sera's sense of relief was overpowering. Thank the gods! "So, if we do anything but the one thing…"

"We won't complete the tie," Logan finished.

"You have no idea just how happy you've made me." Sera sat up and faced Logan. "If I don't have an orgasm in the next ten minutes, I think I might self-combust."

"I can help ya with that," Logan said with a smile. His eyes held a hint of sadness and his tone was sincere. "But I need ya to know that even if we stop now, and never touch each other again—you will always be the keeper of my heart."

"Logan, how can you possibly know that," Sera exclaimed. "We only just met…"

"It's not what I know, it's what I feel. And I feel ya at the core of my being."

"Logan, I'm not sure…"

"Nae, lassie, let me say this. The choice is yours, just as your life is yours. If you allow me to be a part of it, I will be the happiest man alive. If you don't, I will abide by your wishes, and leave you in peace. Just know that whatever you choose, my devotion to you will never fade."

Sera didn't know what to say; his professions were intense and came from a place of honesty that spoke to her heart. Her body was all in, as it had a mind of its own. Her mind, well, it took a little longer to get on board at times.

She leaned forward and kissed him, softly at first and then with more intent. It wasn't acquiescence on the topic, merely a pause in the conversation. Marriage was a huge commitment, as was being the caregiver for someone else's heart. But there was no reason in her mind that they couldn't provide each other some comfort for the time being.

Pulling back from his lips, she smiled at him and rubbed her hands down his soft whiskered face. "I'm okay with seeing where this all goes, if you are."

Logan's smile lit the room, it was as if she had just told him he had won the lottery. "Aye, lassie. I am. What do ya have in mind?"

Sera grinned and leaned up to whisper in his ear. When she was done she sat back on her bent arms and shot him a look of naughty promise.

"I'm alright with that," he said as he straddled her and bent down to whisper in her ear. She could feel his cock throbbing against her leg and wondered how long he would be able to stay that hard. The question he posed had her hopeful the answer would mean for a very long night.

"Where do ya want me first?"

17

The morning hours came too quickly at Logan's the next day, especially since they had spent the better part of the night familiarizing themselves with each other's bodies. They were spooned and comfortable under the blankets, but Sera really needed to get up. Walking up to the house the night before, she spied an outhouse in the rear yard. Just as she stirred to make her way out of the bed, Logan wished her good morning with a kiss on the side of her neck and a gentle squeeze.

He must have anticipated her need since he got up from the bed and wrapped a kilt around his waist, pinning it in the dark as he walked to the fireplace. He lit a nearby oil lamp from the burning embers that were piled on the grate. When Sera's eyes adjusted to the light and she glanced to his chest, her heart rose in her throat.

"Logan, my God, what happened to you?"

She moved quickly to stand in front of him, more concerned about his injury than her nudity and examined the hand-shaped burn that marred his upper chest. She held her hand above the pink skin and felt the heat rise from the blisters forming. It matched her handprint exactly.

"I think that happened the first go round," Logan smirked proudly. "I feel a sting on me back. I think that's where your other hand landed."

"How could this have happened? I feel terrible," Sera soothed as she walked around Logan's body and examined his back. Sure enough, there was another welted handprint that wrapped just above his waist. "I don't remember feeling hot enough to burn you."

"Oh, you were hot," Logan chuckled as he turned to face her. "You were really, really, hot." He waggled his eyebrows and zeroed in on her lips for a passionate kiss. His hands slid up her sides and he pulled her closer. As far as she was concerned, he was in no shape to be messing around. She pushed back on his chest, accidently hitting the same spot she had injured, as indicated by his sharp intake of breath.

"Sorry," she said quietly, taking a step back from him. Perhaps the heat came and went without her realizing it now; Logan said she had been smoking after the conversation with her abuela. If that was the case, she needed to learn to control it before she hurt someone.

Logan stepped forward and attempted to take her in his arms again. She raised her hands and tried not to cave when the look of disappointment etched his handsome face.

"I'm sorry, Logan, but you can't get me worked up again," Sera admonished. "At least not until I know what the hell is going on with me. Just look at the sheets!"

"Don't you worry, lycans heal quickly. In a few days' time you won't even see the mark," Logan said soothingly. "And I can have Mila get us more sheets."

"At this rate, you'll need to get a new bed. I could burn the damn house down if we aren't careful."

"You won't burn the house down, my love. If you're that worried we can be sure to have water nearby when we make love. "

"That would be swell," Sera snarked. "Getting doused right in the middle of an orgasm."

Logan laughed heartily and the sound made Sera's heart sing. Oh what this man did to her resolve! She was starting to feel better and he seemed to be fine. It would be interesting to see if he healed as quickly as he said, especially since the burns were second degree. She wondered if her abuela had any aloe vera, if not, she was sure to have honey that she could mix with a bit of lavender to place on the burns.

His voice interrupted her train of thought. "Would you fancy a bath? I was going to take one before the rest of village stirs."

"A bath would be amazing," Sera answered. They could get the supplies she needed from her grandmother after. It would be better to place on clean skin anyway. "The outhouse is probably first on the agenda for me though."

"We can do that on the way. Just let me gather some things."

While Sera wrapped up in the nearest blanket, Logan went to the kitchen and pulled a basket out from beneath the sink. He also gathered a couple of towels from a nearby cupboard, which looked suspiciously like the ones her grandmother had at the farmhouse. It made her wonder what other things had been moved permanently to her abuela's home in Wisteria.

On the porch, they slid their boots on over their bare feet and walked to the back of the property. Logan gave her the lantern to use in the outhouse and he presumably did what most men do and found a tree to water. He was walking back from some nearby trees when she left the outhouse.

The lantern Logan held lit their way in the dark. The only hint that it was morning came from the birds in the treetops chirping their greetings. At one point she took the basket from Logan so he could guide her over the roots and small branches with his free hand. The path looked as though it had been neglected.

"I'm the only one that uses this path and haven't been home lately to clear it," Logan explained. "This is my private territory. We won't be bothered here."

"I'm assuming I need to be prepared for something cold and quick?"

"Nae, lassie. I have a special surprise for ya."

Sera knew they had come into a clearing since the ground was more level and they were stepping on less debris. She heard the rustle of water spilling over stones ahead, but Logan slowed his pace and walked toward a small pond just inside the clearing. He placed the lantern on one of the large rocks that lined the water's edge; its ambient glow cut through the darkness and reflected from the water's surface. The pond was surrounded by large flat boulders that could easily be used as seating, and it looked as though the river ran right alongside it. She saw tendrils of steam rising from the pond's placid surface, which was in direct contrast to the swiftly moving currents of the adjacent river.

She pointed to the pond with a smile. "If that is what I think it is, I am going to be one happy lady."

"If you're hoping for a hot spring, then ya will be," Logan answered. "I usually wash in the river then soak in the pond."

"Works for me. Lead the way."

Logan left the towels on one of the flattened boulders and took the basket from Sera's hand. He took her free hand and led her to a nearby spot on the river. He pulled soap and a small bottle from the basket before placing it on the ground by the water's edge. He unclipped his kilt and dropped it on top of the basket, turning when he heard Sera's voice.

"Jesus, Logan, your ass!"

"You like what you see, my lo…"

"Logan, I need you to be serious. There are marks there too."

He turned to look behind him, as if he would be able to see his own butt cheeks. Sera stomped up behind him and examined the burns.

"When the hell did this happen?" She questioned.

"I believe it was the third round, my love," Logan said with a chuckle. Either the burns weren't painful, or there was something seriously wrong with him. She hoped for her sake it was the first option.

She looked again at the marks and flushed with the realization of how the burns were placed. The partial palm prints were located on the outer edge, just below his hips, and the four rounded marks curved around them in a quarter moon shape in the middle of each cheek. The location of the fifth rounded mark on each side, right under the globe of his butt, clearly indicated that she had a tight hold on him when the burns occurred. His wolfish smile had her recalling the precise moment.

She covered the grin that spread across her face. "I think I remember the position now," Sera snickered.

"Twas my favorite, lassie. Oh the things you do with that mouth."

"I was so caught up with what you were doing with yours, I had no idea," she sputtered. "I'm so sorry, Logan."

He took her into his arms and kissed the top of her head before looking deep into her eyes. "I'm not," he said with a laugh.

"You're insane," she said with a smirk. "But, I think you're right, we'll definitely need water nearby when we do that again."

She dropped her blanket, kicked off her boots, and followed him into the river. The water was cold, but if Sera was honest, it didn't feel too bad since she always ran hot.

"We could always come here," Logan offered.

"I can't spend the rest of my life in water, having sex," Sera joked.

"Doesn't sound bad to me."

Sera's eye roll had him continuing his thought.

"Once you learn to control your power, it will be better for ya."

"Power?"

"Aye," he said with a nod. "The element of Fire. It will be easier for ya once you learn to harness its magick."

"The element of Fire?" Sera was confused, but at the same time realized that what he was telling her made a weird sort of sense. The way her body heated up, knowing when certain fires she fought were going to be deadly, even the doorway between their worlds opening with a fire was too coincidental. Her mind went back to the symbols in the cave, and she wondered if her grandmother had something to do with them after all.

"Okay, let's say I am meant to tap into some great power. How will I do that? Do you know anything about it?"

"Nae. I'll need to take ya to the witches. We can go in a few days. They'll know what ta do."

He finished rinsing the lather from his body and then helped her rinse the shampoo from her hair. His movements were quick and efficient; she saw that his nipples were tight and the hair on his arms stood on end. He was cold and probably in a hurry to get to the hot spring. She couldn't blame him; she was looking forward to a leisurely soak as well.

Sera waited as Logan dropped the items into the basket, scooped up his kilt and took her hand in his. He hustled to the pond, dropping the basket and lifting her into his arms without a sound. He kissed her soundly before stepping down into the water. The warm water lapped at her skin as he lowered himself into a seated position, keeping her in his arms as he slowly relaxed. When she tried to move out of his lap, he tightened his hold.

"Nae, lassie. I like ya right here."

"Works for me," Sera said with a shrug. "I just thought you would be more comfortable without me in your lap."

"I like ya in my lap," Logan said gruffly.

Sera's eyebrow raised, and she shook her head with a grin. "Now that you say that, I suppose I can tell."

"That happens every time you're near me," Logan chuckled. "It cannae be helped."

She adjusted herself within his arms and lowered her head to his shoulder. "Strangely enough, Logan, it happens to me as well. Although I suppose my reaction isn't nearly as visible."

"I'm glad to hear that," he said quietly, as he rested his cheek on the top of her head. "Or ya might never leave my bed."

Sera closed her eyes, content to listen to his heartbeat. Its rhythmic song caressed her psyche, just as the warm waters that surrounded her soothed her aching muscles. She was blissfully sore. He had spent practically the entire night showing her just how many ways a couple could make love without penetration. He had her trying positions she didn't think were humanly possible. Perhaps, now that she thought about it, they weren't. They were definitely a perfect match when it came to the sex; now she had to determine if they were a match in the ways that mattered. First things first, she needed to find out what was going on with her body.

"I'm curious."

"About what, my love?"

"About the witches," she answered. "And why you think I am meant to tap into some crazy fire energy. I mean, we only just met, but you seem to be making a lot of assumptions about what is happening to me."

Sera felt Logan's voice reverberate against her cheek, his tone was cautious. "Not assumptions so much as pulling the pieces of a puzzle together."

"Meaning?"

Logan cleared his throat, and gave the slightest pause before answering. "Meaning that I was told by the witches that someone would be coming. Someone that would not only be important to me, but that would harness the power of an element. Water and Air have already been found, so that left Fire and Earth."

"And with the things happening to me, and the fact that you pulled me through a portal made of flames…"

"Made me think you embodied Fire. Aye."

"And my importance to you?" Sera heard his pulse quicken ever so slightly, and his arms tighten around her. It made her feel as though Logan was holding back the full story. Not lying, per se, but definitely withholding.

"Your importance to me should be clear," Logan chuckled and started tracing his fingers up and down the outside of her arm and down around the side of her hip. His touch made her thoughts jumble, and she realized there was something he didn't want her to know.

"So they told you that one of the elements would be showing up, and that what? They would have sex with you?"

She felt him twinge; she had obviously hit a sore spot. "Sera, it wasn't like that. And what I did with ya, lassie — that wasn't sex." His voice lowered an octave, and tipped up her chin so he could look into her eyes. "It was so much more. Ya need to know I see my future every time I look in your eyes."

"Logan, you are so intense. Things are going so fast."

He smiled softly. "Aye, my love. And I'm doing my best to rein it in."

Sera laughed and shook her head. "Logan, if this is you reining it in, then we may have to have a chat."

"When you're ready, we will," he said solemnly. "You have the control in all of this and I'm a slave to your decision."

With truth and promise in his eyes, he waited until she moved her face toward his. His lips met hers, warm and firm, soothing her worries with their heated pressure. There was no sense of urgency, even though the sun had started to rise and break apart the dusk that covered them. His tongue tangled with hers and spoke what was in his heart. She knew he would stay there forever if she desired it. He would give her the world—she only needed to ask.

They soaked until the sun brightened the sky and their skin was puckered. Wrapped in the towels they brought and the plaid they came in, they made their way back to the house. The banter on the way back was free-spirited and fun. Sera found herself appreciating Logan's sense of humor more as she got to know him. He came off as an open and honest man, but she just couldn't help feeling that he had a secret.

Sera knew there were questions she needed answered, and it was apparent that she had no willpower when it came to Logan. If he wanted to avoid answering, he only needed to touch her skin and she would melt. She needed to talk to the witches herself, and find out exactly what they told him. Perhaps the answers started with her grandmother.

18

Back at Logan's house, Sera slid into her clothes without the thong. Logan put on a pair of khaki colored trousers that were way more distracting than the kilt in her opinion, especially since he was parading around without a shirt. Sera tried to keep the pheromone fog from affecting her brain and took her panties to the sink to wash and hang them to dry. Logan had just finished cleaning the ash from the fireplace and opening the shutters on the windows when there was a knock at the door.

Logan swung the door wide, revealing the smiling face of Sera's grandmother and her tiny counterpart, Annabelle. The young girl bolted through the doorway with a quick wave to Sera before going into her room. Mila joined the couple, looked up at Logan's chest then looked at Sera with a question on her brow.

"What happened here?" Mila said pointing to the burn. "It looks like a handprint."

"Aye," Logan nodded. "That it is."

Mila looked at Sera, who could only shrug and attempt to hide an embarrassed grin. She honestly didn't know what to say.

Mila entered into the kitchen and set the basket she had brought on the nearby table. She called out to Annabelle from where she stood, waving to Logan and telling him in hushed tones to put on a shirt. Sera felt guilty all over again. Her abuela was probably right; it probably would be best if Annabelle didn't know about the burns. Sera didn't want to give Annabelle the impression she was hurting her papa.

"Annabelle, love. Please come here."

Annabelle ran out, just as Logan left the room. "Yes, Nana?"

"Could you please run back to my house and get the honey from the cupboard near the sink? Also, please snip some lavender from the garden and bring that as well."

"Okay," she answered with a smile. "That will be yummy with the scones."

Sera smiled at her youthful innocence and thought to herself that actually sounded pretty good. Her grandmother's scones were fabulous, and Sera loved honey.

Annabelle bolted out of the door, full of more energy than Sera remembered having in quite some time. She gave Logan a sideward glance as he entered the room, and the smile she had on her face got a little bit bigger. It wasn't until her grandmother cleared her throat, that she had remembered she was there as well.

"We only have a few minutes, Annabelle runs fast," Mila started. "So am I to assume that those marks are burns?"

"Aye," Logan answered. "I believe Sera is the one the witches have been looking for. The element of Fire."

"That makes sense. I won't ask what you were doing at the time," Mila muttered under her breath. She clearly knew the answer since she looked between Sera and Logan and upon seeing their exchange shook her head and blushed.

Mila sat on one of the kitchen chairs with a sigh, she was clearly flustered. "If that is the case, we need to take her to Sevilla's," Mila stated. "She is the best one to guide her while Sera taps into her energy."

"Hello," Sera said with a hint of sarcasm. "I'm here in the room and can hear you two." Wasn't she familiar with the symbols in the cave? Wouldn't she have been expecting her?

"Sorry, Nieta," Mila responded. "It's just you being here was a surprise enough. But you harnessing these powers and being pulled in to serve the greater good is something entirely different. I expected someone to come through. I never thought it would be you. Now that I know, I'm not sure how I feel about it."

"Well how do you think I feel? Once again I am making decisions based on only part of the information. I feel as though my life is all plotted out and I don't have a choice in the matter."

"In a way that is so," Mila agreed. "Destiny plays a large part in all that we do, and is much easier a journey for us once we accept its chosen path for our lives."

"If it is all the same to you, I would much rather get some answers from whoever is considered the source around these parts. I am still very much of the mindset that I am in control of my own life."

"We will get you answers, my love," Logan said softly.

"In the meantime, we need to get some honey on those burns and you need to keep a shirt on," Mila scolded. "No sense in upsetting Annabelle and having her mistrust Sera in any way. Those injuries could be taken for something that they're not."

Sera felt her face flush. What could possibly be worse than her grandmother thinking that she had made out with the resident hunky alpha? If she wasn't mistaken, Mila seemed to be embracing the idea. She knew for a fact Logan was.

"We need to find you some clothes, Nieta. You can hang that scrap of fabric in the other room. I don't think we need to answer questions about that from a curious ten year old."

Good point.

After Annabelle returned with the honey, Sera and Logan went into the bedroom to put a thin coat on Logan's burns. The application took a little longer than it should, and Sera finally had to pull Logan out by the hand to wash up at the sink. He crowded in behind her, circling his arms around her waist and washing his large hands with hers. His head bent low pushed into her hair at the back of her head, and he inhaled deeply, sighing with his exhales like a man at peace. She could hardly concentrate on the task at hand and gave him a playful jab with her elbow before tossing him a towel to dry with.

The leaves were pulled out on the table, and two more chairs had been gathered from other areas of the house, providing seating for all four of them. They sat as a family, enjoyed the scones, biscuits and fresh fruit Mila brought, and discussed what the plans were for the day. Annabelle and Logan decided to go on another hiking adventure, while Sera decided to go back to Mila's place to look through her clothes for something to wear. She would need a few outfits if she was going to be staying, and from the way it looked to her at that moment, she would definitely be staying.

Logan sat beside her at breakfast, and his constant touch under the table aroused her. More than once Sera had to remind herself to breathe, and it became increasingly hard to concentrate on the conversation they were having. Annabelle seemed completely oblivious to the secret winks and smiles between the lovers that Sera was trying in vain to squelch.

The raised eyebrow of her grandmother let Sera know she hadn't been successful. After breakfast, Logan asked for Sera's help in the bedroom while Annabelle and Mila cleared the table.

He closed the door slightly for privacy and cupped her face before lowering his mouth to hers. His kiss undid her, and she allowed herself to get lost in the sensation of it. Between kisses, he whispered words of love in a language she could only understand with her heart. She had no idea how to respond so merely slid his unbuttoned shirt to one side and kissed above the puckered mark she placed there. His skin was sweet and he watched mesmerized as she licked her lips to taste the honey she had smoothed on him earlier.

"I'll be sure to tell Mila to leave the jar," Logan said with a smile. "I may need your ministrations later."

Sera laughed, she knew just where else he would have her spread the honey, and there certainly weren't any burns on that. "We'll have to see about that," she teased. "Much too sticky for the bed, but the hot spring has potential."

He paused as if he had something to say then thought the better of it. He gave her one last kiss before taking a deep breath and adjusting himself. She didn't need to look down to know he was aroused.

"I'll let Annabelle know you will be out shortly," she grinned.

"We'll pick up where we left off—later," he responded with a wink. She left the room with a laugh and called to Annabelle to join her outside. Mila was just leaving for her own house, with the understanding that Sera would join her there.

Sera and Annabelle went out to the garden and the young girl was excited to show her around, even if it would only be for the few minutes it took Logan to get ready. If she didn't need to get some answers from her grandmother, Sera would definitely be going with them. Sera wanted to get to know her better. Annabelle was appeased with the promise that Sera would come on the next hike when she had more clothes to wear.

Sera loved Annabelle's enthusiasm for nature and the fact that she was educated in a large variety of herbs and their healing properties at such a young age. Sera knew her grandmother had a lot to do with that, since she had been on the receiving end of her tutelage years ago. The side of Logan's property was edged with a trailing herb garden, and Annabelle walked down the row properly identifying lavender, sage, garlic, and chamomile. There was even an area with aloe vera plants and other herbs that could be used for burns that Sera took note of. When they strolled by the peppermint, Sera pinched off a few sprigs and chewed them to a paste before spitting them out.

"I like chewing on those too," Annabelle said pointing at the trailing vines of peppermint. "Most of the time I just use Nana's paste. She brought it from her other house."

"I'm hoping she brought other things as well," Sera said with a smile.

"Like what?"

"Well, I need something to soothe my curls, like conditioner or even coconut oil."

"I love your curls," Annabelle said. "I wish I had hair like yours."

"That's funny. I've always wanted hair silky and straight like yours. And the color is beautiful. It reminds me of a sunset, a fiery mix of orange and red."

"Really?" Annabelle looked pleased.

"Absolutely, and that is my favorite time of the day. The sunsets where I come from are spectacular, but the color of your hair has them all beat."

Annabelle's face beamed, and she ran into Sera's arms and gave her a fierce hug. "I really like you, Sera."

"I really like you too, sweetie."

"You should stay here with Papa."

"Well…I…"

"Ready to go, Annabelle?" Logan slipped up behind Sera and gave her butt an inconspicuous squeeze and quickly kissed the nape of her neck. She wondered how long he had been behind her and if he had heard Annabelle's comment. Sera supposed it wouldn't matter, from the way he was acting, he would most likely agree with her.

"Ready, Papa!" Annabelle gave Sera a wave, while Logan gave her a quick wink. The two of them walked hand in hand to the front yard, and up the road toward the edge of the village. Sera smiled at the fading conversation the two were having as they strode away.

"Sera thinks my hair looks like a sunset."

"She would be right, lassie. It's like the most beautiful sunset I've ever seen."

"Well, I like hers too. It reminds me of that picture in Nana's book of the lion, except she has bits of red in hers."

"It does look a bit like a lion's mane, now doesn't it?"

"Yes, but way prettier."

Sera spent some time at Mila's house looking through her clothes and trying to find something decent that fit. Thankfully they were the same size, and her grandmother had several pairs of jeans and some loose t-shirts for when she gardened. Sera took a few of each and took a hard pass on the cotton briefs. She would rather go commando than wear those.

When Sera came out into the living area, she saw Mila placing some items into a large basket. She peeked inside and was happy to see a bottle of coconut oil, toothpaste and a toothbrush. It looked as though she wouldn't have to rough it entirely after all.

"I brought things with me when I traveled back and forth, but it has been some time since I've been to my house in Spain. I think I will have to make a trip soon and gather some more necessities. In the meantime, this should get you through."

"Thanks, Abuela," Sera said softly. "What do you know about this element stuff? Can these witches be trusted?"

"The witches can be trusted. They were the same ones that gave me a fresh start all those years ago. In a way, I think they also had something to do with me meeting your grandfather, although they would probably deny it." She placed a few towels and a wide tooth comb in the basket. Sera was fortunate her grandmother had the same type hair. "As for the question about the element, I only know they are searching them each out. Water, Air, Fire and Earth need to be found in order to re-balance the magick in this land. If balance cannot be restored, it will have lasting effects on our earthly dimension as well. Imbalances are already being seen with the hurricanes, tsunamis and earthquakes. Not to mention the conflicts between humans. I fear it will only get worse if nature isn't brought back into balance soon."

"These witches will have the answers?"

"They will, but they can't always share them," Mila said.

"What good will that do?" Sera was tired of talking in circles.

"Their purpose is not to dabble with destiny, but to give you the tools to make your own way. The right way. Harnessing the magick of an element is an immense responsibility. I am extremely proud that you have been honored with the challenge, but I am also terrified for you."

"If I can run into burning buildings, I can probably handle whatever they deal me."

"You are capable, yes, but don't make light of it. There are forces at work that fight against the good that is being done. With light, there is always dark. With good, there is always evil."

"There was someone who came to the fire one night. At first I thought it was you, but when Logan woke and confronted him, he changed into his real form. I think he called him Erebos? But the man got upset and said his name was Roy."

Mila's eyes grew wide and her face paled. "You need to stay away from him. The Shadowman is toxic and is probably the reason for the imbalance in the energies."

"Yeah, got that. Won't be going anywhere near him anytime soon. He totally creeped me out. But if he is the reason for the imbalance, and the elements are being used to re-balance the energies…"

"Then you may be forced to face him one day," Mila said with a shrug. "However, you will have the power of four with you when that day comes. At least that is what I hope."

Sera helped Mila pack the last of the items in the basket and was happy to see a bottle of scotch slid down between the towels. She and Logan would definitely be tapping into that later.

"So how does Logan fit into all of this? He said he was told that his mate would be coming, and that she would be either the element of Fire or Earth. Since I am doing crazy stuff related to fire, he's made a few assumptions."

"I don't know much about Logan's interactions with the witches, and I stay out of his decisions as an alpha. What I can tell you is that I was given a prophecy long ago that he and I had a bigger part to play in the fate of this world, and that he would need my help."

"What kind of help?"

"I wish I knew." Mila shook her head and poured two glasses of wine, handing one to Sera before walking to sit in front of the fire. It was close enough to lunch in Sera's mind.

"Maybe, it was just that I be here to run things in his absence. Perhaps I am helping by way of raising Annabelle. But, I feel it is more. I do know he is going through something. He has been spending more and more time away from the village. But, he won't share what is bothering him — at least not with me."

"Maybe I can talk to him," Sera offered. "He seems to be somewhat open with me, although I agree that he can be quite evasive."

Mila nodded. "If he believes you are his mate, then perhaps he will share more with you. While I don't know too much about alphas and their mates, I do know that they take their bond very seriously."

"So what about Mom and Dad, did they do the bond thing?"

"Your mother and father fell in love and decided to marry, which is the way of most lycans. Logan is an alpha, so it is different for him. They feel an irresistible pull to the one they are meant to be with. The female does as well."

Sera thought about what she was being told, and so much of it rang true. She wondered if the pull she felt for him explained her tangled emotions. It also made her wonder if the alpha and his mate ever found true love, or if they were merely connected by the physical urges of their plotted destiny. There was no denying the attraction between her and Logan, but she wondered if it could last a lifetime. And considering the lifespan of a werewolf, it would be a long-ass time. Would Logan really want a lifetime with someone physically older?

"With my lycan heritage, will I age slower? Like you?"

"Yes. That is the one benefit we get even if we are mostly human. Some of us are quick healers as well. I believe your father said your injuries healed quicker than most."

"They did," Sera said softly. "Which now makes sense, I suppose."

"Sera, whatever you decide, just know if you choose Logan there is no turning back. It is a lifelong commitment and one that won't allow you to live in the world you were brought up in. Your place will be here, at his side."

"What if he's wrong?"

Mila shook her head in disagreement. "He isn't. Logan takes his position seriously, and is connected with the energies that surround him. He is bound by the laws of nature. If he is feeling something for you, there's a reason."

"It's a lot to take in," Sera said with a shrug. "Who knows, once I talk to the witches and find out what they have in store for me, he may decide that I'm a lot more work than I'm worth."

"I've seen the way he looks at you," Mila said with a smile. "There is no chance of that."

"You are fond of him aren't you?" Sera looked over to her abuela who nodded in agreement.

"Very fond of him, Nieta. He is fiercely loyal, trustworthy, and honest to a fault. He is everything I would have wanted for you in a partner."

Sera raised her glass to Mila's and gave it a clink, before raising it to her lips for a sip. In a way, she had just received her only living relative's approval to proceed with the man who had quickly captured her heart. Now she had to decide what she was going to do about it.

19

A few days later, Logan and Sera had just returned from an early morning bath and were packing for their journey to Sevilla's. While Logan was happier with Sera around, she still hadn't committed to him completely as his mate and he was exhausted from squelching his inner alpha. Before the second moon cycle, Logan needed to get her as far away from him as possible and return to his campsite. He didn't want to take any chances with Sera's safety, he was afraid of what he might do.

Against his natural impulses, he successfully reined in the nature of his beast. Sera knew her mind and had to be given space to make her decisions. He knew that now. There'd be no pressuring her before she was ready, and now that she'd captured his heart, it would mean more to him when she came to him on her own. He would know that he had been chosen, that Sera wanted to build a life with him. Even though they had found creative ways to satisfy each other that appeased his inner wolf, he hoped her decision came soon. He already found it impossible to imagine his life without her.

The past few days had been like being alone in the woods on a crisp fall morning. Perhaps to others they would have seemed mundane and routine, but each of Logan's daily tasks took on new life as Sera took part in them. She was extremely capable, more so than he would have ever imagined with her tiny frame. He had dreamed of his mate, in the years since becoming an alpha, and never once did he envision her chopping wood. The strength in her body as she threw herself into the task stopped his breath and caused his heart to swell with pride. He came up from behind her, slowing his gait between swings, and she scolded him before he had a chance to reach her. She had been right, if he wasn't careful she could lop off one of his limbs, but he couldn't help himself. The sight of

163

her taut muscles and the gleam of her sweat was the most erotic thing he had ever seen. He pulled her into his arms in the light of the day, not caring who was around, and pushed her against the wood pile she had been adding to. After a time, she scolded him for that as well and got back to chopping. He didn't miss the contented grin she sported on her beautiful face.

Logan didn't want to take her to the witches, but she deserved to find the answers she needed to get on with her life. While he feared the changes he faced with the next moon cycle, it soothed him to know she would finally be linked with her destiny. Logan hoped that Zilla was right, and that Sera's fate would be entwined with his, but either way he needed to do right by her. His life was in her wee hands, and it was unbearable to think of how empty it would be if she didn't choose him or the life he offered.

"I have my bag packed, I'm ready when you are," Sera said as she entered the kitchen. She put the bag down and stepped up to him, placing her hands on his cheeks and rubbing the week's worth of growth he had there. The next time he saw her he would be sure to shave; he longed to feel her touch skin on skin. There was no mistaking the concern in her tone. "Logan, what is it?"

He looked into her beautiful brown eyes and smiled softly. "Just gathering wool, my love." He cupped his own hands around her precious face and drew her in for a kiss. She had been chewing on the peppermint again; he tasted its heat on her tongue.

She pulled back from him slowly, and examined his eyes. He had come to learn it was her way to search for the truth. "Are you sure you're okay? Should I be concerned about these people?"

Logan rubbed his hands down the outsides of her arms and took her hands in his with a sigh. He lifted them to his lips and pressed a gentle kiss on her slender knuckles. "Ya don't need to concern yourself with the witches. They will give you the answers you seek."

"Then what is it?"

He pulled her tiny form into his and laid his head across the top of hers. Her arms came naturally around his waist and he marveled at how perfect she felt in his arms. He was trying to be strong, but the worries he carried were getting increasingly harder to hide from her.

"I'll miss ya, is all," he finally said with a slight crack in his voice. Her arms tightened around him and she snuggled deeper into his chest. Her response came with an outward sigh and warmed the very core of him.

"I'll miss you too, Logan. Seems crazy to be saying that since I haven't known you long, but it's the truth." She looked up into his downturned face and gave him a smile. "It will only be for a few days, right?"

"Aye," he agreed. "No more than a week."

Due to the early start, Sera had already said her goodbyes to Annabelle and Mila the night before. Logan's plan was to make introductions, stay a night to get Sera settled, and then leave alone for his campsite. Sera would be at Sevilla's during the moon cycle, which relieved him. Most of Logan's supplies were still at his campsite, so he only carried a change of clothes. It would be a full day's journey to Sevilla's; he planned on making it there by nightfall.

Logan carried her pack, which was slightly larger than his own. Most of the area they traveled through was wooded and dotted with Lycan communities along the way. Logan knew by scent which direction was safe; there were some packs that frowned upon strangers entering their territory. He steered clear of those; he didn't want to risk them giving Sera any trouble. He never allowed Mila to travel alone for the very same reason.

It was a shame really, that Sera might never know the side of her heritage that her father came from. Her father abdicating his place in the pack and running away with her mother created a cut so deep he wasn't sure it would ever be healed. The Cardoso pack now suffered under an unworthy alpha. In a way it was better that Sera's father had passed. It would probably break his heart to know what his legacy bore.

"You've been awfully quiet this morning," Sera prompted. "Makes me feel as if we had a fight, but I couldn't begin to tell you about what."

Logan laughed. "If we had had a fight, lassie, you would be very well aware of what it was about. More than likely something I did."

His comment managed to pull a smile from her lips. He loved that the expressions on her face told a story on their own. Her moods were easy for him to pick up on. He hardly had to rely on his sense of smell anymore.

"Well, I suppose since you haven't done anything lately, that means we're okay," Sera said with a grin. "And last night would have made up for pretty much anything you would have done."

"Good ta know," Logan smirked.

He caught her scent. Sera smelled like sunshine and laughter and her happiness filled his heart. Over the past few days, he had learned to watch for signs of displeasure or irritation, and he was quick to adjust his behavior. It would be dangerous for them both, and others, if tempers were left to simmer. The rhythm of her body was the first thing he tamed, and he learned quickly how to keep things hot without getting burned. He especially loved watching her face as he pleasured her. In his mind, there was nothing more telling of what was in her heart - even if she wasn't listening to it quite yet.

"Is it very far?"

Logan was glad for the change in topic, and for the fact that he was wearing his kilt. The pants would have been way too constricting. He really needed to get a handle on his reactions, Sera only needed to look at him sideways and he was ready to take her in his arms. His nature could only be an excuse for so many things.

"We won't get there much before dark," he answered. "There is a small pond ahead where we can take a break."

"That sounds good."

There was something on her mind; he felt the weight of it. It seemed they had that in common.

"Logan," she began.

"Aye, Sera."

Her face flushed and her chest turned pink, she paused before finishing her thought. When she finally spoke, she stuttered slightly. "Well, I just wondered…I mean…"

"You can ask me anything, my love. I want for us to know each other better."

She smiled at him; he had guessed right. It didn't make him any less nervous though, since he would have to answer anything she asked with honesty.

"Okay. I was trying to wrap my head around the whole… wolf thing."

"Wrap your head around?"

Sera laughed and shook her head with a sigh. "It's just an expression. It means I'm trying to understand."

"Oh, I ken."

"Ken?"

It was Logan's turn to laugh. "Ken means understand."

"It's just that I haven't seen you in your wolf form and I wondered how that all worked. You said it really wasn't tied to the full moon?"

"Aye, that is true to some extent," he responded vaguely. He wasn't sure just how much he wanted to tell her, but she needed to know about the life he was asking her to choose over the one she was currently living. "I can change at will, at any time. But the cycle of the moon calls to all lycans in such a way that it's hard to deny her."

"You can stay in your human form for most of the time, but during the full moon you feel compelled to change into a wolf?"

"Aye. That is gist of it. It is also a time when we connect as a pack."

"Is Annabelle…"

"Aye. She's a natural," Logan said proudly. "She mastered the conversion at a young age. But since Mila has taken to mentoring her, Annabelle has been happier remaining in her human form."

"I see," Sera said softly. There was another question in her tone. "She's so young. When you change, does it hurt?"

"Aye, it can between the cycles. During the three days of a full moon, the pain is no more than a dull ache. Like a sore muscle."

"That's good," Sera said quietly. "I try to imagine it, but it seems so impossible. That you can be a man one moment and a wolf the next."

"It can also seem impossible that someone can burn skin with a touch, yet that is what you can do," Logan responded.

"Good point."

"You'll see my wolf soon enough, lassie. But, I'd much rather spend my time with you as a man."

She smiled at that, and from the way she slid her hand into his, it seemed that she liked him in that form too. He was glad the questions had stopped; he wasn't ready to explain his situation to her. He needed to give her more time; the more human someone was, the less connected to their nature they were. If he could just give her a few more weeks to make her decision on her own, he knew the pull of their species would eventually bring her around. But he also realized if she took too long, the choice he would be left with would be devastating. Most likely, now that he knew her better, to both of them.

They stopped near the pond he had mentioned, and he spread a blanket out for them to picnic on. They shared dried sausage, cheese and sliced apples he packed before leaving his house. The sun was warm on their skin, and it made them lazy. Sera lay with her head in his lap, while he buried his fingers in her hair and massaged her scalp. She was nodding off, hypnotized by the soothing pressure of his fingertips. His mother massaged him as such when he was a pup, and he knew the effects of it.

Logan let her rest. He wasn't in a hurry to get to Sevilla's anyway. He didn't mind having her a few more minutes to himself. Once he got to the cottage, he would have to share Sera's attentions. As much as he didn't want to see her, he hoped Zilla would be at the cottage. He knew her better than her sister Sevilla, and he was more comfortable interacting with a fellow lycan. Even if she was a cat.

There were a few things he needed to ask Zilla. First and foremost, what should he expect when mating with someone who was primarily human. He wanted to be sure that the process wouldn't hurt Sera in anyway, and he was curious if her elemental abilities would aid her. He knew that Sera's parents were successful in having her, but they paid the ultimate price. Sera's mother died much sooner than she should have. Mila never said it aloud, but Logan made the assumption it had to do with complications during the pregnancy.

He also wanted to make it clear to Zilla that questions about him and his situation were completely off limits. He would tell Sera in his own time. While Zilla had agreed to keep his secret safe from Mila, he knew he couldn't trust her to keep it from Sera unless he threatened her. They were the only thing that had kept the witch in line. He needed to be sure they were on the same path before leaving Sera in her hands. There was too much at stake.

"Sorry, Logan," Sera said with a sigh. "I didn't mean to fall asleep, but your fingers are magic. That feels amazing."

"I'm glad it soothes. Ya needed the rest, my love. We still have a way to go."

"We should probably get moving then. You need me to carry anything?"

"Nae. I have it."

Logan gathered the blanket, pushing it into the backpack that held his change of clothes and took Sera's hand. They continued west and reached the edge of Sevilla's territory just as the sun started to set. It looked much the same as it had when he had brought Zilla here after her injury; the only difference was the large dog that came running toward them from the yard. The furry beast hadn't been there back then.

The dog gave mixed signals. Barking ferociously at Logan and wagging his tail each time Sera called out to him. Logan had seen him before with Aleck and watched as he came up the path and calmed the massive wolfhound. It had been several weeks since Logan had last seen Aleck. He wondered if he would still be holding a grudge.

"What the hell are you doing here?"

That answered his question; the irritation in Aleck's tone was clear. Logan supposed it was to be expected; he had played a part in Amie's abduction. Oh, and there was that thing with the clout. Aleck hadn't liked being knocked out cold either. Logan understood pride and deep-down respected Aleck for his.

"I've brought the element to see Sevilla. Zilla too if she's here," Logan replied.

Sera looked between Logan and Aleck. It was obvious that she was trying to determine the history between the two. She held out her hand to Aleck and he took it with a smile. Logan felt a small twinge in his heart when she saw she returned the smile.

"Sera Cardoso."

"I'm Aleck Eyres," he said with a nod toward the dog that sat patiently at his side. "This here is Max."

Sera smiled as Max raised his paw and waited for her to take it and introduce herself. She shook it and then rubbed him behind the ear, causing him to tilt his head into her hand and shut his eyes tight. Max was already putty in her hands. Logan knew just how he felt.

While introductions were being made, Sevilla and Zilla came out with a man using a large stick to support himself. He seemed to be favoring his right leg. When Sera looked up to the group, she tilted her head in confusion and walked to meet them in the path.

"James, is that you?"

"Sera!"

She closed the gap and raised her hands to circle his neck.

The man put his arms around her waist as best as he could while leaning on a stick and gave her a hug. He kissed her on the cheek before he continued. "What on Earth are you doing here?"

"I was just about to ask you the same thing!"

Logan's stomach knotted and his fists tensed. What was that stranger doing with his hands on his woman? Logan was getting warmer, even though the sun had almost set and the air was cool.

"The story is mental really. I'm still sorting a thing or two out," the man said conversationally.

Logan looked into the worried faces of the two sisters as his ribs started to lengthen and constrict his breath. He was panting now. Zilla moved forward and raised her hand as if to soothe him. He ignored Zilla and tried to concentrate on Sera's voice to soothe him, but she wasn't talking to him. She was still talking to the stranger.

"There has been so much that has happened to me as well. I…"

Max snapped and snarled, and Aleck took a hold of his collar, pulling him back with both hands in an attempt to settle him. There were chesty rumblings coming from both the dog and Logan, as the two growled for very different reasons. Zilla jumped back from Logan as he snapped at her hand.

Logan watched as Sera turned, and her eyes grew wide with confusion. The man, the interloper in Logan's mind, was looking at him as well, but there was fear in his eyes. The fear made Logan's chest widen and his fingers lengthen. His teeth were sharp against his tongue and clenched so tightly they drew blood.

The two sisters took a few more steps back, and Aleck managed to pull Max back to the door of the house. Logan saw him call for someone and then pass the dog through the doorway before coming back out onto the lawn to stand near the stranger. Aleck waved the sisters back and said something to them. Logan couldn't hear the words; the red haze in his mind muffled the sound.

He hadn't taken his eyes off of the man, who was now closer to the door with the sisters. Aleck ushered them all inside. They were leaving. He had won.

"…ong with you?"

Logan's pulse pounded in his ears. He saw see Sera's lips moving, but he couldn't hear the words. Why was she frowning at him? She placed her hand on his chest, in the same place where the burn had been just days before, and looked directly into his eyes. Hers were the same beautiful brown, with flecks of gold sparkling in their depths. He wanted to lose himself in those eyes; they seemed different somehow. More mesmerizing. His chest wasn't as tight and it was easier to breathe. The danger had passed, she was safe. The threat was gone. More than that, she had calmed him.

Sera's other hand cupped his cheek, and her frown was replaced by a gentle sadness. She spoke again, and this time he heard her.

"Logan, what is wrong with you?"

She lowered both arms and took his hands in hers. He looked down watching as the nails pulled back into his fingertips and the hair receded. He was feeling more like himself and could only imagine what she was thinking about him. She dropped his hands just as he sensed her tremble.

His voice sounded as though he'd been chewing on glass. "Sera, I can explain…"

She shook her head at him, she wasn't having it. "Honestly, whatever it was it was uncalled for. James is just a friend, Logan. A friend. There was no good reason for you to give everyone a heart attack."

"I'm sorry, my love. I truly am. By the time I realized what was happening, it was too late."

"Are you telling me that you can't control this? What the fuck, Logan? You looked like you were ready to kill someone. Your hands turned to claws and your teeth are like razors."

"I can control it, but there is something going on right now that makes it difficult. It's too hard to explain."

Sera's discerning gaze rested on his face. Logan took a deep breath and shook off the last of the unwanted change. Her next words were quiet but firm.

"I think it would be best if you head for your campsite tonight instead of waiting until tomorrow."

"I cannae leave you here with strangers," Logan mumbled. "It doesn't feel right."

"I'll be fine, Logan. From what you explained to me I'm sure they're expecting me anyway. I'm a big girl, I'll figure it out. And if you think about it, up until a few days ago you were a stranger to me too."

Logan felt as if his heart cracked. She had lost faith in him. There was nothing he could do or say that would cause her to change her mind. He wouldn't want to anyway, she was right. He should be on his way. They each needed time to think. And he couldn't be trusted to be around others.

Her eyes held worry and pain. As he took a step forward to soothe her, she took a step back. It was cold without the warmth she once looked at him with, and he feared he would never see it again. It was best that he leave and give her space. Perhaps there was an area nearby he could camp for the night.

"I'll go, my love. You're right, it'll be best. Thig rium mo ghaol."

Sera took his hands in hers again and Logan was lost in the warmth of her touch. He put it to memory, an imprint in his mind that he could pull out on a cool night and relive. She was looking down at his knuckles, running the pads of her fingers over them and feeling their length. They were back to normal. When she raised her face to look at him, there were tears forming in her eyes. The sight of it nearly undid him.

"It's called trust, Logan. When you decide it isn't too hard to explain to me, you know where I'll be."

Sera rose up on her toes and placed a kiss on his cheek, before turning her back to him and walking toward Sevilla's house. He couldn't recall ever feeling so empty. As he watched her pass through the doorway and shut the door, he realized something that made his heart ache. She had never once turned back to look at him as she walked away.

20

Sera stood with her back against Sevilla's front door, having closed it against the image of Logan standing in the yard alone. She closed her eyes and took a cleansing breathe, not quite ready to answer the questions she knew were coming. How could she possibly answer the things that she needed answers to? She looked around the room filled with curious faces staring back at her. There was only one she recognized; the rest were strangers to her.

James was the first to speak. "What the hell was that? Sera, who was the guy…or…whatever he…"

"Be careful what you say, human," one of the women with long black hair warned. Her rounded breasts were practically spilling from the corset style top she had on, and Sera was secretly glad Logan wasn't around anymore to see it. There was no way Sera's tiny B's could compete with that, especially in the tee-shirt she was wearing.

"Human?" James repeated. "Did you just say human? Aren't we all…" He shook his head in utter confusion. Sera watched as the woman raised her eyebrows in challenge. It made Sera wonder if perhaps this woman was a lycan as well.

"We are," the woman said slowly as if she were speaking to a child. "However, you will find in Wisteria, there are many variations of that description. Some are more sensitive than others when you question their nature, or abilities for that matter."

James looked into the serene faces of the two women, then looked around the room at the others. He shrugged his shoulders; he was clearly embarrassed. "You're right. I apologize, meant no offense. Sorry, Sera."

"You don't need to apologize to me, James," Sera said. "Logan and I just met. He brought me here to find some answers."

The other woman with long black hair came toward Sera and directed her to take a seat next to James at the large wooden table in the center of the room. The two women were twins, identical in practically every way except for tone and style. Their eyes were slightly different as well, both green, but one more hazel than the other. In a lot of ways they were similar to Logan's.

"I'm Sevilla," she said with a welcoming smile. "You are most welcome in my home. This is my sister, Zilla. She is opinionated and passionate about her beliefs but otherwise relatively harmless."

Zilla gave Sera a wink and a wave. She was the one with the more hazel eyes and harmless wouldn't be a description Sera would use. She sensed Zilla was a handful. From the way Sevilla shook her head at her antics, it looked as though she agreed. Sera waved at Zilla while the rest of the group settled into their respective chairs. It looked to Sera as though she and Logan had interrupted a late supper. Sevilla continued the introductions after she moved back to the other side of the table to stand near Zilla.

"You have already met James, Brooke's brother. Brooke is the lovely young lady sitting on the other side of him." James sat back so Sera and Brooke could lean over and make eye contact. Sera noticed that one of Brooke's eyes was emerald and the other was a brilliant blue. She knew what heterochromia was from some of her medical classes, but had never actually met someone who had it. The woman pulled it off beautifully, sporting colorful streaks in her beautiful blonde hair to match. Sera's initial thought was that she would make an amazing mermaid.

Sevilla walked behind the couple sitting across from Sera and placed a hand on each of their shoulders. "This is Amie and her boyfriend Aleck, who also happens to be James' best friend." Aleck gave Sera a quick nod and smile, but was quick to break eye contact. His shoulders were rigid and his jaw tense. She wondered if it had anything to do with the altercation with Logan. They seemed to have some history when Aleck greeted them outside.

Meeting Amie's direct gaze over the table, Sera noticed she had hair a slightly lighter shade of red than Annabelle's but just as striking. Her pale blue eyes looked tired and softened with her smile as she reached across for Sera's hand. Sera squeezed the tips of Amie's fingers as she addressed her. "It's nice to meet you, Sera."

"It's really nice to meet you, too," Sera said with a smile.

"Welcome to wonderland," Aleck muttered under his breath. Amie gave him a playful jab with her elbow before lowering her hand beneath the table. From the way their arms were angled, it looked as though the couple was holding hands.

"What Aleck means to say is welcome to Wisteria," Sevilla said with a smile. "Now, I'm not sure how much Logan shared, or how much you have found out on your own, but I imagine you have quite a few questions to ask us."

"I do," Sera answered honestly. "And now that I'm here, I can't imagine how I'm going to pose them. The whole way I got here and what I've experienced since seems so crazy."

James placed his hand over Sera's on the table and gave it a gentle squeeze. "Well, I'm the newbie and even I've come around to embracing a totally new reality," he said with a grin.

Sera looked past him to Brooke who nodded in agreement. She had the same crisp accent as James when she spoke. "Really, there wouldn't be much that could surprise us at this point."

A glance up to the sisters gave Sera the briefest glimpse of a secret look, as if they disagreed with Brooke's statement. Perhaps they knew of things that could still surprise them all. Sera wasn't sure she wanted to know what those things were.

Sera smiled at James and Brooke, and then across the table at Aleck and Amie. Something inside her clicked. It was similar to the feeling she had with Logan early on, and with Annabelle since. She knew in her bones that these were people she could trust, and they would play an important role in her future. In a way, it saddened her that Logan didn't feel the same way about her — that he had an issue with trusting her.

She took a deep breath, calmed by the warm look in James' eyes. He was patiently waiting for her to tell her story and rubbed his thumb over the top of her hand on the table. She was glad for the support, but so many things had changed since she had last seen him. Their last conversation was spark and fire, and although she still thought he was extremely handsome, she saw him in a new light. It was amazing that she could go from being ready to have sex with someone, to looking at him as a brother in a matter of weeks. Of course, that had been before she spent time with Logan. What was she going to do about Logan?

Sera looked up. She had been gathering wool, as Logan had called it, and everyone was waiting quietly to hear her story. She had nothing to hide, and perhaps the others could fill in some of the blanks along the way. Slipping her hand from beneath James', she placed both her hands on her lap. Even though she wasn't sure where she stood with Logan, it didn't seem right to her to hold another man's hand. She decided to keep her story more about the magick and less about her relationship with the alpha. Especially since she was still trying to sort out how she felt about him.

"James, you asked about Logan. The truth is — the first day I saw him was the day I pulled you out of the Wellness Center building. He was standing in a burning circle of fire."

Brooke's voice squeaked as she leaned to see Sera's face. "You're the Sera that saved my brother? Sorry to interrupt, but that is brilliant! Thank you, by the way."

"You're welcome," Sera laughed. "After I saw Logan in the fire, I started to have strange things happen that I didn't think much of until I went looking for my grandmother. Things like cotton wraps burning into dust in my hands and my body temp getting so hot I would dry instantly after a shower. I thought perhaps my grandmother could help me figure out what was happening. She knows a lot about otherworldly things. Anyway, when she didn't respond to my calls, I went to her home in Spain. I ended up searching for her where she worked, at the Cave of Zugarramurdi."

Sera heard an intake of breath and looked up at Zilla who was beaming. "You're Mila's granddaughter!" she exclaimed.

Confused by the familiarity, Sera confirmed the statement with a nod. "That's right — but how did you…"

"I've known Mila for years, and she and I have become very close." Zilla smiled warmly, the sass in her demeanor was gone. If the two sisters weren't dressed differently, Sera would have a hard time telling them apart now.

"How honest were you with Mila about your friendship I wonder," Amie muttered softly.

Sera felt the tension in the room rise as Zilla's cheeks flushed. Zilla ignored the comment and finished her thought. "She's very proud of you, you know."

"That means a lot to hear, thank you." Sera wondered why her grandmother wouldn't have mentioned her close friendship with the witch. She had made it seem that the witches had only helped her transition to her new life in Spain. Based on Amie's comment, Sera thought perhaps she shouldn't trust Zilla entirely.

"So how did you get here?" Amie questioned. "Did you come through a portal like Brooke and I did?"

Sera thought about what Logan said about Water and Air being found, and the dots were instantly connected in her mind. "You are the two elements?"

Amie nodded. "I'm Air and Brooke is Water. Her guy Will has some residual magic from coming through the portal with her. He harnesses lightening."

"Holy shit," Sera exclaimed. "Is he here?"

"No," Brooke answered. "But he will be tomorrow, we can introduce you then."

Sera nodded and looked back to Amie. "So did Aleck come through with you?"

Amie nodded. "Yes, his ability seems to be to repel magick. He has a natural barrier against it. How about you?" She questioned. "Did someone come through with you? Was it Logan?"

Sera winced internally and wondered how on Earth she was going to explain it. "I suppose in a way he did. He actually pulled me through the wall of the cave. There were symbols that somehow allowed for it to happen. Next thing I knew I was in the middle of a forest."

Sevilla nodded and added to the conversation. "There were two circles of symbols that supported Mila's travels back and forth. The third portal would have shown up when you were near enough to it to activate it. You may have seen triangles?"

"That's right," Sera agreed. "There were triangles all the way around the circle, with other symbols around them. I ended up seeing the symbols carved in the trees where Logan was camping."

"She must mean the site where we hold the summer solstice celebrations," Zilla said to Sevilla. "Logan has been camping there."

Sevilla nodded in agreement. "That would make sense. The circle is in the south and the symbols are meant for protection. That must be where the elemental portal ended up being for Fire. I'm assuming that is the element you are connecting with?"

"It seems to be," Sera laughed. "Unless this is menopause I am going through, which is also a possibility."

Zilla laughed abruptly. Perhaps they would get along. She had the same sense of humor. "No, it is definitely not that. You are way too young for that to be happening. Perhaps there are other reasons you are overheating."

Sera was taken aback by her comments, then realized she might be aware of Sera's heritage. Zilla knew her grandmother; it was also possible she had even known her parents. Could some of the things be happening to her because of her genetics? Zilla looked into her eyes, and Sera saw answers there that needed to be uncovered. Tonight wouldn't be the night, though. It was late and she needed some time to think. She went back to the subject at hand.

"Logan mentioned he thought the symbols provided protection," Sera mused. "Anyway, once he pulled me through, he took me to his village, which is where I found my grandmother. She has connections to this place that I never knew about."

"It's mental how everyone seems connected," Brooke exclaimed. "Like links in a chain. James to all three of us, your grandmother to Logan and Zilla..."

Sevilla answered with a sigh. "Yes, the connections do seem coincidental, don't they — almost as though they were designed by Fate."

The comment gave Sera the impression there was more on Sevilla's mind than she was letting on. Especially when she saw Zilla's sideward glance her sister's way.

"I think for now we should finish eating and get some rest. Tomorrow will be a long day for us all. We will need to see what Sera can do, and if the journal has provided us with any more clues to aid us."

"I can bunk with Brooke if you need me to," James offered.

"That won't be necessary, James, but thank you. I have a room ready for Sera. Brooke knows the one. Zilla can stay in my room for the time being."

"I have a few things to do," Zilla said as she gave Sevilla a kiss on the cheek. She sashayed to the door and swung it open, turning back over her shoulder and giving James a saucy wink. "Don't stay up, darlings." One second she was a stunning woman, the next she was a silky black cat.

Well, that answered Sera's earlier question.

James stared with his mouth open, and Sera looked from him back to the cat who winked again over its tiny furry shoulder before sauntering up the path. It was definitely Zilla; she had the same color eyes and the same sexy strut. With a swish of her tail, the door slammed shut.

"Definitely not something you see every day," James said in awe.

"Stay here and you will," Aleck muttered. Brooke and Amie made half-hearted attempts to keep in their giggles. Even Sevilla was smiling at her sister's antics.

"Pay her no mind, she has always been the most flamboyant in the family," Sevilla said. "Sera, please help yourself to anything you would like while I go make some last minute adjustments to your room. Brooke, perhaps you would like to open a bottle of wine?"

"None for me, thanks," Amie said with her hand up. "As a matter of fact, I'm beat. I think I'll head up to bed. It was really nice meeting you, Sera. See you in the morning. I'm excited to see what you can do."

"Not sure I can do anything, but have a nice night Amie," Sera said with a smile. "It was nice to meet you both." Aleck gave a quick nod, while he pushed the chairs in. He looked preoccupied and kept his hand on the small of Amie's back as they went up the stairs. Sera assumed all of the bedrooms were on the second floor, since the majority of the lower level seemed to be one open room. Sevilla followed the couple up the stairs, lingering a few steps behind.

Brooke got up from the table and pulled three glasses from the cupboard, as well as an unmarked bottle of something pink. Sera assumed it was wine and decided she would try whatever it was since she was in dire need of something alcoholic.

The wine glasses were filled and distributed, and Brooke sat across from Sera in Amie's vacated seat. It would make the conversation easier. Brooke pulled some chunks of cheese and a slice of bread onto a clean plate and nibbled on them as Sera made her plate.

"Brooke, you realize all of this is a bit hard to take," James said with a smile in his tone. "I mean really, love, shape-shifters and magick? What's next — a pumpkin from the garden turning into a carriage and Max morphing into the horse that pulls it?"

"Max would hardly need to turn into a horse, James. He is big enough for the job, don't you think?" Brooke's laugh tinkled over the table, and Sera glanced to see James' grin. She could see the resemblance between the siblings now. "Sera, you mentioned you hadn't known Logan very long?" Brooke asked.

"That's right," Sera said between swallows. "I saw him in visions, but didn't get to know him until he pulled me through about a week ago."

Brooke nodded, and contemplated her wine. It looked as though she was sorting something out. "And your grandmother is here in Wisteria?"

"That's right," Sera said cautiously. "Is there something wrong?"

"Not at all," Brooke smiled so openly it removed the hesitations that Sera started to have. "It's just that I have this journal that shows me things. I'll show it to you tomorrow. Anyway, it showed me a few things about you, and it gave me the impression that you were connected to Logan in a – well, a boyfriend- girlfriend way."

James turned in his chair and faced Sera. It seemed he was very interested in how she would respond. Not that she had anything to hide; at the time she had met James she hadn't been seeing anybody. Well, except in her dreams, but she could hardly count that.

Brooke looked between James and Sera, while Sera's face flushed pink. She was starting to feel a bit warm. Thankfully Brooke picked up on the cue immediately.

"I'm sure I read into it wrong, we can sort it later," Brooke said kindly. "There are a number of things happening right now that we need to get to the bottom of, but for now we will concentrate on you tapping into your element."

"I'm not sure how that will work, but I am willing to give anything a try. I haven't felt in control of my life for quite some time," Sera confessed.

"I know just what you mean," Brooke said with a grin. "You just stick with Amie and me, we can show you some tricks. Pretty soon you will have more control than you ever could imagine."

"Fire, huh?" James said with a grin. "Had I known about Brooke's world sooner and your part in it, I could have called that one."

"Because I'm a firefighter?"

"Nope," he said with a wink and a waggle of his eyebrows. "Because you're hot."

Sera rolled her eyes and they all had a laugh. It was amazing how being around others going through the same type of journey could lift such a large weight from her shoulders. She wished for a moment Logan could have been with her; he could have benefitted from the camaraderie. Although, now that she could see that James was still showing interest, she decided Logan being there would have been bad news after all.

While she made assumptions before, she was sure now that Logan sensed James' attraction and reacted to it. She needed to find a way to explain to James it wasn't going to happen. Whether she ended up with

Logan or not, she knew there would be too many complications dating someone related to someone who could wield the powers of water. Sera was excited to see what Brooke and Amie could do, and even more excited to see what powers she possessed.

Sevilla came down the stairs to announce that Sera's room was ready, and the three women cleared the plates from the table. James gave them each a kiss on the cheek, thanking Sevilla for the meal, before heading off to bed. He left his stick near the door and called Max from the other room. The dog had been asleep in front of the fire and hurried to James' side wagging his tail. James told the dog they were going to bed, and used the dog's head for balance. As he hopped up a step, Max walked up a step as well, always staying in line with his master.

"That is a really smart dog," Sera said with appreciation.

"He really is," Brooke said. "He's been a great therapy dog for both Aleck and James."

"I can see that. Max seems like a natural."

"Yes, there's something really special about him. It may be that he comes from here," Brooke said with a shrug. "Who knows, maybe he has a bit of magic in him as well."

Sevilla dried the rest of the dishes Brooke handed her and placed them in the cupboard. "You two head upstairs, the room is all set, Brooke. I can finish up here."

Brooke gave Sevilla hug, then waved to Sera to follow her up the stairs. "Your room is amazing," Brooke gushed. "The sauna is to die for."

"But the house is so…"

"Rustic?" Brooke finished with a grin. "Sevilla likes to have it that way where she spends most of her time, but upstairs is primarily set up for us. So it has the comforts from home, and then some. I have no idea how the electricity and indoor plumbing works up here, but I don't question it," she said with a laugh.

"Works for me," Sera said with a sigh. "I've been taking my baths in a river for the past week."

Brooke opened the door and switched on the light. At first glance the room looked like a sunset, glowing with bright oranges, crimsons and lemon yellows. Sera entered the doorway and turned back to Brooke who was pointing up the hallway.

"I'm just there, straight across, if you need anything. Sevilla should have a supply of items in the bathroom for you to use, towels will be in there as well."

"Thank you, Brooke," Sera said softly. "Have a good night."

"Good night, Sera. So glad you're finally here."

Sera spent a full twenty minutes in the sauna before cooling off in the shower. She was never so happy to see a razor and shaved everything she could possibly think of. Not that the hair on her legs had stopped Logan from getting frisky, but it made her feel better having it gone. She finished up in the bathroom, slipping on a clean tee-shirt before padding out into the bedroom.

The patio doors had been left open, and the cool night breeze came through, causing the orange sheers to billow toward her. The moon shone just on the other side of the curtains, giving them a glowing effect that warmed the room. She pulled the sheers apart and stepped over the threshold to the small balcony.

The moon was swollen, almost completely rounded and bright. The night was clear but not silent, and she was soothed by the creaking of the tree-frogs and the whistling chirp of the nearby crickets. She closed her eyes and heard the sounds beneath the sounds. There was the rush of water hitting the stones in a nearby river and the plunk of a small fish dropping back into a pond after catching its unsuspecting prey. She even heard the faintest rustling of steps, the distinct whisper of something moving through tall grass in the distance. The steps were getting increasingly louder. Something was coming.

She opened her eyes and looked out into the darkness. It didn't take her long to see him, a magnificent gray wolf with glowing golden eyes. He had to be massive, since from that distance he looked like a large dog. He seemed much larger and more muscular than Max, and his fur shone like diamonds in the light of the moon. He didn't change his pace, merely continued walking toward the house and came to a clearing just beneath her balcony. He sat with a whine, never once looking away from her eyes. Now that he was closer, she could see the heartache within them.

"Logan," she whispered in awe. Seeing him there in his wolf form did strange things to her. As she looked into his eyes it was as if she could feel him standing behind her nuzzling her neck and wrapping his arms around her waist. Sera leaned up against the railing, getting as close as she could to him without going down to the lawn.

She heard another high-pitched whimper, and then muffled barks from a few rooms down. James must have settled Max quickly, since after a few seconds she didn't hear any more disruptions.

"You need to be quiet," she whispered softly as his head pitched to the right. "Otherwise, they will let Max out to attack your ass." She heard a snort, and then watched as the wolf stood and shook the hair on his body. It made him seem bigger, if that was at all possible, then he sat back down and continued staring at her.

"You've been warned. So, it won't be my fault if that happens," Sera joked. "And I'm not going to talk any louder than a whisper. I know you can hear me."

The wolf nodded slowly while maintaining eye contact. The intensity was doing strange things to her resolve. Why was it that she was upset with him again? Oh yes — the trust.

"Listen, Logan, I'm really sorry about earlier. I really should have gone somewhere with you to talk it out, but you made me so angry. In my mind I have placed a lot of trust in you without really knowing much about you. But, I feel as though the trust has been one-sided."

The wolf lowered his head and looked at the grass for a few moments before looking back up into Sera's face. She found her strength to continue in his silence and apt attention.

"You said that fate brought us together. That we are meant to be together, to be mated. If that's the case there needs to be trust between us. It seems that you are going through something you feel you need to protect me from, but you need to know I have done pretty well for a number of years protecting myself. I don't need a man to complete me, Logan. I need to make that clear to you. That isn't what this relationship, if there ends up being one, will ever be."

He was still listening quietly, and she was curious to know if he was able to talk while in wolf form. Either way, she was enjoying getting her point across uninterrupted. "What I want is a partner, someone who instinctually knows what to say and do, just by knowing me, heart and soul." Sera's voice started to crack; she was getting emotional. "Someone who can look into my aging face and say with genuine honesty that I have never been more beautiful in the days leading to that moment. Someone who accepts me as I am, that will embrace a life without children, since in all honesty, I think my chance at that has come and gone. And above all else, I need someone who can trust me with his secrets, and if it came to it — his life."

Sera looked down into his beautiful eyes and felt the tears form in her own. She wasn't sure what he would decide; she had dumped a lot of expectations on his shoulders. "Take care of yourself, Logan, and don't worry about me, I'll be fine. Everyone here has been wonderful, and I think I will be able to piece together answers to the questions I have about what is happening to me."

There was a rumble that could have easily been mistaken as thunder, but she knew it was coming from the wolf's chest. Considering the reason for him getting upset in the first place, she decided to ease his mind. "And nothing will happen between James and me. You will just have to trust me."

Sera felt as if a weight had been lifted from her shoulders, and she hoped that even though he hadn't spoken, Logan felt better as well. "You know, you are pretty easy to talk to like this," Sera whispered with a smile. "Goodnight, Logan."

A whimper came to her ears as she walked through the doorway and closed the balcony doors. She needed to get some sleep; she was completely drained. She turned out the lights and walked to the bed, slipping under the cool sheets, before blowing out the nearby jar candle on her nightstand. There was a salt lamp as well on the same table, which Sera decided to leave on as a night light. Its glow caught in the sheer canopy above her bed, and shone back to her from the silky threads.

As her head pushed back on her pillow and she let out a contented sigh, she heard a muffled sound coming through the panes of glass on the doors and windows. It was the lonesome howl of a majestic wolf, sharing his woes with the darkness. It was the most heart-wrenching sound she had ever heard in her life. For the first time in years, Sera cried herself to sleep.

21

Sera, Brooke and Amie were out in Sevilla's yard practicing spells, while James, Aleck and Will attempted to catch dinner at the pond Sevilla directed them to. The guys had taken Max with them, although Brooke mentioned he loved to swim so Sera wasn't sure how many fish the men would actually catch.

As promised, Will had gotten there the day after Sera arrived and she watched as the tension Brooke carried in her shoulders disappeared with his firm embrace. They were good for one another, from what Sera observed, and while she had gotten bits and pieces of each woman's story, she would be interested to know what the men thought about this whole magick thing. Sera found the point of view of men much more familiar, but kept her space from the guys so she wouldn't upset either of her new friends. She had noticed that Amie was particularly clingy with Aleck, and he in return, so decided she would keep her distance just to be safe.

Zilla still hadn't returned since the night Sera arrived. No one brought up her name, or even seemed to care that she was gone, which Sera thought was rather strange. Sevilla kept herself busy baking and making meals for everyone. For someone who supposedly had a magical arsenal at her disposal, Sera found it odd that Sevilla liked to do so many things by hand. She was amazed at the amount of food she produced from her small garden, and while there were only a few chickens roaming the yard, there seemed to be an endless supply of that to bake as well. Perhaps she was using a bit of magic after all.

The full moon had come and gone, and there had been no further sign of Logan. Sera stayed busy during the days, but at night she found her mind couldn't help but latch on to the memories of him she had created in such a short period of time. She wasn't able to connect with him in her dreams as she had done in the past, and found that she missed his challenging banter and engaging smile. Mostly, she missed the comfort of his arms; she had quickly gotten used to sleeping in them. She missed his solid warmth against her back, especially surrounded by so many new faces.

Over the last few days she had gotten to know the other two elements pretty well, and while she wasn't used to having female friends, she was having a wonderful time bonding with both Brooke and Amie. They each had very different personalities, but seemed to have solidly connected in the short time they had known each other. From what Sera pieced together, Brooke met Amie right before James arrived at the Wellness Center about a month before. You would never know it; they seemed like forever friends.

In Sera's mind, Brooke was a natural leader, always searching for clues and sharing her findings with the rest of the group. She had a natural team mentality that used each person's strengths to their best potential, and she attempted to fill the gaps where there was weakness. She also came off as being comfortable with her magical skill set, which made sense since she had also been the first to come into her power. Sera immediately trusted Brooke. She and her brother James were genuine people.

Amie had only just recently tapped into her element, but already had a strong sense of her ability. She seemed naturally gifted, able to do new things by seeing them demonstrated and then asking a few pointed questions. Amie had a brilliant mechanical mind, but at the same time had an ethereal quality about her which Sera thought was beautiful and frightening at the same time. Like one minute she could blow a gentle breeze your way, and the next suck you up into a wind funnel.

Sera hadn't had as much opportunity to chat with her alone, since Amie and Aleck often went off to nuzzle and whisper amongst themselves. Sera noticed a few times that they seemed to be arguing, but then realized they were just passionate in the way they communicated. Sera couldn't get over the feeling that there might be something going on with them that they hadn't shared with the group. When Aleck wasn't around, Amie seemed more focused, but was still slightly distracted. She could relate, since thoughts of Logan distracted her every waking moment. It made Sera wonder if she could rely on Amie in a life and death situation.

"Sera, watch out!" Amie screamed, pushing her arms in front of her and sending a powerful force Sera's way.

Sera was pushed backwards by the gust, which caused her to skid across the ground on her butt. Sera felt the anger rise; she had just washed the khakis she was wearing. But, when she sat up she immediately cooled off. A large column of molten rock shot up from the ground where she had been standing. The roar was deafening and the heat coming from it was like a blast furnace.

"Shit!" Sera had no idea what to do; she wasn't even sure what triggered the lava-like burst. She got to her knees, still stunned by the sight, and watched as the column of liquid heat reached toward the sky and then bent back toward the ground. She would have been burnt to a crisp had she still been standing where she had been. Perhaps she could trust Amie with her life after all.

Brooke ran toward the molten mass and blasted it with a cooling force from one side, while Amie spun the air around and controlled the heat from the other. The column cooled into a twisted black pillar in a matter of seconds. Amie looked up and realized the sprays that had bent back to fall back to the earth had cooled also. The entire structure glinted in the mid-day sun.

"If we ever need to recreate Stonehenge, we know who to come to," Brooke cracked.

Amie laughed and held her hand out to help Sera stand. "Yes, except Sera's would be much nicer. This is beautiful, it looks like a tree made from black glass."

"I feel terrible, you guys. I have no idea what happened there," Sera said with confusion. "Why can't I control my powers like you guys can? It's like they're all over the place."

"Cut yourself some slack, Sera," Brooke soothed. "You've only just arrived. It took me a while to figure out how to focus my powers."

"Sevilla is going to shit. I've burnt half her trees and now this?" Sera grinned. "What the hell are we going to do with this thing, we can't leave it here."

"Oh yes you can," Sevilla answered, as she walked through the garden and to the center of the yard where they all stood. "Obsidian is hard to come by, let alone having a tree made of one. This will be a powerful protection for us once Zilla and I charge it."

"Charge it?" Sera asked.

"Yes," Sevilla nodded. "We chant with intent, visualizing the power we intend for whatever we are going to use as a tool later. I am only able to do small things, but Zilla is able to help with things that are much larger. She's better at it than I am."

"Where is she anyway?" Brooke asked. Sera thought perhaps she was only asking to be polite. It was pretty clear that most of the group didn't like Zilla.

Sevilla shrugged and sighed. "Zilla keeps her own schedule. I'm sure she will be along soon enough." She turned her attention to the row of trees on the outer edge of the property that were now smoking stumps, then looked at Sera. "So I take it that your power has been a tad unwieldy."

"That is putting it lightly," Sera groused. "I can't seem to control it at all."

"It's possible you just need something to ground you," Sevilla offered. "I will see what I have that you might be able to wear."

Brooke nodded. "Of course, Sevilla has stones that helped Will and I when we first arrived. He had issues controlling his power, and once Sevilla gave him hematite to wear it settled him right down."

"I'm sure I have something that will work," Sevilla nodded sagely. "So what have you ladies discovered so far? Any luck figuring out next steps?"

Brooke shook her head and walked over to her journal, which had been left on a nearby rock. She had been looking inside of it off and on for the past few days, and had explained to Sera that clues would appear on the pages as each of the elements was found.

"The pages aren't showing us anything new for Sera. We've already gone through all the clues for Fire. It's as if something else needs to happen before the secrets are unlocked," Brooke mused. "It is the strangest thing really, although if I'm honest, Sera's powers aren't acting the same as ours were."

That seemed to perk Sevilla's interest. "Meaning?"

"Meaning that her powers are much more volatile," Amie chimed in. "Like they are tied to her emotions, similar to Brooke and her rainstorms, but in a much more primitive way. It's almost second nature to Sera, something she doesn't notice she is doing."

Sevilla looked at Sera with worried eyes. "Is this true?"

Sera nodded slowly. She might not understand everything Brooke and Amie were talking about, but she definitely knew that she wasn't in control of her power. The scariest parts were the pieces of time she couldn't account for.

"Yes, everything Amie says is true. It's crazy really. One moment I will be making campfires, and the next minute I am waking up with half the yard in flames."

"Well," Sevilla said, "I think there is a piece to this puzzle that we are missing. Something inherently off with Sera's nature, and we need to get that in balance. I will see what I can do about getting Zilla back here, she has connections with the lycans that I don't."

"What do the lycans have to do with it?" Sera asked.

"Remember when we looked at the writings in the journal that showed connections between you and Logan?" Brooke said as she pointed to the book she was holding. "Well, the book shows this thistle, which we know represents you. I noticed the tattoo on your chest."

"Logan has one on his back," Sera said. "It's identical to mine, only larger."

"Interesting," Brooke mused.

"This picture of the half-woman, half-wolf, along with this phrase here 'Ceann-uidhe' linked us to the lycan community and to someone Scottish," Amie added.

"The only person we knew that fit that bill was Logan," Brooke said. "Now looking at this picture, there is no denying the resemblance to you. The dark curly hair is a dead giveaway. And now that we know about the matching tattoos, we definitely have the right girl."

"I thought that, too," Sera agreed. "The human half could definitely be me, and now that I know about my connection to the wolf half, the picture makes sense." Earlier, when she had seen the picture, she realized she could no longer deny her link to Logan. It made her wonder just how much of her genetics would come through now that she had come back to her roots. Perhaps her heritage was interfering with her abilities as an element.

"Well, not so much for you, but as a connection to Logan maybe," Brooke said. "It was why I got the boyfriend-girlfriend vibe."

"Yeah, makes sense," Sera agreed and looked at the unasked question reflected in all of their faces. They wondered about Logan. She decided to answer, without answering. "Our relationship is complicated."

"Got it," Brooke said with a nod. Thankfully, she had picked up on the let's-change-the-topic tone. "When Amie and I each came into our powers, the pages connected to our elements filled in and provided guidance for us to harness or control our abilities. But, if you look here on your pages, the ones with the triangles, they are still blank. That hasn't happened before, and I'm not sure what it means."

"It may mean that she hasn't completely fulfilled her destiny," Sevilla prompted. "Sera, is there something you can think of that was left undone, or that has to be addressed?"

Sera thought of Logan and his insistence that she was meant to bind herself to him for life. Could that truly be her destiny? Impossible. How could she have spent her entire life putting herself in danger's way, saving the lives of others, only to have everything she worked for devalued by the silly destiny of becoming someone's wife? She wasn't buying it, especially considering the power of the element she had been gifted with.

She looked up into Sevilla's face and decided that there might be a worse fate than going to hell for the lie she was about to tell. However, since she harnessed fire, she decided it was worth the risk. "No, Sevilla," Sera answered softly. "There isn't anything I can think of."

The men coming back into the yard saved Sera from prolonged scrutiny. It looked as though Max hadn't put a damper on their day's catch after all.

"Wow, you guys did great!" Brooke exclaimed. She gave Will a peck on the cheek before examining the variety of fish he had strung through the gills.

"Lovely catch, gentlemen," Sevilla agreed. "I have a table over here I use to clean them. I'll get you some knives."

Aleck and Will took the fish over to the bench and Amie and Brooke followed them. It looked to Sera as though they planned to help, since Brooke was busy making ice and filling a basket that Amie was holding.

Sevilla came back out long enough to hand a few knives to the group, along with a plate for the fillets, then glanced at Sera before heading back into the house. More than likely, she was getting things ready to cook their catch. And, more than likely, she didn't buy the bullshit Sera was selling.

James sat down on a stump near the creek; he looked worn out. It made Sera wonder how far of a walk the pond had been. Max looked tired as well. He was probably exhausted from doing his doggie investigations as the men fished. Lying at his master's feet, he let out a contented sigh. Sera decided to keep James company and walked to where he had settled himself.

"Looks like you pooped him out," Sera laughed.

Jim nodded in agreement. "I think he pooped me out. Pull up a stump."

"Don't mind if I do," she said with a grin.

"So how did you ladies fair today?" James pointed to the obsidian tree sculpture in the middle of the yard. "Is that black thing your doing?"

"Afraid so," Sera laughed.

"And it is a...?" He left his question open ended, so she could answer.

"Sevilla tells us its obsidian. I guess it helps with protection."

"There was a volcano in the center of the yard that what...erupted?"

"What do you mean?" Sera asked

"I'm not an expert, but I do know that obsidian is formed when lava is cooled quickly. I saw it on National Geographic one night at the Wellness Center."

"Well, the girls cooled it quickly, so I suppose that makes sense," Sera murmured. "I didn't do it on purpose though. It was somewhat of an accident."

James' eyes widened and a grin split his face. "Lady, if you have those kind of accidents, you have nothing to worry about from anyone — human or otherwise."

"I'm not even sure what I'm doing here to be honest."

"All I know is I've seen you all do some pretty amazing things these past few days. And if what Sevilla is saying is true, we are going to need all the help we can get when the battle comes to our door."

"How do we even know what we are fighting against, or the reason for that matter?" Sera looked into his eyes and saw excitement snapping like a live wire.

"The what and why doesn't matter as much as the being ready to face the inevitable — when. If you are prepared for anything, then you can face everything."

"I suppose," Sera nodded. "Definitely had to do that in my career. Suppose this won't be any different."

"I would imagine that fighting against magical beasties could present its own set of challenges."

"You are right about that," Sera laughed.

James motioned his head with a glance to the front walkway. "Looks like Zilla is back."

When Sera looked up, she spied Sevilla's sister. She watched her make her way slowly up the walk and head straight to the house.

"Is it just me, or did it look as though she was limping?"

James nodded slowly, his eyes still fixed at the front of the house. His voice was quiet, as if he was deep in thought. "She was definitely limping, and…"

Sera waited for him to finish, and when he didn't she prompted him. "And?"

He looked at her with his clear gaze, and answered softly, "And, she went to the house straight away because she didn't want us to know. Not sure about that one honestly. Have heard some bits about her."

"Yeah, I'm not sure about a lot of things," Sera agreed. "She is definitely one of them."

After cleaning the fish, the group went inside and Sera spied Zilla near the fireplace in the adjacent room. The couples went up to take naps and ground their excess energy. The way Sera understood it, Brooke needed to be in water and Amie in air after they'd overused the magic they tapped into. Brooke and Amie weren't used to using so much of their power, and the last few days had drained them. The sauna in Sera's room made sense to her now, but strangely she didn't feel the same as the other ladies. The more she used her power, the more balanced she felt.

James was in the kitchen keeping Sevilla company as she cooked. The questions he was asking her were from Brooke's past, and Sera felt that she really didn't have much to gain from or add to the conversation. She decided the timing was right to chat quietly with Zilla. She poured herself a glass of wine from the wet bar and sat on the small couch near the rocker Zilla was perched on. She was sipping on the wine she poured herself earlier and staring into the fire. She broke the silence without looking at Sera.

"You have questions about our kind," Zilla said quietly.

"I do," Sera responded. "Specifically as it relates to me and Logan."

Zilla visibly winced. Sera wasn't sure if it was because she was in pain, or because she was swallowing a secret. Her voice came out in a squeak. "I will answer what I can."

"Fair enough," Sera responded. She took another sip of her wine and rested back into the cushion of the couch. The room was dark and cozy and gave Sera a sense of privacy. Even though Sevilla and James were in the next room, their conversation was muffled. She kept her voice low.

"I'm curious about your relationship with my grandmother. How long have you known her."

Zilla sighed and Sera could see the smallest of smiles on her face. Her voice was laced with melancholy. "I've known Mila since she was born. I know most members of pretty much every lycan community there is. But, I have always felt most at home at Logan's."

Sera nodded, she knew what Zilla meant. There was a sense of welcome in Logan's community that she felt almost immediately. She was sure that her abuela had a lot to do with that, since that was the type of person that she was.

"Were you involved in helping her find a place to live?"

"She told you that?" Zilla seemed surprised, then nodded her head in agreement. "Yes, her mother came to me when she realized she was showing no signs of conversion. She wanted a better life for Mila than exile, so she asked if I could help. I was already traveling between our dimensions, so was able to take her with me on one of my trips without drawing too much attention to myself. She met your grandfather and eventually made a home there. Their ceremony was beautiful. They were such a lovely couple."

"You were there when she was born and at the wedding?" Sera gasped. "How the hell old are you?"

Zilla laughed into her wine. "Next question."

"Fair enough," Sera smiled. "Obviously you knew my mother."

"And your father," Zilla added. "They had a beautiful ceremony as well." She turned in her seat to face Sera, adding intimacy to their conversation. Zilla seemed more comfortable. Sera couldn't help but note the scratches on her lower arms.

"I guess you guys go way back. What about Logan? What's his story?"

Zilla paused, as if she were carefully selecting her words before speaking them. "His leadership is more open than most. He believes that every person, no matter their lineage, has something to contribute to the whole." She smiled fondly, and it made Sera wonder if she and Logan had ever had anything between them. "He's a good man, Sera. And I believe you will challenge him, which is what I think he could use in his life."

"What he is offering will completely change everything I know," Sera answered quietly.

"Having the power you do, and using it to overcome the obstacles that I feel are coming, will change everything anyway. The question you need to ask yourself at the end of the day: What will bring you happiness?"

Sera pondered her statement. "Finding happiness is all well and good, but what about trust? I'm not sure he is being completely honest with me. There is something that he's holding back."

"About?"

"About the whole lycan thing. About my part to play in it. He wants me to agree to be part of his life, but he isn't giving me the whole story."

Zilla nodded and took another sip of wine. "There are things destined by Fate that we can't change, and I believe your relationship with Logan is one of them. He is fighting against his nature to give you the time you need to make your decision." Zilla looked up from her wine glass and Sera saw a mottled yellow bruise on her cheekbone. "I will only say that it would be in our best interests for you to make your decision soon," she finished with a sad smile.

Sera hardly had time to make sense of Zilla's statement when there was an urgent pounding on Sevilla's door. James rose to his feet and held a barking Max back by his collar. Zilla and Sera entered the kitchen to see what was happening.

"Sevilla, it's me," a deep voice called through the door. "Open up."

Sevilla scurried to answer the call, looking completely flustered by the unexpected visitor. She opened the door a crack and poked her face through, speaking to the man in hushed tones. It looked as though she lost the argument, since in the next moment the door swung wide and the man entered the house. Sera didn't miss the gentle squeeze he gave Sevilla's hand as he entered, nor the loving smile that warmed Sevilla's face as she gazed at him. He lowered the hood on his cloak and lightly ran his hand on her cheek. The motion was over almost before it had begun and Sera and Zilla's collective gasp interrupted the intimate moment.

"Kadar?" They looked at one another, and then at the stunned face of Sevilla, who seemed shocked that either of them knew the man's name. Her cheeks were rosy, as if she had been caught in a lie. There was no mistaking the man Sera met at Logan's campsite. The scar on his face was a dead giveaway. Sera wondered how Zilla knew him and at the same time was curious how Sevilla had kept the relationship from her sister for so long. It was clear to Sera there was something between Sevilla and Kadar; the pheromones were hard to ignore.

The rest of the group came down the stairs, having heard the disruption. James stopped Max from barking, but kept his hand on his collar just in case Max decided the man was a threat.

"What's he doing here?" Will asked, looking between Sevilla, Zilla and Sera.

The man didn't wait for the women to respond, answering Will's question himself. "There's been an attack. There are many who will require healing."

Sevilla scurried to the kitchen cupboards and pulled bottles down from the shelves, placing them in a nearby basket. "Brooke and Amie, I need you to go upstairs and gather towels and sheets from the hall closet."

Her tone didn't give room for delay. The couples went upstairs to gather supplies.

"I'll gather the crystals from the mantle," Zilla offered. Sevilla gave her a quick nod and returned to gathering her selections of herbs.

Kadar's gaze met Sera's and the pity in it caused her stomach to flip. The acid rose in her throat and when her tattoo started to burn, she could hardly voice her dreaded question.

"Kadar, what happened? Who needs our help?"

"The village," he said. "The entire lycan village."

Sera knew by the screaming in her heart which village he meant. One hand covered her stinging tattoo, while the other covered her mouth. She dropped her hand and looked into his eyes, unafraid to show the tears she couldn't hold back.

Although she already knew the answer, she had to ask. "Which village?"

Kadar walked up to Sera and put his arms around her, giving her a hug meant to reinforce her resolve. It only managed to make her cry even harder. She felt his response vibrate through her, more than she heard it. It broke what was left of her strength.

"Logan's," he said quietly.

22

The entire group worked quickly to pack supplies to tend to the injured. Kadar mentioned there were quite a few. Sera didn't have the strength to ask him if he recognized any of them. She worried not only that her grandmother would be among them, but also Logan and Annabelle as well.

Sevilla thought it would be best to leave Max behind since he didn't seem to like Zilla and she was afraid of how he might react to other lycans. Aleck agreed with Sevilla; he said Max hadn't liked Logan much when he met him either. He had no doubt the dog would stay put, he listened well to instruction. They left a side window open wide and showed it to Max, having him jump through it a few times to be sure he could get in and out easily. Sevilla topped off his bowls with food and water, since they weren't sure how long they were going to be.

Sera helped Sevilla and Zilla load the items they were taking with them into a small wagon and waited outside for the rest of the group. There wasn't anything she needed to take with her; most of her things were back at Logan's.

The group walked quickly up the path with Sevilla, Kadar and Zilla in the lead and Aleck and Will pulling the wagon. Brooke and Amie carried baskets filled with linens they anticipated would be needed for bandages. Sera and James picked up the rear, and while he seemed to be moving around easier, he still walked with the branch-crutch Max had found him.

"You must be worried about your grandmother," James said quietly. "I hope she's alright."

"Thanks, I do too," Sera said softly. "Once I get there I'll be fine. I have seen just about everything you can imagine in an emergency. It's just the anticipation, and knowing the vics personally that is getting to me."

"I get it more than you'll ever know."

It didn't take long for them to get to a place far enough into the woods that Sevilla was comfortable with. She had explained that the doorways were never made near her house, in order for her to keep magical creatures from stumbling across it.

Zilla took a few steps forward and waved her hands quickly, first in a circular motion and then with a push forward. The move was quick and efficient and created a doorway edged with a crackling energy Sera assumed they intended for everyone to walk through. Like the portal in the cave, the scene in the circle was much different than the area around it. Sera recognized the village in the distance. Zilla seemed to be taking them as close as she could to Logan's place.

"You go first," Zilla said as she waved Sera through. "Check on Mila and Annabelle first. We can tend to the others."

Sera nodded and handed Zilla her basket before running through the portal. She didn't hesitate when she got through to the other side, nor did Sera wait to see if the others were behind her. She ran as if her life depended on it, and when she got close enough to see the blood in the streets and the first house smoldering – she ran even faster.

She made it to her grandmother's door, just as it was being opened. Her abuela stepped out, surprised to have Sera run up to her and pull her into a firm embrace.

"I was so worried," Sera said, as her grandmother's arms came around her waist and hugged her back.

"I'm fine, Nieta. But there are so many others who are not. I was just going to pick some herbs from the garden. The lycans heal quickly, but sometimes the wounds need a little help at their age. The humans should be helped first."

"I've brought help," Sera explained. "Can't that wait until we give the others instructions?"

Mila ignored her so Sera had no choice but to follow her grandmother out to the garden. Mila took a gathering basket down from a hook on the side of the house and slowly snipped and gathered herbs and vegetables.

"Zilla, her sister, and some others that I have met, are just behind me. Abuela, you need to focus. Where are Logan and Annabelle?"

Just then, Zilla ran up to them in the garden and Mila stood to give her a hug. Her grandmother started to shake, and Zilla said a quick chant and snapped her fingers in front of Mila's face. She started to cry, but had stopped shaking and her eyes looked clear.

Sera looked into the street and saw James speaking to an elderly woman. She nodded and pointed at the houses down the street, leading the way as he waved to the others to follow. Sera was glad, it was one less thing for her to worry about for now.

"I'm glad you're okay," Zilla said to Mila. "Where should we go first?"

Mila was more focused; it seemed the shock had passed. "The house across the street has a man who has lost a lot of blood. He isn't a shape-shifter. I only had long enough to bandage the bleeding. He hasn't been checked on since."

"I'll go there," Zilla said as she pulled a few things out of the garden and added them to the basket of linens she carried. She hurried up Mila's path and into the street.

With the chaos, Mila still hadn't answered Sera's question. "Abuela, where are Logan and Annabelle?"

Mila looked up with tired eyes. The pain and worry in them caused Sera's heart to drop. She dreaded the answer that she would be given.

"What is it?" Sera demanded. "Where are they?"

"Logan isn't here, Nieta. I'm not sure where he is. As for Annabelle, she is inside lying down. I gave her a sedative, her injuries are severe."

"How severe?" Sera asked, not waiting until she received an answer. Her grandmother moved too slowly for Sera's taste. Her eyes were blood-shot and glassy, she was still in shock. Sera dropped the basket filled with herbs at Mila's feet and ran to the front of the house. Sera needed to see Annabelle for herself.

The house was quiet and dark and Sera could taste the copper tang in the air. The kitchen would need to be cleaned; there was blood on the floor. She didn't call out for Annabelle; she didn't want to disturb her sleep. She crept to her room and creaked open the door. In the pale light of room, Sera saw her form on the bed, covered in blankets with her fiery hair braided into a rope that lay ac0ross her pillow. She heard Annabelle's deep breaths and the slight rumble of a congested snore. More than like-ly she had been crying before her abuela managed to calm her down enough to fall asleep. It broke Sera's heart to think that.

Sera went to Annabelle's side and sat on the edge of the bed. Her weight bowed the bed but didn't disturb Annabelle's slumber. It made Sera wonder what her abuela had access to here in the woods to bring relief; it wouldn't surprise her if she had used a pinch of belladonna with whatever concoction she had come up with. She had been given that when she was younger as well, although in extremely small doses.

Since Annabelle was lying on her side with her back to the door, Sera had to lean over her body in order to examine her face. The injury there caused her to gasp and put her hand to her mouth. There were three slash marks across the left side of her face, deep and ragged with the bruising just starting to show. It looked as though she had been swiped at by a bear. There was also a shallow cut on the other side of her head, which didn't seem to be part of the claw marks. It was almost as though Annabelle had been knocked off her feet and hit her head on a rock. Sera's stomach churned, her body realizing what her mind was struggling to come to terms with. Gently, she pulled the blankets from Annabelle's arms and examined the minor injuries there as well. Thankfully, the cuts weren't as deep as the ones on her face; however, with someone her size, the loss of blood would weaken her.

Annabelle stayed asleep for the entire examination, even as Sera pulled the blankets up and snugged them under her chin. She took a well-loved fabric doll from the nearby toy basket and slid it in beside Annabelle on the pillow before tucking the blankets the rest of the way around her sleeping form. As Sera took one last look at the resting child before leaving the room, she noticed the doll had been found and was now tucked under Annabelle's chin. Sera felt crippling waves of inadequacy; she wished there was more she could do.

Her grandmother had come into the kitchen and was hanging bunches of herbs along the fireplace hearth to dry when Sera left Annabelle's room.

"What happened?" Sera questioned angrily. "Who the hell would do that to a little girl's face?"

"Nieta, it is complicated. Things aren't always what…"

"Tell me!" Sera shouted, instantly regretting the volume and peeking into Annabelle's room to ensure she hadn't disturbed her. She was still sound asleep. "Tell me," she said in a softer tone. Her stomach was in knots, the tattoo on her chest was on fire. Sera already knew the answer her grandmother was going to give her, she just didn't want to believe it.

"Logan," Mila responded softly. "It was Logan, Sera."

Sera sat on the nearest chair. She just couldn't believe what she was hearing. "It had to be someone else, another lycan."

The look of pity on her grandmother's face just about broke her. "No, Nieta. It was Logan. At one point he stared right through me as if I wasn't there. I don't believe he was in his right mind."

"That's impossible. He wouldn't hurt a hair on Annabelle's head, or yours for that matter. It had to have been someone else." Sera's head spun, her mind racing with all of the possibilities.

Mila walked to her and placed her hands on Sera's upper arms. The warmth of her palms somehow braced Sera enough to hear the truth of it. "Sweetheart, I care for Logan very much, and I know you do now as well. But, I know what I saw."

Sera stood and gave Mila a hug, leaching as much strength from her as she could before facing her new friends with the truth. She realized now why Kadar had been acting strange. He had already known.

"I'm going to find him; something isn't adding up."

"Sera, I'm not sure that is a good idea."

Sera was already heading out the door, refusing to take no for an answer. "There are plenty of people here to help, but someone needs to talk to him. If there is something going on, and he is out of control, he needs to be stopped. I think I have the best chance of calming him down."

"Sera, wait," her grandmother said, before taking a small basket and putting a few herbs and some clean cotton bandages in it. She put a bottle of whiskey in the basket as well and handed it to Sera. "He is bound to have injuries too."

"What's the whiskey for?"

"To clean his wounds," Mila answered with a smile. "And perhaps, to keep you calm."

Sera smirked. "I'm not sure you gave me enough."

"You need to get to the bottom of this, Sera. I believe in my heart that you were sent here to help him. I believe you two are destined, and whatever is going on with him needs to be stopped. The next time he could kill someone."

"I'll find him and get answers. And if it was Logan who injured Annabelle, he won't have a chance to do this to anyone else!"

Once outside, Sera walked up to Kadar who was repairing the door on a nearby cottage. He stopped his work when he noticed the question on her face.

"You're going to seek him out, aren't you?"

"I am. I need directions. I'm not sure where I'm going."

Kadar nodded, and put his hammer down, wiping his hands on the front of his pants. "I can take you to the edge of his territory then point you in the right direction. I wouldn't dare go further than that."

"You believe he did this too?"

Kadar looked at her with pity. "I know you care for him, Sera, but all of the villagers are describing the same scene. It would be hard to believe that it was a different beast with a caged white stone like yours hanging from his neck."

"Will there be enough help for the villagers? Should I plan on staying?"

Kadar shook his head. "I think you will be more help to Logan. He will be devastated that this happened. There has to be a logical explanation for his actions, but I'm not sure knowing the truth will help him."

"Why do you say that?"

"Even though the villagers aren't holding him responsible, he will still never be able to forgive himself, especially when it comes to Annabelle."

"Wait a minute, I thought you guys just met," Sera said. "How could you possibly know all this?"

"Technically we have just met," Kadar shrugged. "Let's just say we have common friends and enemies and travel in the same circles. Word gets around. Besides, Logan's an alpha. He would have a hard time staying hidden from those who wish him harm."

"What do you mean? Who wishes him harm?" Sera's pulse quickened.

"Calm down. I didn't mean me," Kadar laughed. "I'm just saying he has made a name for himself and his strength of character doesn't go unnoticed."

Sera nodded. It seemed to her that Kadar was being forthcoming, yet something in her gut told her he too was hiding something. She was really getting tired of the bullshit. Perhaps these common friends or enemies were people that wanted to remain in the shadows. In that case, Kadar could be playing both sides. She decided Logan was right; she should be cautious with him.

They walked past pools of blood and torn clothing as Kadar led her down the path to the outskirts of the village. The villagers with minor injuries were securing doors and shutters that had been torn from their hinges. Sera walked past a broken chair and shattered pottery that had been thrown from the nearby houses. Viewing the destruction, Sera wondered how one person, or beast, could have created such havoc. Even if it had been Logan, there was no way he would have been able to do all of this without realizing it. Could he?

Sera noticed Brooke and Amie leaving one house and entering the one next to it after a quick knock. Like Annabelle, the villagers with injuries were inside resting. She was sure Sevilla and Zilla were also tending to the injured, while the men helped secure the homes. Sera kept her head down and followed Kadar, since she was sure everyone would try to talk her out of seeking Logan out. She didn't have the strength to argue with them.

They entered the woods without anyone noticing they had left. Though Sera was shorter, she managed to keep up with Kadar's quick pace. They walked between endless rows of identical trees, and she wondered how Kadar was able to determine the direction he was going in. Was he going by sense of smell like Logan had? Was he a lycan too? She pondered everything she had seen and heard, and it still wasn't adding up in her mind. There had been something bothering her since her abuela announced that Logan had been responsible for the attack.

She jogged a few steps until she was side by side with Kadar. He slowed his steps slightly and smiled with a brief side glance. She decided it was enough of an invitation to talk. "Do you remember the night we met?"

"How could I forget," he said smoothly. "I remember never meeting anyone so lovely. I also remember Logan was a bit, shall we say, territorial."

"I suppose he was now that I look back," Sera mused. "But that isn't why I brought this up. Something happened that night."

"I don't remember anything."

"That's the thing, you weren't there," Sera said.

Kadar was confused, his brows furrowed and he shook his head. "I was there all night, although I suppose I may have left early the next morning."

"I have no idea what time it was, but when I woke you weren't there and there was someone at the edge of the circle of trees calling my name."

She had Kadar's interest. "Who was it?"

"It was my grandmother," Sera answered. "Except the eyes were wrong, they were bright blue and glowing. When she started speaking to me, Logan woke up and stopped me from going to her. When I looked back she had changed into a man."

"Erebos," Kadar whispered.

"That was what Logan called him," Sera agreed. "Although the man got upset and said his name was Roy."

"Roy?" It came out as a question, but his face told a different story. He knew both men.

"That's right. Anyway, my point is, if there is someone out there who can shapeshift into other people, maybe he is the one who attacked the village."

Kadar nodded, pursing his lips and pondering what she had told him. She knew her argument had weight. Honestly, Logan said he didn't trust Kadar, so for all she knew it could have been him that night in the forest.

"The Shadowman does indeed have that ability. And if he took the shape of Logan, he could have easily done the amount of destruction we saw in the village. But, I'm wondering to what purpose."

"Logan used the term Shadowman as well."

"He goes by many names," Kadar said with a shrug.

"He was trying to lure me out. I think he knew about my ties with the elements. Even though, at the time, I had no idea what was going on. Honestly, I'm still not really sure I do," Sera said. "He warned Logan that he couldn't be in two places at once, and that he would be waiting."

Kadar was uncomfortable. He looked like he had swallowed a sugar cube that was lodged in his throat. She was right, her argument did hold weight, and Kadar had other pieces to the puzzle that made him squirm. It made her wonder about his relationship with the others, since pretty much everyone recognized him when he arrived at Sevilla's house. He seemed to be right in the center of things, which meant perhaps Sevilla was too.

"What you say is possible," Kadar finally agreed. "But I would urge you to be careful with Logan anyway. I haven't known him long, but I have noticed a change in him. He angers more quickly."

"Yeah, he and I have talked about that," Sera nodded. "I just find it impossible to believe that he intentionally hurt his own people."

Kadar stopped walking and turned to face her. His dark eyes met hers with honesty and truth. "The hurt we give isn't always intentional. Sometimes it is the product of our circumstances or mood."

A wolf's distant howl broke the silence as Kadar took Sera's hand in his and raised it to his lips. He pressed his warm lips on the ridge of her knuckles with a smile. "This is where I must leave you, he knows we're here." He pointed through the trees to his right. "Follow that path there about another mile and you will find Logan's camp."

"How can he possibly know we're here from this distance?" Sera said unbelieving.

"He's a wolf," Kadar said simply, as if it were common knowledge that a wolf could sniff things over a mile away. "Trust me, he knew we were here about a mile ago. That howl was a warning. Be careful, Sera. Even if your theory is right and Erebos had something to do with the attack, Logan still has something going on right now. He might not be ready for company."

"Even if he's not, he's left me no choice," she said. "Thanks, Kadar. Let everyone know where I am and that I'm okay."

Kadar nodded, and Sera took that as her cue to continue toward the camp. She just hoped that when she got there her theory was right and Erebos was the one to blame. If Logan was anything like he was the day he dropped her at Sevilla's, she wasn't sure she would be able to reason with him.

<h1 style="text-align:center">23</h1>

Logan paced his campsite with the realization that Sera would be there soon. Her scent was both calming and arousing and he could tell by the intensity just how far off she was. He was glad Kadar picked up the warning in his howl; his scent faded shortly after Logan's call. It would have been bad if Kadar had come all the way to the camp with Sera. It was too close to the most recent moon cycle and he was still extremely edgy.

He went to the wagon and pulled out a bottle of Scotch, draining the last of the bottle with four large swallows. He needed to be in control of his beast when she arrived and the liquor would help take the edge off. He popped the cork on another bottle and poured some on a rag before taking four more swigs. He used the rag to wipe the last of the dried blood from his knuckles and hid the rag with the others that he had used to clean himself up. He had been too weak when he first woke to go down to the river to bathe, so was forced to wipe up as best he could. The bloodied rags piled in his wagon made him wish he could remember what he had done the days and nights before.

While he was still concerned for her safety, he was glad Sera would soon be with him. Perhaps if he took her into his arms and buried his nose in her hair her essence would infuse his body with serenity. Her calming effect might help him piece together his memories from the moon cycle. While he couldn't remember what happened, he knew it was something truly horrible. He felt it in his bones. The last time he had woken up cut and bloodied with no memory of his transition was when he was a pup and had made his first kill. He just hoped whatever it was he had fought with was truly deserving of the beating it received.

Leaving Sera at Sevilla's nearly crippled him; the pain couldn't have been worse if he had severed a limb. In hindsight, he might have been better off having someone chain him to one of her trees for three days. But, Sera's safety was his priority. Every night away from her in agony was worth it, with her approach to his camp, he knew leaving her had kept her safe.

An intake of breath halted his pacing, and he turned to the light of the fire to face his beloved. Her eyes were pained, and her hand trembled as it covered her mouth. He followed her line of sight and realized too late he should have put on a shirt.

"It's a mere scratch, my love. T'will heal soon enough."

Sera dropped her hand and her steps quickened. She came around the fire and lifted her hand quicker than a viper struck its prey. He heard the crack of her hand as it slapped his face, long before he felt its sting.

"You bastard. How could you?"

"Sera, I can explain."

"Explain what Logan? That you attacked your own village?"

"I don't know what ya mean."

"That you injured countless people and damaged god knows what?"

"My memory is dark...I dinnae have control the last..."

"Don't even talk to me right now about control," she seethed. "You have no idea just how much control I am struggling to maintain with you right this very second. You are lucky I don't go cremation chamber on your ass."

He had no idea what she was talking about, but she was livid. He worried he had finally gone too far. Had he really attacked his own people?

Sera dropped a basket at his feet filled with linens and what looked like another bottle of scotch. Mila must have sent her with them and he thanked the Gods. Mila must be okay. But what else had he done?

"My love, I can explain..."

She pointed at him and a scowl covered her beautiful face. Her eyes disappeared into a ferocious squint.

"I was giving you the benefit of the doubt," she yelled. "I wanted to believe that Erebos was the one who attacked the village. But yes, Logan, I would like you to explain why you look like you were dragged behind a truck along a gravel road for three miles and there is enough blood here to warrant it a crime scene. And while you are at it, please explain why there are gaping slash marks across poor Annabelle's face."

Sera covered her face and her body shook with sobs. Her anger turned to a bone-crushing sorrow. The sound of it tore at his soul. He knew he had done something the night before that he couldn't account for, but he had no idea it was something so horrific. Her wailing broke what was left of his heart. It shattered at the realization that he hurt his precious Annabelle. Hot tears streamed down his cheeks as he shook his head in disbelief.

"It cannae be so. Not Annabelle." Logan couldn't remember anything, but what kind of monster was he if he hurt the ones he loved? He needed to explain what was happening to him. It wouldn't excuse him from his actions, but it was important for him to tell Sera the truth. "I don't remember," he cried. "Nothing since I left ya at Sevilla's."

"You blacked out for days?"

"My last memory is of you speaking to me in Sevilla's yard, the next was when I woke here."

"Logan, it's been almost a week."

"Aye, my love," he said with hitch in his throat. He wiped the tears from his face and took a cleansing breath. The truth tasted bitter on his tongue. "The pull to be mated is taking control and soon I'll have no humanity left."

"Honestly, Logan, I'm not sure what you are talking about." She was annoyed with him; he felt it coming off her in waves. He wondered how much of what he said was going to get through.

The sorrow that filled him slowly ate at his resolve. How could she ever look at him the same way again? And his Annabelle. How would he ever be able to face her? He needed to be comforted; he needed to know he was forgiven. He tried to take Sera into his arms, but she pushed him back. The heat of her touch burned the tender skin around his wounds.

"Don't you touch me," she hissed, before pacing back and forth like a large cat checking its territory. She wiped her cheeks and took a deep breath, her eyes traveling across every cut and bruise showing on his body. The lines on her face softened, there was worry reflected there now. She was evaluating his injuries. It gave him hope that they could get through this.

She pointed to one of the stumps near the fire. "Sit down."

He sat. Followed her instruction without comment and watched as she bent to pull some torn cotton strips from her basket. She pulled out a larger rag, along with the bottle of scotch. She popped the cork from the bottle and took a healthy swig before wetting the rag with the alcohol.

She handed him the bottle to hold while she walked behind him and started to clean the wounds on his back. He tried not to flinch as she cleaned the dirt out of some of the cuts. The alcohol burned worse than her touch.

Her voice came to him over his shoulder. It was laced with anger and hurt. "I am having a really hard time understanding how the man I have come to care for could have possibly done the things I saw."

Logan flinched.

"Sorry," Sera muttered. One of the cuts had been rubbed so hard it was bleeding again; he felt the wet heat of it dripping down his back. Her hand came around to the front, palm up with fingers wiggling. He put the bottle in her hand, and then took it back when she waved it in front of his face. Her touch was much gentler as she cleaned the freshly opened wound. She was quiet, still waiting for a response from him.

Logan took a deep breath. She deserved the truth, as much as he knew or could remember at least. He only had until the next cycle of the moon before all of his choices would be taken from him. She said she had come to care for him. He couldn't wait any longer; he prayed what she felt was enough.

"I've told ya I'm the leader of my pack."

"Yes."

"I've also told ya my heart recognizes you as my mate."

"I remember. But, Logan I still don't unders…"

"Hear me out, lassie." Logan paused and took in a deep breath. "I dinnae want to pressure you. To force you to jump into my life so different from your own. I thought there'd be time for love to grow, not only in my heart, but in yours."

"Logan…"

He twisted around on the log to face her and took both her hands in his own. The rag hung between them, pink with the blood she had been cleaning from his back. "Nae love, let me finish. Please."

She nodded slowly, giving her undivided attention to the truth he would tell. It was what she had asked from him before, but he had been too afraid to give it.

"A lycan alpha in my world needs to be mated, truly mated, by their sixtieth year. If they're not, they can no longer convert."

Her eyes squinted in confusion, and he continued.

"Without a mate, they remain a wolf and the pack finds another alpha."

Her eyebrows raised in realization as he completed his confession.

"My sixtieth birthday is next month; during the next moon to be exact."

She paused for a moment, weighing all that he had said to her. Her tone was soft and unbelieving. "So, if I'm understanding this correctly, you can no longer be a man if we don't have sex by the next full moon."

He was thankful she understood and was amazed she could sum it up so simply. If he had been strong enough to speak the truth earlier, he realized they would have still come to this moment. She wouldn't have abandoned him. She was truly everything he could have ever hoped for in a life mate, and it made him wonder if he fulfilled her desires in the same way. He prayed to the universe he did, he needed her in his life more than she could ever know.

"Aye, that is the small of it. It would also mean that my pack would be left without an alpha to defend them. There is no one to take me place."

She pulled her hands from his and wrapped them around herself. Her head lowered in thought and she was silent for a few seconds before responding. "And you didn't tell me this before because?"

"Because I dinnae want to put that pressure on you. To feel obligated to base your decision on the needs of the pack. I love ya, Sera, and I wanted you to choose me because ya felt something for me as well. I hoped against all hope that you would grow ta love me."

"And you're positive these feelings you have are real. That they aren't just some crazy pheromone induced…"

"Nae, my love. You have the whole of my heart, in this world and the next. You challenge me to be a better man, you work at my side as my equal, and you soothe my soul like a honey balm. I could never love another as much as I do you. Fate choosing you as my mate was an added boon."

She was quiet, lost in her own thoughts. She took a deep breath and on the exhale he heard her question come out on her sigh. "And if I chose not to be with you?"

His heart sunk, but he answered with the truth that she had asked for and the honesty she deserved. "I would face the next moon alone and try my best to find a worthy replacement before then."

"And what would become of my grandmother and Annabelle?"

"I had hoped that Mila would take Annabelle back with her to Spain. I fear for their care under another alpha's rule."

He stood and put his hands on her upper arms. Her head lifted and she met his gaze. Her eyes sparkled like fireflies in the dim light. She had never been more beautiful to him as she was at that moment. A moment when despite all of his flaws and mistakes, she was willing to hear him out.

"Sera, please believe me when I say I would have never intentionally hurt anyone in my village, especially Annabelle."

"I know that, Logan," she said with a sigh. "And while it could still be the Shadowman, I can't help but think with all of your injuries that it was you. That was what was so upsetting when I first saw you. Plus, the villager's mentioned seeing your necklace."

"Zilla gave it to me. She said it helps balance anger."

"Sevilla gave me one just like it." She pulled the caged stone from her neck to show him. "Neither one of them seem to be working very well."

"Agreed," he said shaking his head. "I still can't believe I could do such a thing. But, with the cuts on my body and what the pack members witnessed, it must have been."

Sera nodded slowly, her response was barely a whisper. "It was horrible, Logan. It broke my heart."

He heard worry in her tone, but he also picked up on doubt and confusion. It was important that she learned more about their people. She was now part of their culture, whether they were together or not.

Logan looked into Sera's tired eyes and wished he could see the embers of love he once fanned. The spark that had been there had all but died; it was covered with a layer of mistrust. Her lack of response made him desperate to explain.

""Everyone, including Annabelle, will heal. I need you to know that," he said. I know it doesn't forgive what happened."

"No, it doesn't forgive what happened," she said. "This could have all been prevented by being honest with me, Logan."

"I know, lassie. I'm sorry. I wanted to give ya more time. I dinnae want to make the choice for ya."

Sera sighed, allowing Logan to pull her into his embrace. He didn't know what she would decide, and at this point he didn't care. He was just happy to be back in her arms once more.

They stood by the fire, each contemplating their decisions. Logan felt the weight of Sera's concerns and remained silent as she weighed her options in the comfort of his arms. He felt lighter than he had in months, having shared his burden with another. Whatever she decided, he would love her until the end of time. But, it was his hope that somehow, someway, he would be able to do it as a man.

△

Sera felt like her heart had been put through a meat grinder. Her stomach churned with the thought that the man she loved could have done something so terrifying. At the same time, the part of her that loved him had a hard time believing it, even with the proof Logan had gouged into his back. She had a lot to sort out, not only her feelings for Logan, but also her place in this new life that she was part of. But, all of that would have to wait.

She needed to get Logan back to the village; there was much to be done. While she still had a glimmer of hope that it hadn't been Logan who attacked his own people, the evidence seemed clear. Not only did he look like he had been in a fist fight with Wolverine and Freddy Kruger, but he also admitted something even worse. He had no memory since the night she had seen him from the balcony. He could have done any number of things in that amount of time. Besides, everyone, including Mila, said it was Logan. He needed to go back and make amends.

She finished cleaning his wounds. Most of them were scratches, like he had rolled naked in a bramble bush. But there were a few deeper ones as well, which made her wonder if some of the villagers had converted during the attack. Would Annabelle have changed to defend herself? The lines on his back and lower abdomen looked very much like the marks on Annabelle's face. They must have been made by claws.

"You realize you'll need to face them," she said quietly, while dabbing the last of his cuts near his tattoo. She looked at the familiar symbol, the thistle that matched hers, and the tears in her eyes welled. There were so many things that connected her to this man.

"Aye," Logan said on a sigh. His shoulders slumped in defeat. "My people need their alpha, even if he is unworthy."

Her heart broke and her emotions teeter-tottered at the sound of his voice. He was taking the blame for something he couldn't remember doing. It was both honorable and frightening. She finished the last of her ministrations and then threw the bloody rags into the fire.

"You aren't unworthy, Logan," she responded quietly. "Sometimes, we get dealt a shitty hand. It's how you handle your loss that determines your worth."

"Never liked cards. More of a dice man meself," Logan laughed. "Lost me shirt most of the time with those as well."

Sera laughed, glad for the change in the mood. The damage was done, there was no sense wasting energy worrying about the what-ifs. There was work to be done.

"I missed your laugh, lassie." Logan stood to face her and gave her hands a gentle squeeze.

"Me too," Sera responded with a soft smile. "I'm done with the last of your cuts. You should put on a clean shirt and pack what you need to go back."

His next thought came out in a whisper. "What if she doesn't forgive me?" He walked abruptly to the wagon, rummaged for a shirt and pulled it on. He wiped his eyes and collected himself for a few seconds. He returned to her with his pack slung over his shoulder.

She smiled softly at him, wishing she could kiss the haunted look from his eyes. She responded with something she hoped was true. "You're her papa. Of course she will forgive you, Logan."

"I hope you're right, lassie."

After Logan shoveled dirt onto the fire, they walked out of the camp-site together at a brisk pace. Night was falling and the distance was far. It made Sera wish she had learned how to make the portals she had seen Zilla create. Brooke explained that in time Sera would know how to manifest one as well. The skill sure would have been handy; it would have cut their trip down to seconds.

She slipped her hand into Logan's, needing the warmth and comfort it provided. He didn't turn his head, merely laced his fingers between hers and smiled softly. By offering her hand, Sera had given him forgiveness and acceptance, and the tiny gesture spoke volumes to them both.

Once they pulled the village back to rights she would need to decide on what would come next. Logan was devoted to his people, loyal and honorable in his views and was the most passionate and generous lover she had ever been with. With him her comfort, her desires, her needs came first. That was why she was having such a hard time with every-thing. Was the part of him he hadn't allowed her to see truly that un-predictable? And if so, how would a commitment from her change that?

She needed to see how it went at the village, especially since the decision affected more than just the two of them. Sera needed to decide if committing to Logan and changing her entire life outweighed the impact it could have on countless people if she didn't. Well, no pressure there.

24

The sun painted the sky yellow, orange and candy-apple red by the time Sera and Logan made it back to the village. Logan went straight to Mila's and Sera slowed her steps, allowing him a private conversation. Mila had been out in her garden feeding the chickens and looked happy to see them. Impossible as it seemed, Logan looked small next to her grandmother's tiny frame, like a shamed child waiting for a scolding. Sera's eyes watered when her grandmother pulled Logan in for an embrace, acceptance written in the serene smile she had on her face.

Mila said something about Annabelle then, pointing to the house. Sera could only hear bits and snatches of the conversation; she was trying to give them their privacy. Logan looked back to her and held out his hand. Sera took it as a request for support. She went to him, placing her hand firmly in his, and kissed her grandmother on the cheek. Logan thanked Mila before ushering Sera into the house. The next visit would be much harder for him.

When Sera walked in, she was happy to see that Annabelle was up and bundled near the fireplace looking at her picture book. There was a small basket at her side, filled with the animals Logan had carved for her. She was comparing a giraffe he had recently made with one of the pages in her book. The sight of it made Sera's heart swell.

Annabelle smiled at Sera, then past her to Logan entering the room behind her. The change in her smile was impossible to miss. When she saw Logan, her smile warmed the room.

"Papa!" Annabelle screeched in delight and made motions to move from the rocking chair she was perched on.

"Nae, my sweetling," Logan said as he moved forward. "I will come to ya."

Annabelle's face was still puffy, but the harsh red gouges from the day before were now faded pink. Logan was right, she was healing quickly. The cut on her forehead had all but disappeared.

Logan bent down and kissed Annabelle's forehead before getting on his knees and examining her face. He put his face to the top of her head and pulled in a deep breath before raising his head to examine her face. His fingertips ran gently along the claw marks on her cheek. His eyes were pained, but there was something more that Sera couldn't quite put her finger on. Relief?

"It doesn't hurt anymore, Papa," Annabelle said as she patted his large cheek with her tiny hand. "Nana put a salve on it that took out the sting. I didn't want to, but she made me stay in bed yesterday."

Logan smiled and cupped her other cheek. "I'm glad you listened to her and that you are feeling better, my heart." His voice cracked as he continued, Sera came up beside him and placed her hand on his shoulder for support. His eyes were watering. "I'm so sorry for what I did to ya, Annabelle. I would do anything to take it back."

Annabelle tipped her head before shaking it, clearly not understanding Logan's apology. "Papa, you didn't do this to me," she said in confusion. "It was the bad papa."

Sera's heart caught and she held her breath.

"Bad papa?" Logan repeated in confusion.

"Mhmm," Annabelle nodded. "He looks just like you, but for the eyes. Plus, he was missing the thistle. After I saw that I..."

Just then Mila burst through the door, which was when Sera heard the screams. "Logan, we're being attacked."

Logan jumped to his feet, barking orders as he ran to the front door. "Mila, take Annabelle into her room and stay in there until I come back for ya. Sera, I need ya to make sure nothing comes through this door."

"Logan?" Sera called, as she met him in the doorway.

He turned to her, his face cracked wide with the biggest shit-eating grin she had ever seen. The pointed teeth made it hard to miss. His eyes had changed as well, they were glowing gold and crinkled in glee. His throaty growl and lengthening nails confirmed he had started his change.

"My love?"

Oh, what this man could do to her with those two little words. She grinned back, unable to help the joy that was in her heart. The tiny shred of hope she had carried had been right.

"Tear him to shreds," she said before giving him a quick kiss on the lips. There was no denying what choice she was going to make moving forward. She couldn't imagine her life without him or the family she was now part of for better or worse.

He left the house, calling behind him as he ran. "Aye, my love. That's the plan."

Sera shut the door and helped Mila get Annabelle moved to the bedroom. She wouldn't leave without her figurines, so Sera scooped them into the basket before hustling in behind them. Annabelle had already pulled pillows and blankets off the bed and was on the floor tucked between it and the wall. Sera leaned over the edge of the bed and handed her the basket, along with the book she had been looking through.

"Stay down, sweetie," Sera said, kissing the top of Annabelle's head.

"I will. And be careful, he looks just like my papa. Except for his eyes are blue."

"Thank you, I'll be sure to tell the others."

Mila came out to gather things from the kitchen as Sera made her way to the door. "There are a few things I need to gather before you go," Mila said. She pulled open the drawers pulling out large carving knives and her rolling pin.

"Seriously, Abuela?"

"Well, I know you won't be staying like he asked you," Mila answered with a grin.

"Well, yeah. But not sure that will help you much if he makes it in here."

"It did last time."

Muffled screams came through the door, along with distant growls and snarling. Sera had no idea what to expect, but it sounded like a war zone. There was no way she was staying inside, and her grandmother could obviously defend herself. "Okay, I have no worries about you. I will be more help out there, and chances are he won't even make it this far."

"I have faith in you, Nieta. I'm sorry I ever lost it in Logan, I had no idea."

"I didn't either," Sera said as she opened the door. "I won't be making that mistake again." Sera hustled out of the house into chaos. She scanned the street, looking for the place where she could be of the most help. Logan was nowhere to be found, but she could hear snapping and snarling in the distance. She had to trust that Logan had things under control with the Shadowman, since she had more pressing things to handle in the Village. Things were going south quickly.

The village was being destroyed by three large creatures that looked like they were each made from earth-like substances. One was the color of stone, the other reddish clay and the last looked as though it was made from wood. They were large, bulky creatures without features that moved at a snail's pace. If Sera remembered correctly, these types of beings were called golems. How on earth would they defeat something made from earth itself?

One of the slow-moving creatures was using a log to smash the corner of a house, while the villagers who lived there ran from the front door. The creature didn't give chase; it was as if it had a single purpose in mind. Sera heard the guys calling to the villagers and spied them at the end of the street. They were waving the residents to safety. Brooke, Amie and Aleck came running up to Sera out of breath.

"We heard you went after Logan," Brooke said quickly. "Is that why all hell is breaking loose?"

Sera tried not to take offense. They wouldn't know at this point that Logan wasn't guilty of the earlier attack. "The Shadowman was the one who made the first attack. I believe he's back."

When the three of them looked at her with confusion, she continued. "He disguised himself as Logan. Long story."

"I believe you," Brooke said. "The wanker did that to me constantly."

"I'm not sure where Sevilla and Zilla are, but we need to do something," Amie said. "Any ideas?"

"I say we stick together and target the one working alone," Aleck suggested. "Figure out its weakness."

"Let's go," Sera said.

They ran down to the gray creature bashing on the house Sera spied earlier. The reddish colored and wooden golems were smashing their way through a house up the street.

"Water isn't going to do anything to stone," Brooke yelled over the sound of splintering wood.

"For the reddish clay one it might," Amie answered back.

"I could probably use fire for the one made of wood," Sera said. "If they aren't too close to the houses."

"It may not matter much longer anyway," Aleck said. "Maybe wind with something abrasive would work on this one? Amie?"

Amie nodded. Aleck and Brooke took a step back, so Sera stepped back as well to give Amie space. Sera watched as Amie raised her arms and quickly disappeared. The only indication that she was still there, was the small air funnel that crossed the street and moved toward the stone golem. The funnel gained size and speed, and whistled like a turbine.

At first the golem didn't seem affected. He continued his single-minded mission without pause. But soon his arms stopped rising, and Sera saw that there was a blurred haze around the creature keeping it contained. It looked like she was spinning dirt along with her force.

"What is she doing?" Sera asked Aleck.

"She's trying to get enough of a force around him to slow him down," he explained. I thought that perhaps like wind erodes stone over time, that Amie might have some effect."

"Not sure we have that kind of time," Sera said. "Could she maybe work her way out from the inside? Find a fissure?"

"Brilliant!" Brooke exclaimed. "Amie, find a crack and spin your way out," she yelled.

Sera wasn't sure how she heard it, but the next minute the haze around the creature was gone and his arms started to move again. Instead of continuing his destruction of the house, he picked up his log and started moving to where they were standing.

"I'm not sure that I like where this is heading," Sera said. She put her hands out to her sides, just in case she needed to create some fire fast. Not that she thought it would help.

"Give her a minute," Brooke said quietly. Sera noticed her hands were at her sides as well.

They all watched as the gray mass lumbered toward them, each of them taking steps back with its steps forward. It stopped when it reached the street, dropping the small tree it had been using as a club. The sound emanating from it was like ice cracking in a glass, but on a much larger scale. Sera watched as cracks started to spider across its entire body, and puffs of powder blew out of them.

"It's working, babe!" Aleck yelled.

"If you could go a little faster!" Brooke added.

Sera caught the worried look Aleck gave, but he didn't say a word. The golem had come to a complete standstill, no longer able to control its movements. The fissures were the size of the slash marks she had cleaned on Logan and there were shards of stone falling from them the size of gravel chunks. When the high pitched hum turned into a whistling shriek, Aleck yelled.

"Get down!"

Sera was tugged down by her arm and crushed by the weight of Aleck's body. She barely had time to register that Brooke was pinned under him right beside her, when she heard the explosion. Sera turned her face and closed her eyes, just as stones in all shapes and sizes came raining down on them. Thankfully, none of the stones were any larger than a golf ball, since Aleck took the brunt of the peppering on his back. When the stones stopped falling, Aleck stood and helped each of them up. He was visibly shaken.

"You guys okay?" He asked, looking behind him toward the house. Sera didn't see Amie, but Aleck held his arms open wide as if he expected her to appear in them. Sera looked over to Brooke who gave a nod. She looked fine.

"Yeah, we're good," Sera answered. She watched as Amie appeared in Aleck's embrace, and smiled when he cupped her face with both hands and looked into her eyes.

"How are you? You feel okay?"

Amie smiled and gave him a quick kiss. "Stop worrying about me, Aleck, I'm fine. I feel good."

"That was extremely impressive," Sera said. "Now let's see what Brooke and I can do!"

"We should have timed it, honey," Amie said with a grin. "Not sure these ladies could do it any faster."

"We'll just see about that!" Brooke said with a wink. She took off in a run, with Sera close behind her.

"Game on!" Sera yelled.

The clay and wood golem were both working on destroying the same house, so Aleck lured the clay one away so Brooke could do her thing away from Sera. There was nothing worse than trying to burn something when someone was watering it down. Aleck, Brooke and Amie were behind the house with the clay golem, while Sera stayed up front with the one made of wood. She assured them that she wouldn't need any help; she had finally learned to control her powers during their training sessions, and by practicing what she learned when she couldn't sleep at night.

The creature noticed her and moved away from the house where it had been crushing the porch. The people that lived there had long since left, more than likely moved to safety by the others. She assumed that Sevilla and Zilla were with the guys, but who really knew at this point. It seemed to Sera that those two each had their own agendas.

As the creature lumbered toward her, she spread her feet shoulder-width apart and stretched her hands in front of her. Sera focused on the golem, who was as thick as a hundred-year-old oak. The heat would have to be hot and fast, and she thought of the quip she had made to Logan about going cremation chamber on his ass. That was definitely what she needed to shoot for. She concentrated, feeling the heat blister in her core, and channeled it using the techniques Brooke and Amie had taught her. It was all about visualization and focus for the most part, and Sera had used the same techniques in her firefighter training.

Before the golem had gotten to the street, Sera sent a blast of molten fire from her fingers. The bright blue color was what she expected for the heat level she was shooting for. Once it hit her target, she focused her energy at the creature's center, and gave an extra mental push. Pulses of energy shot out from her fingertips like the rings of Saturn, burning a hole straight through the golem's core.

The energy sparked and hummed through her veins. The feeling was intoxicating. She pumped her arms forward, first right hook then left, sending pulses out, wave after wave. Within seconds, the golem was riddled with holes, weakened by its missing wood. What was left of it turned to ash in the heat. It took no time at all for the wood between the holes to burn away, causing the golem to collapse on itself. The embers continued to burn where it fell. It didn't look like it was moving anymore, and from the hooting and hollering in the back, it sounded as if Brooke had managed to defeat the clay golem as well. Sera still heard the sounds of fighting beyond the village; it was time to help Logan.

△

If anyone would have told him that one day he would be kickin' his own arse, Logan would've thought them daft. But, here he was, in the middle of the woods doing just that. For every move the Shadowman had, Logan had a countermove ready. The creature not only looked like him, but fought like him as well. Logan had changed into his half-wolf form, which was the best way for him to fight hand to hand, and Erebos had chosen that form as well. The difference was that the creature was beginning to tire, he wasn't used to hand to hand combat, at least not against an alpha. Logan wondered why Erebos wasn't using magic but realized that his abilities must be tied to the entity he mimicked. If that was the case, he would have no magic to use himself, which is why he had animated the golems and brought them with him.

He knew the Shadowman sent three creatures into the village; Logan watched him send them off as he caught up to him in the woods. Hopefully, Sera and her friends would find a way to defeat them quickly. He knew how much damage they could do in a small amount of time. Will and James had gone off with Kadar to help the villagers find safety, and Zilla and Sevilla seemed to be holding their own against the three golems that had stayed behind. Knowing that things were being handled allowed Logan to concentrate on fighting solely against the Shadowman. He had just given the false alpha a sock in the snout when he felt the tattoo on his shoulder start to tingle. Sera was nearby.

Logan felt her presence seconds before he heard her voice. He was confident that she had seen to the safety of Mila and Annabelle, first and foremost, which meant that the village was secure. While holding the Shadowman by the throat up against a tree, he made eye contact with Sera and gave her a wink. Wide-eyed, she started toward him, and he shook his head.

"I'm fine," he told her in a gravelly voice. "Help the witches."

She nodded and turned to join Zilla and Sevilla, which distracted Logan just enough for the Shadowman to give him a knee in the groin. The instant pain shot through Logan like a bolt, causing him to bend at the waist and take in deep breaths of air. By the time Logan straightened up, the Shadowman was behind him with his arm around his neck.

"Ya play dirty, Erebos" Logan sputtered.

"I told you my name is Roy," he growled. "And if it gets me what I want, of course I do."

Logan stomped down on Roy's instep, which loosened his grip long enough for Logan to break free. He spun around and punched Roy in the abdomen before giving him a left hook in the snout that made his own teeth ache. Roy was disoriented and bleeding, stumbling to stay in a standing position. He grabbed both sides of Roy's skull and pulled it down quickly to meet his own rising knee. The movement knocked Roy down like a notched maple.

"Two can play at that game," Logan said to Roy's prone body before giving it a kick in the ribs. He watched as Roy shifted back to his own form. He no longer looked like a wolf, nor did he resemble Logan. He was back to his own bruised and bloodied, semi-scrawny body with shoulder length black hair. Logan wondered what Zilla saw in him; the guy was an ass. Still, Logan abided by her wishes and kept him alive. The creatures he created, on the other hand, were a different story.

Satisfied that Roy wasn't going anywhere, he converted back to his human form and picked up the kilt that he had tossed along the edge of the tree line. He quickly secured it as he ran over to help the ladies with the golems. By the time he got there, the rest of the elements had arrived with Aleck, and they were working on the last creature. With their combined efforts it didn't take long, and the stone golem exploded in a shower of pebbles.

Sera ran to him and jumped into his arms, linking her arms around his neck and hooking her legs around his waist. She kissed him eagerly, her energy contagious as he sank into her euphoria. He knew how she felt; he always felt the same way after a good fight. He pulled back from the embrace and whispered in her ear. "We'll need to pick this up where we left off. Later."

Her smile was brighter than a hundred fires as she whispered back. "You can count on it, my love."

Zilla ran to Roy, kneeling down next to him and making sure he was still breathing. Sevilla made her excuses to join her, which suited Logan just fine. The sooner they locked him away somewhere, the better off everyone would be. Sera took a step toward them, but Logan stayed her with his hand.

"Let the witches deal with him," Logan reasoned.

"We should deal with him now and be done with it," Aleck argued. "That guy has been nothing but trouble."

Logan shook his head. "Aye, he's a bastard. But often, there are reasons we don't understand for the things that happen, and for those we are forced to deal with. The witches made their wishes known. We stay out of it for now."

"So we just let him go?" Brooke's tone was disbelieving.

"It's not letting him go, as much as letting the witches navigate Fate. She's not one you want ta mess with."

"You're right about that," Amie agreed. "We've met her."

"I need to check on Will and James," Brooke said as she started back toward the village.

"Sera and I will head to Mila's and check on her and Annabelle," Logan answered.

"I'll find you later, Logan. To help with some of the rebuilding," Aleck said. "In the meantime, I think Amie needs some rest."

Logan tried not to look too surprised at Aleck's offer. He was a good guy; they had just gotten off on the wrong foot. "Thanks, Aleck," he said as he shook his hand. He smiled when Aleck's grip was a little tighter than it needed to be.

The group walked back toward the village, with Logan and Sera the last to leave the area. When Logan looked behind them one last time to the clearing where he fought the Shadowman, the sorcerer had disappeared along with the witches. It made him wonder what Fate had in store for them all, and if finding the last element would be the key to ending the Shadowman's reign. He hoped so, since Logan was ready for some peace. It had been a long time coming.

25

Sera and Logan went directly to Mila's cottage. Thankfully, there was little damage done to the structure. When they walked through the front door, they saw that Annabelle was back in front of the fireplace and Mila was cooking lunch. It was as if the attack had never happened.

Mila insisted Logan and Sera stay and have lunch. Neither had eaten since the night before, so they agreed. Logan went to the fireplace and sat across from Annabelle, while Sera gathered first aid items from Mila's cupboards. She carried an armful of supplies over to Logan, and started cleaning his newer scratches.

"You know, if this is going to be a habit I might need to run home," Sera joked. "I have a much better first aid kit at my apartment."

Logan grinned. "Nae, my love. This doesn't happen often. No need for ya to go anywhere."

Sera looked over to Annabelle and raised an eyebrow. "Somehow I don't believe him," she said with a wink.

Annabelle laughed, delighted to get in on the fun. "I wouldn't believe him either. He gets hurt all the time. Just last month he punched his fist bloody. And then there was the time that an entire building fell on him and he had to crawl his way out."

"Traitor," Logan laughed. "Whose side are ya on?"

Annabelle answered with a grin. "Hers."

Mila's laugh floated over from the kitchen. Sera mouthed "thank you" to Annabelle, who nodded and grinned. If the heart could burst from happiness, Sera was pretty sure hers would be close to erupting. She absolutely adored Annabelle, and it seemed that she liked Sera in return. It was important that she did, since Sera knew that Logan and Annabelle were a package deal.

She was dabbing peroxide on the fresh cuts on Logan's back when his voice startled her out of her thoughts. His low tone made her tummy flip, and she was agreeing before he even spit the last of his sentence out. "I was thinking after lunch we could go for a soak."

Sera leaned over his left shoulder, her chest resting slightly on his back. She felt her tattoo pulsing, but it wasn't the same feeling she got when she received a warning. This felt different, it felt like her heartbeat. Visions of the moments they had spent together were wrapped inside the potential of their future. Their smiles, the sounds of laughter and the undeniable truth that she would be part of something special, came to her in a blinding flash. She belonged here, as a part of Logan's life, as well as Annabelle's. She looked across at the top of Annabelle's bowed head, playing with the figurines so lovingly made by her papa, and smiled. This was Sera's chance at a family and she would be crazy not to take it. She responded to Logan's comment, but also to so much more.

"That sounds perfect."

After lunch, they had a leisurely soak at the hot spring. Logan had taken his shaving kit and spent time down at the river scraping the whiskers from his face and neck. Sera wasn't sure how she would feel about it, since she liked the feel of coarse hair on her skin, but when he finally came to her in the tub she was pleasantly surprised. The man was a god. She couldn't stop touching his smooth cheeks, kissing his chiseled jaw. They were both content to relax in each other's arms, languidly stroking each other's skin and placing tender kisses on any fresh bruises that appeared. Before they knew it more than an hour had passed.

They walked back to Logan's cabin wrapped in blankets. Once inside, Sera waited in the rocking chair while Logan built a fire. As far as she was concerned, they were in for the night. She was glad Mila had thought to send them with some baked goods, fruits and cheese. She sipped at the scotch she poured herself. The delicious burn was making its way into her stomach, warming her from the inside out.

The marks on Logan's back were much better after the soak. Sera could still smell the lavender salve she applied to them on her hands. The combination of the alcohol and the soothing scent completely relaxed her. She watched with a warm smile and interested eyes, as Logan finished with the fire. He must have felt the touch of her gaze since he turned to look at her with his head cocked.

"What's goin' on in that pretty head of yours?"

Sera breathed in the sound of his voice, one more layer of relaxation in her soul. "Not so much a thought but a feeling," she said simply. "Contentment sums it up."

He liked her answer, she could tell by the way he puffed his chest, but the comment also gave him pause. He slid over between her knees, taking the glass out of her hand and setting it on the floor before taking both of her hands in his. He knelt before her, rubbing his thumbs over her knuckles and looking her directly in the eyes. She hadn't been ready before for what he was about to ask her, but she knew she was ready now. She shifted in the rocking chair, perching herself closer to the edge so she was inches from his face and smiled softly. Logan immediately relaxed, relief loosening the grip on her hands. He let out the breath he was holding with a sigh.

"I'm glad to hear that, my love. I want ya to be happy here."

"I know you do, Logan," Sera said softly. She lifted one of her hands to cup his face. "I know now I could be very happy here."

He turned his head into her palm and closed his eyes, breathing in the scent of her like she was a rosemary sprig. A moment later, he pulled her hand down to the other and clasped them both in her lap.

"Sera Cardoso, my love," his voice cracked with nervousness. Sera had never heard anything so adorable. "My heart. My life mate. Will you take my hand? Will you walk at my side, along our life path, until the end of time? There is no other for me, in this life or the next. Will ya be my wife?"

With tears threatening to spill and a smile splitting her face, Sera gave Logan her heart-felt answer. "I will, Logan. I absolutely will."

He pulled her forward, showering kisses on her face, cheeks and hands, before pulling her into an embrace. Before she knew it she was lying on the bearskin rug in front of the fire with Logan on top of her. Words came out between his kisses.

"You make me so happy... I love ya so much... are ya sure... about this life..."

"Logan," Sera laughed holding his face in her hands and looking up at him. "I need to you understand that I am choosing this life because of how I feel for you, no other reason. The family we will make with Annabelle is... what did you call it?"

"A boon?"

Sera smiled. "Exactly. An added boon. Yes, I am sure. And yes, I love you — to the moon and back."

He kissed her swiftly, then stood and scooped her off the floor. "I think this conversation is better suited for the bedroom, my love." He hustled to the bedroom, almost hitting her head on the doorjamb in his haste.

"You don't want to wait until the wedding night?" Sera joked. She squealed as he tossed her on the bed and he pulled the blanket from her body. He made quick work of the pants he had on as well.

"Nae, lassie. Not unless you want to do something more formal this second. It can be arranged, but we'd be naked."

Sera squealed as he dropped down on the bed and slid on top of her. He rested his weight on his arms on either side of her head.

"I think something a bit more formal can wait. I think my abuela would want to be involved in the planning," she said.

"Whatever you want, my love." He kissed her on the forehead, then gently on the tip of her nose, before lowering his lips to her mouth.

"Right now, I only want you," she said with a sigh.

"Ya have me, Sera. Heart and soul."

Sera lost herself in the moment. The warm heat of Logan's lips branded her as he placed fevered kisses along her neck and shoulder. He quickly moved lower, taking her breast into his mouth, and her back arched in response, already ready for what he would offer her. She knew every inch of his body, neither of them was shy when it came to sex. The anticipation of finally feeling him inside her almost caused her to climax before he got going. She could feel his smile as he gave her nipple a gentle nip.

"Impatient?"

Sera growled as she wiggled her hips beneath him. "Aren't you?"

Logan slid up and pressed his length up against her. "Aye. I'm always that for ya. But tonight is special."

Sera reached her hands up, cupping his cheeks and rubbing his smooth skin. "Tonight is special, you're right. But Logan?"

"Aye, my love."

"Have you seen me when I get impatient?"

"Good point," he chuckled.

She pulled his face down to hers and put every ounce of heat she had into a single kiss. He got the hint fast. Licking his way down her body, he plunged his tongue between her folds and moved his thumb rhythmically across her nub. Sera was primed and it didn't take long for the orgasm to take control. He kept up the pressure with his thumb, moaning endearments on his way up to her neck. As her back arched and a pleasured moan escaped her lips, he moved his hands to her hips, lifted her slightly, and plunged inside.

Her nerve endings were still tingling when he slid inside her, and she couldn't help the small scream that came out when he did. He pulled back and thrust forward again, this time pulling a moan from her lips. Her moan was quickly squelched by his mouth, as he thrust his tongue and hips in unison. Every nerve in her body was thrumming; he filled her body and soul.

Still pumping, his face moved down to her neck. "Thig rium mo ghaol," he moaned. She had heard those words before, and while he had told her they were an endearment, she still didn't know what they meant.

"Mine airson beatha." The words he was saying between kisses were foreign, and doing strange things to her. "Dà chridhe a-nis on." Her second orgasm was building and she lost control raking her fingernails across his back. The tattoo on her chest pulsed to the same rhythm as his frantic thrusts.

Logan's words came in pants. She could hardly hear what he was saying, she was so focused on the euphoria he created. He pulled back far enough to look into her eyes, and she tried to focus on them as he said what was in his heart. They were glowing gold and shimmering with the tears of emotion that she felt as well.

"Is thusamo bhean."

Sera didn't know what his words meant, but they caused the strongest reaction her body had ever had. As another orgasm ripped through her, her hips fought to rise against the pressure of his hands holding her in place. He was seated deep inside of her, and she could feel him pumping against her swollen flesh. Logan's head dropped to her neck, as he continued to push forward. The intensity of the moment made her jaws ache, but she didn't want the feeling to stop. She felt a sting on her shoulder, and tasted blood on her tongue. Had she clenched so hard that she bit it?

Her thoughts were jumbled; she could no longer think straight. Still deep inside her, Logan licked his way up her neck and whispered in her ear. "Gu ruig am bàs tha mise agadsa."

An unearthly growl escaped her lips as she pulled Logan's body closer and sank her teeth into his shoulder. She tasted the salt on his skin, flavored with the copper tang of his blood. She pulled back with a gasp, what on earth was she doing? Had she really just bit him? She had no idea what compelled her to do it, but even more strange was that Logan didn't seem to mind. If anything, he was ecstatic. He looked into her eyes, tipping his head sideways and looking at her as if he was seeing her for the first time.

"Logan, I am so sorry," she said softly. She started to wipe the bite with her fingers, but there was hardly anything there. She looked back into his face, and he was grinning like a fool. If she wasn't mistaken, his semi-hard erection was growing firmer inside of her.

His voice was comforting, and his tone was deep. "Nothing to be sorry for, my love," he said softly. "You just made me the happiest man alive."

Sera shook her head in confusion. "What are you talking about?"

"The nip," Logan said. "It can happen the first time with lycans."

Sera wasn't a lycan, at least not a full one. Who even knew what she was anymore. It was like she couldn't control her own body.

"I'm not sure what just happened. It was like something came over me."

Logan grinned. He was definitely getting harder, she could feel it inside of her. "Aye, the words can have that affect."

"Words?"

"The vows I just took for us."

Sera was having a hard time concentrating, he was intoxicating. "You were saying things I couldn't understand. Some things you have said before."

"Aye. The gist of it is, come to my love, mine for life, two hearts are one, ya are my wife."

"Didn't you say five things?"

"Aye," Logan said. "The last bit was until death I am yours."

Sera smiled with the realization that he had made it official. "So we're married."

"Aye," Logan said with a grin. "And you will nae be sleeping tonight, Mrs. Blackwood."

He started to thrust again; she wondered how he managed to recover so quickly from the last eruption. Then she realized that her body was starting to hum again just as quickly. Sera had no idea where the energy burst was coming from, but she would take it. If the last hour was any indication, she would need a lot of it moving forward to keep up with her new husband.

△

Sera woke to the sound of Logan whistling. His mood light and playful, and he gave her a wink when entering the room. He placed a tray on her lap and crawled into the bed next to her. Placing his arm behind her, he supported her back and used his other hand to take pieces of fruit from her plate. It was obvious that they would be sharing the breakfast, since he had cut up enough fruit and bread for a small family.

"How are you feeling, my love?"

Sera looked up into his face and smiled. "Amazingly good actually," she said. "I think the soak we took yesterday soothed my back. I can't remember the last time it didn't ache."

Logan kissed her nose and grinned, then pulled apiece of buttered bread from her plate and took a big bite. He talked around mouthfuls. "Aye. The soaks do have healing properties."

She took a sliver of apple topped with a piece of cheddar. The salty tang went well with the sweetness and soon she had eaten most of the apples on the plate. Their lovemaking had worked up an appetite.

"I'm usually not this hungry first thing," she exclaimed. "Thank you for this, Logan. It was really sweet of you."

He ate the last of his bread and a few pieces of fruit before sliding off the bed. He leaned over, kissing her soundly before taking the tray back to the kitchen. She heard him pumping the water and filling the sink, presumably to wash the few dishes he had dirtied. Enjoying the few minutes to herself, she relaxed back on the pillow with a sigh, and pulled the blankets back up toward her chin. Her eyes swept over her hands as she smoothed the blankets, and it was then that her mind caught on something. There was something odd, a tickle in her mind, but she was having a hard time registering what it was.

She lifted her arms from the blanket and examined her hands one by one. Her skin was smooth and unmarked. They looked well hydrated; she couldn't see any of the lines that were usually present. Logan was right; the hot spring really did have healing properties. She was curious about the rest of her skin and got up out of bed just as Logan walked back into the room.

"I thought we could go down to Mila's to tell her the news," he said as he put on his clothes. "Then we could take Annabelle out for a short walk. She could probably use some fresh air."

Sera nodded, sliding on the clothes he brought over to her. For some strange reason they didn't fit right. They were much looser than they had been before. Sera decided that it meant that they needed to be washed.

"That all sounds good," she said. "I would like to spend more time with Annabelle. But, first I think we should meet up with the others, and figure out next steps. I want to be prepared if the Shadowman comes back."

Logan shook his head. "He won't be back. He isn't strong enough to fight the three of you yet. Once you find the fourth, you'll be unstoppable. I think he realized that last night."

"Let's hope so," she said. "Where do you think they've taken him?"

"Who? Zilla and Sevilla?"

She nodded. "Mhmm."

Logan shrugged. "Impossible to say. Not even sure at this point if they took him, or he took them."

Sera's heart sunk. She hadn't even thought of that before, but it was a real possibility.

After he was dressed, he walked over to her and pulled her into a warm embrace. "Ready to go, my love?"

"I am," Sera said. "Let's go to Mila's first, then we can head to the cabin where the others are resting."

Sera felt fantastic, being married definitely agreed with her. They walked to Mila's and knocked on the door before entering. Annabelle sat at the kitchen table and was bottling some of the herbs Mila dried. Sera smiled, remembering having done the same thing when she was Annabelle's age. The young girl looked up with a grin and stood to give Logan a hug. When she looked at Sera, there was a question creasing her brow.

"You look all glowy today," she said a-matter-of-factly.

Sera felt her cheeks flush with embarrassment. She knew it was impossible that Annabelle was picking up on what happened between her and Logan, but she couldn't help but think that perhaps it did show on her face. Logan cleared his throat and saved Sera from her discomfort.

"Sera's as beautiful as ever, but the hot springs seemed to work their magic. Do I look glowy as well?"

Annabelle squinted, examining Logan for differences. "Not really," she answered with a shrug. "Maybe the magic only works on ladies."

"Perhaps it does," Logan laughed.

Annabelle sat back down at the table and continued her chore. Sera looked up into Mila's questioning gaze. She was looking between Sera and Logan, doing her own examination. She walked up to Sera, and took her chin in her hand, rotating her head left and right then looking deep into her eyes. After a few seconds, she then took Sera's hands in her own and looked down at the tops of them. Sera looked down as well, which was when she saw something she had not noticed before. The spots that had started forming on her skin a few years back had disappeared. It made her wonder about the one on her cheek.

Mila smiled and pulled Sera into a hug. "Congratulations," she whispered quietly. Sera wondered how on earth her grandmother had known. Then again, her abuela had always had special talents. "There's a mirror on my dresser. You may want to use it."

Why? What was wrong with her face? She left the kitchen as Mila was hugging Logan as well. When Sera looked back over her shoulder before entering her abuela's bedroom, he had a huge smile on his face and was nodding to her whispered questions.

Sera picked up the small hand mirror and looked at her image. The face staring back at her was her own, but she now realized what everyone else was seeing. She took her fingers and moved the skin near her eyes. The skin that was once lined was now smooth as a baby's bottom. The age marks that started to form were gone as well, from both her hands and her face. She hadn't looked this good since she was thirty.

The realization caused her to look down; it seemed even her breasts were a bit perkier. The sudden sound of Logan's voice made her jump.

"I've only ever seen you with my heart. Ya haven't changed in my eyes."

"Haven't changed?" she said unbelievingly. "Logan I haven't looked like this in over ten years."

"About fifteen, I would suspect," he said with a grin.

"What are you talking about?"

He pulled her into his arms, and she could feel the vibration of his chuckle. "Ya need to calm your wee self, my love. You're starting to steam."

"Logan, you need to explain yourself right now, or I am going to do more than steam!"

"When we mated, the lycan in ya came out. I didn't know that would happen. It was a pleasant surprise."

"And the changes? Why am I younger? That is what happened, right?"

"Aye. You are younger," he answered softly. "I think nature matches the female to the male after they commit to each other."

"I'm back to being thirty?" She was having a hard time believing it. Although, if she would have been told weeks ago that she would be able to wield fire from her fingertips, she wouldn't have believed that either.

"It seems so, my love," he said apologetically. "Are you okay with the change?"

She grinned and shook her head at the wonderful man so concerned with her comfort, who had only ever seen her through the eyes of love. She was a lucky lycan. "Of course I'm okay with it, what woman wouldn't be? I've married the equivalent of the fountain of youth."

"I suppose ya have," Logan chuckled and kissed her soundly. He took her hand and led her toward the living area. "Time to tell Annabelle. She and Mila have a party to plan."

Sera allowed him to make their announcement and was swept up in both Annabelle's and her abuela's excitement. Her mind wandered to the implications of her newfound youth. Would her insides be younger as well? Could there possibly be siblings for Annabelle in their future? She thanked whatever power had brought her a second chance and tried not to worry about the what-ifs. Her ability to morph into a wolf, combined with her recently acquired powers, was just one of the many that niggled at her mind. Knowing she had Logan by her side moving forward was the only thing that kept her grounded.

26

Sera and Logan spent a short time with Annabelle and Mila, after the announcement that there would be a wedding. Annabelle was thrilled that Sera would become her new mama, and Mila pulled out a paper and pencil and started jotting down ideas for the ceremony. Their excitement was contagious, but Sera found it a bit overwhelming, especially since her realization that she had not only changed emotionally, but physically as well. She and Logan left Mila and Annabelle discussing decorations, with the assurance that they would be back later to take Annabelle for a walk.

They didn't have to go far to find the others, as they were just up the street at the houses destroyed by the golems. Brooke and Will were helping Amie stack the salvageable wood planks. It looked like James was in charge of burning the splintered pieces that Aleck carried over and piled nearby.

Logan slid his hand into hers as they neared the bonfire where James stood, and Aleck gave an abrupt nod before walking back toward Amie. Sera would have been able to pick up on the tension between them, even if she hadn't been told the story of why they didn't get along. Their first meeting hadn't been the best, from what Amie had explained, although to Sera it sounded like Logan had restrained himself. She understood both sides, and hoped for everyone's sake they would find a way to get along. They would all need to work together in the coming months.

James smiled fondly at Sera before clearing his throat and giving a polite nod to Logan. He glanced briefly at the couple's clasped hands before greeting them. He hid his surprise pretty well, although Sera could tell he was shocked. It was better he find out this way, so there would be no more confusion on his part. She hoped it wasn't too late to be friends.

"Good morning, Sera. Logan."

"Good morning," Sera said with a smile. Logan muttered a greeting under his breath; it was almost as though it pained him. She poked him in the ribs with her elbow, which provoked a louder response.

"Good mornin', James."

James nodded, then turned his head to hide a smile under the guise of picking up more wood to put on the fire. Sera knew better. James had seen that she had prompted Logan to play nice. Logan was too busy posturing to notice. She tried not to laugh; the whole scene was ridiculous.

"I don't see Kadar," Sera said looking around.

"He left last night," James answered with a nod. "He was worried when Sevilla didn't return by nightfall, so went to check a place that he thought she might be. He said he'd be back in a few days."

Sera remembered the loving glances between Kadar and Sevilla and realized that his worry probably ran deeper than most. She looked up at Logan who gave her a pained look, he was clearly uncomfortable with polite conversation.

"Where are we going to be the most help?" Sera asked with a grin. She decided that everyone would just need to get over themselves if they were going to continue to work together. Besides, Logan hadn't had control over his temper for very good reasons. She was sure from now on he would be better.

"Logan could probably help Will and Aleck," James offered quickly.

Logan muttered under his breath, which prompted another poke of her elbow. Perhaps he wouldn't be better. He lowered his head and whispered into her ear.

"I'll do it, my love. But I cannae promise it won't come to fisticuffs."

Sera answered with a fierce whisper, she could practically feel the fire in her eyes. "It better not, Logan, these people are my friends."

He chuckled and gave her a kiss on the cheek. "I'll be a good boy for ya." He nodded once more to James before joining Aleck by the rubble.

Holding her breath, Sera watched him interact with Aleck for a few seconds. She released it with a sigh when it seemed that they would be able to refrain from beating the crap out of one another, at least for an afternoon. She looked up to James when she heard him clear his throat.

"He's a lucky bastard," he said simply. "If this is what you want, I'm happy for you."

"Thanks, Jim. I'm lucky too, to be honest. He really is a great guy."

"I'm sure he is," he cracked. "Once you get past the fact that most of the time he looks like he wants to break you in two."

Sera laughed and moved closer to the fire. "There was something going on that he was dealing with," she explained. "I think things will be different now."

James looked thoughtful, as if he were trying to solve a puzzle, then nodded in agreement. "I'm sure they will be. As long as he's good to you, he won't have any trouble from me."

Sera looked over at Logan, who had found a hammer and started making repairs on the house. Amie and Brooke said something to him that made him laugh; the sound of it pulled at her heart. Logan paused and looked over at her, cocking his head and waiting for her acknowledgement. He wanted to be sure she was okay. She waved and smiled, prompting him to blow a kiss. Brooke and Amie smiled at the exchange and started toward the spot where she and James stood. Logan resumed his repairs on the house as Sera responded to James' comment.

"He'll be good to me, James. I know it in my heart. Finally, I'm where I belong."

Sera watched as Brooke and Amie chatted with Will and Aleck, and then made their way to the burn pit. Brooke was looking well rested, but Amie had bags under her eyes. Sera made a mental note to have her abuela mix something up for Amie to help her sleep later. Perhaps she didn't rest fully in strange places.

"Amie and I think we should head to Sevilla's and see if she and Zilla made it back," Brooke said. "We need to find out where they took the Shadowman, and what to expect."

"I agree," Sera answered.

"Also, I think that our help is needed here," Amie added. "I'd like to get our things so we can stay while repairs are made."

"That's a good idea. I have a few things I can pick up as well."

"I should go and get Max," James said. "He's been alone too long."

"I keep forgetting about Max," Brooke admitted. "Will he be okay here?"

"He can stay with me," James offered. "I'll be sure he behaves."

"Brilliant," Brooke said. Plans made, Brooke looked over at Sera. "Did we still have a wagon available to use? I think that might help."

"I know right where it is, I can get it," Sera offered. "Thank you all so much. Logan especially will appreciate everyone's help. Let me go tell him what we are doing. I'll be right back."

Sera crossed the yard, walking to Logan with a smile. He watched her every step with his sexy gaze. She wasn't sure she would ever get over how hot he made her feel, each and every time he looked at her. He gathered her in his arms and buried his face in her neck, breathing deep before looking over her shoulder. When she looked behind her, she saw James turn away and continue to put wood on the fire. She looked at him, a knowing look raising her brow.

"I came over to let you know that I am heading back to Sevilla's with the others. The plan is for Will and Aleck to stay here and help you."

His eyes squinted, and he nodded toward James. "He going with ya?"

"He is actually," Sera grinned. "There won't be a problem with that, will there?"

Logan looked sheepish for a split second before his face split with a toothy grin. "Nae, my love."

"Good. Because if for whatever reason you were feeling a bit jealous, I would have to set you straight."

"Not jealous, as much as concerned. He fancies ya."

"I didn't choose him though now did I?"

Logan leaned down and kissed her tenderly. "Nae, ya dinnae. I trust you, Sera."

She threw her arms around his broad shoulders, pulling him tight in a hug. "I will never give you a reason not to."

"Safe journey, my heart," he whispered softly. "The Shadowman is still out there somewhere."

"We won't be long, I promise."

Sera led the group to the outskirts of Logan's territory, far enough so that they were able to create a portal safely. Amie stepped back and allowed Brooke to create the magical doorway. Sera had been right, Amie was tired. Perhaps when they got to Sevilla's she could take a nap. Sera wouldn't mind one herself; she had been kept up all night by her new husband's attentions.

Amie went through first, then Brooke waved James through pulling the wagon. Sera went in behind him, commenting to Brooke as she went through.

"You're teaching me that next, right?"

Brooke nodded. "Absolutely. Although, I have a feeling you will be teaching us a few things soon. You catch on quickly."

"Hello," Sera laughed as she wiggled her fingers. "Fire."

Brooke laughed and shook her head at the terrible joke. Sera decided she was really going to like having girlfriends.

The portal took them to an area near a crystal blue pond that looked familiar. If Sera remembered correctly, Sevilla's was just a short walk through the woods. She could see the path they needed to take from where they were standing. Brooke and Sera walked side by side in the lead, while Amie helped James pull the wagon. Even though his leg had healed, he still tired easily. He really needed the benefit of some physical therapy sessions.

Brooke kept glancing sideways at Sera, the curious gaze was hard to miss. It seemed to Sera that there was something on her mind. Brooke wasn't one to mince words; Sera had learned that quickly enough, so she waited for the inevitable round of questions. She had a feeling she knew what they would be about.

"Okay, what gives with Logan?" Brooke asked with a grin. "And you look amazing by the way."

Sera shook her head, she had no idea where to start. Brooke looked at her expectantly and Sera laughed. "So much has happened; it is hard for me to keep it all straight."

"Okay, so start with the major points."

"Basically, Logan and I are married. And, I found out I'm a lycan."

"Those are some pretty major points, lovey." Brooke said. "Married? And you're a werewolf? How?"

Sera looked back to see if their conversation had been overheard, so far it hadn't. She lowered her voice to respond.

"It runs in my family," Sera shrugged. "It seems that my grandmother is from Wisteria. She's known Logan his whole life. She thought I was born human, so never told me."

"My mind is blown right now," Brooke said. "If you don't mind me asking, is that why you look so young?"

"I have no idea," Sera answered honestly. "But I guess it could be that. Lycans heal quickly and I guess the genetics catch up to you when you commit to an alpha. I only just realized what happened this morning. I'm still sorting it out."

"Blimey," Brooke exclaimed. "I mean you looked amazing before, but you look…well…I can't get over it, you look close to our age."

"The kicker is I feel like it too," Sera admitted. "I haven't felt this good since I was thirty. At least now I feel like I can keep up with Logan."

"Well if anyone can, it will be you," Brooke grinned. "Although he does seem more balanced since you met. Less grumpy."

"He's been through a lot, but I know things will be different from now on. He really is the sweetest man I have ever met. I think we'll be good for one another."

"I love it when it works out that way. So will we be having a party?"

Sera nodded. "Mila and Annabelle are planning it as we speak."

"Brilliant! So glad you found happiness," Brooke said with a smile. "And I'm really glad to have you as part of our crew."

"Thank you, Brooke. I've always been part of a team, but now I feel as though I am part of a family."

"Just so," Brooke nodded. "I suppose this explains the picture of the half-woman, half-wolf in my journal."

Sera laughed. "Yes, I suppose it does."

"Can't wait to see what you do with all of these changes in your life."

"Me either," Sera said with a wink.

The first thing Sera noticed when walking up to Sevilla's, was that the door was wide open. Max heard them coming and met them on the path. He seemed happy to see them, and didn't seem distraught in any way. If someone had been at the house, they were long gone.

Brooke hurried in through the door and called out for Sevilla. As Sera came in behind her, she saw what Brooke had already seen — no one was home. There were cupboard doors and drawers open, and a few pieces of furniture tipped over. Someone had definitely been searching for something.

"I'll be right back," Brooke said, running upstairs to the bedrooms.

James and Amie came inside with Max and looked around the room.

"Someone tossed it," James exclaimed. "Wonder what they were looking for."

Brooke came back down the stairs, her journal in her hand. "I think they were looking for this. Thankfully, they didn't rummage around upstairs. Max must have scared them off."

Sera looked at the pages as Brooke flipped through the book. There seemed to be much more writing on it now than there had been before. While she still didn't understand much about the journal, she knew that the writing would give them more clues as to what came next.

"I don't think it's safe to stay here," James said firmly. "We should get our things and go back to Logan's village."

"Agreed," Sera nodded. "Whoever was here might come back. We don't want to be here when they do." She couldn't help but wonder if it had been Kadar that searched the house. Would he have been looking for something to help find Sevilla?

"I'll get your things, James," Brooke offered. "It might be best if you keep watch out front. The girls and I will pack up. We'll meet you in five minutes."

James nodded. "Good plan. Come on, Max."

It didn't take long for Sera to pack her few belongings, since she hadn't brought much with her. She hoped that her grandmother could take her back to Spain for a shopping trip; she had some things she needed to get. She also needed to get her hands on a computer so she could arrange an extended leave of absence by email. She doubted she would ever be back to work, but she wanted to leave her options open for the time being.

Sera met the other women downstairs in the kitchen. Brooke was putting a deck of cards and a pointed stone on a chain into a small pull string bag. Sera assumed it was Sevilla's tarot deck and pendulum. Her abuela used tools like that as well. Brooke also took a few sage wands from the bowl in the center of the dining table. Sera had been making similar wands for as long as she could remember, and Sevilla had done a nice job on hers. They included colorful sprigs of dried flowers and were wrapped with sparkling twine. Sera thought she would ask Brooke if she could have one. Sage was used to remove negativity among other things. It might not be a bad idea to walk around the perimeter of Logan's territory with it.

"I don't want to leave these tools behind," Brooke explained. "Just in case Sevilla and Zilla show up at Logan's, these might help them figure stuff out."

"I don't think they should come back here if they do show up, regardless," Amie said. "It could be too dangerous."

"I agree," Sera said. "Is there anything else you want to take?"

"I don't think so," Brooke said as she shook her head. "I think we have everything we need."

"Okay, let's get James and go," Sera said. "We've probably been here too long already."

James had been outside for over five minutes and was wondering what was taking the girls so long. It wasn't as though they had loads of packing to do. Max ran off to explore, leaving James alone to wander the garden. It hadn't been tended in a few days, there were several ripened tomatoes and some well-formed peppers. He spied a gathering basket near Sevilla's shed, and got to work gathering the vegetables. He would take them back to the village; if he didn't, they would surely go to waste.

Tossing some green beans on top of his growing vegetable pile, he caught movement out of the corner of his eye. It startled him and he stood up suddenly, almost dropping the basket to the ground. At first, he thought it was Sevilla, although after his eyes focused, he realized the woman didn't look much like her after all. It was more the way she held herself that gave him the impression, with her back straight and her chin slightly raised.

The woman was stunning, with thick silvery hair that fell in subtle waves to her waist. Her long flowing gown flared at her feet, white as the hair on her head. It had gossamer threads that ran through it that shimmered in the sun. It made him wonder how she would have walked up the dirt path without ruining the hem.

"Hello," he said softly, afraid to shatter the illusion with a voice any louder. Her being here was like magic. He took a few steps toward her, in awe of her porcelain complexion and trim figure. She was like an otherworldly doll.

She nodded, then smiled and blinked. It was then that he realized there was something strange about her gaze. He waved his hand, and she waved back with a grin. It was impossible — how on earth could she see him with those eyes? They were entirely white. He assumed she was blind, but he didn't see a cane. He took a few more steps, mesmerized by the beautiful creature that had come up to him in the yard.

"I'm James," he said, as he reached the space in front of her. He held out his hand and she took it, smiling as he gave it a gentle squeeze. Her palm was warm, and a tingle of awareness buzzed up his arm to the back of his neck. A slight breeze carried her fragrance, which was light and feminine and reminded him of dessert. He waited patiently for her to respond.

She didn't answer, only stood with her hand in his and a compelling smile on her lips. James was aware of his pulse; she made him nervous and more excited than he had been in years. His heart racing, he was desperate to learn her name. He was glad now that the ladies were taking so long to pack; he didn't want to disrupt the magic of the moment.

He put on his most charming smile, vaguely aware that she might not actually be able to see it. "This is where you tell me your name, love."

She took a deep breath, as if to gather strength, and then whispered softly. "What is on its way, but never arrives?"

James hadn't been prepared for that response; he wasn't sure anyone would have been. He looked up into her face and she stood there serenely, as if she had given him a straight answer and he was too daft to get it.

"I'm sorry, I don't understand," he said to her honestly. "But I really want to, more than you could know."

His comment prompted another smile, as she slid her hand from his and lowered them in front of her. She clasped them together, and he was happy to see her ring finger was bare. He pulled in a breath to ask her something else when Max came into the yard behind him with a playful bark.

James turned to Max, putting both his hands up in surrender to slow the dog down. While Max didn't typically jump on strangers, James didn't want to take any chances. Her dress was too pristine.

"Max, slow down," he said, giving the dog a pat on the head when he sat on his haunches at James' side. He heard conversation coming from the front of the house. It seemed that Brooke, Sera and Amie were on their way out and interrupting his moment as well. When he turned back to the woman to apologize for the disruption, she had vanished. Had she ever been there? Was he just seeing things?

James puzzled over the riddle, whispering the words the woman had given him. "What is on its way, but never arrives?"

"What was that?" Brooke must have noticed the confusion on his face. She walked straight to him and put a hand on his arm. "What is it, James? You look as if you've seen a ghost."

"I don't know," he answered. "Not sure she was real." He shook his head, maybe he had been hallucinating. He wondered if perhaps he needed to get back to the Wellness Center and complete his therapy.

"She who?" Amie asked, looking around the yard then down at the dog. "There's no one here but Max."

"I could have sworn I saw someone," James said quietly. "Perhaps I am too worked up by all that has happened."

"I suppose," Brooke said. She sounded unconvinced.

"If you're ready we should probably get out of here," Sera suggested. "We have everything we need."

"Right," James nodded. "The wagon is over there; you can put your things in it. Let me grab the vegetables I picked. They were ripe, figured someone should get some use out of them."

"Good idea," Brooke said as walked toward the wagon.

Sera looked into his eyes with a slight squint, then sniffed the air so subtlety that he wouldn't have noticed had he not been looking right at her. It reminded him of something Max would do. He knew exactly what she was picking up on, he could smell it too.

"You're sure you're okay?" Sera had chosen not to acknowledge it. He was thankful for that since he wasn't sure how he would explain himself.

"I'll be fine, Sera," he said with a smile. "Let's head back, before some-one decides they want to come back and give the place another toss."

Amie and Brooke pulled the wagon up the path, while Sera picked up the basket of vegetables and James walked after them. He gave a sharp whistle to Max, who barked and pranced behind the group. As James walked past the area where he had imagined the woman, the scent of vanilla tickled his nose once more. He looked around but didn't see her. Now that he knew that she was real, and not a figment of his imagina-tion, he hoped it meant that he would see her again. She was not some-one he would soon forget.

27

The group made it back to Logan's village by nightfall, and Mila put the fresh vegetables to good use for dinner. They all ate outside together by the light of glowing lanterns. There was much more room for them this way, and before too long they would need to stay indoors. The nights had turned colder and the leaves had turned quickly. It seemed winter was well on its way.

The women sat together at one end of the table, with blankets covering their shoulders, while the men sat on the other chatting away. Sera was happy to see they were getting along; the afternoon together working on the house repairs must have done them some good. More than once, Logan caught her staring down his way, and would give her a wink or blow her a kiss. For someone so alpha, he had absolutely no problem showing his affection for her in front of others. That turned her on more than he could ever imagine. She decided she would let him know later when they were alone.

"I've looked at this journal every way but sideways, and still can't figure things out," Brooke admitted. "Most of the pages that filled in are about Sera, and are things we've already learned."

"I did notice drawings in there that looked like the circles I found where I found the portal," Sera said.

Brooke nodded. "Those were instructions for creating portals tied to your element. We should be able to train you how to make them, even without Sevilla being here."

"We should try to do that tomorrow morning before we leave," Amie suggested. "Sera may need to get back home for something before we get back."

"Mila can help me with that as well," Sera said. "She's been traveling back and forth for years."

"Yes, but my magic is tied to an item that was given to me," Mila added. "You will be able to create yours through your element."

"It's just crazy to think about," Sera said. "But exciting at the same time."

"I'm excited to see it," Annabelle blatted. "Can I come watch you, Sera? I promise not to get in the way."

"Of course," Sera said with a grin. "But, we will be sure to have you at a distance, since fires can be unpredictable."

"Brilliant," Brooke nodded. "We will start first thing in the morning. The boys can pack up while we train. We need to get James back to the Wellness Center and come up with some kind of a story why he's been gone."

"It will be good for him to finish his therapy," Sera agreed. "He seems to be struggling with something right now, just the impression he gives me."

"I agree," Brooke nodded. "The issues that took him there have only been added to by the crazy life I've found myself living."

"If anyone can get him through this, it's the staff at the Wellness Center," Sera soothed. Brooke felt guilty; Sera heard the heightened anxiety in her tone. "And although I won't be there volunteering, your brother knows where to find me if he wants to talk about the magick stuff. We'll get him through this."

"Thanks, Sera," Brooke said. "That means a lot."

"When will you all be back?" Mila asked.

"Will and I will come back for a few days to help finish the projects after we drop off James. After that, I would say it might take as long as three weeks by the time James finishes his therapy and Will and I get things settled at home."

"It should be about the same for Aleck and me," Amie added. "I need to make some adjustments to my schedule anyway. In the meantime, Brooke and I will do what we did when we were looking for you."

"You guys were looking for me?"

"Absolutely. We had gotten pretty close too. I think we would have found you, especially with your link to James, if Logan hadn't pulled you into Wisteria like he did."

"It's pretty cool the way we are all connected," Sera agreed. "It makes me wonder about the bigger picture. What parts we all have to play."

"The threads that connect us are more tangled than you realize," Mila said with a smile. "Untangling them is the fun part."

Sera shook her head and laughed. "Which is precisely why I leave that kind of stuff to you, Abuela. Patience isn't my thing."

"Patience will come," Mila said. "And you will all learn to work together and balance the good and bad."

"I believe that," Brooke said. "Sevilla is always talking about balance. I think it is our job to make sure it is maintained."

"If you can find the last element that might stop him from getting any more of a foothold." Will added. "I'm not sure the witches will be much help to you. I'm surprised that they aren't back yet, honestly."

"Me too," Brooke murmured. "I'm really worried about Sevilla."

Will put his arm around her and gave her a gentle squeeze. "I'm sure she'll be fine, Angel."

Amie nodded her head in agreement. "Zilla is with her Brooke. If I know anything about her, it's that she can work her way out of any situation she doesn't want to be in. Perhaps they went to find Fate."

"Perhaps," Brooke responded unconvinced.

"With their help or not, figuring out our purpose is going to involved working as a team," Sera said. "It will be up to us to stop the Shadowman from dabbling in our lives."

"Agreed," Amie said.

"Logan and I will see what we can find out from here, while you guys do what you need to at home," Sera said. "We will see you back in three weeks."

"That's perfect," Mila exclaimed. "Just in time for the winter solstice! That will be the perfect day for a wedding!"

Amie and Brooke both agreed that they would come back a few days before the big event to help set-up. The group spent the remainder of the time after dinner seated around a campfire with wine for the ladies and scotch for the men. James had quietly declined, as did Amie, who decided she was tired and needed some rest. She and Aleck said their goodnights and walked back to the cabin where they were staying.

Sera thought James was acting strangely since their return from Sevilla's, although the other men didn't seem to notice. There had definitely been a female presence in the yard at Sevilla's; she had even smelled her vanilla perfume. Sera wondered if that was what was bothering him. Perhaps he thought that he was hallucinating? She wondered if that was why he was in such a rush to get back to therapy.

James watched everyone take sips of their drinks, and she looked down to see his hands fidgeting near his side. When he excused himself to take a short walk, she remembered that Brooke had mentioned part of the reason he was at the Wellness Center was for alcohol abuse. His sudden change of mood made more sense to her in that case. It was probably uncomfortable to be around the liquor.

Sera told Logan earlier that she would be staying behind with him in Wisteria for the time being, which prompted a full-body bear hug. He had also been grinning like a fool all night, even more so now that the scotch was kicking in. As happy as he was, she knew he would have questions for her, questions they would discuss later when the night covered them and they whispered secrets under his tartan blankets. He knew the weight of her decision; he would want her to be sure.

She would let the chief know that she would be taking an extended leave of absence. She wasn't going to break ties completely, at least not for now. She still had affairs to settle. Once she was trained to create portals on her own, traveling back and forth would be easier; at that point she could cut all ties if she chose to.

They had all just finished their drinks when Will stood up, taking Brooke's hand in his and helping her rise. "Brooke and I are going to call it a night," he said with a nod. "Can we help with anything?"

Sera nodded, she was ready for bed as well. "That would be great, Will. If you and Logan can get the lanterns, Brooke and I will clear the last of the dishes."

Annabelle stifled yet another yawn, so Logan pulled her to her feet for a quick hug before sending her off to bed. She hugged Sera as well and said her goodnights before following Mila into the house.

After Will and Brooke left, Sera and Logan walked in the opposite direction to his place. Actually, their place, she supposed now. It was all so strange to think about. So many changes happened so quickly.

"So are you okay with what Mila has planned? The day of the solstice for our wedding?"

"Aye," he said softly. "The winter solstice is a time of new beginnings.

That'll be perfect for us."

"I think so too. Besides, I have always dreamed of a winter wedding. I never thought in a million years I would be having one. Especially growing up in the desert."

"You'll make a beautiful bride, my love."

Sera smiled; this man could warm her with the simplest of phrases. "Thank you, Logan. By the way, is there anything special that you want included? We will need to tell Mila before she gets too carried away with her planning."

Logan laughed. "I've already given her my ideas. Annabelle was in on the conversation, so I know it is as good as done." He held the door open for her and followed her inside, lighting the lantern on his way. "Stay put, I'll make a fire."

"Logan, don't be silly," she said with a grin. "Just give me a second." She walked to the hearth and set some fresh logs down, before taking a step back and sending out a targeted blast of heat. The logs caught in an instant.

"Well, that's handy," he said with a chuckle. "What other tricks do ya have, lassie?"

"Well you will just need to come in here and see, won't you?" She pulled him by the hand into their bedroom.

"As anxious as I am for that, we need to talk about the next moon."

"What do you mean? I thought since we…"

"Aye," Logan interrupted her, "I'll be fine from now on. It's you that we need to talk about."

Sera realized what he was saying, and her breath caught. She hadn't even thought about it until now. She had been so busy with the craziness with the other elements. "I'm going to change, aren't I?"

"Aye. I believe so. But, there's no need to feel nervous. I'll be with you every step of the way."

Sera nodded and walked to the window. It was a comfort that she would be going through it her first time with Logan. She wanted to be as prepared as she could be and looked outside at the sliver of moon that shone into their bedroom. Thankfully, he had some time to prepare her.

Logan walked up behind her, the heat of his body warming the back of hers as he cradled her in his arms. Her hands caressed the coarse hair on his forearms, and she remembered the beautiful wolf that he had become at Sevilla's. She also remembered Zilla's quick conversion to a sleek black cat; they made the change seem so simple.

"What will I become?" She couldn't help the crack in her voice. She had never done well with the unknown.

"Hard to say, my love. If I had to guess I would say a wolf, however, some have been known to turn into other creatures, like Zilla." He gave her a gentle squeeze and rested his chin on her shoulder. The whisper of his breath tickled her ear. "I'll love ya no matter what fate has in store for ya."

"Well, considering I'm linked to fire as well, we could be in for a surprise," Sera laughed. She tried to make light of it, but her mind was racing.

"I've thought of that," Logan admitted. "But, we will face whatever comes at you, together."

"I love you, Logan," Sera said as she turned around in his arms. "You are the best thing that has ever happened to me."

"I'll take it as a compliment, considering all that's happened to ya."

Sera smiled and raised her hand to his prickly chin. His whiskers were starting to grow back which pleased her. "I have a feeling the best is yet to come."

"I'll move earth and sky to make it so for ya, Sera. And, I love ya too. You are the light of my life."

The rest of the evening was spent just as Sera imagined, covered in Logan's plaid and whispering plans for the future they envisioned. They talked about Sera's part to play in the Shadowman's defeat, and he filled her in on the history as he understood it. In between the talking, they stroked, kissed and embraced. She was ready to rise to the new challenges that would come her way with the help of her new family. There was no doubt that this was the life she was meant for.

Δ

James sat on the porch in the dark, listening to the crickets and tree frogs, and trying to calm his jitters. He knew now it was way past the time for him to go back to Sedona. It had been nearly impossible for him to resist drinking with the others at dinner. Especially after the stress of the last few days.

Max had gone inside to lay by the fire when Brooke and Will went off to bed. Amie and Aleck said their goodnights earlier, the busy days were wearing on her noticeably.

The night was cool, winter was on its way, but the chilled bite didn't seem to be bothering him. The wool blanket he had covering his lap seemed to be enough to keep him warm. He looked across the moonlit street to Logan and Sera's place. The only light that came from their windows was from the glow of their fire. In a way he was envious, although he realized now Sera wasn't quite the right fit for him. But now that he'd been weeks sober, he knew he wanted what she found. He was tired of filling his time with momentary comforts in an unforgiving world.

He looked away from the house, scanning the balance of the village, making his mental rounds to ensure that his loved ones were safe. She came around the corner of the house from the rear yard, quiet as a whisper and as pale as a ghost. All his anxiety melted away, he hadn't realized it until he saw her, but he had been edgy since she disappeared.

"Hello again," he whispered. He didn't want to wake anyone in the house, especially Max.

She nodded her head and her hair spilled forward, shining in the moon's light like molten silver. He had never seen someone so stunning; she took his breath away.

"I've thought about the riddle all afternoon," James confessed to her. "It drove me mad, actually. What I came up with didn't make much sense for your name though."

The same enigmatic smile came to her face as she tipped her head. She was curious as to what he came up with, he could tell. The movement confirmed her interest in him, in his mind, and gave him the strength to proceed. It was important that he got this right, this woman was special. He had already decided by the way she quieted his soul whenever she was near, that he had to get to know more about her.

He stood and waved his hand toward the seat next to him before reaching his hand out to her. She took it and allowed him to guide her to the open seat. He sat back down turning his body toward hers and moving slightly closer. It would be much easier to talk quietly now.

"So the riddle, if I recall correctly, was 'what is on its way, but never arrives?'" He paused, waiting for her nod of confirmation before continuing. "I've been thinking a lot about my future lately, and it dawned on me that the answer could be just that. Tomorrow is on its way, but never arrives, since by the time it does, it ends up being today."

Her smile lit the night; he had gotten it right. She reached her hand out just then and placed it over his. He hadn't realized how cold his fingers were until she warmed them with her own. Her motion prompted him to move a bit closer.

"What confused me was that it isn't a proper name. Is it?"

She shook her head; he was on the right track.

"I thought about names that could mean tomorrow. There was Destiny, but I didn't think that suited you for some reason. I also thought of Moira, which means destiny or fate. I know this because I had an aunt Moira. Lovely lady, but talked up a storm. The name didn't suit you."

She laughed aloud, the first sound he had heard her utter since the riddle she gave him earlier. The sound erupted from her like a blast, which she quickly covered with her hand. It made him laugh as well, but he quieted himself quickly with a finger to his lips and got up to listen at the door for movement. He came back to the seat with a nod.

"Not everyone is keen on my sense of humor," he admitted with a laugh.

She placed her hand back over his. This time he turned his palm over and took hold of her fingers. He looked for the smile, which she gave freely combined with her exotic blank stare. If he wasn't mistaken, the reflection in them was moving, similar to smoke or mist swirling in their depths. He could stare at them all day.

"That was when it came to me, really. Not Tomorrow, Destiny or Moira, but something more simple and elegant. Fate."

He heard a small squeak, then allowed himself to be tugged forward toward her. The excitement on her face was contagious, and his gaze dropped to her full lips as her face drew near. The kiss was quick but pleasant, warming him like no fire ever could. Her smile was beaming; he had guessed right.

"Nice to meet you, Fate," he said softly. He looked into her gorgeous face, feeling her soothing effects on his nerves, and wondered if she could possibly be his tomorrow as well as his fate. There was something about her he just couldn't ignore.

She pointed to his chest, then waved her finger back toward her own.

"The two of us?" he whispered.

Fate nodded then said to him softly. "To have me, you must share me, but if you share me, I'll be gone."

"I'm terrible at riddles, lovey. It's more my sister's thing really."

She stiffened and shook her head adamantly. It was clear he wasn't to tell anyone else.

"But, you intrigue me like no one else ever has. I promise I'll work on the answer. Alone."

She relaxed and leaned in for another kiss, this time the attraction couldn't be denied. James knew it definitely went both ways. He moved his hands up, one to cup her face, the other to the back of her head. He bent it to the side, deepening the kiss and was delighted to feel her tongue tickle his. She was sweet like the vanilla scent she carried and the moment was over much too soon for his taste. In a way it was better; if the kiss had been any longer he would have gotten carried away.

"I'm leaving tomorrow," he told her with a sigh. "But, I'll be back in a few weeks. There's to be a wedding."

Fate nodded and sat up straight. He looked for signs that he upset her, but she still smiled and took hold of his hands.

James brought her knuckles up to his lips and gave them a gentle kiss. "Will I see you again?"

Fate nodded and smiled, slipping one of her hands out of his grip and placing it on his cheek. She leaned forward for one more kiss, then stood to leave. As she walked away soundlessly from him, he whispered, expecting that someone as magical as her would be able to hear him.

"I'll solve your riddle by the time you see me next."

She turned to face him from the middle of the yard and graced him with a glorious smile, then slowly faded from sight like a mirage. He still felt her on his lips, and his hands smelled sweet from running them through her hair. Although he knew in his heart she wasn't a hallucination, he decided it would be best to keep her to himself. If he was wrong, and she was in his imagination, his stay at the Wellness Center could be way longer than even he intended.

Δ

EPILOGUE

3 weeks later...

It was a beautiful day for a wedding. Although there was snow on the ground, the sky was clear and the winds were warmer than they had been all week. Mila had chosen a beautiful location for the ceremony, a short distance from the village, in a clearing of trees similar to Logan's campsite. They had been working for some time on providing seating by way of log pieces and creating structures out of willow branches and twigs.

As promised, Brooke and Amie had come back a few days before to help with the decorations. They had created an ice blast between the two of them that they used to cover the entire archway with sparkling crystals and icicles. Brooke let Sera know that Will had a special decoration in mind as well that he would install right before the guests arrived.

The full moon had come and gone. Although Sera had felt the pull the night Logan had taken her out, she hadn't connected to her wolf. In a way, she was disappointed; she had hoped she would have something special to share with her new family. Logan explained it could take time for her to connect, especially since she lived so long as a human. He kissed her and said even if she never was able to convert, she could join them for the runs they went on. And no matter what, he would love her until the end of time. That would be pretty long, considering her lifespan had been extended to match his. She tried not to worry that the lack of conversion could mean that she was meant to turn into something else entirely.

Sera and Annabelle were at Mila's house getting ready for the ceremony, with some of the items she had brought back from Spain. Sera made sure that Annabelle only used the light shimmery shades of makeup, and kept the darker ones for herself.

"You'll want to be sure you are sparing with it, Annabelle," Sera warned. "Just bits on your lids and a few sparkles on your cheeks should do it."

"I'll be careful. Yours looks really pretty too. That color makes your eyes look so big."

"That was what I was shooting for," Sera laughed. She gave her hair one more fluff, the coconut scent surrounding her like a mist. "You ready?"

"Yes," Annabelle nodded as she picked up her muff. "I almost forgot! I'm supposed to be helping Nana with the platters."

"We'd better get in there then," Sera grinned. "You know how she gets when she's under pressure."

Mila had spent several days cooking and preparing the meal for the day. The breads had all been done days before, and she was putting the final touches on the roasts that would be served for the main meal. They brought food back with them from their trip to Spain, since they had so many people to feed. Sera and Annabelle poured the pre-sliced vegetables and fruits on the trays her abuela lined up, which didn't take long. The days of prepping made their jobs quick and easy. It was all too soon before her abuela was instructing them to have a seat; she didn't want them staining their clothes.

Sera had been practicing creating portals and was quick to show Brooke and Amie how much she improved from the last time they saw her. She finally felt that she had the hang of it. The first few times they had gone back to Spain, her abuela created the portal with the ring the witches had given her all those years ago. It wasn't long before Sera was creating and opening her own doorways. Since she was familiar with the clearing that her elemental portal lead to, it was just a matter of finding a place just outside the outskirts of town she could link to. She and Logan had gone in the woods and practiced every chance they could, and had made a fun game of hide and seek with Annabelle on their walks as a family.

Brooke and Amie had been distressed to hear that she and Logan hadn't been able to find any clues about Sevilla and Zilla's whereabouts. It was as if the two witches disappeared completely. She explained that she and Logan had gone back to the house with Kadar several times, but it was just as they had left it when they had gone back to collect their things. Nothing more seemed to be disrupted, and Kadar had not been able to find any trace of them in the places he knew to look. There was one more place he intended on trying, so would be leaving right after the ceremony.

It worried Sera that something horrible had happened to the women, but she stayed strong in front of Brooke. She didn't want her to worry anymore than she already did. Thankfully, they hadn't seen any sign of the Shadowman either.

Brooke brought the journal with her, and between decorating for the ceremony and helping Mila prepare food, they looked through it and tried to solve some of the newer puzzles that showed up on the blank pages. Amie explained that the drawing of the tree on some of Earth's pages, looked a lot like the dragonblood trees they had seen in Fate's domain. Sera thought they looked like something you would see in a Doctor Seuss book. It made her wonder if perhaps the clue to the last element would be found in Wisteria and made a mental note to ask Logan if he had seen the trees in his travels. It might be worth checking it out. She even considered that it could represent the tree she created at Sevilla's. With as strange as this place was, anything was possible.

James finished his session at the Wellness Center, and even though Sera could tell he was happy, he did seem a bit distracted. He helped, but kept his distance, and scanned the area constantly, almost as though he was looking for someone. Threats perhaps? Aleck seemed to do the same thing, and Amie had explained that with their military background, it made sense. Sera didn't have the heart to tell them that Logan would smell a threat way sooner than it would be visible to them, so she bit her tongue and allowed them to feel good about their attentiveness.

"Are you ready, Sera?" Mila said quietly.

Sera was so absorbed in her thoughts she hadn't heard her walk up to her side. She stood and nodded, taking a cleansing breath in and releasing it slowly. It was ridiculous really; they were already married, but this ceremony would make it so much more formal in her mind.

Mila helped Sera into her fur cape and Annabelle into her muff. She had made them from the rabbit furs that Logan had given her weeks ago and had only just completed the final touches the night before.

The satin lining was smooth against Sera's skin. "You did a beautiful job, Abuela. I absolutely love it."

"You're stunning, Nieta," Mila said lovingly. Tears pooled in her eyes, and she glanced over with a smile to Annabelle.

"Time to go you two," Mila said with an approving nod. She took off her apron and hung it by the door, sliding a woolen shawl over her shoulders. As she left the house, Sera turned to Annabelle and gave her a quick wink.

"Let's go see your papa," Sera grinned.

Annabelle led the way, with Sera right behind. They were both dressed in Logan's plaid, Annabelle with a long skirt, and Sera with a sash tied at her waist, belting her white strapless dress. She considered draping it across her shoulders like a shawl until Mila presented her with the white fur cape that had taken her breath away. Sera had wondered, at the time, why Mila insisted on shopping in Spain for fabric. Now she knew why. Annabelle walked with her hands warm in her muff and her head held high, beyond the yard where the tables were placed, to the clearing where the guests sat waiting. Sera noted she was careful with her pace; they had practiced that on their walks as well.

The winter solstice was the shortest day of the year, so the daylight was fading fast. There were lanterns in place to light Sera's way, hanging from metal hooks that lined the aisle. The archway they created was filled with sparkling lights that looked like fireflies, and there were orbs of light hovering overhead in all shapes and sizes. It was a truly magical setting and she knew she had Will to thank.

Everyone stood when she finally arrived, turning back to look at her and smiling with love and warmth. She passed her neighbors, the ones that she had come to know over the past few weeks, and accepted their whispered blessings with a nod as she passed. She looked in the seats in front, with the members of her new family, Brooke, Will, Amie, Aleck and James, who were smiling at her with misty eyes filled with admiration. James even went as far as giving her a jaunty wink; she was glad to see he was back to feeling himself.

She finally looked up at the keeper of her heart. The man she had joined herself to, and with whom she would spend the rest of her days with. She had never seen him look more handsome, as he proudly wore his plaid to match her and Annabelle. It was the one thing he had insisted be part of their special day, and Sera couldn't be happier.

The hand-fasting ceremony confirmed their commitment as a family, and as such, Logan had felt strongly that it include Annabelle as well. Sera walked up to Logan, noting that he was clean shaven once again. He had explained to her once that while he knew she liked his whiskers, there were times he wanted to feel her warmth against his cheek. He pulled her into an embrace, and she lost herself in a moment of loving warmth. They separated, and each took one of Annabelle's hands, standing before the archway as a family.

Kadar officiated the wedding for them. His kind face and humble tone soothed the jittery nerves in Sera's stomach. Being the center of attention unnerved her, but she found if she focused on Logan's warm and loving gaze, she could imagine that it was only the three of them and no one else. She completed the circle with Logan's other hand, anxious to have them bound with the ribbons she and her abuela carefully selected at the fabric store. It would be a physical sign that she was bound to him for life, and that she was committed to being not only a lover and a wife, but also a mother and friend. It was all she could have hoped for, and she thanked fate for the turn in destiny that had brought them into her life.

There were rings for all three of them. Simple gold bands with engraving Sera couldn't read. She couldn't wait to ask Logan what they said; she was positive it was something meaningful and lovely. His traditions were part of who he was, and Sera loved that most about him. Knowing he would give them a strong base to build on, was the best way to start their new life together. She was anxious to see what the future had in store for them.

△

Beyond the edge of Logan's territory two figures watched the ceremony from the darkness, keeping their distance for more reasons than the fact that they were uninvited. They could see the crowd easily with the glow of their lamps and the sparkle of the magic lit the night sky like stars. It made it easier for them to slip into the shadows, since all eyes were on the couple — all eyes, except for the single man who searched the darkness.

The couple watched as the ribbons were wrapped around the couple's hands, and then around the hands that grasped the tiny wolf known as Annabelle. Roy had never understood the need for commitment; he saw it as a sign of weakness. When he gained control of their body, his and Erebos', he realized that Erebos's feelings for Zilla would be their demise. Erebos was the weak link. The first thing he did, when he took over their body, was to put her in her place. She was soon doing things for him completely against her nature. With the information he learned from Ryker, he was finally in control.

He was feeling better, but still wasn't at full strength. The fight with the elements in their world, then creating the golems in his, had weakened him. The stones Ryker found were no longer channeling the magical energy to him from the others; he needed to find the weapon the last element held safe. Only with that would he be able to absorb the power he needed. Ryker told him what he should look for, but he wasn't able to tell him where start. Not before he blacked out anyway. Too bad really, since Ryker missed his chance to visit with his beloved.

Roy would never go back to being a phantom in his own body. He had only just taken control and fully locked Erebos out. Erebos didn't deserve a corporeal form; he was weak and a fool. If Roy had to pull every star from the universe, he was going to find a way to make the change permanent. Once he no longer had to keep Erebos's essence alive, he was going to take great pleasure in crushing the vial that contained it under his boot heel. Then he'd decide what to do with Zilla, he was growing tired of her too.

His companion tried to dissuade him from attending the wedding, but he hadn't been able to stay away. He was curious if the women had made any progress on finding the final element. When they first arrived his companion seemed nervous, looking into the crowd and shrinking behind him. It was as if she didn't want to be seen. He looked around, curious as to who would prompt the change in her. His eyes looked again at the man searching into the dark places of the forest, even though his eyes should be on the ceremony. Gazing back to her, he examined her face and saw something more than her usual stoicism.

"Why is he searching, do you wonder? Does he sense us here?"

She shook her head, gazing back at him with her blind stare.

He didn't wait for her to speak — it was rare that she spoke, and frustrating to no end when she actually did. The man turned his back to the woods and looked back at the werewolf and his new mate. They were clapping as the couple kissed; their happiness irritated him.

"It's time to go," he said abruptly.

He heard her take a breath, deep and cleansing as she had done before. She was preparing to say something, he could tell by her face. It was a struggle for her to communicate. It made him curious as to what caused it.

"It can be measured," she whispered softly. "But it can't be seen."

"I don't have time for your riddles," he said in exasperation. "If you weren't so powerful I would chain you to the wall along with your sisters."

"Soon it will pass, and the great tree will grow into a power only the intended can know."

The last comment stopped him, there was a clue in there, he was sure of it. Or a warning. He never knew with her until it came to pass. The only thing he knew for sure was that it would come to pass, whether he was ready for it or not.

The crowd was breaking up; it was time to leave. He created a portal, hardly visible in the dark, and waved his hand toward it as an invitation for her to go first. He made it a habit to keep her in front of him; destiny had a funny way of changing in an instant. There was no way he would want his back to it.

They walked directly into his dungeon; it was the best place to create his portal since no one would ever dare follow. And if they did, they would be trapped like the rest. He walked to the largest of the cells, peering into the darkness to the figures strapped to the wall. The chains that criss-crossed their chests glowed bright and kept them weak and motionless. They had all been a disappointment. He had hoped they would give him enough power to remain in corporeal form, especially since he had been unable to secure any of the elemental magic.

He didn't want to be forced to keep Erebos' essence in a jar; it made him much too vulnerable since it had to either be hidden or carried with him at all times. He needed to find a way to sever their tie forever. The final element had the key. He knew it.

Fate stood beside him, staring into the cell at the two women whose features matched hers in almost every way.

"You do realize the only way to save them is to give me what I need," he said.

She nodded slowly, raised her hand to quickly wipe underneath her eye, and then turned to await his instructions.

"Very well," he said over his shoulder as he made his way up the stairs. "Tell me more about this tree."

△△△

Fate's blindness doesn't prevent her from seeing the future, but her visions don't always agree on the way to get there.

The spirits who once guided Fate are silent while dark energy leaches across Wisteria. Fate once had control over all destinies, but now is helpless as mystical creatures die. Without the internal voices to guide her, she is afraid of her own path for the first time in her immortal life.

Fate and her two sisters represent Past, Present, and Future. They struggle to maintain the balance in a land intrinsically connected to Earth. Their magick must be combined to defeat a growing evil that transcends time, but at what cost to the nature that binds them?

Loyalty to the men they love battles their divine purpose. In a universe where all energies are connected, the corruption of one can spell devastation. Fate's blindness mustn't prevent her from finding the light. It will be the only way the earth will survive the darkness.

Desperate to find the source of his power before it falls into enemy hands, a powerful Jinni must accept help from a widow, whose caution might eclipse even his. Will they discover that trust in each other is the biggest risk of all?

If you liked *Twist of Fate*, you'll love *The Jinni's Wish*! Get your free copy today by following this link: https://bookhip.com/TWLTXJ

In a land that parallels ours, a great evil lies in wait. To defeat it, Brooke must face her greatest fears.

Just when Brooke Fisher thought she had a handle on her anxiety, strange things start to happen. In addition to her hair turning green, she's had nothing but cold showers and iced coffee for weeks. When the man starring in her nightmares walks into her reality, she fears what their connection truly means.

The beautiful woman Will Engel has met is complicated in a way that speaks to him. As he helps her unravel the clues in a mysterious journal, he finds that their pasts are intertwined in a way that defies all logic.

As the threat of the Shadowman grows stronger, their journey takes them to a magical land that parallels their own. What they find there not only confirms Brooke's destiny as the element of Water, but Will's role in her future as well.

Amie must unlock the secret to her destiny. One in which she embodies the element of Air.

A persistent ex-boyfriend is the least of Amie Petridis's concerns. After a cryptic tarot reading, winged creatures start to show up more noticeably in her life. Their energy is especially prominent after a sexy U.S. Air Marshal breezes into her life.

Although Aleck has a painful secret that had kept him from getting close to anyone in the past, his attraction to the feisty pilot can no longer be denied. During a romantic getaway to the land of her heritage, they stumble upon a portal to a magical world. Amie's connection to the element of Air is brought to light and her destiny is sealed.

They have both been dealt a hand by Fate which they will have to embrace. They will also learn they aren't the only ones who have had to make sacrifices. Amie is the second element that has been found, and what they do next will determine the fate of the others. Balance must be restored.

Pulled into a struggle between balance and chaos, Tara must embrace her burgeoning powers and fulfill her destiny as the element of Earth.

Tara Varela secretly communicates with animals. Even stranger is her ability to heal others, which is getting stronger by the day. After tending to a mysterious man through an otherworldly connection, she embarks on a journey in a parallel realm she never knew existed.

Her journey to Wisteria is only the beginning. As she comes to terms with her magickal gifts, she finds the man she has befriended understands more about her purpose than she does. As they unravel the mystery of their connection, they each struggle with their growing attraction.

The healing energy that Tara harnesses is powerful, but as with most magick, there's a cost. Theo's desires can't be acted upon without draining her powers, but Tara has made it clear she's willing to chance it. The choice between following their desires and doing what they must is something they will struggle with. Little do they know, neither has much choice in the matter.

ACKNOWLEGEMENTS

I am amazed and humbled when I get to this point. At the tail end of a project, when I work on the bits of the book that don't have to do with the story, I recap the year before and think of all of the people that helped me turn my story into reality.

The acknowledgements are extremely near and dear to my heart, as are all of the people listed. I try my best to include everyone, but please forgive my memory if you have helped me in some way but I forgot to thank you here.

To my loves, as Logan would say — my amazing family. Thank you for all you did to support me during another crazy year. The dinners were amazing, the cleaning appreciated, and the hugs the only way I could have possibly made it through my self-imposed deadlines. I love you all more than you could possibly know.

To retired Fire Chief Mark Hogrebe, a much delayed, but no less heart-felt thank you. Your thoughtful considerations on Sera's work scenes and what she would be able to do gave me a powerful opening scene. I appreciate your help more than you will ever know.

To the Muse Crew, Judy Bobrow, Madelyn March, Sharon Quiroz, Linda Grischy, Kathy Wheeler and Leslie Barrett. We made it through another book you guys, and I owe you big time! Sera and Logan's journey has been all the richer because of your insistence that I could dig deeper. Thank you for challenging me every step of the way!

To my content editor, Jennifer Melzer, you have become a very important part of my growth as a writer. Thank you for making rethink scenes, and for seeing things in my story that, once polished, help make my book shine.

To Jen Sumeracki at Sumo Design, thank you so much for taking on the relaunch and making my covers sparkle! You are amazing and I am so glad to have you in my corner!

A special thanks to my beta readers, Catt Pryde, Brittany Campbell, and Laura Gibson, who read through the "almost ready" version and provided invaluable feedback and support. You guys are amazing and I love you!

To my BFFs, Nettie McHugh and Barb Thompson, who know how to make me laugh when I want to cry, who encourage me to keep moving when I want to give up, and who are ready to pour the drinks when I get thirsty. The next round is on me — preferably on a beach!

Last but not least, I want to thank the amazing community of writers I have met on social media, with a special shout out to the #Turtlewriters and the #Dolphinwriters. You have been amazing to connect with and have been supportive of my journey like only other creatives truly can be. You guys get me! I appreciate that most of all on days when I need a little pick me up. Thank for your amazing support network and #keepwriting!

While it hasn't always been part of her occupation, writing has always been part of D.A. Henneman's life—poetry and song lyrics through teenage angst (no, you won't get to read any of them), short stories in college classes (perhaps you will get to read some of them), and random marketing materials during her stint as a flower shop owner. Even with all of that writing in her life, ten chapters of a book stayed buried in her file cabinet until she closed her flower shop. The timing was finally right, and the Power of Four series was born.

Most days she can be found on her blog posting about her writing journey. You can find her at www.dahenneman.com. You can also follow her on multiple social media plaforms.

www.ingramcontent.com/pod-product-compliance
Lightning Source LLC
Chambersburg PA
CBHW021111110726
47900CB00007B/2132